The Banshee

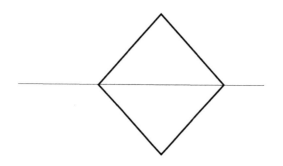

Written By
Eric Fitzgerald

Although this is a fictional story that I made up, there are stories from people claiming they have indeed witnessed banshees and fairies.

If you hear a loud scream at night or find a hair comb on your bedroom window tomorrow morning… I wish you luck, my friend.

Disclaimer – this book contains brutal and horrific content that some readers might find disturbing.

You have been warned.

To my mother,
who taught me strength and
endurance

To my father,
who taught me precision and care

To my brother,
who taught me kindness and
patience

CONTENTS

I THE MCNEEVE ORCHARD (1924)

The ghostly pale light of the crescent moon lit up the dark fields reflecting the ominous hills in the mirror-like puddles spotted around the orchard. It was shining liquid silver in the still water. The McNeeve mansion towered above the surrounding structures sitting in the heart of the plot, deep in the lushes County of Mayo. The mansion had a fickle candle burning in the downstairs window, not enough to blind the ongoing deep black but enough to light up the kitchen table so the McNeeves could enjoy their dinner utterly oblivious to the ancient creature that loomed outside, crouching in the shadow of the woods behind the house. Its poignant yellow eyes blatantly tore the silent night. It would have its fun, but it just stayed silent at that moment. The family already had their own trouble, so it would wait patiently for its turn. The darkness slowly devoured the gold-plated lettering on the stone archway on the edge of the land.

'McNeeve Orchard est. 1892'

An empty bottle of Jack Daniel whiskey was carelessly thrown on the kitchen table, almost spilling two glasses of mirky water and knocking a fork off the table. It bounced on the ground and danced on the spot while lamenting a melancholy jingle until it stopped dead.

Joe reached down beside his seat and picked up his fork, carefully restoring it beside his knife, not making eye contact with his father, and being as quiet as possible. He did not want to attract any attention.

'Why don't you tell your daddy how your day was?' Tommy spoke with a slow mumble; the whisky was slurring his speech, but it was evident he was trying to speak clearly.

Joe shifted uncomfortably, wishing he could disappear. You wouldn't guess it, but Joe loved his father. Tommy was a very caring father. But the drink turned him into a monster. He only started drinking that week. *Why*? Joe thought.

'Whash about you, Matt? Huh? How wash school?'

Matthew looked at his older brother for advice. Joe nodded discreetly at him.

'Fine, daddy; I saw nineteen cows when I was coming home.'

Tommy smiled and sat back, basking in his whisky perfume. 'You shure you were at school and not Cleary's farm?' He laughed, a choking, sad sound.

Maggie swept around the table, placing plates of bacon and cabbage in front of her family. Joe noticed that she pulled her chair a few feet away from her husband before sitting. He assumed she was afraid of him too when he was drinking.

The sound of muffled chewing was deafening, and the odd screech of someone aggressively cutting the bacon and catching the delf plate felt like an incision on the soul. The family was about midway through their taciturn dinner when Maggie finally sliced the tension by speaking:

'Have you finished your homework?' Joe and Matthew nodded in synchronisation.

Tommy, who was halfway through his second bottle of whiskey, blurted out. 'My day wash fine; I'm sure David has told you anyway.'

Maggie awkwardly sipped her water.

Tommy continued: 'Did you shee him today?'

Maggie sullenly continued eating.

'What, you don't want to talk to me now?' Tommy shouted, 'Why don't we talk anymore!' He slammed his fist down on the table, rattling the dishes, and aggressively rose from his chair.

Matthew jumped to his feet before Tommy gained his footing. He ran out of the room, pressing his hands to his ears.

Maggie was filled with rage. 'I don't want to speak to a no-good drunk!' Her face was as red as her neat ponytail. Her deep brown eyes concealed a fear awoken by her haste.

'A no-good drunk?' Tommy repeated with surprise. 'I am not a drunk! You drive me to drink, you shnake! Always shneaking around with David!'

'Then why don't you fire him if you don't trust me?' she screamed in a pitch that could crack a window, pushing up from her chair. 'Ohh, I forgot because he is a better man than you will ever be.'

Tommy slapped Maggie across the face, hard.

Joe, who was frozen with shock, feeling he had to intervene, shot from his seat and hurried around the table to his mother's side. When he reached her, Tommy had a hold of her by her hair. Maggie screamed in pain as Tommy shouted in her ear. Instead of slowing down, Joe transferred all his momentum into strength and pushed his father.

Tommy went flying back and crashed into a cabinet. It exploded in a storm of broken glass. Maggie now darted to her feet to preclude Tommy's vengeance.

Trying to hold Tommy back, she turned to Joe: 'Get out of here, Joe!'

Tommy docked a furious fist under her chin, lifting her off the ground. She crashed to the floor, unconscious.

Joe stood petrified as he watched his father approach him impassively.

Tommy clumsily gripped his empty bottle of whiskey from the table and, as quick as a whip, smashed the bottle on his son's head. Joe's body went limp as he dropped to the floor like a ragdoll, while blood gushed from an open gash on his left temple.

Tommy was looking bewildered and scared at his actions.

As Joe's eyes darkened, he could make out his father sitting cross-legged on the floor holding Maggie. His screaming ears could hear his father muttering; he focused his fading senses on listening before he blacked out.

'I'm so sorry, honey! What have I done?'

Joe could very hazily make out the sound of someone sobbing before his head lulled over and he faded to sleep.

Joe woke in the familiar warmth of his bed. He heard a song his mother always sang when he was sick and opened his eyes.

'How are you feeling, poor boy?'

Joe sat up and groggily raised a hand to rub his aching head. His fingers slid across a bandage. He looked curiously at his mother. I'm hanging in there like a loose button... what happened to me?'

Maggie sat on the bed beside Joe and sighed sorrowfully. 'I vexed your father too much last night, and things got a bit out of hand.'

Joe pointed to the bandage on his head. 'Did he do this to me?'

Maggie shook her head. 'You fell and hit your head, sweetie, that's what your father said, but I have tended to it and bandaged it, just like my mother did to me when I got injured back when I was a small girl.' Maggie began to dream of her past. After a moment, she snapped out of it. 'Yes, a foolish little girl I was. Anyway, all you got is a scratch; it won't kill you. It should heal nicely assuming you don't engage in any levities.' She chuckled. 'Breakfast is on the table eggs, sausages, and apple juice. Your favourite.'

Maggie smiled and kissed Joe on the head. 'Get dressed and come downstairs. You have a lot to do today.' Maggie vanished. Joe collected himself and pulled off his bed clothes to get up. He gathered the same clothes he wore yesterday and began dressing. Joe made his bed and left his room.

In the kitchen, Joe sat at the table beside his brother Matthew, who had finished his breakfast and was now licking his fork clean.

'Mornin Matt,' said Joe.

Matthew dropped his fork on his plate. 'Hi, Joe! Why do you have a plaster?'

'Ahh, I fell and bumped my head, that's all.'

Matthew burst out laughing at that. He was trying to say something else, but he was laughing so much nothing came out, only gasps and wheezing sounds.

Maggie came over to the table and served Joe his promised breakfast. She noticed Matthew laughing and smiled.

'Good to see we are happy today.'

'Joe bumped his head.' Matthew struggled to say, then exploded laughing again.

Joe tucked into his breakfast. Maggie sat across from Joe.

5

'Your father wants you to help trim all the trees in Big-Hill Field,' -both fields were named by Matthew- 'then pack the graded apples in the shed.'

Joe dropped his fork and knife. 'But it's Saturday!'

'I know, sweet child.'

'I was going to help Matthew catch more butterflies. How many have you got now?'

Joe turned to Matthew. Matthew smiled and stuck up four fingers.

'I will never get all that done today!' Joe sulked.

Maggie looked at Joe with pity. 'Please try for me.'

Joe reluctantly nodded and continued eating. Matthew jumped from the table with alacrity at the thought of butterflies and made a dash outside while playfully screaming.

Maggie got up and followed him out, shouting: 'Wait, Matthew! You're only wearing one shoe.'

Joe was now alone. He drank his apple juice with a sullen expression, wondering if Matthew was born lucky or not.

Joe left the house and stood still for a moment; closing his eyes, he allowed the hot sun to kiss his skin. He looked up and quickly shut his eyes at the sudden exposure to the brightness of the gorgeous summer day. He took a deep breath and marvelled at how beautiful the world was. He looked around the orchard and spotted three men in Robin Field, trimming the trees and harvesting apples. He saw another man carrying two buckets crammed with apples to the shed. Joe sighed at this sight, knowing it was more work for him.

He spied his father, wearing his red plaid shirt and overalls, holding a notepad in his hand while also shouldering a shovel. He was talking with a man. He locked eyes with Joe; his sober blue eyes pierced him.

Joe made his way to the tool shed. Opening the door, careful not to knock off the opened padlock, which was never locked for quicker accessibility, a waste of a padlock, Joe thought and approached the wall adjacent to him. Noticing all the loopers were gone, which is what Joe always used because the long arms of the loopers compensated for his height and allowed him to sheer even the top of the trees with ease. All that was left were a blunted and rusty pair of folding saws. Like two archaic switchblades. Joe took one of them in his hand and examined it. *This wouldn't cut paper,* he thought, and left the shed.

On his way to Big-Hill Field, Joe once again peered up the hill at the out of use well beside a towering sentinel, a pale oak tree. Every time Joe looked at it, he was filled with uncomfortable stress; perhaps it was fear. He was not sure why; it could have been the tales he heard at school of monsters living in it or the warning his father gave him and his brother about what he would do if he caught them there. - He was being hyperbolic, of course, but still. Joe liked his backside with the skin on it. - It also could have been the shrill screams he could hear some nights and the dark figure he sometimes spied walking away from the well. His mother was convinced he was seeing things, and everybody put the screeching sound down to the mule and horse acting up in the barn.

Either way, Joe never approached it, but he looked at it every single day, expecting something to jump out and drag him down to the deep unknown. He had an active imagination for a sixteen-year-old.

The Banshee

Finally, Joe continued making his way to Big-Hill Field, when his heart was uplifted. In the middle of the field, David, one of the men who worked there, picked apples from the tallest tree. Joe loved spending time with David; he was funny and easy to speak with.

Joe entered Big-Hill Field through an open gate on a white picket fence. The refulgent sun illuminated the footpath like a golden road to bliss. Joe decided to sneak up on David and scare him while his back was turned. Very silently, Joe tip-toed to David. When he was three steps away, he inhaled deeply to build up a terrifying scream. As quick as a bullet, David turned around and screamed very loudly at Joe. Terrified, Joe lost his footing and fell backwards onto a cart of freshly picked apples, knocking it over. David, laughing very loudly, managed to collect himself and pick Joe up from the overturned cart.

Embarrassed, Joe dusted himself off and looked up at David with awe. David beamed at him through bright green eyes.

'How did ya know I was coming?' Joe asked.

David skimmed a dirty hand through his messy hair. 'Before I started working here, I was part of a very secret group of assassins named the Shadow Dancers.

'We were a highly trained group of killers; we could hear enemies approaching no matter how quiet they were. And we were trained to kill people even with loopers.' David aimed his loopers at Joe. Joe looked amazed and scared. David burst out laughing.

'I made all of that up. I saw you coming down the field.'

Annoyed at how credulous he was, Joe raised his folding saw and shook it menacingly at David. 'I will get you back someday!'

David continued laughing. 'Why are you using a folding saw to prune the trees?'

'All of the loopers are gone. This is all that was left.'

David nodded and handed Joe his loopers. 'You take this, and I'll take the folding saw.'

Joe made the trade.

'Because,' David continued, 'I am much bigger than you, so I can reach everything easily. I will be a gentleman and give the loopers to the small boy so he can reach,' David said mockingly and smiled evilly at Joe.

'Someday, I will be much bigger than you, and I will plant you in this field on your head!' Joe retorted and pushed David as hard as he could.

David did not expect such strength and went flying backwards into a line of apple trees and fell over.

'Get up. We have a lot of work to do.' Joe laughed.

David stumbled back to his feet. 'I am sorry, Mr McNeeve, I will get on it immediately.'

Joe smiled smugly at this title. David looked at Joe and only then noticed the bandage on his head.

'What happened to your head, mucker?' David asked.

'Mum said I fell and hit my head. I really can't remember what happened to me.'

David stared at Joe with concern then restored his cocky smile. 'As long as it won't slow you down, we have this whole field to do today by ourselves.'

'And then after this, I have to pack every apple in the storage shed,' Joe said with a sigh of defeat.

David kissed his bottom teeth and chuckled. 'Sucks to be you.'

A few hours later of tedious branch cutting and apple picking when the sun was on the downclimb from her pinnacle. Joe and David met in the middle of the field again.

David smiled and wiped the sweat off his brow. Joe returned the smile.

'We are making excellent progress, a few more hours, and we'll have the lot done,' said Joe.

David pulled out an apple from his pocket and bit into it. Joe pulled an apple off a nearby tree, examined it, and then chowed into it with a moan of respite. They sat on the ground side by side, eating their apples.

'You can go and pack the apples. I can finish up here; it will only take a few hours,' said David

Joe beamed as if a significant burden had been lifted off his shoulders. 'Are you sure you don't mind?'

'No, I find this very recreational. Just leave me the loopers.'

Joe laid the loopers down. His smile faded. 'Do you know anything about the well at the top of the hill?'

David wore a sullen look and stopped eating his apple. 'Promise you will never go near it, Joe. There is an evil woman that lives there.' David got to his feet.

'A woman?' asked Joe, bewildered.

'Don't ever disturb her,' David commanded and strutted down the field, the loopers swinging idly by his side.

Joe was bemused at David's sudden mood change. Also, a bit creeped out. Not knowing if it was another of his jokes or not, he got up, threw his apple core away, and left the field.

Joe was halfway to the big, galvanised shed at the bottom of the field behind the mansion. The shed was expanding with new extensions to increase productivity and processing.

The sun was almost cracking the rocks on that monumental summer evening; there was not a single cloud to hide the sun's light on the world.

The McNeeve Orchard

Of course, Joe is young and, according to his father, a malingerer. He was never allowed in the factory part of the shed, just a tiny nook of a room on the side, where the packing was done. Joe approached the wooden side door, left his hand on the handle, halted.

He could hear laughing and screeching behind him, and he cast his gaze over his shoulder to see his brother Matthew, running around in circles, seemingly trying to catch something. His heart was filled with a mournful longing to join his brother and play, but if he did not do the work, his father would be very annoyed and possibly lash out again. Joe's memory began to return to him. *I didn't fall and hit my head. He hit me with a bottle!* Joe rubbed his bandaged head. *He was hitting mum!* Joe faced the house. He felt helpless and small; he loved his parents. Why *do they have to fight?* He thought, *and why do they keep mentioning David?*

Upon entering the shed, he was impacted by the aromatic fragrance of fresh apples. After closing his eyes and inhaling a deep scent of the sweet aroma, he reopened them, and his heart sank.

Apple upon apple, rank upon rank an absolute myriad of apples to pack! *I will never get this done today.* He morbidly approached the desk on the opposite side of the room carefully stepped over the overflowing baskets of apples left haphazardly on the floor. Joe sat at the table and exhaled loudly. He reluctantly retrieved an empty box on the floor beside the desk and placed it on the table. He picked out an apple from one of the many baskets compacted on the table and pulled it close to his eyes, examining it for any bruises or other imperfections. After a thorough inspection, Joe deemed the apple healthy and placed it in the box. A few apples later, he came across a dirty, bruised apple; he slid a wastebasket from under the desk with his foot and dropped the rotten apple

11

into it. When Joe had finally filled his box with good apples, he closed the box, sealed it, and stamped *The McNeeve Orchard* brand on the box.

He then carried the box to the side of the room decorated with many empty shelves and left the box on the lowest shelf. Joe returned to the desk and continued the ritual until the sun began setting,

A single ray of light penetrated the small window facing Joe. Dust spores danced in the light, glistening like tiny fireflies, informing Joe that the day was ending. He had spent so long perusing apples he almost forgot about his life. He had decided enough was enough. He did not want to spend what was left of his Saturday packing apples. He was going outside to find Matthew and play with him before dinner. Joe got up from the table, leaving the almost full box of apples. He stretched, cracking half of his skeleton, and made his way outside. He passed by the shelves, which now had thirteen full boxes on them.

Joe covertly left the shed, looking left and right to ensure his father was not around. As the sun set on that beautiful day, the haggard light exaggerated the beauty of the nearby flowers and apple trees that adorned the orchard while shading the nearby woods, giving the trees a somewhat unwelcoming and almost sinister appearance.

Joe sneakily crept around his house, looking for Matthew. As Joe continued his silent search for his brother, he passed by Big-Hill Field to find David was no longer there. *He must have finished the field.* Joe did not bother to put much thought into it.

The longer Joe spent sneaking around, the more he became careless; his slow, precise footfalls were substituted with longer, heavier strides. Until Joe either forgot or did not care about his father spotting him. After a while of not being able to find Matthew. The sun was disappearing behind the hills. Joe was about to resort to calling out Matthew's name, despite being found slacking by his father.

The orchard was full of men working, but no red plaid shirt to be seen. Joe thought that maybe he went into town or something. Either way, the coast looked clear.

Joe glanced at the well and felt a cold shiver run up his spine. He was now at the front of the mansion. *There was no way Matthew would venture out into the woods,* he thought, so Joe did not even bother looking on the west side of the house. He was about to go inside and ask his mother when out walked David, finishing buttoning up his shirt.

'Hey, Joe, did you get them apples packed?' David said coolly.

'Most of them, why were you in the house? And have you seen Matthew?' Joe asked.

David started walking down the footpath to his bunkhouse; Joe trailed at his heels.

'Oh, nothing. I ripped a hole in my shirt earlier, and your mum stitched it for me, bless her good heart. I haven't seen Matthew in a few hours. Is he lost?'

'I don't know; I mean, he's got to be around here somewhere, right?' Joe asked, concern betraying his devil may care attitude

'Exactly, don't go worrying; you will find him, detective McNeeve.' David smiled at Joe as he continued walking.

Joe stopped following David and stood still, thinking he could hear Matthew's screechy laugh. Joe looked over his right shoulder and saw his brother playing beside the well by the great oak tree. Joe felt his heart drop to his guts. He sprinted to the tree screaming his brother's name.

13

When he finally reached the tree he was gasping for air. He saw his brother was no longer climbing the tree but was now hunched over the rim of the well, shouting down into it. Joe grabbed Matthew by the arm and threw him backwards onto the ground. Matthew landed with a crash.

'What are you doing, Matthew?' Joe shouted in a more angry tone than he wanted.

Matthew climbed sorely to his feet. 'Playing.'

'We were told never to come near the well.'

'I wanted to know what the woman wanted,' Matthew replied, holding back tears.

There is an evil woman that lives there.

'What woman?' Joe asked.

'The one in the well.' Matthew started crying and ran back to the house.

Feeling like his soul just turned to steel, Joe approached the well to look down.

Don't ever disturb her.

When he reached the well, he hear a quiet chanting. Listening carefully, it sounded more like a song with incomprehensible lyrics. He craned his head over the edge to look down. Suddenly! From the darkness, the face of an old, decayed woman emerged into sight. Her terrible yellow eyes streaked with thin bloodlines stared not only at Joe but also through him. The deep empty holes in her yellow eyes seemed blacker than the darkness she absorbed. She was clawing her way up the well, her long pale claw-like fingers scraping and scratching the old stones as she groped for the next ledge. Her mouth hung open, revealing jagged fang-like teeth. Her jaw was rigid, but she was muttering something; the sight of the inescapable abyss in her throat was enough for Joe. He screamed and fell backwards, splashing a round frantically, gasping for air. He finally got to his feet, and he followed Matthew.

While sprinting back to the house, he frequently glanced over his shoulder to the well to see if it was following.

He saw an old woman with long red hair wearing a weathered green dress, covered by a grey cloak in front of the well hobbling towards him. Joe screamed again and ran quicker than he had ever run before.

Joe dashed in the front door, slammed it shut, and pressed his hands and body against it to make sure that it would not budge. He took one deep breath before realising Matthew was standing at the foot of the stairs, hugging his mother, who wore a look of pure shock. Matthew was crying in his mother's arms.

'Joe! What on God's green earth is going on,' she yelled.

'She's coming!' said Joe, terrified, panting for air. 'The old woman in the well!'

Maggie started to get scared, seeing how terrified Joe was. she outstretched her hand to him while cradling a crying Matthew. Joe, sobbing, cowered in his mother's protective embrace.

'There, there, don't be afraid anymore, my poor boys,' she said softly. 'Dinner is almost ready.'

Matthew clapped his hands joyfully and ran into the kitchen screaming, 'Dinner, dinner, dinner!'

'No running in the house!' Maggie yelled after him.

Joe was tapping Maggie's shoulder until he had her attention. He looked at her with serious eyes. 'There was an old lady following me, I swear it.'

Before Maggie could reply, there was a steady knocking. Joe began crying loudly and pulled Maggie away.

'That's her, the old lady! Don't let her in.'

Maggie pushed Joe aside ignoring his warnings.

It was not an old crone, but a beautiful young woman, her radiant red hair and beautiful green eyes seemed to enchant anybody who looked upon her. She wore a very cool minty sun dress accompanied by a well-tailored straw hat. After a brief silence, she noticed Maggie was too enthralled to start speaking, so she decided to break the silence. She smiled, dazzling Joe and Maggie with her pearly fluorescent teeth.

'Sorry, I don't mean to disturb you at this hour. My name is Anne. Would you be Mrs McNeeve?' Her voice was as smooth as warm milk.

Maggie nodded and finally collected herself. 'Yes, I am she, Maggie, if you wish. I'm sorry, who did you say you were?'

Anne stepped closer. 'Anne Sullivan.' She took another unconflicted step inside and saw Joe staring at her with blatant attraction. She smiled at him.

'Aren't you a handsome young man; what's your name?' she asked—bending slightly, so she was at eye level with Joe. Joe seemed to be under a spell and had forgotten how to speak.

'Hmm?' Anne tried prompting Joe to answer her question.

'Ohh, for goodness's sake!' Maggie blurted out, ashamed of her son's behaviour, 'His name is Joe.' Maggie walked over to her son, walking around Anne to squeeze Joe's shoulder, trying to revive him from his empty state. Joe felt as if his blood had frozen in his body, making it impossible to speak or move.

Anne smiled once more, staring at Joe; she brushed his cheek with an ice-cold finger.

Maggie watched with slight horror.

'I will be seeing you soon, Joe.' The way she said his name sent a biting chill down his spine. He could never imagine a beautiful young girl having such a shrill broken voice.

Anne turned to leave. She stopped in front of Maggie. 'Maggie, isn't it?'

Maggie nodded. 'Yes, it is. Do you live around here?' Annoyance and disgust in her tone.

Anne smiled mischievously. 'Yes, yes I am. I just moved here, and I just wanted to meet the neighbours.' She smiled again, and left before any more questions could be asked about her. Maggie watched her leave, dumbfounded.

Anne started humming a song on her way down the road. Joe, who finally came back to himself at the sound of the song, ran to the window to watch. Anne turned her head to look at him, only she was no longer the beautiful "Anne Sullivan," she was a wretched decomposing old woman. Joe looked to see if his mom was watching; to his distress, she had gone into the kitchen. When Joe gazed back down the driveway, he did not see anybody, but he could still hear the faint humming of the song. It was only then his mind had caught up enough for the song to become discernible. It was the same song he heard coming from down the well.

<u>II</u> OF DREAMS AND FOXES

Joe lay in bed, the dim light from his gas lantern was not enough to illuminate his room, but he was thankful for any sort of comforting light tonight. His eyes wide and his head turned to the side, looking out a small gap between the dark curtains, at a stary sky. Constantly picturing the wry smile of that old woman and the song she was humming. Joe remembered the song so clearly in his mind; for a moment, he was not sure if he was thinking about it or really hearing it.

I will be seeing you soon, Joe.

There was a knock on his bedroom door, it peeled open, and in emerged Joe's father, Tommy. Joe turned his head. Tommy approached Joe's bed gently, picked up a clay sculpture off a nearby shelf on the way, and sat on the bed.

'How are you doing, son?' Tommy asked.

'Tearng away like a hole in a sock. Thank you,' Joe replied stiffly and uncomfortably.

Tommy began fidgeting with the sculpture of what appeared to be a dragon—examining the poor craftsmanship with his fingers. Tommy raised the dragon to his eye to better make it out. It was not detailed and looked like a lump of clay, poorly carved to appear as a dragon.

'This is a terrible figure; where did you buy it?' Tommy asked, continuing to turn the dragon over in his hands.

'I made it in school.'

'I am sorry... how is your head?' Tommy asked quickly, blatantly changing the subject while carefully peeking under Joe's bandage, looking at the gash that had begun to scab. 'I am very sorry, Joe.'

Joe stared with knowing eyes at his dad. 'Mum says I fell and hit my head.'

Tommy met his omniscient eyes and smiled shamefully. 'Yes, that is what happened, but I am sorry for fighting with your

mom, arguing all the time; it's not the way a man should behave.

'I am setting a bad example for you and your brother. For that I am—'

'It's alright, dad.'

'It's not alright; I am the man of the house. Recently I have been acting so puerile. I know you didn't finish packing the apples, and I don't blame you. It was too much work for one boy to do, so I will help you tomorrow, hmm? We will make a day of it, eh?' Tommy beamed.

Joe smiled back, momentarily forgetting the woman in the well.

Tommy placed a firm hand on the bed sheet where Joe's knee was. 'That woman you saw today, Anne... whatever it was, is just some child-minded fool. I promise I will never let her hurt you.

'Even your mom seemed a bit put out at dinner,' Tommy shifted uncomfortably. 'She is a dangerous woman, Joe. I don't want you or Matt to ever speak to her. She didn't... touch you... anywhere, did she?' His face flushed white.

'No!' Joe answered immediately, unsure what that meant but not wanting his father to be upset.

'Good, I tell ya boy, if I ever see her around here, I'll plant my foot so far up her arse, when she drinks, she will be washing my toes!' They both laughed.

Joe swallowed the real reason he was terrified. At that moment, he did not know what frightened him more, the horrible face of the woman in the well or telling his father he was at the well—disturbing *her.*

Tommy smiled and got off the bed. Putting Joe's dragon back on the shelf.

He turned around. 'Goodnight and I'll see you tomorrow,' Tommy said softly and left the room.

Joe rolled over in his bed and continued staring out the tiny gap in the curtains at the stars thoughtfully. Joe lay there in deafening silence, knowing he would get no sleep that night.

I will be seeing you soon, Joe

The next morning, Joe woke up as always, on the brink of dawn. During the week, his father rang a bell outside the bunkhouses to wake the employees. However, being the weekend, there was no bell, but being woken at the same time every day had left him with a mental alarm clock. Joe rubbed his haggard eyes, wondering if he fell asleep at all or not. It seemed like an endless night, but here it was, ended. Joe pulled himself out of bed and dragged his feet to his wardrobe, getting dressed. He made his bed by carelessly throwing the duvet across the mattress and went downstairs.

Joe slid his hand down the bannister as he descended the stairs. He entered the kitchen to find his mother sitting at the table, elegantly sipping a mug of tea, an empty plate in front of her with segments of a good breakfast littered around the plate. She was wearing a maroon dress with her hair flowing down to her shoulders. She watched Joe enter the room and smiled at him.

'Good morning sweetie, how did you sleep?'

'Morning, I slept fine, thank you, what about you?' he approached a cabinet to get a box of cereal. Maggie finished her cup of tea and used a nearby napkin to dab her top lip. Joe filled his bowl of cereal with milk and poured boiling water into a mug with a teabag sitting on the bottom to make himself a cup of tea.

After stirring the teabag around in hot water, he removed the tea bag and added a splash of milk; he stirred again, briefly. Satisfied with the golden brew, he carried his breakfast and tea to the table and took a seat. He shovelled his cereal into his mouth with his spoon. - He was not in a hurry; this was just how he ate. - Maggie watched him, trying to look for the best time to strike a conversation between his bites, but between his rapid arm filling his mouth and his incessant chewing, she decided to make her own time. Maggie cleared her throat. Joe stopped munching and devoted his attention to his mother.

'Your father told me you were terrified last night about the woman we met yesterday, Anne or whatever her name was.'

Joe's eyes widened at the name; he gulped. 'Were you not scared?'

'I'm not sure who she was, but like your father said yesterday at dinner, we will never let her near here again. She will not hurt you or Matthew.'

I will be seeing you soon, Joe

Joe attempted to smile, but he still felt in danger. He knew he could not explain what happened at the well, his mom would never believe him, so instead, he nodded at Maggie, 'Thanks, mum. Is Matthew awake yet?

'I am not sure; I will check on him now.' As Maggie was about to leave the kitchen, she almost walked into Tommy, who was entering the kitchen. He caught her by the waist and playfully spun her to preclude a collision. He kissed her on the cheek, smiling. Maggie returned the smile while continuing the twirly dance and then placed her hands on his face. Joe could slice the tension with a dull blade, but they were trying to move on as nothing had happened. Maggie continued up the stairs.

A forgiving interaction, Tommy thought, but he could not sense the deep coldness of Maggie's feelings for him.

Tommy entered the kitchen smiling; he approached the still hot kettle on the stove. Joe, who had just finished drinking his tea, brought his dishes to the sink and washed them. Tommy softly slapped his son on the back.

'Did you have a good breakfast?'

'Yes, sir,' said Joe.

'That's great to hear, boy; we got us a day today.'

Joe felt cheerful at how chirpy his father was, but he didn't ask why. *He made up with mum, and now we will be a happy family again.*

Tommy sipped his tea carefully, doing his best to avoid burning his lip while pouring his breakfast.

'I better head out to the shed and get packing the last apples.'

Tommy sipped his tea again. 'Good lad, I will be out as soon as I finish my breakfast.'

Joe left the house through the back hall, connected to the kitchen; the back hall was mainly used as a storage room—packed with unused blankets and cabinets filled with God only knows what.

Joe stepped out and was instantly smothered by the heat of another beautiful day. He smiled warmly and took a deep breath. He was inhaling the fresh perfume of apples, blooming flowers, and pine trees from the woods to his right. He squinted his eyes from the blinding sun to look at the rolling hills and fields in front of him, beyond the fence. Stretching on as far as the eye could see, dotted here and there, hungry cows. Joe once again found himself pondering how big and spectacular the world really was when a sharp easterly breeze slapped his face hard and forced him to turn his head.

He opened his eyes and saw he was facing Big-Hill Field, and beyond that, he could see the top of the oak tree crowning the hill, guarding the well. Joe felt suddenly queasy at the thought of the woman.

I will be seeing you soon, Joe.

Peaking from behind the great tree, Joe could see a figure watching him. Hoping it was David, Joe waved. The figure did not wave back. Wondering who it could be but dreading the worst. Joe shielded his eyes from the sun with one hand and strained his vision to discern the figure. To his horror, he saw the silhouette was coming towards him, not walking or running, but floating rather quickly.

With a cowardly screech, Joe began sprinting to the shed, the anxiety of feeling sharp, ice-cold claws slicing through the back of his neck and ripping his head off intensifying. Not looking back this time. His shaking hands easily found the latch sealing the door and slid it open. He threw himself in, falling to the floor. He jumped to his feet and forced all his weight against it. He panted heavily without blinking. This would be his last moment alive, and he spent it cowering and crying. Rational thought left him; he had never felt so afraid. He croaked out his father's name, a final plea for rescuing, but his voice shattered in his trembling throat, his hands were shaking violently, and his heart hammered in his chest. Tears flooded his eyes. All he could do was wait. Wait for an unrelenting force to knock him to the ground, wait to see those wicked eyes as she slowly tore his head from his shoulders. Listen to his neck muscles and tendons pop and tear as he watched his body grow smaller as his detached head rolled away behind the table, into the bin with the bad apples.

After what felt like a lifetime with nothing happening, Joe built up enough courage to look out the window next to him, hoping not to see her but expecting to. Feeling both comforted and uneasy at the sight of the empty pathway. There was a crash. Joe suddenly fell back with a petrified scream. He shut his eyes tight and began crying uncontrollably. He felt two strong arms grab his shoulders and pull him up.

'What the hell is going on, boy?' a familiar voice boomed.

Joe opened his eyes and saw his father standing in front of him. Flushed with relief, Joe hugged his father tightly.

'What happened to you? Did you fall? Are you hurt?'

'No, I was—' In that instant, Joe realised he could not tell his father the truth about what had just happened. Instead, he lied: 'I fell and I think I twisted my ankle.'

Tommy looked at his son suspiciously. 'You fell and twisted your ankle?' he repeated unconvinced.

Joe nodded.

'You screamed.'

'It hurt.'

'… loudly.'

'Badly.'

'Do you need to see the doctor?'

Joe shook his head. 'No, I'm okay, just needs a bit of time to heal,' he said, dangling his foot loosely.

Knowing he would not get the truth from his son, Tommy decided to press the matter no more. He lightly slapped his son on the shoulder. 'If, you're sure. Now, there is no point in standing around with our hands in our pockets. We have work to do.'

Tommy walked over to the shelves with the boxes of packed apples, making a mental note of Joe limping to the desk across the room.

'Thirteen boxes? Did you do this all by yourself? Or did you have help?' Tommy said, amazed.

'No, I had no help. Me and David pruned all the trees in Big-Hill Field, and I packed these apples after.'

'It was dark when I looked in here last night. I thought you only packed four boxes. There are only a few hundred apples to get through so. When we get done here, you can go play, assuming your ankle will not give you trouble.' Tommy shot Joe a doubtful look. 'You're becoming a very hard worker; you will be the man of the house soon.' He laughed.

Joe avoided eye contact, smiled, and began examining apples, 'Hopefully, it will be just fine.'

In the stuffy little apple-scented shed, Tommy and Joe spoke no words as the time passed. They were mainly focusing on working so they could finish and enjoy the rest of the glorious Sunday. Every now and again, Tommy whistled a tune and abruptly curtailed it, only to restart it a few minutes later. Joe never learned how to whistle. After they examined the apples and put them in the box or the bin, depending on their state, Tommy would carry the box to the shelf. After two hours of silent labour, Joe's mind strayed to the well and what lurked in the deep dark.

At last, Joe cut the silence: 'You know when you bought this land thirty years ago?'

'Thirty-two,' Tommy corrected proudly.

Joe nodded, acknowledging his mistake. 'What was it like?'

Tommy was taken aback at Joe's uncharacteristic interest in the history of the orchard. 'Well, your mother and me were just married. We lived in Tipperary, that's down South. I wanted to become a farmer, so I started looking for some cheap, prolific land we could settle in. We heard about this very affordable plot of land in Mayo, so we came up here to look, and well, I fell in love with it.

'So, we bought it that day and moved in.' Tommy smiled, reminiscing on his youth. 'I was always interested in a lovely country lifestyle since your age. Me, Uncle Luke, and a good few local lads built the main house; my father was a builder, you see, and I was always good with my hands and a quick learner.

'After that, we realised apples were the easiest thing to grow here; it already had a few apple trees scattered around, so we planted more. Before we knew it, we had a whole orchard; I built them bunkhouses and hired some lads to help harvest. We built this shed.' Tommy smiled with pride. 'We built fences to divide the fields; then we extended the size of the main house.' Tommy placed the last apple in the box on the table, closed it, and sealed and branded it. He brought the box over to the shelf and put it down with a sigh of relief.

Joe noticed Tommy never mentioned the well, which was the only thing he wanted to learn about.

'What about that old oak tree and the well?'

Tommy fell dangerously silent. Like a quiescent sky about to unleash a boom of thunder. 'I told you, boys, before, don't ever go near that well or even talk about it. It is cursed. I will hear no more about it... you didn't go near it, did you?'

'No, of course not,' Joe lied, then he realised his father was also... scared of the well; maybe he knew more about the woman. *I better not ask.* 'I'm going to go play now.'

Before his father could make any further inquiries, Joe left the shed and ran down the beaten path to the woods. Tommy watched his son runoff without limping. A terrible suspicion aroused in him: *why was he lying? Did he go near the well?* Tommy desperately hoped Joe did not awaken the banshee.

The tree line grew closer; he slowed his pace down to a walk as he joyfully gazed at the luminous green leaves on the trees, exaggerated by the bright, warm light of the sun. Without hesitation, Joe disappeared into the bushes on his very own fabricated path. Joe had travelled that trail many, many times. You came to a clearing if you continued through the woods for about two hundred steps. And in this clearing lay a pond. Joe had never told anybody about his hideout, nor did he ever intend to.

That was Joe's private paradise. He elegantly danced through the trees, dodging all the low-hanging branches and skipping aside to avoid the blatantly rude branches that always tried to rip his clothes. He could not help but smile and sing along to the bird's harmonious songs. He laughed again and mused about little houses in the trees as if little people lived in them. A ludicrous thought, but it was an occurring fancy when he walked in those trees. All his fears left him, and his heart was uplifted, as it always was when he passed through that wooded gateway to serenity.

Joe emerged from a thicket into the glade. The opening was almost a perfect circle, crowned with trees. As if a round fondant cutter was used to remove a patch in the forest and replace it with beauty. There was the pond, looking like a sparkling pool of sapphires in the bright rays of the sun's grace. And in the centre of the pool, a large, white protruding rock, like that of a closed hand, pointing to the sky with a crooked index finger. The pond itself was adorned with flowers of all colours: bog cotton, primrose, foxglove, and even Irish lady's-tresses. Joe once thought this was a fairy summoning ground, where they tried to summon a giant from the pond.

He smiled and plonked himself down on a cleft by the water. His back against a smooth angled rock, perfect for lounging. As he gazed at the pinnacle of the rock in the pond, his peripherals decorated by the many colours of the lucid flowers, his eyes got heavy, very heavy. He closed them, heightening his sense of smell which was drowned in the poignant odour of nature. And his hearing, full of critter dialect he could not translate, bird song he could not understand, and the continuous whoosh of a dormant wind. Joe dozed and, before long, was comfortable in a wild dream.

He was in a dark pit with a luminous blue lid. He could faintly hear high-pitched voices, chanting, seemingly in another world. as the chanting grew louder, so did the blue roof grow closer until Joe could touch it. It felt soft and squishy yet plaint to the touch, like a balloon filled with water. The chanting morphed to cheering and plaudit as Joe vivaciously tore the shield attempting to hold him back from the world. The blue wall fell away like water on a rock as Joe breathed in the free air. Carefully he stood up as if he had been crunched up in the pit for four lifetimes. He began to rise slowly, and he rose higher than the trees, and he kept rising until the tall trees was waist-high to him. Bewildered and fascinated, Joe began to look around.

The orchard was no longer there. He could see for miles over trees and hills. His attention was snapped to the high-pitched laughing and cheering, so he looked down to figure out the source of the squeals. To his surprise, Joe was looking down at curious creatures he somehow knew were fairies from the stories his mother used to read to him. Tiny, winged, almost humanoid creatures. Green, they were all different shades, seemingly all females. Some were a dark evergreen; some a bright topaz, and the rest were every colour in between. They all had bright ginger hair and short yellow skirts. None of them wore shoes as there was no need. They always flew. As Joe watched the hundreds of little colours rushing around and laughing, he pictured a field of bright flowers dancing in the wind. Catching a glimpse of his own arm, he discovered his body was made entirely of stone. However, he did not feel concerned; he was too gladdened by the singing fairies to be troubled.

Suddenly the once clear blue sky morphed into a crimson shade. A murder of crows flew overhead, squawking in their horrendous croaks. Everything went quiet. Then the peace was ripped apart by a shrill, blood-curdling scream that shook the very foundations of the earth. The fairies were crying and screaming, attempting to hide, echoing the words, *she found us, she found us* Joe looked up, a resounding crash of thunder seemed to rip the sky in half, revealing nothing but a vacant dark, devoid of anything. A shape began emerging from the tear. A prodigious head took the face of the old crone. Her blood hair flowed onto the tiny trees. Her eyes were giant empty pits. A monstrous boney hand gripped him around the waist, squeezing with an unbearable force; Joe could both hear and feel his stone body being crushed to dust. He tried to scream but could not. In a whimpering breath, the large eyeless face seemed to wheeze the name, *Joe.*

Joe woke with a jolt to find he was still sleeping against the rock in the glade. Judging by the sun's position in the sky, he reckoned he was asleep for about an hour. Shaking with fear, he quickly looked around to confirm that he was only dreaming. He was. The bright colours waving around the pond caught his eye, and he remembered the fairies, zooming back and forth. *It was only a dream*; there *are no fairies or giants as* he thought his eyes were drawn to the protruding rock in the pond resembling a giant's hand. He remembered being a stone giant. *It was only a dream... it had to be.* Joe groggily rubbed his eyes when he saw, on the adjacent end of the glade next to a tree. A fox, a beautiful red and white fox with a twitching nose and curious eyes. Joe could not help but smile at that chance encounter. Being a lover of wildlife, he was afraid to make any sudden movements in case he scared the critter away. As the minutes passed on, Joe started growing uneasy with the intimidating fox; it was pretty content, silently staring at Joe. The fox opened its mouth and barked; the bark sounded much too near the name *Joe*.

He was now filled with a frightful threat. He briskly got up and walked to the thicket behind him where he came from. He stopped and turned around to take one last look at the fox, making sure it was not following him. The fox was no longer where it was standing; it slowly crept towards him, maintaining eye contact. The fox picked up its pace and slowly trotted towards him, forcing Joe to hurry back to his house.

Running through the woods to get home, Joe was a lot clumsier. He fumbled his way through the branches. A terrible feeling of being savaged by the fox drowned him. He almost fell over a thick stem that snapped under his foot, but it did not go without a fight. A smaller rogue branch connected to it broke free and slashed him across the cheek, painting a warm red line on his face. Joe stopped and turned around. He wiped the thin wet slit on his face.

He froze as if he had indeed turned to stone. Crouching behind a tree was a hooded figure, just staring. It pulled off its hood. There was no mistaking the crimson red hair and personable smile of Anne Sullivan as she stood dormant.

With a deep swallow, Joe took a step backwards. Anne screamed his name *Joe* and started sprinting towards him. Instantly Joe's flight instinct kicked in. He turned around and ran as fast as a superhero through the trees. He stumbled over low-lying branches and had his shirt torn by higher ones. It did not seem to slow him down in the slightest until his foot caught on a thick old root that tripped him. He took such a hard fall that he could not recover instantly; it knocked the wind out of him.

Seeing his house through the last few trees filled him with translucent hope. A shrill cackle grew louder and louder until he could feel it bouncing in his ears. *She finally got me,* he thought. Feeling hopeless and helpless, Joe tucked his head in his arms and raised his knees to his chest. He was lying on the ground like an overgrown fetus. A warm surge ran down his leg. He was waiting for the worst to happen. Waiting.

III TUATHA DÉ DANANN

He Watched his son run off into the woods, noticing he was not limping. Tommy contemplated the conversation in the storage shed between him and his son. Joe asked questions about the well; he was terrified and lied about injuring himself. *Why*? Tommy pondered deeply as he walked back to the house. *Did Joe go near the well*? *Could he have woken the evil that lurks there*? *The banshee*. Tommy feared this would happen someday. He had told his kids never to go near the well, but he could not stop them. He was told not to block off the well or seal it. There was only one man who could help, a man who had looked evil in the eye more than once. It was time to visit an old friend.

The gentle breeze cooled his sweat-drenched back as Tommy walked around the house. The grass swayed to the music of the wind; the trees were too lazy to dance in the heat. The scent of apples and wildflowers filled Tommy as he approached the shed connected to the house. He pulled open the two white wooden doors. As spacious as the shed was, the centre space was taken up by a large carriage that was used to transport the apples into town, tucked away beside this large wagon. Sat a smaller cart, large enough for two people to sit on. Tommy pulled this small cart out of the shed. When he got it out, he brushed the dust off the seat and made sure the harness was sturdy. Firmly shaking the wheels to make sure they were tight and kicking the spokes to test the axel connection. Pleased with the results, he shielded his eyes from the sun with his hand and gazed down the field to the barn. He then looked behind him to the house, wondering if he should get the mule from the barn first or tell his wife he was going to town.

David approached him. He was wearing a clean white French shirt with green town pants. His short light brown hair combed over, and his bright green eyes smiled at Tommy.

'Mornin boss!'

'Mornin.'

'Lovely day isn't it?' said David.

'Divine.'

David could almost feel the tension between them. He laughed awkwardly. 'Divine, quite right.' *There is no way he knows.* 'You wouldn't happen to be heading to town, would you? Any chance I could tag along? I have to post a letter to mum.' David reveals the letter to Tommy.

Tommy thought hard. He needed to speak to David to find out what was going on with him and his wife if indeed would truly move on. 'Yeah, sure thing. Would you mind hooking this up to the mule? I had better tell the wife where we're going.'

Tommy passed into the house.

'No problem, are you gonna start paying me for weekend work now?' David joked in the distance.

Tommy entered the house through the front door. His eye was drawn to a table hugging the wall across the stairs. The table was intricately carved, with a lion's head protruding from each side. The top of the table was finished with a soft layer of marble, and the cabinets were ornamented with silver crescent handles. Pricey, yes, but a fine piece to spruce up a boaring hallway. Lounging on the table was a framed family photo; Matthew, Joe, Maggie, and himself were all smiling in front of the Eiffel Tower. Tommy laughed because he had never been to France, or anywhere outside Ireland for that matter, *them drop screens at the gallery make a very convincing portrait.* Tommy tried to remember what they did that day after the portrait; They spent the day shopping for shoes; Maggie was the fussiest, as always. He laughed. They had a picnic by the Lake. Matthew was trying to see the fish and fell in; Tommy had to jump in to save him. He never did get around to teaching Joe and Matthew how to swim; it did not feel as important anymore, the family has not had a day out since. Nor did it feel like they ever would again. he gently retired the portrait on the table with a longing for happier days. He could hear voices down the hall. Maggie and Matthew. He continued down the hall towards the voices.

Tommy entered the room on the left at the end of the hall. The sun was glaring through the window shades, making the wall look as if it were locked up behind shadow bars.

Maggie and Matthew were sitting at a simple wooden table in the centre of the room. Maggie was trying to teach Matthew his letters. Matthew, who kept fidgeting uncomfortably, just wanted to go outside and play.

Maggie looked up when Tommy. 'Go outside and play; we will finish this later,' Maggie said to Matthew while ushering him out.

Matthew stopped just in front of Tommy.

Tommy scuffled his hair and smiled. 'How are you doing, Matt?'

'Good. I'm going outside now to play with the buzzing B's and even C's.' He laughed.

'As long as you don't, P,' Tommy said.

Matthew burst out laughing and ran down the hall.

Maggie closed the children's alphabet book aggressively, and she sighed with frustration. 'Come to hit me again?'

Tommy sank into the nearest shabby armchair chair, taken aback. 'I am so sorry. I will never touch alcohol again, I promise. I don't want to lose you.' Tommy jumped out of the chair to Maggie, holding her hands in his. 'You mean the world to me. And Joe and Matthew, you all mean the world to me. I never want to hurt anybody again! Can we not go back to the way things were before David came along?'

Maggie slid her sweaty hands out of his. 'What is your obsession with David?'

'Maggie. I know about you two. I have always known.' Tommy paused to select his following words carefully. 'You are a married woman Maggie, my wife with two children... maybe I messed up, perhaps I should have been a better husband.

'I'm sorry, but please put an end to whatever you're doing. I will forgive everything.' A tear pooled in his truthful eyes. 'I will forgive you, and we will forget everything. All you have to do is tell me.' Pain flowed down the wrinkles of his ageing face. 'Tell me t-t-that you still love me.' Tommy breathed deeply and looked into Maggie's eyes, searching for her soul. 'I will forgive it.'

Maggie turned ghostly pale, almost translucent. She could not bring herself to see the agony in her husband's eyes, agony she caused. At that moment, she wanted to say it. Needed to say it, *Tommy, I do love you. I will not see David anymore.* But she couldn't lie to him, and she couldn't be honest without shattering him, so she stared at a curious knot on the wooden floor. She stared at it; it looked like a snake coiled up, ready to strike. Maggie wished it would strike her; Then, she would not have to answer. At length, she tried to speak but choked on saliva. She lifted her regretful gaze to address Tommy but could not speak. He stepped very close to her, and she sensed a rage off him. A wave of dangerous anger that made her muscles constrict in terror. He understood the implicit message in her silence.

'I'm going into town,' Tommy said, 'and David is coming with me.'

Maggie pulled back. Her sorrowful face twisted into worrying disapproval. 'Ohh Tommy,' she cried, 'please don't hurt—'

'What? You think I would kill him?' he interjected.

Her frightened appearance confirmed it. He left the room, slamming the door behind him.

Maggie collapsed on a chair and drained her teary eyes.

Before leaving the house, Tommy stopped to look at the family portrait on the table one more time. A heartbroken sobbing filled the hallway. Tommy admired how happy they were in the photo. He looked at Maggie's smile and beautiful happy eyes, then Joe's smile and dark blue eyes, then Matthew. He looked even closer at Matthew, smiling at him with his green eyes.

David had secured the mule to the carriage and had placed some boxes of apples behind the seat when Tommy emerged from the house. David sat on the leather bench in the small carriage and held the reins. Tommy climbed in beside him and took the reins off David without saying anything.

David laughed. 'I thought you might have got lost in that big house of yours.'

Tommy remained silent and gave the reins a flick to propel the mule forward. It was a forty-minute walk to the town of *Hollystone,* but on such a glorious day as that, there was nothing better than enjoying the beautiful scenery.

The cart rolled up the main path under the arched stone gateway and turned west. The sun seeped onto their faces from above. David retrieved two worn grey caps out of the compartment in the wagon; he gave one to Tommy and slotted the other one neatly on his head. Tommy did the same. The wagon rolled on along the country track. The two men rode in silence.

David was looking out, enjoying the view, fields of green and yellow hills as far as the eye would allow one to see. Some fields were decorated with blooming green trees: pine there was, fir, beech, ash, and even some oak. Some fields were spotted with daisies, others with daffodils. Some fields were dressed in flowers and unkempt grass others were manicured. The countryside was alive with birds flying to and fro the trees busying themselves, singing away while they worked. The curious cows could not help but look to the road to investigate the clip-clap of the mule's footsteps followed by the gentle thunder of the wagon. The smell and air of this country were unequal powerful. The sun was now as high as she would rise, radiating her beauty across the land. The wagon rolled across an old but reliable stone bridge laying on a stream. David looked down at the water to see a crystal-clear stream of liquid silver gently flowing down the hill accompanied by the relaxing sound of busy water. The sunlight danced on the surface of the water, looking like hundreds of shy glistens that hid when you looked their way.

David breathed deeply, inhaling the pungent fragrance of mother nature herself. Tommy, however, did not look content.

He possessed a troubled look and a quivering lip like someone who needed to know the answer to a question he did not want to ask.

Tommy edged in with small talk: 'It's a lovely day.' If not particularly interesting, a comment on the weather was always a safe conversation starter.

'It's gorgeous; about time we had some good weather. The constant rain is depressing.' David laughed and softly elbowed Tommy's arm.

Tommy did not return any friendly gestures. He stared ahead, hoping the refreshing breeze would spark the courage he needed to get to the point in that "conversation." 'What brings you into town today? Just the letter? You know the post office doesn't open on Sunday'

'I know yeah, I'll just leave the letter with Michael, and he'll post it tomorrow, instead of coming in to post it Wednesday with the delivery.' He paused, admiring the cloudless, deep blue sky. 'That's not the only reason I'm going in today, though.' David shuffled cheekily. 'I am meeting a girl.'

Tommy considered David curiously.

'Some lovely girl came by the orchard yesterday, and she invited me out today. So, I told her to meet me at the pub,' said David dreamily. 'She is an angel of a woman Tommy, enchanting brown eyes, and long red hair. A voice like silk, and she smells like flowers; exotic flowers, flowers I have never seen, but I know how they look by the smell of them. Does that make sense?'

Tommy shook his head; however, he was thrilled, no, relieved to know David had another woman instead of his wife.

'Why are you going into town today? If you don't mind my asking,' said David.

'I have to see the priest about a...' Tommy hesitated to utter the name. Then he taught better of it. 'Well, about a private matter.'

David nodded. 'I have brought a few crates of apples from the shed; it should lighten the delivery for us next Wednesday.' His green eyes were glowing.

Tommy nodded, feeling stupid. He never thought about bringing the spare apples. *He is too smart and handy around the orchard to get rid of.* Tommy thought, but the affair with his wife meant David could not stay. Or maybe he could. Tommy was internally perplexed. He thought long and hard about Matthew and his green eyes. David was hired ten years ago; Matthew is nine. *How long had they been sneaking around*? Tommy did not want to confront David on the matter, knowing it would turn ugly, meaning David would leave, which would lead the orchard into ruin. And no doubt Maggie would leave with David, sundering his family and life. Tommy felt his existence being strangled, knowing he could not stop it. Focusing on the bigger picture and the reason he is going to town. Tommy held his silence.

The cart rolled into a small town, Hollystone. A village might be a more accurate word. There were six white-washed wattle and daub houses with finely trimmed straw roofs. The town was compacted inside a significant clearing of the forest. One of the buildings had two stories; the rest were bungalows. Every building in the town had flower boxes on the windows, adding an elegant colour scheme of red, blue, and yellow to this otherwise bland town. The two-story building was the post office; beside that was a small, tidy house with letters over the door. *Burkes Groceries* a small, faded sign on the rain-washed blue door in an obnoxious bold font read: *Closed.* A longhouse with a newly built outdoor seating area was across the wide trail that cut its way through the town. Over the heavy brown and white door hung a big round sign. On this sign was a picture of a freshly pulled pint of Guinness with the words: *The Irish Oasis* written in bright yellow text around it.

Further up the road was a pretty little building *Forde's photography.* That was where the McNeeves visited the Eiffel Tower. The last two houses just appeared to be accommodation. A middle-aged woman was outside the nearer house on the left, watering the flower boxes on the windows.

When the cart reached the centre of the town, David jumped out.

'I better get out of here; I have never been a churchman, and I don't intend to start now.'

'Maybe now is a good time to start,' Tommy retorted sullenly.

'Hah?'

Tommy stopped the wagon and helped David unload the crates of apples.

David slipped his letter safely into his pocket. 'Letter' he looked down at the crates. 'apples' David combed his hair with his hand and pointed to the pub. 'Lady.'

Tommy climbed back in the wagon and urged the mule on with a flick of the reins. Over his shoulder, David was piling the crates on top of one another,

'I'll be here in two hours if you want a lift home,' he shouted back to David, bringing the crates to the grocery shop.

David waved a hand nonchalantly. 'Would you like any more bottles of whiskey?'

Tommy shouted back: 'No, thank you,' he then quietly continued, 'I will never touch the drink again.'

Tommy drove the cart through the town, around a corner on the far end. There he met a woman and her daughter picking berries from the hedges.

'Hello, Teresa, and good heavens that can't be little Mary?'

The young girl nodded her head and smiled. Teresa was a middle-aged woman with bright brown hair tied back in a ponytail. Freckles concealed her bright grey eyes and stubby nose.

'How old are you now?' said Tommy.

'Fifteen,' Mary answered.

Mary was Joes best friend at school. She had two brown pigtails adorning her head and looked like a miniature version of her mother, with fewer freckles.

'You are nearly as old as my Joe, a few more years, and you will be older than all of us.' Tommy laughed, and Teresa and Mary joined in.

'We're picking berries for a pie,' Teresa said.

Tommy beamed at Mary. 'That sounds yummy. Can I have some?

Mary nodded.

'Joe would love some too, I bet; he loves pies. I'll bring him round.' He winked knowingly at Teresa. They laughed; Mary hid her blush.

'Well, I better keep going, goodbye!' He waved.

Tommy proceeded down the road. Around the corner that cut off the town with dark evergreen trees. Amid the forest sat a small church. The steeple brushed the canopy of the trees. The tall hedges on both sides of the road were speckled with wild violet fox-fingers and ripe blackberries. The cart was halted outside the small wooden gate which was hanging on the listlessly built stone wall outside the church. If he continued down that road for 50 meters, he would come to the Gardaí barracks.

Tommy stepped down off the cart, leaving his hat on the seat, and passed through the open gate to the church. He placed one hand on each door and pushed hard. *Locked*. Tommy walked around the church, inspecting the building. When he was behind the church, he espied a small wooden cottage with clear smoke emitting from the spotted. He exited the churchyard and entered the tended grounds of the cottage. He noticed the lawn had recently been trimmed, the flowers had been watered, and there were ornaments of rabbits and other critters scattered around the garden.

Tommy knocked three times and waited quietly, listening. A few moments passed, then a kind, smiling man faced Tommy. His black shirt and white collar marked him as a priest.

'I am afraid you are a bit late.'

Tommy stared in bewilderment.

'Mass ended four hours ago,' the priest said with an accompanying chuckle.

'Ohh.' He laughed, 'Father Waldron, you probably don't remember me; my name is—'

'Tommy McNeeve, your wife is Maggie McNeeve. You own the orchard down the road,' the priest answered with enthusiasm.

Tommy stood there, impressed. 'You have a good memory, father.'

The priest chuckled and beckoned Tommy inside. 'Won't you come inside? I have just boiled the kettle, and I have egg sandwiches.'

Tommy nodded politely and entered.

The cottage was indeed very small but very comfortable. The heat from the stove was enough to warm the whole room. Tommy made his way to the table and sat down on a wooden dining chair. He was admiring a picture of a lake hanging on the wall. Father Waldron busied himself making tea for two and dishing up the sandwiches.

'Milk? Sugar?' asked the priest.

'Just a spit full of milk, please,' retorted Tommy.

The priest walked over to the table, holding a plate of egg sandwiches and two cups of tea. He placed everything on the table across from Tommy. Tommy gladly reached for a sandwich and his cup of tea. Father Waldron did the same.

'So, Tommy, I assume you're not here to say the rosary,' the priest said while biting into his sandwich.

Tommy shook his head. 'I fell out with God when he took my mother,' Tommy answered. 'Do you remember when I first moved here... you told me there was a fairy ground around my land and I shouldn't desecrate it?

Father Waldron carefully sipped his tea. His radiant blue eyes shone behind the mug.

'My sons were playing up there yesterday, and father, they are not acting the same since. I am worried. My oldest son Joe seems to be petrified, and I don't know what's scaring him, and he won't tell me the truth. All I got from him was the mention of some woman and the well.' Tommy took a swig from his cup.

The priest sat back and closed his eyes, shaking his head. 'The banshee.' At the mention of the name, the bright room seemed to be swallowed by transient darkness, and there appeared to be a strong breath of wind blowing the trees eastward for a moment.

Tommy shivered. 'Ever since you first told me that name, I never liked it. I don't even know what it is, and I still fear it.

Father Waldron leaned forward in his chair. 'When you first moved here, I tried to admonish you about the fairies, and if I remember correctly, you laughed and told me not to worry. Do you believe in them now?'

Tommy stirred uncomfortably. 'I don't know, and I just want to help my son.'

The priest nodded. 'Fairies are believed to be Tuatha Dé Danann. One of the first tribes to arrive in Ireland. A magical people. They fell in love with the beautiful land, so they decided to shrink themselves and live underground. For generations, they have sat quietly and watched as people immigrated to Ireland. They farmed the land and built wondrous things. They reside in wonderfully beautiful places known as fairy circles.

'The fairies and the Irish people co-existed unanimously. Our ancestors revered them and built monuments for them, and out of appreciation, the fairies summoned spirits and even giants to aid us in building and other assortments. They created leprechauns, spirits that took the form of small, jolly bearded men. That gives people luck and wealth. They created giants to help us build with larger stones. They created a spirit called the banshee. This spirit took many forms.

'Legend says if you hear the cry of a banshee or see her in whatever form she has chosen. It warns of a family death. Or if you find her hair comb, it's the same result.'

Tommy leaned forward inquisitively. 'I don't understand. Is my family in danger?'

'Yes and no.' He finished his tea. 'The banshee herself was not meant to be a dangerous spirit.'

'Was not? You mean she is now?' Tommy interjected.

'The banshee was the creation of the fairies. They created them to inform mothers if their sons were killed in battle. But, somewhere along the way, the banshee spirit became too powerful for the fairies. Maybe they underestimated her for too long, or perhaps the fairies blinded themselves with her supposed loyalty, or maybe the banshees were very deceitful. No one knows for sure.

'There is only one discernible fact. The banshee is no longer under the control of the fairies. They are a liberated spirit; some are peaceful, benign entities who still perform their duties. Some are hateful demons with an insatiable hunger to destroy fairies and anyone who gets in their way. I fear the banshee tied up with your family is evil!'

Tommy sat back heavily, both perplexed and scared. 'What do you mean tied up to my family?'

'The fairies created the banshee for their friends, the first people who settled in Ireland. Anybody who can date their lineage back to the first settlers.'

'The first settlers? Jaysus father, I don't even know my grandad's name.'

'Your family was among the first in Ireland.'

'How do you know?'

'Your name...' Tommy still looked confused; Father Waldron continued, 'if your surname is Mac, Mc or O', your family has more than likely had a banshee since your great great great gre—'

'Okay, I get it.' Tommy put down his empty mug. 'Why is it in the well?'

'I read somewhere that banshees use wells as gateways between worlds; that's how they get around, you see.'

'Excuse me, father. You keep saying banshees, and they... do you mean there is more than one?'

Father Waldron locked Tommy in a severe stare.

'How can you know all this?'

'I am a priest; I have heard it all. Also, in my youth, I acquired a rather strange book. It has no author's or title, for that matter., but whoever wrote it is sage. It possesses a rather ethereal account of all the spirits that traverse this country. I am not sure where I left it, but I will get it to you when I find it.'

Tommy bowed his head. 'So... how do I get rid of them, father?'

'There is only one power greater than a fairy.' The priest's retrieved a silver crucifix tucked away under his collar. 'God almighty is the only one who can help you.'

'Forgive me, father, but I have never been a religious man, so somehow I doubt the Lord will make any time for me and my problems.'

The Priest smiled a toothy grin. 'The Lord never turns his back on his children, even if they have turned their back on him. The Lord forgives; all you need to do is ask.'

Tommy laughed.

'You don't have to get rid of "them"; only one banshee was assigned to each pure-blood Irish family,' Father Waldron continued, 'Your banshee is malignant. I sensed it twenty-four years ago when I blessed your home—A potent, evil spirit. You must be careful. Their power grows with fear and hate.

Tommy gulped, 'You said she takes many forms. How will I know her?'

'There are many accounts of banshees in different forms. Sometimes an old crone wearing a grey cloak with red eyes from crying so much. Sometimes she is a beautiful young lady; some say she can even turn into animals. And there are a few accounts of her changing her size. Sometimes she is very tall other times, she is hunched over, and other times she is described as a feeling. However, she is always described as having blood-red hair in all her forms.

'Except for a scarce case when she has silver hair and a white dress. But that's a very rare thing. It means the banshee

46

has devoted her life to one person and becomes somewhat of a guardian angel.'

Tommy instantly remembered the account his wife gave him yesterday evening of the beautiful woman.

(Beautiful crimson hair, lovely brown eyes.)

What was her name, Anne something? Suddenly David jumped to his mind.

She is an *angel of a woman Tommy*, *enchanting brown eyes and long red hair.*

Worry took hold of Tommy. 'Thank you very much, father, for everything,'

Father Waldron shuffled as quick as he could and shouted after Tommy as he hurried off: 'Should I be expecting you at mass tomorrow?' His voice fell dead upon the dormant breeze; Tommy was already gone out of earshot.

Tommy sprinted back out onto the road through the churchyard, past his mule and wagon; he figured that would be too slow, so he continued running into town. The day had grown colder. Not just because there was a sharp chill, the temperature seemed to have just dropped. The once loud sun was now hid behind a heavy dark cloud. The world no longer felt like a bright, happy place. The ostentatious flowers which adorned the hedges along the road were cowering into their grassy fortress. The sweet scent of berries had faded into a fetid stench of putrid meat. The singing birds had fallen dumb.

Turning the corner into town, Tommy looked up the main street and saw no one. It seemed a lifeless town. He ran up to Burkes grocery store, where the crates of apples were left outside. Tommy pushed the intractable door. He called out for David, but there was no answer. Tommy ran to the post office, the same outcome. Next, he went across the road to the pub, yelling David's name. There was nothing but silent echoes floating through the ghost town.

Suddenly Tommy heard a high-pitched, blood-curdling scream vibrating around the quiet village; it came from the woods behind the post office. Tommy took off running towards the scream, David might not have been his favourite person, but he needed him. *He needs me!* He jumped into the nearest thicket and ran like a charging bull through the trees, pushing some branches aside and snapping other ones by running through them. As he sank deeper into the woods, he noticed it was getting darker. Not because the shrinking sun on his right shoulder was disappearing behind the trees, it felt almost unnatural; it felt emptier and colder. He could faintly hear a whimpering which grew into sobbing, like an animal caught in a trap when it realised it was about to die. *Does it know it's going to die?* he briefly thought.

Tommy passed into a small field, hidden by thick trees. The image that greeted him petrified him. There was David, lying on the ground, squirming. A horribly grotesque creature with red hair was stooped over his body, eating him alive. The creature appeared to be clouded in a shadow, making it barely visible. Tommy had never seen so much blood. David seemed to be alive because he was twitching and sobbing, but other than that, he appeared to be dead. He was not fighting back. The creature looked up at Tommy with its bloodshot yellow eyes and screamed. The scream was so loud and powerful it knocked him off his feet. With all the energy his adrenaline gave him, he quickly got to his feet and bolted heedlessly through the trees.

Tommy, who was not one for running, could have left the fastest man on earth behind in the dust. He ran for what felt like an age of the world in a straight line, with the feeble sun on his left side, until eventually, the adrenaline wore off.

Tommy now realised how exhausted his limbs were and collapsed onto the ground. Shutting his eyes and falling into an unwanted sleep before he even realised it.

He awoke several hours later. The sun was sinking behind the dark silhouette of the hills and was being relieved by the moon. Tommy was groggy but swiftly remembered why he was there. Then he was terrified, he was freezing, and he was lost. Reacting instinctively, he turned around, putting the sinking sun on his back, and walked east, hoping he would find the road or the town or even the orchard. He might not have been the most intelligent man alive, but Tommy always had a good sense of direction.

He finally came to a road he knew to be the road from his house into town. He breathed a sigh of relief and kept heading east. Tommy walked on through the impenetrable darkness. Stirring at every twig break, tree rustle, and beast that dared disturb the silence.

David, was that real? Cold tears pooled in his blurry eyes. He shivered from the bone aching chill, but he knew he was almost home. He remembered that he had left his mule and cart outside the church. He knew Father Waldron would look after the mule. But David? Despite everything that he had done, David was still Tommy's friend. And no man, friend, or enemy deserved to die like that. Inadvertently Tommy started remembering David lying helplessly on the ground and the monster that killed him. Its yellow eyes, terrifying scream, hideous body, and red hair. That was her, the banshee. She would go for his family next. He started walking faster as he looked about the darkness and began to see animated shadows everywhere.

It started raining, heavier and heavier until the road was drowned in a deluge. A crack of Thunder violently shredded the perilous silence. Suddenly a bright white bolt of lightning lit up the unassailable dark, revealing what the icy light of the dim pale moon could not—Tommy's house in the distance. With a crazed chuckle of relief, Tommy began running as best as he could.

The incessant rain made it difficult to look up; Tommy was exhausted and sore. His clothes were soaked, adding substantial weight to his movement. Still, he carried on. Through the arched gateway, up the track, past the barn and the bunkhouses, to his house. He began knocking, exhaustedly.

Maggie opened the door wearing her bed robes, with a look of stress and relief on her face. 'Tommy! Where have you been? Why are you back so late? And where is David?' Maggie asked in a quick, whispered shout.

Tommy, managed to say: 'David is dead.' Before falling face-first on the floor, blacked out from exhaustion.

$\underline{\mathrm{IV}}$ THE CLIFF

Three long shadows glided along a wet dirt road towards the descending sun.

'Miss Harrington is a horrible teacher. Look what she did to my knuckles for not knowing how to spell cousin. C-u-z-i-n. That is how it's spelt.'

'At least she used the cane on you,' Joe said through a busted lip, a fresh bruise stained the left side of his face.

Joe wrapped a comforting arm around Matthew, who was sobbing incessantly.

'You shouldn't have called her an eejit,' Mary said, feeling rebellious and laughing.

'So, I was just meant to watch her beating Matthew? It's not his fault he doesn't know what five times four is.'

Matthews's hands were bloody and bruised. Joe was shouldering his school bag and Matthews. Mary was carrying her own.

She smiled at Joe. 'You are so brave.'

Joe blushed a feminine pink under his black bruise. 'I wonder if my dad is alright. He was asleep on the couch downstairs when we were going to school. He went into town yesterday, and I didn't see him for the rest of the day,' Joe said with a touch of worry in his voice.

'I saw him. He was heading to the church,' Mary said.

'The church?' Joe looked deeply confused. 'Why would he go to the church?'

Mary shrugged her shoulders. 'Then we met David in town. He had boxes of apples. I like David; he's hilarious.'

A blatant flash of jealousy zapped across Joe's face. 'Yeah, he's great, not as strong as me, though.' There was no humour in his defensive tone.

Mary laughed. 'Are you jealous?'

'No!' Joe stated confidently but was betrayed by the red tint of embarrassment.

'You've gone red!' Mary pointed mockingly to Joe's face and laughed.

Matthew stopped sobbing and added his screechy laugh to Mary's innocent girly giggle.

'Shut up,' said Joe, visibly nettled. The laughter died down as they continued walking.

A gentle rain soothed the sun-kissed landscape. The birds sang in a choir of happiness as the grass and flowers drank deeply from the soggy soil. The fields were coated in a blanket of moisture, twinkling in the sunlight like a world of diamonds. The trees stood solid and proud even with their soaking wet hair. The lazy cows did not mind being wet; they enjoyed eating slippery grass. The heavy clouds were threatening another downpour. The sun peeked in and out of the quiescent clouds, reflecting a bridge of many colours from the water drops in the sky.

'Look a rainbow!' Mary said while pointing into the adjacent field. 'We should follow it and get the pot of gold.'

Matthew clapped his painful hands carefully yet excitedly. 'Yeah, yeah, let's go!' Matthew screeched with ebullience.

Joe held him back. 'No, we are going home. Besides, leprechauns aren't real.

Mary looked devastated. 'Excuse me, Joe McNeeve, they are so real!' Mary took Matthew by the arm. 'Come on, Matthew, you and me will go.'

Joe tightened his hold of Matthew's other arm. 'We are going home!'

Mary released Matthew's arm, and he was fired back to Joe, who went crashing to the ground.

'Is big strong Joe gonna beat me up?' Mary teased.

'Don't be so childish. I just want to get home.'

'Childish? Me? You're the one acting childish.' Mary did her best impersonation of Joe: 'Don't do this. Don't do that. My name is Joe. I'm big and strong, and I never get scared!' Mary laughed.

'I don't get scared,' Joe confirmed with pride.

'Yes, you do, I saw it; you were crying yesterday, and you peed in your pants!' Matthew said, accompanied by a loud screeching laugh.

'Shut up, no, I didn't!' Joe snapped defensively.

Matthew continued laughing.

Mary gently left her hand on Matthew's shoulder. 'What are you talking about, Matthew?'

Joe stirred uncomfortably. 'He is only joking, trying to make a fool out of me.'

Matthew shook his head, laughing. 'No, you got chased by a fox and started crying and peed your pants.'

Mary shielded a laugh with her hand. 'Joe McNeeve scared of a fox?'

'Leave it!' Joe spat and walked ahead of the other two.

Mary, who felt guilty about teasing Joe, looked at Matthew. He returned the stare while licking his chin. She smiled and shrugged her shoulders, linked arms with Matthew, and followed Joe's shadow.

Joe trudged angrily; he knew what he saw. It was her. She was chasing him. Anne was running after him. *She was going to kill me, wasn't she?* Indeed the last thing he remembered before fainting with fear was being curled up on the ground crying, feeling like a helpless bird about to be devoured.

His mother found him lying alone at the foot of the woods; she approached him worriedly and tried to rouse him. When she rolled him over, she realised his face was glazed in tears, and he was lying in a puddle of his excretion. After managing to shake him awake, Joe seemed to be stunned. He was muttering some incomprehensible nonsense. Maggie helped him walk back to the house. They met Matthew, who had just left the kitchen with stains all over his face from his playful lunch. Matthew took one look at Joe and burst out in his screechy laugh, clapping his hands excitedly. Matthew had never seen anything more humorous than his pee-drenched brother babbling to himself. Maggie pushed him aside impatiently to bring Joe up the stairs to his room. Matthew followed noisily.

Maggie gently laid Joe in his bed and removed his wet clothes and undergarments. Joe stared at the roof, muttering:

'She got me.'

Matthew screamed, seeing Joe naked on his bed. Maggie was beyond fed up with Matthew's silliness, and she hastily beckoned him out of the room. After placing a blanket over Joe, Maggie sat down beside him and put her hand on his forehead. She was checking his temperature. He was icy to the touch, his eyes wide open, staring at nothing, and was muttering the word *fox* over and over.

Maggie starting to make assumptions about the event, asked: 'Did a fox attack you?'

Joe gave no reply.

Maggie persisted. 'Were you chased by a fox?'

Matthew, eavesdropping behind the closed door, pushed it open, laughing. 'Joe got chased by a faw-awks, Joe got chased by a fox. Matthew sang in a mocking singsong.

Maggie was now visibly irritated; she got up and shoved Matthew away, commanding him to go downstairs.

Matthew descended the staircase with heavy footfalls and his iconic screeching laugh. The sounds echoed around the dormant house like the morning sun spilling light into the dark corners of the night. Maggie stood, watching Matthew go downstairs. She turned around to look at Joe. He was lying dumbfounded in his bed. She shook her head in worry, unsure of how to treat her son—hoping Tommy would know what to do when he returned from town *with David*. A new terror gripped her. *Please, God, don't let anything happen between them.* She stepped out of the room.

Thankfully, Joe was feeling better later on and came down to the kitchen for dinner because Tommy did not show up until very late that night. And David was dead.

Joe tried to remember more about Anne and the woods yesterday but was suddenly snapped back to the present from his thoughts by Mary calling his name from behind.

Joe turned around to see Mary and Matthew, standing arm in arm by a tangential country road. The long dirt trail climbed gently uphill to a small, white-washed cottage with a damp straw roof. Across from the house was built a barn. Chickens were pecking the ground for seeds, harmoniously clucking, as they followed the rooster around. A man was busying himself around the farm, carrying a brown sack to the barn. Sheep were grazing around the field carelessly, secretly being watched by a silent sentinel. He was indeed very good at his job of being a guardian. He had watched his sheep for six years with no casualties. As ferocious as he was, he did very much enjoy being scratched behind the ears and having his belly rubbed. Sam the sheepdog he was called, and he was very obedient, but he had a soft spot for Mary and would often abandon his watch to greet her when she returned from school.

Joe returned to his companions.

'I will see you tomorrow. Me and mummy are going to bake a blackberry pie today. Shall I bring some into school tomorrow for you?' Mary asked.

Matthew nodded his head.

'Yes, please. I love pie,' Joe answered gratefully.

Mary chuckled knowingly. 'Mummy said she is going to teach me how to bake it. We were out picking blackberries yesterday when we met your dad,' Mary said.

Joe instantly remembered all his worries about his father, like a bucket full of horrible thoughts, were dunked on him; he remembered the well and Anne.

Mary watched Joe's face turn sallow under the bruise. 'Are you alright?'

'Yes.' *No.* 'I was just thinking about our homework.' *I was really thinking about the well, and Anne. And how she wants to kill me! Ohh, God, why can I not stop thinking about her?*

Mary laughed. 'Homework? Alright. Well, see you both tomorrow!'

Mary waved at the boys; she smiled at Joe.

Matthew yelled: 'Goodbye.'

Joe readjusted his shoulders to secure his tenuous grip on the backpacks. He gently took hold of Matthew's hand, and they continued walking down the road.

The Cliff

It was a fifteen-minute walk from Mary's house to the orchard by the road, but Joe had learned if you cut through the field with the chestnut tree looming at the gateway, you can cut the journey down by half. There was a long, precipitous drop on the hill at the back of the field, which Joe had climbed up and down multiple times, but Matthew had never seen it. And the wet ground would make it more deadly,

Joe, being Joe, figured it would be grand and decided to risk it. Also, he had had enough of this new game Matthew began playing, where he jumped into every single puddle in proximity. Joe and Matthew continued down the road until they reached a gateway beside a towering chestnut tree. Instead of climbing over the gate as he usually did, Joe looked at Matthew's sore hands, pulled up the gate's latch and swung it open with a metallic screech, and guided Matthew inside. The field was empty. Sometimes it housed some carefree cows, but not now.

While walking up the gentle slope of the knee-high wet grass, Joe released Matthew's hand and allowed him to skip cheerfully through the daisies. While Matthew was skipping happily through the flowers, he started humming a song Joe was quickly able to recognise; his uncontrollable mind raced back to the song emitting from the well and what the fairies were singing in his dream. *Yes, it was only a dream!*

He lost himself in his head but quickly snapped back to consciousness just in time to find Matthew at the top of the precipice, dancing.

'Matthew, stop!' he yelled. Panicking. Joe sprinted to his brother. Matthew froze and turned at the resonant hollering of his name. He was then vigorously pulled back by Joe, almost losing his footing in the process.

'You have to be careful, Matt. There is a big fall here.'

'I can see it,' Matthew replied.

The Banshee

Joe took a step in front of Matthew, looking down the drop, trying to find a safe path to climb down to the bottom. Turning to his brother, Joe commanded him to wait there and said he would go first. Joe dropped to his knees, swinging one leg out over the drop, rubbing it along the soil wall, trying to find a foothold. He found one. He prudently lowered himself to find another solid place for his other foot while test gripping the sturdy-looking rocks before he trusted them with his weight. Joe continued that arduous climb down, all the time growing more cautious about how he would get Matthew down. The rain certainly did not help; everything was wet and slippery; three times, Joe's hand slipped off stationary roots, and rock's almost falling to a deadly fate if it was not for his body strength. The fall was not high enough to kill, but a hard fall on sharp rocks would be perilous for anybody. The climb was not made any easier by the two heavy schoolbags dangling pendulumlike from his shoulders and his rain-heavy clothes.

Finally, Joe's feet hit the ground ending the difficult descent. He took a step back and looked up at the cliff wall. He was very hesitant about asking Matthew to attempt the climb, having himself just about being able to do it. He could not let his brother find his way home alone, and he had not had the energy to climb back up. So, there was only one option.

Joe would stand directly under him, so if he did slip and fall, he would theoretically catch him. An insane plan, but Joe was never really a vital thinker.

'Alright, Matthew, climb down,' Joe shouted through a megaphone created with his own hands to amplify his voice.

Matthew's leg appeared over the edge, followed by the other one. He was now clinging helplessly to the wall, too afraid to move. He started crying and screaming for Joe, standing directly under him with open arms waiting to catch him but naively hoping he would not have to. There was a very lucid path Joe found, and he tried his best to get Matthew to use it:

'Put your left foot lower; come on, Matt, you can do it!'

The sun hid behind a loud cloud, obfuscating the light. The once lucid path was veiled by shadow. Joe could no longer see the trail for Matthew to use. He was about halfway down; his arms ached badly, sweat trickled from his forehead and mixed with tears. And then, the panic kicked in. Matthew trashed around recklessly, trying to hurry his decline by recklessly throwing his weight on whatever looked sturdy enough to hold it. He grabbed hold of a rigid-looking branch and, before testing its steadiness, shifted his weight onto it. The branch snapped with a thunderous crack. Matthew desperately clawed at the wall trying and failing to prevent his inevitable fall.

Down he fell with a scream that would make a banshee block her ears, an eight-foot drop onto the sharp rocks.

Alas! He did not hit the rocks. Instead, he landed in his brother's open arms and knocked Joe to the ground with a crash. Joe smashed the back of his head off a rock and was momentarily dazed. There was no response from Matthew. Joe collected himself and tried to rouse his brother, shaking him, calling his name, and slapping him on the face softly. Nothing. Joe sat there holding his unconscious brother, wondering what he should do.

Suddenly a burst of heartwarming laughter lit up Joe's face.

'I got you! You were scared, huh.' Matthew laughed.

Joe smiled with sudden relief. 'Don't do that to me, Matt; I thought you were hurt,' Joe said sternly but playfully.

'My hands hurt,' Matthew said while displaying his cut and bruised hands. Joe stood up and patted the wet dirt off his pants. He picked Matthew up and gave him a small brush down with his hands. The two brothers continued walking arm in arm through the field over the hill, where the orchard was visible.

The sun leapt in and out from the clouds to spit light on the world. The gentle breeze personified the grass and flowers, making them dance to its sweet song. The innocent birds chirped in their happy orchestra. Matthew was cheerfully skipping through the long grass, picking flowers and chasing butterflies. Joe tightened his grip on the two schoolbags and gently rubbed the bruise on his face. As they got closer to the orchard, the powerful scent of apples and home filled his lungs. Joe and Matthew carefully climbed the small fence enclosing Robin Field and made their way to the house. He snatched two plump red snacks from the trees.

Joe first noticed how quiet and deserted the orchard was, which was very unusual for a Monday evening. None of the workers appeared to be around. Matthew sprung into the house,. Joe followed him and paused beside him in the hall. They could hear raised voices coming from the kitchen. Joe and Matthew quietly sneaked down and saw all the workers and Maggie and Tommy in the kitchen.

'David went into town with you,' said Paddy. 'and he has not come home! Where is he?' Paddy had a big voice and a bigger belly.

'He said he was just posting a letter! Why did he not come home with you, and where is the wagon?' John said.

'Yeah?' The remaining three men protested in synchronisation.

Tommy quietly sat on a chair, staring into his clasped hands.

The Cliff

Maggie spoke on her husband's behalf: 'David attacked Tommy and stole our wagon and some money we had lying around.' The lie came quickly and effortlessly to Maggie.

Tommy gazed at Maggie dubiously; he could not even entertain the fancy that she would try to defend him over David.

'He would never do that, and you know it!' John shouted.

'If he is not home by this time tomorrow, I'm going into town and bringing the Gardaí out here,' Paddy said. On that note, he turned around and left the house, followed by his entourage of colleagues. They all ignored Joe and Matthew on the way out. Matthew ran upstairs.

'She was eating him alive Maggie, oh God, what was I supposed to do? So, m-much blood!' Tommy buried his head in his hands.

Joe walked into the room. Maggie was standing by the stove, and Tommy was crying in a chair.

'What happened with David?' Joe asked.

Tommy continued to ignore everything,

'He attacked Tommy and stole the wagon,' Maggie said, looking distressed. She did not believe it herself.

She knew David was dead, and as far as she knew, Tommy killed him out of anger and vengeance. Then why was she defending him? She loved David, but maybe she loved Tommy more. Perhaps she loved her children and did not want to sunder her family. Or perhaps she was just scared.

'How much money did he steal?' asked Joe.

'What?' Maggie snapped.

'You said he stole our money too.'

Maggie avoided looking at her son. 'Ohh, about a hundred pound.'

'About a hundred? How do you not know the exact amount?' Joe asked and was instantly cut off by his enraged mother.

'For Christ's sake, Joe, stop pestering me! Do you have homework? Go help David with his.'

Joe looked bemused at Maggie. 'Matthew.'

'What?'

'You said David, but you meant Matthew,' Joe clarified.

'Yeah, right go.' Maggie ushered Joe out of the room with a swish of her hand. Joe took one last glance at Tommy, who was still in a stupefied state. Without another word, Joe left the room.

When Joe was halfway up the stairs, the kitchen door slammed closed like a gunshot in an empty graveyard, and Maggie quietly shouted at Tommy. Joe sat on the stairs, listening as best as he could.

'Is it true; what you told me last night?' Maggie asked with no reply. 'Tommy McNeeve, you had better speak to me right now! What is the matter with you?'

Joe heard a very audible sigh, then the click-clack of his mother's heeled shoes growing louder and louder. Joe crawled quietly but quickly up the last few steps and hid behind the bannister

'You need to get to thinking before the Guardaí gets here!' Maggie said, with many notes of worry in her voice. She left the kitchen, and cried. Her howls and sobs made Joe picture an injured Doe. Eventually, she retreated down the hall to the living room.

Joe's heart was cleaved in two. He wanted desperately to comfort his upset mother, but he knew he had better leave her alone and do what she said, so he continued up the stairs to Matthew.

Some hours had passed, the haggard sun was now slipping below the hills. Joe had finished his homework and had helped Matthew complete his. He was not much use when it came to algebra and Matthew less, but he was very persistent.

They had been playing tic tac toe for who knew how long. Joe was too afraid to leave the room in case his mother was still upset, and he did not even know what was wrong with his father. *David attacked him, but he was acting so strange. David wouldn't do that!*

Matthew announced he was hungry, and a deep rumbling in Joe's stomach confirmed his shared need. Usually, Maggie had dinner ready around that time; Joe began wondering if she would make dinner at all. Assuming the worst, Joe stood up and quietly sneaked out. He looked left and right to an empty hallway; dust particles floated wildly in the last light of day. He turned around to Matthew before he left.

'I will get us a sandwich. You stay here, Matt.' He knew the second he left, Matthew would follow; unless: 'Let's play a game, I will sneak downstairs and you keep watch up here. Let me know if you see anyone. We can't get caught, do you understand? By mum or dad.'

Matthew laughed and jumped around.

'Sssshhh.'

Joe didn't understand it, but he felt getting caught by his parents would be very dangerous. He left the room.

When he reached the bottom of the inconveniently squeaky stairs. He paused for a moment, listening intently, and heard nothing. He tip-toed to the kitchen. To his surprise, his father was no longer sitting there. So much for his stealth mission. He wondered where his parents were, but at that moment, he had only one objective: make sandwiches for

63

himself and his brother. Joe busied himself around the kitchen preparing ham and cheese sandwiches; just as he put the last slice of cheese on the bread, he glanced out the window. To his astonishment, he saw David standing at the foot of the woods and staring in the window at him. Joe dropped the cheese on the floor; it landed with a wet *FLUP*. He raced out the back. His idea was to confront David himself and find out what has happened. Hear the tale from the horse's mouth, as it were. David would never hurt him; they were best friends; at least, that is what Joe kept telling himself. He descended the three steps and out to the woods.

As he got closer to David, he called his name. No reply or acknowledgement came from David; he remained standing like a statue staring at Joe.

'David, what is going on?' Joe asked; he was slowly creeping towards the dark silhouette of the looming woods. When he was about a stone's throw away from David, he quietly turned around and walked into the woods. Joe cautiously followed him, calling out his name. Joe was always terrified of the forest in the dark but need drove him on. David was headed deeper and deeper into the woods. The quiet moonlight barely lit up the woods, and the dying sunlight could not penetrate the dark girth. Go. Joe picked up his pace to a slow jog to catch David; no matter how slow or quick Joe moved, David always remained the same distance away from him; even when he was running, and David was walking, he still seemed to equal Joe's pace.

Out of the woods, David led Joe. Behind the shed going west towards Big-Hill Field. The final strand of sunlight had faded, leaving the world in darkness save for the weak gloom of the pale moon peeking out behind large sailing clouds. Joe's soul turned to steel when he realised David was heading for the well. Joe stopped in his tracks. David stopped moving also. Joe was now staring in anticipation at David.

David slowly turned around; only it was not David. The old woman with glowing yellow eyes and blood-red hair was hobbling towards him. Joe was frozen in fear. She seemed to absorb the darkness. He could do nothing but stand there and watch the woman approach him.

He tried to get his legs to move but could not. The woman was now standing directly in front of Joe. She dropped her jaw grotesquely low. The smell of death was the first thing to pierce Joe, followed by an echoing scream, which was enough to revive Joe. He attempted to run but suddenly felt a scorching pain in his right wrist. He screamed and looked down to find the woman had a hold of him. Her grip singed his flesh. She stared into Joe's soul, smiling; she wheezed Joe's name. A sound best described as a harsh storm mixed with death.

Suddenly a booming yell came from the house. It was becoming louder and clearer, rapidly approaching where Joe was. It was Tommy calling Joe's name. The woman released her firm grip on Joe as Tommy got closer and stepped back, facing him. The darkness around her seemed to grow thicker until it consumed the woman, and she was gone leaving nothing but the faint humming of her song.

Joe was now lying on the ground, crying, holding his wrist. Tommy dropped to his knees and examined Joe's arm. The flesh on his arm was red raw, and glowing. There was a symbol burned into his skin as if he were branded by the hand of Satan himself.

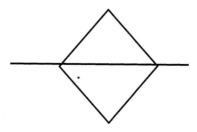

Tommy put his arms around his son and carried him into the house.

Joe was laid on the couch in the living room by his father. As he lay there, searing pain emitting from his wrist and sudden exhaustion from the adrenaline dying out. Joe passed into a deep sleep while his father did his best to wrap up the wound with a sheet he found, covering a nearby armchair.

<u>V</u> A FATHER' S DUTY

Tommy paced back and over the room, all the while glancing at an unconscious Joe, trying to rationalise what he just saw. *Was that the same thing that killed David? It didn't look the same, but that hair, that red hair. Maybe Father Waldron was right. It must be the banshee.* Tommy looked down at Joe's arm, covered in a white sheet saturated with blood. *Maybe I should wake Maggie up and get her to look at it.* Suddenly, the living room door cracked open with a screech. Tommy snapped around.

'Why is Joe asleep there?' Matthew asked.

Tommy relaxed. 'Hullo Matthew, how are you, sport?'

'I'm hungry,' Matthew briskly replied.

'That's right; we didn't have dinner. I am sorry, son. I will get us something to eat. Could you do daddy a big favour and go upstairs and get mommy?'

Matthew turned and ran upstairs. Tommy wiped the cold sweat from his brow. He hadn't really spoken to Maggie or anybody since he returned from town. His wife undoubtedly thought he killed David. *How can I explain what really happened? Is she going to think I did this to Joe as well?* Tommy had so many questions and no answers. The sound of hurrying footsteps from upstairs coming down the stairs pierced his eardrums. It was time to plead his case.

Maggie burst into the room, wearing a maroon nightgown. Her hair was tangled in a mess, and her eyes were a heavy red from crying incessantly. 'Oh my God,' she cried while looking at Joe. She gently picked up his arm and unwrapped the sheet. Inspecting his burnt wrist, she glanced up to Tommy, an indiscernible thought behind her eyes. 'What did you do?' she asked fearfully.

'No, no, no, I did not do this. Maggie, you know I'd never.'

Tommy tried to reach for Maggie's hand. Like a shot, she rose to her feet and grabbed an iron poker from the fireplace. Aiming it at Tommy, she built up all the courage her drained body would allow.

'Get out of this house right now and never come back, you, animal!'

Tommy was taken aback and frightened. He approached Maggie to hug her. She swung the poker at his head; he reacted quickly and jumped backwards. The poker ended up just missing his right temple.

'GET OUT OF MY HOUSE!' she screamed.

Tommy, seeing there was nothing more to be done, there was just no way to convince Maggie he did not do it; he turned tail and left the house.

Standing outside, Tommy was quickly cloaked by the icy breath of the bitter wind. The white glow of the failing moon barely illuminated the orchard. Everywhere he looked, the looming darkness slowly devoured the world. And every silhouette looked like a monster waiting to lunge.

Tommy felt petrified; unforeseen danger lurked in every direction. He felt alone and naked in a hostile world. Every sound was intimidating, from the wind shaking the trees to the hungry badgers foraging and all the nocturnal insects crying. All those sounds dampened into a susurrus noise.

Tommy could hear crying emitting from everywhere. The ubiquitous wailing sounded like Maggie. Thinking she had stepped out of the house to cry, Tommy did not hesitate to find her.

He could see (barely) that she was not at the front of the house, so she must have left through the back door. Tommy ran around the west side of the house, all the while the crying hammered louder in his ears. When he turned the final corner of the house to the back, he noticed Maggie walking up the hill towards the well. 'Maggie, wait!' he called after her. She continued heading for the well, crying.

The crying almost sounded like she was saying, 'Tommy, please help.'

She sat on the edge of the well with her head in her hands, sobbing gently. Tommy approached her and caressed her softly.

'It's alright, Maggie; it will all be alright; I can explain everything.' Tommy rubbed her shoulders. The crying stopped, and she was now chuckling very quietly. Tommy, perplexed by this sudden mood change, took a step back. She began cackling frantically. Tommy stumbled backwards and fell to the ground. She raised her hands to her head and slipped off her hood.

That hair.

Tommy was terrified to see it was not Maggie, but instead an old crone with dark red hair and a wrinkly odious face. She smiled grotesquely and lunged for Tommy, wrapping her long cold fingers around his throat. She picked him up with unperceived strength and held him over the well. She dropped him. Tommy did not know how long he was falling for – the well was only ten foot deep - and what he would find if he finally landed. All he knew was that he was afraid; he was very afraid. Until suddenly, he hit the ground.

Tommy groggily opened his eyes. Nothing but blinding darkness could he see. He repeatedly opened and closed his eyes, trying to adjust to the blackness, but he could not. The darkness was impenetrable. He moved his arms, then his legs, and to his surprise, he did not break any bones from the fall, although his limbs did hurt, and he felt a cold, wet liquid running down his head. His heavy breathing echoed in the well. He could hear water dripping in the distance; by the sound of the angry wind and lazy water drops echoing around, he guessed the well connected to a large cavern. Unable to see anything, Tommy switched his gaze upward. The cold moonlight glimmered on the lip of the well, some fifteen feet above him. Tommy knew his best bet for escape was to climb up the wall. He stretched his arms and legs as best he could and flexed, limbering up. When Tommy stood up, he grabbed onto the rock wall of the well; he was about to start the climb when suddenly he heard a noise coming from inside the cave. It sounded like a faint whisper. 'Please help me.'

'David? Is... that you?' Tommy replied. He could not see anything, but it sounded like David. It could not be. The silence was broken again by a crude sound of flesh dragging on stone.

Again, the voice wheezed. 'Help me.' It now sounded like the voice was all around him. And whatever was crawling towards him sounded like it was right in front of him. It was; he could feel its breath. Tommy jumped up as high as his legs would allow, grabbed onto the rocks, and began climbing. It was a dangerous climb. Cold, sharp, wet rocks were not easy to keep hold of and climb, but Tommy dreaded to find out what waited at the bottom of the well more than the pain. His nimble hands found the rock above with ease, and he climbed like a spider., using both hands and feet. The shrill cackling coming from the deep dark below had motivated Tommy to climb faster.

Tommy threw himself over the well's lip and effortlessly rolled out onto the ground. He continued to crawl until he was a safe distance from the well. Only then did he stop to catch his breath. Listening intently for any sound of pursuit, he heard nothing. It was only now when the adrenaline wore off; his arm pained him terribly. He examined it to see a blood-soaked sleeve. He rolled up the sleeve and discovered a deep wet gash on his elbow. He rolled the sleeve back down and held his sore elbow.

Tommy knew he could not go into the house to look for any sort of first aid, so instead, he wearily got to his feet and decided to check the toolshed for anything that might help. While limping away from the well, Tommy couldn't help but think of David. If that was him in the well and if he could have done anything to help him. Then Tommy remembered:

if he is not home by this time tomorrow, I'm going into town and bringing the Gardaí out here.

He is home, but he is in the well. He laughed half crazed knowing nobody would believe him. He approached the toolshed. Tommy found loopers, plyers, and saws hanging on the wall inside the shed. The floor was littered with empty sacks and in the corner of the room was a table with a clipboard full of writing, a pen, and a bottle of ink. Tommy approached the desk and opened the drawer on its side; he reached his hand inside and pulled out a dirty towel. Unbuttoning and removing his shirt, Tommy briefly examined all cuts and bruises on his body. Painful as it all was, there was nothing serious other than the cut on his elbow.

Tommy pressed the towel to his bleeding elbow and tied it using his shirt. With a cry, he tightened the knot with one final pull. It was not a surgeon's performance, but it would suffice for the night.

He hobbled over to the corner and rolled up a couple of burlap sacks to make a makeshift bed. With a grunt of pain, he lowered himself onto the bed and pulled a sack over himself to keep warm. Tommy lay there for hours, unable to sleep because he was shivering with pain or the cold; the discomfort of his bed did not make it any easier, but eventually, a deep sleep caught hold of him.

The clippity clap of hooves followed by the thunderous roll of a wagon was enough to recall Tommy from his sleep. Opening his eyes, he saw the early sun gleaming through the dirty window. To the best of his ability tried to remember the events of last night. His eyes darted to his painful arm. The towel was painted with dry blood. He carefully untied his shirt around his arm, removed the towel, and looked at his elbow. It was wet and gooey and red around the wound. It was infected and would need to be tended. Tommy threw on his shirt and buttoned it up, leaving the shed.

A cooling breeze sent a shiver down Tommy's spine as he stood there basking in the warm light of the sun, watching the busy birds flying to and fro, chirping happily to one another. The grass bent and waved, carrying the sweet scent of apples. A dark cloud loomed in the distance, threatening heavy rain.

'Hullo Tommy, how fare you this morning?' Tommy looked over his right shoulder.

'Ahh, hello, father. What brings you out here?' Tommy asked, turning towards the priest.

When Father Waldron approached Tommy, his blood-soaked shirt and the dried, crusty blood stain running down his face came into notice.

Father Waldron backed up two steps. 'My God, Tommy, are you alright?'

Tommy examined his appearance and laughed. 'It's nothing, father, just had a little accident, that's all.'

Farther Waldron shifted from one leg to the other uncomfortably. 'I brought back your wagon and your mule. You left them outside my church last Sunday. She has been well fed and cared for, don't worry. I would have brought it back yesterday, but I was rather busy.'

'Don't worry about it, father. I'm sorry to have put you through such hardship. How I managed to forget my wagon is beyond me,' Tommy said with a nervous smile.

'Yes, also…' the priest said while pulling a black book out of his robes. 'I found this book buried at the bottom of a box in my room. It's the book about the fairies I mentioned Sunday; I thought you might find it rather interesting. I was also hoping to have a chat with you about the banshee.'

Tommy's eyes lit up in terror at the word. 'Sssssssssshhh,' he said. 'Not here, follow me.' Tommy led the priest to the toolshed, ushered the priest in.

Father Waldron hesitated. The sight of a bloodstained, wild-eyed, haggard man leading him into a toolshed made him rethink his plans. 'Actually, Tommy, I just remembered I have to prepare for a sermon; is there any way we can have this chat some other day?'

Tommy stepped too close to the priest. 'Father, I need your help… I am in a lot of trouble. It's about… the woman we spoke of,' Tommy said.

The priest stepped back shakily. 'Of course, I will help you, but first, I need to know what is going on. Can we not speak in your house?'

'No father, Maggie has kicked me out; she thinks I hurt Joe last night; it was the banshee father, I swear. And David… oh God.' Tommy wept uncontrollably.

73

A voice interrupted them from behind. 'This is the wagon that David stole; is he back? I need to talk to him,' said Paddy inspecting the wagon.

'I have brought that wagon back from my church this morning; Tommy left there last Sunday,' Father Waldron declared curiously, watching the events unfold.

'He left it at the church on Sunday? He told us that David stole it and attacked him.' Paddy stabbed a venomous glare at Tommy, ' have you seen David father?'

'I am afraid not,' replied the priest.

Paddy clenched his fists and stormed over to Tommy, punching him hard in the mouth, breaking a tooth.

'Please, Paddy, there is no need for violence. I'm sure this is all just a misunderstanding,' said Father Waldron.

Paddy noticed Tommy was covered in dried blood. 'Whose blood is that?'

Tommy could not answer; a warm lake flowed down his throat; it tasted like copper pennies. The door of the house swung open with a disturbing screech. Maggie hurried down to the group crowded around the shed. She looked at Tommy, traumatised. 'Whose blood are you covered in?'

Tommy lay silently on the ground dreading the reality that nobody would believe him, except maybe Father Waldron. Paddy approached Maggie.

'Father Waldron here brought this wagon back from the church: apparently, Tommy left it behind him on Sunday, which means David never took it, so that story you cooked up for us was nothing but a pile of horse shit.'

Maggie turned pale. Tears sat on the edge of her eyes. She looked reproachfully at Tommy. He stared back, drenched in blood and fear.

'I lied.' The prepared tears streamed, and she chocked between loud sobs; 'I made up that story because I was afraid,

I was afraid, Paddy. The truth is Tommy came back to me late Sunday night and told me David was dead, and just last night, he tried to kill Joe; my poor boy branded his arm.'

Paddy unleashed a pernicious kick at Tommy's head, knocking him back disorientated. John quickly came from behind and subdued Paddy. Tommy stood up dizzily: feeling like he was out of options and time; he decided to tell the truth.

'I did not kill David, and I did not hurt Joe. It was the banshee; I know it sounds ridiculous but ask Father Waldron he will vouch for me; we need to find a way to stop her.'

Everybody looked to the priest. Father Waldron stuttered nervously. 'Well, w-what I mean is, I a-am in no position to j-j-j-judge this man for actions he may or may not have committed; perhaps we can take him to the Gardaí?'

'John, get the big wagon from the shed and connect it to the horses; we're going paying the Gardaí a little visit.' Paddy grinned while staring at Tommy.

'Be easy with him. I do believe there are supernatural forces at work here,' Father Waldron said.

Paddy flicked his tongue off the top of his mouth in disbelief *tsk*.

'Could I ever go in and see Joe? Maybe even say a prayer over him,' Father Waldron said.

Maggie nodded and invited the priest inside with a nudge of her head. Tommy watched his wife and Father Waldron pass through to the house.

John wheeled the big carriage from the shed and left it there, making his way down the road to the barn. Tommy sheepishly glanced at Paddy, squinting his eyes from the refulgent sunlight. He swallowed a lump of fresh blood. Paddy stood across from him, waiting for Tommy to make any move: he did not. Tommy was very fearful of going to the Gardaí; he did not kill David, but unfortunately, he had no evidence to prove his innocence and had more than one reason to commit the crime. Standing there, unsure of what to think, a new terror struck him; what would become of Joe. What did the banshee do to him? Would Joe ever understand what really happened? All those thoughts grabbed hold of Tommy. John brought the horses up from the barn and attached them to the carriage.

He ambled over to Paddy and Tommy, smiling: 'Your chariot awaits.'

Paddy grabbed Tommy by the scruff of his neck, forcing one arm up behind his back so forcefully Tommy was sure the arm snapped. Paddy aggressively pushed Tommy towards the cart, throwing Tommy in the ample opening in the back of the carriage. Leaving Tommy on the floor, Paddy took a seat on the built-in, faded red leather bench, watching Tommy. John climbed into the driver's seat.

'Go offer Father Waldron a ride home,' said Paddy.

John climbed back down and made his way to the house with a sigh.

'You will get the death penalty for this, Tommy, mark my words,' Paddy said in a deep, threatening tone.

Tommy began to cry, 'I didn't do it, Paddy; I didn't do any of it, you have to believe me.'

'I don't have to do anything; if you didn't do it, who did.'

'The banshee,' Tommy said in a weak whisper.

'You're crazy. Do you believe in fairies as well?' Paddy said with a pitying laugh, silencing Tommy with a brisk kick to the stomach.

John and Father Waldron emerged from the house and made their way to the carriage, climbing the cockpit. Once everybody was seated, John flicked the reins, and the wagon began moving. Tommy gasped for enough breath to ask the priest how his son was.

'He will live, I think, but I implored Maggie to bring him to the doctor all the same. That mark on his arm; Joe was touched by a curse: a hateful curse. I am not sure what it means; however, I will make regular house calls to pray for Joe. and hopefully banish any present evil.

'Oh, come on, Father, you don't believe that story he's pulled out about banshees? Said Paddy.

Father Waldron chuckled, 'Is it not my job to believe first and ask questions second? I cannot confidently state that fairies exist, the same as I can't say if God exists or not; all I can do is believe and help to spread the light, and right now, there is a boy who is hurt, so if I can help him I will.'

The wagon rode on in silence, along the dirt road into town. The curious birds flew around tweeting questions to one another about the strange company in the carriage. The heavy air choked on the grass's perfume, and the sun's heat made the flowers stretch in laziness. Tommy could not help but shiver; from pain and fear for what was going to happen. He darted his eyes around the back of the carriage and at Paddy and the exit, contemplating whether he should try to escape. The beautiful, peaceful day contradicted Tommy's feelings. He was not calm and relaxed; he had never felt so stressed out and worried. He knew he would go to jail; there was no way anybody would believe him. Tommy ground his teeth and lay back, feeling every bump and stone the wagon rolled over on his sore back. He had to escape; he had to get back to the orchard and find a way to kill the banshee. It would not stop him from going to jail, but his family would be safe. One thing was sure: he could not save them from a prison cell or, more likely, *the grave*.

Tommy sat up and searched the wagon with unsteady eyes for anything he could use to overpower Paddy. Even if Tommy were unhurt and well-rested, he could not take Paddy on, and he knew it. He found nothing. The wagon was completely empty.

It would have to be a sucker punch, but Paddy was cautiously watching, waiting; how could he make Paddy drop his guard. He thought about maybe asking Father Waldron something, but the sound of his voice would put Paddy on alert. Tommy was frantically thinking about ways to dupe Paddy; he was very strong but not very smart, *outsmart him,* he thought. Tommy lay back, with his eyes closed, listening intently; the wagon wheel was ever so slightly squeaking when it rolled over rocks. Tommy allowed himself a cunning smile.

'Paddy, did you ever fix that back wheel as I asked you to do weeks ago?' Tommy asked.

Paddy, who did not look phased, stared down at Tommy. 'You never asked me to fix a wheel.'

Tommy felt like his plan was transparent; probably because of his over-enthusiastic tone, he collected himself. 'Do you hear the way it's squeaking? It's about to fall off,' Tommy said as convincingly as he could.

Paddy looked vexed, gawking at Tommy; he glanced up to John. 'Stop the wagon a minute; I need to check the wheel.'

Paddy jumped off the wagon, leaving Tommy lying there on his own. He disappeared around the side. Tommy smiled in amazement, shocked that his plan actually worked. He looked behind and saw that Father Waldron was staring down at him, shaking his head. Tommy ignored him and leapt out the back of the wagon. As soon as his feet connected with the ground, his head felt as if it were sliced down the middle with a loud *clonk*. He fell to the floor.

'Do you think I was born yesterday?' said Paddy, putting a spade back in its holster on the side of the carriage. Paddy was now on top of Tommy, pulling him to his feet by his shoulders; standing face to face, Paddy was about to say something clever judging by his wry smile.

Before he realised what had happened, he was sitting on the floor with a bloody nose. Tommy began running east, through the thorny thickets, into a field adorned with trees, breaking any lines of sight that might track him. Tommy continued to run dizzily.

He ran until he was winded, stopping and listening for any pursuing footsteps, leaning on a tree. His plan did not go as well as he hoped; rubbing his forehead gently, he never thought he could throw such a damaging head butt. If Paddy was not unconscious, he definitely had a broken nose, Tommy heard a sharp click, and he was fine. Hoping the carriage was still going to be heading into town to drop Father Waldron back at his house, and more than likely bring the Gardaí over to the orchard, to arrest him, because they knew that is where he would go. Tommy sighed in frustration. He had to go back to kill the banshee, but he could not be seen. He figured he should wait for the cover of darkness to continue.

He found a wide hallow grove in a nearby oak tree, removing the stones and anything else that might prohibit his entry; he squeezed in, raking leaves and dirt onto his body to camouflage himself because he felt he might still be hunted. Tommy got as comfortable as possible and slipped quickly into a dreamless sleep.

He woke with a start, by a squawking crow, who seemed to be displeased with his new neighbour in the hollow tree trunk. Tommy did not know what time it was, but the sun was setting, darkness began washing over the land. It was a short walk back to the orchard. He stood up, and with a bone-cracking stretch accompanied by a yawn, he was ready to go. He gazed at the falling sun, setting in the west; he knew the orchard was east, so he looked where the sun had come from and breathed deep. His elbow still hurt, his bones were stiff and sore, and he was ravenous. Onwards, he walked, listening to all the birds wishing each other good night from their nests. A harsh breeze shook the trees: its cold touch fondling Tommy; he shivered. Tommy stumbled his way over the hills like a blind man, unable to see the holes in the ground and the peevish rocks hiding in the dark. Before long, the looming roof of darkness covered the shadowless land, the crimson remanence of the sun, and the pale crescent moon emitted little light. Tommy continued walking as the crows flew, climbing over hedges and jumping over dikes; he had to be near the orchard.

He came to a dark forest which he believed to be the woods right behind his house. He paused for a moment, thinking: *it would be dangerous to go through the woods at night with no light, but it would be smarter*; in case a group of officers at the orchard was looking for him: taking cover in the dark trees would be a rational move.

He moved very slowly through the trees, carefully placing every footstep, making sure not to trip on roots or twist his ankle. Things were now pitch black; he could not see his hand in front of his nose; the going was very slow; he was not even sure he was walking in the correct direction anymore. Suddenly the air opened, and the trees felt like they had fallen away. The crescent moon revealed itself behind a sinister cloud, unveiling a hidden glade.

The hopeful moonlight became more and more bright so that Tommy could see all around him. He stood still in amazement, taking in the beautiful sight; the deadly breeze seemed to have faded into a gentle whisper; the air was filled with a deafening silence. Tommy's eye was fixed on a protruding rock from a crystal-clear pond; a sudden urge overcame him to approach the stone. The closer he got to the stone, the more he realised that deafening silence was, in fact, hundreds of tiny voices pleading for help. Tommy looked around left to right to find the source of the squeaking supplications; he could not see anything but could feel a crowd of innocent eyes watching him.

He fingered his ears, unsure if he was imagining it or not; he approached the moon-kissed pond to splash cold water on his face. When his hands penetrated the calm surface of the water, he was astonished to find the water was warm without knowing why he plunged his face into the water. He could hear a voice as slick as marble, swimming in the nebulous tide.

He is the only one who can stop her, it said; *the boy is the promised prophecy,* said a higher-pitched voice. *It must be the boy.,* said a cheery third voice, *you must help him, TOMMY.* The way it said his name; such a deep, resonant sound, like an earthquake in ice, made Tommy withdraw his head in shock, and he fell backwards to the ground. Hair dripping, he dried his face with his sleeve and rose to his feet; he no longer felt tired or sore as if he were bathed in enchanted water. Tommy scanned the clearing with befuddled eyes trying to make sense of what had just happened. He could not hear or see anybody. He curiously inserted his hand into the pond only to find this time it was ice cold; reluctantly, Tommy once again plunged his head in the water, this time only to hear the constant roar of the flowing water; he retracted his head and shook the water off his hair.

I am losing my mind; he thought; *only the boy can stop her. Joe*? He was not sure if the was real, but the magical, unusual feeling he got from this place; made him wonder if this glade was a fairy circle, like the areas Father Waldron mentioned. *No*! he thought *I am tired and hungry… did that happen?* He paused, *but if the banshee is real, the fairies must also be real.* he slapped his head. '*I don't know*! *Oh God, I don't know*! he raised his hands and gazed to the heavens. *What do I do?* Falling to his knees, Tommy wept. Wiping the tears from his eyes, he stood up wearing a sullen face. *I must protect my family.* Tommy thought and continued marching east, looking behind him to recall where he came from. He disappeared into the darkness of the trees.

After countless minutes of stumbling through the dark trees, he came to the edge of the tree line. He sat in a shady bush looking out at the orchard surveying the land; his own house seemed to lie dormant in the dark, with only the low gloom of a candle in Joe's room window. The silhouette of the large shed hiding in the night was silent. The sour scent of apples clouded the fields in a translucent mist. Tommy continued to look left and right for any sign of movement; he then noticed the whispering light of a lantern bobbing around his house. The man walking the light was clad in the Garda Síochána uniform. The dark navy coat adorned with brass buttons, matching trousers, and a black police cap: embroidered with the Gardaí signature: a gold and blue badge.

Tommy felt his heart sink, he could only see one guard, but a deep dread inside of him told him there was more. He cupped his face in his hands, wondering how to proceed; he did not even know where the banshee was or how to find her. The only time he had seen the banshee was at *the well. But it's not me who can kill her.*

Tommy knew what he must do; he waited for the guard to move on along the other side of the house and then made his move.

Tommy moved soft and quick towards the house like a shadow, skulking from bush to bush. He reached the front door and tried the handle. It was locked. Not wanting to be caught on the porch, Tommy quickly made his way around the back of the house. When he was at the side of the house, he heard footsteps coming from in front of him and spotted a small light getting brighter as it turned the corner. Tommy exhaled suddenly, panicking; he turned around on the spot and tried to head back; but to his dismay, a light was coming from where he was, followed by loud footsteps. Feeling hopeless, Tommy quickly looked around, hoping to find somewhere to hide. Maggie's beautifully maintained flower beds lay neatly by the fence; she adored those flowers.

He unscrupulously dived into them, lying as still as he could, hoping the dark would obfuscate him. Tommy could hear footsteps clearly to his left, and he could see the lukewarm glow of the lights bouncing off the wall. He remained silent, too afraid to breathe in case his panicked breath betrayed his location.

'Was that you at the front a moment ago?' said an unfamiliar voice.

'I was at the front of the house, yes,' said another voice.

'No, I mean, was that you trying to enter the house?' said the first voice. 'I saw a shape walking from the front around this side of the house; I ran up as quick as I could. So, that wasn't you?'

There was a silence. A long silence, too long. Tommy felt his suppressed lungs clench up so tightly he thought they would burst into flames. The pale reflection of light on the wall was slowly consumed by darkness, not natural darkness, the permanent black of closed eyes.

'He must have run up here to the trees,' said the second voice, 'come on!'

Tommy distantly heard the footsteps fading away, followed by the shrinking light. He gasped desperately for air, drinking deep of the apple-flavoured oxygen. He waited a moment and then rose from the crushed flowers.

Tommy quickly came to the back door. *Locked*. Tommy took a step back from the house; to look for any potential entry points like open windows, like a thief. He could not see any. Tommy bent down to the ground and picked up a small stone; he threw the stone at Joe's window, and stood still, waiting, a few lifeless seconds passed, Tommy picked up another stone and again threw it at the window; shortly after, Joe appeared at the window and groggily opened it.

'Dad?' said Joe rubbing his haggard eyes.

'Yes, son, it's me. I need to talk to you.'

'Let me get mum,' Joe said, but Tommy vigorously cut him off.

'Joe, please, you have to trust me.'

Joe hesitated for a moment; then he nodded his head, and with that, he disappeared from the window. Tommy stood quietly, listening for any footsteps. The back door was opened, Tommy stepped inside.

Tommy and Joe sat down at the kitchen table. Joe looked very nervous by his father's bloodstained appearance. Tommy knew he did not have the time to explain how he got there. He started by saying: 'How is your arm, Joe?'

'It's very sore, and I can't move it too much,' Joe answered, showing Tommy his bandaged arm.

'You know I didn't do any of the things they're saying, don't you, Joe?' He paused, 'The reason I have come back is I need to keep you all safe. It's a father's duty to take care of his family. I am the man of the house' another uncomfortable pause. 'We must kill the banshee. I am not sure how or where to find her; she might come to you. Will you come with me down the well?' He did not want to risk his son's life, but *he is the one that can kill her.*

Joe stirred uncomfortably. 'No, dad please; I-I-I don't want to,' he wept.

Tommy froze, thinking he could hear movement coming from upstairs. He jumped to his feet and grabbed Joe by the unwounded arm, standing him up. Tommy briskly pulled Joe, begging him for silent cooperation. Joe screamed in agony. Tommy looked down at Joe, thrashing wildly on the floor, tears soaking the stone tiles. Tommy's eyes were drawn to Joe's bandaged arm. The branded symbol was glowing neon green, burning brighter and brighter behind the bandage. Tommy stared at it without blinking, transfixed. It blasted a blinding green flash that stunned Tommy, knocking him backwards onto a counter. Joe was crying uncontrollably. Tommy shook the disorientation from his head. When he could see again, he saw the banshee was standing at the kitchen door smiling and laughing. Without hesitation, Tommy grabbed a sharp knife from the counter and approached the banshee, and as quick as a cornered snake, slashed her throat with a smooth, fast motion. The banshee fell to the ground, gurgling. Tommy looked down at the banshee bleeding and clawing for air.

Breathing heavily, Tommy triumphantly dropped the knife. Maggie rushed in and screamed in horror; she dropped down to the body, screaming and crying. Tommy looked down at the body and almost fainted with shock. Matthew was lying on the floor in a pool of blood.

<u>VI</u> THE MAN OF THE HOUSE

Joe stumbled sluggishly up the stairs, cradling his right arm in his left hand. After two months of healing, his right hand was still powerless and painful, bearing the fading image of the grotesque symbol. When he reached the top of the stairs, Joe attempted to flex his limp hand, trying to touch all his fingers individually to his thumb, just like the doctor told him. An arduous struggle, but Joe persisted and completed his exercise. He entered the room, Matthew's room. The phantom laughter of his brother echoed in his sullen heart; he collapsed onto Matthew's bed and wept. There was nothing sadder than an empty room. Collecting himself, Joe walked over to the window and looked out of it. It was a cold, miserable day on the orchard; the autumnal chill buried the summer warmth. A heavy blanket of rain clouded the air; Joe could faintly hear voices rising and lowering in argumentative song outside. Joe looked down and saw Paddy and John shouldering packed bags, arguing with Maggie. Joe quickly turned, glancing at Matthew's empty bed; he wiped his eyes with his sleeve, and left the room.

Hurrying down the stairs to find out what the conflict was about, he stopped at the foot of the stairs, spying the family portrait on the table in the hallway. A tear streamed down his face. *How could such bad things happen to my family?* He thought, *you are the man of the house now, Joe, you are not allowed to cry*! and with that, Joe aggressively smeared the remaining tears from his cheek and continued walking.

'We are the only two people left working here,' said the muffled voice of John, 'you have to understand two people cannot maintain the orchard.'

'If you leave, we will have nobody', Maggie said, 'the orchard will go out of business. Please don't go. We will hire more people.'

Paddy interjected with a cruel laugh. 'Hire people? That's a laugh. After the news got out about that psychopathic murdering husband of yours, nobody will ever come near this place!'

His bandaged arm burned painfully, and a dormant rage consumed Joe. He swung the door open forcefully and closed the distance to Paddy; his nose twisted along the bridge where the bone broke and would never sit right again.

'My father was not a murderer; it was the banshee! Why won't anyone believe that?'

'Look, son,' said John sympathetically, 'it's lovely you are defending your old man like this, but the reality is there is no such thing as a banshee or fairies, your father is a sick man, and I'm afraid he has poisoned your malleable mind.'

Joe's lip quivered on his clenched jaw; he stared into the odious eyes of Paddy. He wanted to hit him, keep hitting him until his face was a discombobulated mess of blood and goo staining the ground.

you are the man of the house

It won't fix anything. He swallowed his anger and reluctantly turned around, clenching his fists.

'Back to fairyland, good lad,' Paddy said.

Joe, dwelling in rage, turned swiftly to that clown: Paddy and fired a heavy punch at his jaw with his left hand.

Paddy, who was fully expecting a belligerent response, dodged out of the way in the nick of time; the momentum from the missed strike pulled Joe forward, and he tripped on his misplaced feet, falling to his knees.

Paddy laughed hysterically. Both Maggie and John lifted Joe back to his feet, trying to calm him with soothing words. Once Joe was on his feet, he approached Paddy again, now with a burning need to inflict pain. Paddy ducked under another punch.

Paddy was now fed up with Joe's outburst and seized his bandaged right wrist. Joe again fell to the ground, this time screaming and crying. Maggie quickly intervened, slapping Paddy across the face, forcing him to release Joe's arm.

Paddy's stern face flashed with shock. He pulled his fist back, staring with malevolence at Maggie. John quickly grabbed Paddy's arm before he could hit Maggie.

'I think we all need to calm down,' John said, 'there is no point in denying that we are all angry and confused; the best thing we can all do right now is get away from this place. I'm sorry to say this, Maggie, but I doubt this orchard will ever thrive again, not after what happened.' With that, John released Paddy's relaxed arm. He picked up his suitcase and walked away. Paddy picked up his bags, took one last look at Maggie and Joe, spitting on the ground before their feet. Paddy followed John off the orchard.

Maggie helped Joe up again, tears welling in her eyes. 'Ohh Joe, my poor boy. Are you hurt terribly?' she cried, 'I don't know what we do from here.'

Joe stood up and slapped Maggie's helping hand away. Without a word, he stormed back into the house, unable to process the many emotions he was experiencing.

Joe entered his room. He limped back to his bed and collapsed onto it, burying his face in his pillow. He screamed and cried as loud as he could, but the sounds never left the room, thanks to the muffling pillow. He rolled over on his back and stared up at the roof through a cascade of tears. You are the man of the house, he said to himself, and you are not allowed to cry; you are not allowed to be sad. You have to look out for the family. Joe faintly recalled the sound of his father's words, like the ringing of familiar but distant bells chiming out from an alien-like planet.

Joe sat up as straight as he could on the side of his bed and swallowed his grief. *I am going to make them believe us.* He did not know where the sudden burst of courage was coming from, but it felt like there was a fire in his heart. 'I am going to kill the banshee, and then you can come back home, dad.' The words tasted odd in his throat, but he was determined.

Joe shuffled around to his bedside table, picking up a tattered, black book off the surface.. A plain black book, torn with years of existence, a weathered leather strap sealed the book. On the front of the book was written in a flourishing bronze font: *Fey*, no pictures and no author. The book Father Waldron left him the day they took his father, the day Matthew—he did not want to think about it.

He tried to remember what Father Waldron had said to him that day. "*How is your arm?*" Joe recalled, "*I believe your father about the banshee*" Father Waldron's voice flooded Joe's memory. "*This book might have the answers you need about her.*"

It was almost the end of the second month; Father Waldron should be visiting any day now. Joe was going to ask him about the banshee, but then he taught, *why wait?* Joe sunk back on his bed; with his back to the board and unbound the leather strap of the book.

Upon opening the book, Joe felt a hush whispering rushing all around him, rustling his hair and the curtains and disturbing the peaceful air until Joe struggled to draw breath. The air he inhaled felt like a poisonous cloud, filling him with despair, but Joe would cower no more

the man of the house

he would cry no more; the man of the house was never afraid. Joe said to himself. And he began reading.

The book lacked proper layout; it looked more like somebody's diary than a novel: some of the pages looked older than the others, discoloured and fading; every entry seemed to be written by a different hand, and the pages were crudely taped into the book, but Joe did not care, skimming carefully through the frail pages, he saw there was information of different lengths on different creatures. Joe mused as he flicked through the pages

accompanying the creature's name. There were sometimes poorly hand-drawn images of the monster. Joe allowed himself a chuckle when he saw a drawing of a leprechaun. He read to himself,

The leprechaun is a generous spirit who offers luck and wealth... blah blah blah, Joe skipped through the paragraph. *They take the form of a small man with a long ginger beard wearing a green top hat and carrying a bucket of gold—created by the* fairies *in goodwill to the humans.* Joe turned the page.

The púca. The accompanying drawing sent a shiver down Joe's spine. It looked like a cross between a werewolf and a rabbit with glowing red eyes. *It gives either good or bad fortune by helping individuals or devouring them.* Joe turned the page with a gulp, thankful he did not have to look at the púca anymore.

Fairies. There was no drawing beside the name. Although Joe pictured a small colourful winged creature, like the ones in that dream he had. *Yes, the DREAM.*

The fairies are the Tuatha Dé Danann, the first tribe to settle in Ireland. A magical people who allegedly shrunk themselves down and live underground. Fairies are responsible for creating all the magical creatures that roam the land today blah, blah, blah. Joe flipped the page.

Some of the spirits they have created have become more powerful than anticipated and broke away from the command of the fairies. Becoming their own masters; they no longer help people but instead feed off them, growing more powerful, always seeking out their creators to feed off them and obtain such power; that they believe will satisfy their insatiable greed. He skipped ahead.

Fairies have many different forms and are more commonly described as a voice or feeling experienced by those who encountered them. Fairies are believed to reside in fairy circles or Grounds, a patch of land encircled by flora or trees. Outside of these realms, fairies have no power.

Joe laid the book down on his knees and looked up at the ceiling, trying to process what he had just read. Powerless outside their realm, the glade in the woods behind the house popped into Joe's mind. He thought back to the last time he was in the glade. *The fox*! he thought. *She was in the fairy circle. Why didn't she fight them*?'

(Because it's not real!)

Joe picked up the book and read the final line in the paragraph.

92

These fairy grounds are inaccessible to those the fairies do not allow access to and radiate with magic to those who have been chosen.

Joe recalled the unabating bone-rattling hum he could not understand when he was there. *Maybe I should go back there?* He thought, *perhaps the* fairies *can help me.* Joe flipped the page and continued reading.

Far darrig… no. He flipped the page.

Cú Sith' The accompanying drawing of a giant hound aroused Joe's interest, but he flipped the page and continued through the book. And lo! There it was.

Joe felt an uneasy shift in the air as if an unseen presence was watching him. He shivered.

The banshee, accompanied by a drawing of a cloaked old woman, crying, sitting at a tree, her eyes were scribbled out. It is a *benevolent spirit created by the fairies to notify worrying mothers of their children lost at war. The wail of the banshee or the finding of her hair comb; means somebody close to you will die. Joe paused, thinking he could very faintly hear a long scream. The banshee grew hungry and vengeful; no longer wanting to help people or answer to the fairies, she grew malevolent. Tirelessly hunting people and fairies alike. She has many forms and can shapeshift even into animals; she can change her size and manipulate the darkness surrounding her. Not much else is known about her. She commands powerful magic; her known magic includes shadow magic and deception. But every drop of evil magic used leaves a secret to destroy the one who uses* it. He pondered the last statement.

Joe shut the book shaking with fear. Only now realising what he was dealing with.

He stared for a moment at the bronze font on the front of the book *Fey*. He turned the book over, hoping to find an author's name on the back; absolutely nothing whatsoever. Curiosity took control as he opened the book again to check the front cover. Nothing. The writing was dripping down the pages, melting. He quickly flicked through the now incoherent pages until he hit the back cover. Joe vigorously skimmed back through the entire book gasping at the now virgin pages. He shut the book and noticed that the title "Fey", which was once written in a flourishing shiny bronze text, was no longer visible. Joe, who was now utterly afraid and bewildered, looked in the book one more time.

The page he opened on did have writing on it; Joe read it with bewilderment: *The banshee will find you, Joe, I will consume your being, you will fade away in the Underworld. I will find you!* The accompanying drawing of the old woman flipped her hood off. Her eyes which Joe felt were penetrating him, glowed a sinister yellow, and she screamed very loudly. A dark black fire engulfed the book. The flames spread quickly; in seconds, the shadowy tongues licked Joe's hands, confused shock caused him to launch the book across the room, not taking any notice that the fire was ice cold. Joe breathed a sigh of relief when the fire burned out without spreading.

He got to his feet and carefully stepped around his bed to where the burning book landed. It was not there. He spent a few wasted moments searching. The book was gone. Twisting his face in wonder while looking confusingly around the room, thinking about what he should do next, the answer became lucid in his mind *I need to find the* fairies. Such an unexplainable change came over Joe; he was no longer that frightened boy he was yesterday; he was now the man of the house.

Presently Joe was in the kitchen when Maggie entered the room and called his name. Joe stopped where he was and turned around to his mother.

'Joe,' she cried, 'Joe, could we speak for a moment? Please.' and taking a seat at the kitchen table, she beckoned Joe to an empty chair.

Joe took a seat but remained silent.

'Joe, you have been ignoring me since the night Matthew... since they took Tommy away.' Her voice broke. 'And then this morning, what has gotten into you, Joe?' Tears welled in her baggy, red eyes. 'Please don't go mad like your father.' She held a rag to her nose and sniffled.

Joe felt the same rage from earlier spread through his veins like poison. He punched the table. 'It wasn't dad; it was the banshee! She is real. I don't understand why nobody will believe me!' His wrist burned.

'Honey, I don't know what your father has told you... but the banshee is not real,' Maggie said in a calming tone, hoping to palliate her statement.

'Dad was a good man!' he shouted, 'And you let them take him.' He was filled with angry contrition; he could no longer control his overloading emotions. Tears streamed down his face, and his voice, like brittle glass, kept cracking.

Maggie jumped to her feet and walked around to Joe, hugging him. 'It's okay, Joe. I am here,' she cried, squeezing a broken Joe.

'No!' he screamed, pushing Maggie away and standing up. 'You can't protect me! Only dad could, and it is your fault he's gone!' Joe did not fully believe that, but the unquenchable rage in him; made him say it. 'You couldn't even protect Matt!' Joe screamed, wiping his tear-filled eyes, vibrating uncontrollably with both rage and shock. A shock that he was saying these horrible things. To his mother.

Maggie stood as still as a tombstone and silent as the grave at midnight. Her face was devoid of any emotion that might betray her feelings; her sore, haggard eyes were locked on Joe. She remained still for what seemed like forever. She seemed to grow larger, now towering over Joe. His bravery left him, and he remembered that he was just a boy. He fell to the floor, crying and begging for forgiveness.

Maggie finally spoke in a voice as strong and threatening as a winter blizzard, 'How dare you say that to me.' Her voice now rose into a scream, like the battle cry of a bloodthirsty barbarian. 'I AM YOUR MOTHER! HOW DARE YOU SPEAK TO ME LIKE THAT!'

Joe crawled awkwardly backward from Maggie; using his only abled hand; but she followed him, never breaking eye contact. Joe had never felt so afraid before, not even his confrontations with the banshee frightened him that much, or maybe they did; Joe could not remember; in fact, he could not remember anything just then. He begged for his mother to stop, water streaming from his eyes like small waterfalls, shaking like an innocent puppy in a snowstorm.

Joe backed up against a wall, and Maggie stood over him. She crouched down to Joe's level.

'I am your mother. Don't you ever speak to me like that again!' Maggie stood up and left the room.

Joe remained in a heap on the floor, sitting with his knees to his face crying.

The sun was still sitting on her high throne, watching the planet, when Joe finally exited the house. He stopped to wipe his eyes. The orchard's perfume was no longer as powerful as it had been a few months ago. Either due to the autumn breeze smothering it or the dearth of productivity.

The Man Of The House

The sky was a cold, pale blue, splashed with a dramatic orange glow. The contradicting shades met in the middle in an apologetic pink tone. The clouds were a shy transparent mist that wanted nothing more than to pass unnoticed. Silence drowned the world. Save for a single crow, shouting curses in the distance. A cold wind blew around Joe, kissing his wet cheek. Joe shivered and began walking towards the woods.

He clumsily made his way through the trees, his itchy, blurry eyes aggravating his vision; he walked through the rigid branches, attempting to bar his passage, grabbing with clawed fingers at his blue shirt. Joe cared not and continued making his way through the trees.

A tedious journey finally brought Joe to the clearing. He exited through a thicket and stood in the circular glade, amazed as always at just how beautiful it was.

Joe remained still, breathing in the magical aroma and listening to that low buzz, now guessing its arcane origin. A gentle breeze flowed through the glade, inviting the flowers to dance to its whispering song, and gracefully, they accepted; the constant flicker of colours of the animated flowers confused Joe to believe something was beckoning to him.

Joe stood still and silent as a tree for a long while, hoping for something to happen. As the uneventful time passed, he began doubting the book, the glade, and the fairies. Curious about his sanity, *maybe I am going crazy,* he thought, *perhaps I just imagined reading that book? No. Father Waldron gave it to me: it was real* Joe anxiously looked around the glade.

'Hello', he called out, 'is there anyone here? Please, I need help.' Joe stood silently, anticipating an answer but heard nothing. 'Please,' he cried. And collapsed on the soft grass; he whimpered.

The Banshee

The sun began descending from her dais when Joe finally collected himself. He stood up and took one last hopeful look around the glade and saw nothing. 'Fine,' he said aloud, 'I don't need your help.' Joe slowly retreated to the bristly ticket he entered from. To his shock, he did not enter the woods but instead found himself on the opposite side of the glade. Scratching his head at that most peculiar happening, Joe passed through the thicket he just emerged from, and lo! He was again on the opposite side of the glade, where he first entered from.

Filled with wonder and fear, Joe tried to leave the glade from every direction but always ended up on the opposite side of the circle. Feeling claustrophobic and imprisoned, he started to breathe heavily and move around recklessly, trying to leave to no avail. He was filled with a terror he could no longer ignore and called loudly for his mother until his throat hurt.

He curled up on the ground feeling trapped, heard a noise, a voice it sounded like. A very high-pitched ethereal voice, chanting his name. More voices similar to the first joined in the singing. Joe opened his eyes and saw a radiant, bright white circle of light hovering on the tall rock in the pond. Joe blinked his eyes in disbelief.

Come to us, Joe, come to us, Joe thought he could hear the voice saying. As if under a spell, Joe approached the light. He got to the foot of the pond and stood still. Not knowing what to do next, he waited in anticipation.

Jump. The voices squeaked. Without hesitation, Joe closed his eyes and stepped forward, falling into the pond. He was expecting to be engulfed by the cold kiss of the water, but instead, he opened his eyes and, to his amazement, was not at the bottom of a shallow pond; he was, well, floating in a bright liminal state of existence. Joe did not know where or when he was. Through the air that surrounded him, Joe could see outlines of large trees and small beams of yellow light zooming around. The harder Joe stared, the clearer the world became. The space was now filled with large trees. Joe looked around in awe.

Welcome, Joe McNeeve, said a ubiquitous, resonant, but somewhat sweet voice.

Joe struggled to find his voice. 'Where am I? Who are you?'

The voice laughed, and now it became clear to Joe why the voice sounded so strange; it was not one voice; it appeared to be many voices combined into one. Despite everything that was going on, Joe did not feel afraid; rather, he felt strong, warm as if he were made of volcanic stone.

You are in our sacred forest, said the voices*; we have brought you here to ask for your help. We must stop the banshee. She has grown much too powerful.*

Joe shivered at the name. 'How can we stop her, and what is she?' He felt his feet land on solid ground.

She used to be a fairy like us, we created her to notify the humans of a family death, and for centuries, she obeyed, but then she grew hateful and started to kill and consume humans. She has been hunting us for an age.

Joe was surprised that none of this felt odd to him. 'How do we stop her?'

There is a way to stop her. The voices rose up and then sank back down*; there is a ritual that can bind her to the Underworld.*

'A ritual? said Joe, 'What kind of ritual and what is the Underworld?' As he spoke, he could hear the gentle twinkle of little wings beating as the yellow lights zoomed around.

The banshees were gifted by us to the first settlers in Ireland. Any family whose' surname begins with Ó, Mc, or

Mac, sang the voices. *You are a McNeeve, meaning she cannot herself kill you unless she brings you to the Underworld, which is her realm.*

Joe looked around in bemusement as the once misty realm became clear to see. Joe saw clearly now the fairies. Strange they looked; They bore a certain similarity to humans, but on each hand had three fingers, glowing green eyes, and they were clad in leaves, with all different hairstyles and colours. They were small, tiny, and they did not walk here and there but instead were carried by their large, almost translucent rounded wings. They all seemed to be a pale yellow colour.

They busied themselves flying from one large tree to another; it was only upon closer examination; Joe realised these giant trees were littered with houses and shops and other fairy needs. A large city it was. Joe looked around in amazement at the beautiful world.

Will you help us? asked the voices.

The thing addressing him now also became clear to Joe; he was startled to see that it was an enormous entity; it did not have pale yellow skin, rather thick brown fur covered its body. It had long pitch-black, sharp claws, like shadow blades. Joe traced the beast with his eyes up to his head, which shocked him the most. Its head looked like that of a bear, but its prolonged snout full of sharp, protruding teeth seemed out of scale. On the top of its head were long, erect ears like a bat's. But its most distinguishing feature was its eyes. Its glowing red sagacious eyes seemed to be burning with an unobtainable knowledge.

Despite this beasts' horrifying appearance, Joe did not feel threatened; instead, he felt comforted, being in the presence of this guardian. Joe was still bewildered by the harmonious voice emitting from the creature.

We represent the fairies, so we speak with all their voices. It said as if reading Joe's thoughts. *Will you help us?*

Joe thought for a moment. 'If you cannot defeat her, how do you expect me to do it?'

She is too powerful for us to control, but you are a McNeeve; you can perform the ritual we mentioned earlier to banish her to the Underworld. said the many voices of the beast.

'I thought the Underworld was her realm?'

It is, but if you perform the ritual, she will be bound there and will not be able to leave.

'Okay, how do I perform this ritual?' Too distracted by everything he was seeing to pay close attention.

You will need this said the beast, groping with a giant paw at the ground.

Joe noticed he was standing on a curiously engraved, white stone platform. Joe watched in bewilderment as an alter rose from the platform bearing a stone tablet.

There is inscribed an ancient spell on this tablet, a spell to bind a spirit to its realm. The voices said, *to perform this ritual, you will need to acquire a drop of her blood, smear it on the tablet and throw the tablet down the portal chanting the spell.*

Joe studied the tablets language: *Bí spiorad beidh tú i do chónaí anseo go deo níos mó. Cuirim cosc ort*

'I can barely read simple Irish; how am I supposed to say it?' Joe asked in a concerned voice.

Have no fear; the voices said in many encouraging tones as if feeling Joe's emotions. When *the time comes, you will be able to read the spell.*

'Okay,' said Joe no less anxious, 'where is the portal?' He stuffed the stone down the seat of his pants, held tightly by his belt.

We do not know.

Joe stood waiting. 'You don't know? Have you any idea?

We have no idea we have not left our realm in an age. Have you seen her interact with anything in particular?

'Hmm, I mean she—' *The well,* he thought.

A well! of course, that's it, the portal to the Underworld. Can you read my mind? Joe thought.

Yes.

'Class,' said Joe. 'Can I just jump into the well?'

No, that will not work. The portal will not open for anyone unless the master of the realm invites them. We invited you to us, that is how you are here. Otherwise, the realm is invisible.

'So, she has to invite me? Great.' Joe shifted awkwardly, 'Is there another way?'

We do not know, perhaps there is an ancient, powerful spell, but of such, we know not.

Joe pondered. 'How do I get her blood?'

This will be no simple task; we need to know her weakness.

'Do you not know it? You created her.'

It is different for each one, some earthly mineral. Banshees have laws to live by. They must possess weaknesses. That is why they can not use magic without leaving a mark of personal liability.

'A mark!' Joe began removing the bandage on his wrist. He displayed the symbol to the beast.

It studied the mark and made a strange noise, laughter maybe? Two fairies came flying down to Joe from the large trees holding between them a shiny object; as they got closer, Joe realised it was a golden dagger: its handle encrusted with rubies and sapphires and other unknown gems, giving it a

102

mysterious yet beautiful appearance, and its pommel was that of a delicately carved bird: a Robin.

Joe held the knife carefully in both hands, afraid of breaking it. He studied it carefully, tracing his finger along the gem-encrusted hilt. He has never seen a thing so beautiful in his life.

'Can I kill her with this?'

Yes, but it is too dangerous. You can only kill her in her Underworld; I must insist you not even try it. Focus on getting her blood with the knife for the ritual.

He nodded in understanding, sliding the dagger carefully between his belt and his hip. The cold gold slapped his skin. 'If the ritual works,' Joe said, 'is there any way she can get free?'

It will work, said the voice dogmatically; only *your blood can release her.*

Joe finally asked the question that danced on his heart. 'Will you not help me?'

The beast sighed; I *am afraid we can do no more; we cannot intervene; we have no form in your world, and our magic will not work on the banshee. Once a fairy item is used in your world, it becomes disenchanted and returns to whatever it once was. That is why you have only one chance with the ritual.*

Joe puffed in dismay as his hope diminished. 'I suppose you sent the book to me as well?'

What book? the beast's tone raised in curiosity.

'The book titled "Fey", it was a black book with every description of every mythological creature,' said Joe confused, 'after I looked through it; it just burned in a black flame.'

That was not our book; perhaps it came from other fairies. said the beast, now lowering its tones.

103

'Wait, there are more of you?' said Joe in amazement.

Once there were many of us, but now… it paused, *burned in a black fire, you say? It sounds like shadow magic… but how could she—*

Suddenly! The beast was interrupted by a poisonous ear-throbbing scream that seemed to vibrate the forest.

Quick, show me that. The beast grabbed Joe's wrist and saw the symbol was glowing a dangerous green. *She is tracking you. She knew you would come here.*

The beast let out a loud, impressive roar.

The colony came alive with worried fairies crying. *She found us how did she find us*, as they darted to and fro without perceptible heading. The beast stood on all fours and roared again, a terrifying resonant sound to behold.

The fairies flew around the trees aimlessly, screaming and crying: *she has come, we are doomed*!

The beast took one last hopeful look at Joe. *You must stop her! Remember what I have told you. Now go!*

Joe was pushed off the dais by a gentle stroke of its colossal paw. He was seemingly falling through the floor of the world. The last thing Joe saw was the beast roaring and adopting a fighting stance. Joe looked down and saw a white surface, presumably the ground, rapidly approaching him. He shut his eyes.

Joe felt himself land softly on solid ground; He opened his eyes, and to his surprise, he was lying on the grass in front of the pond. Joe brushed his hands on his clothes and realised he was not wet. With an unclear urgency, Joe rose to his feet; and began running back to his house, making it through the thicket into the woods. He stopped for a moment to question if that was real, then he felt the familiar shapes of the dagger and the tablet against his legs. Joe hastily ran through the woods, back to his house; Hearing or imagining hearing the cries and screams of fairies experiencing genocide in a different world.

Joe emerged from the woods behind his house and caught his breath. He contemplated for a moment bringing the dagger and tablet to his room and hiding them under his bed but soon realised that would be foolish for two reasons. If his mother ever caught him with these objects, she would take them off him, leaving him defenceless. Also, he would need to be near the well with these objects; he would not have time to run up to his room, retrieve them and run back down.

Approaching the well, Joe stood thinking: *If I put these by the well,* Joe thought while fondling the bulging dagger in his pants, *and she finds them, I will not be able to stop her.* Joe thought long and hard. *The toolshed!* He turned his head to the small wooden shed at the front of the house; smiling, and as quick as his tired legs would carry him; he hurried to the hut.

Upon entry, Joe looked around the room; he saw a pile of old sacks stuffed in one of the corners like a bed, splattered with bloodstains. He did not want to think about where the blood came from. Kneeling, Joe picked up a bag from the ground and approached the desk. He carefully left the dagger and tablet on the table and threw the sack over them: concealing them. He left the shed.

He noticed a wagon parked outside on his way back to the house. Even without the discerning Christian crosses engraved on each side, Joe knew the wagon and the Pinto mare that drove it to be Father Waldron's. Joe rushed inside, knowing Father Waldron would believe him and perhaps even help him.

Joe entered the house and his attention was immediately drawn to his right, where he heard the soothing voice of Father Waldron speaking with Maggie in the living room.

'Ahh, there he is now,' said Father Waldron while standing up. 'I was just asking after you.'

Joe entered the room smiling.

'Right, I'll leave you two at it,' said Maggie rising from her chair. 'If you need me for anything, farther, I'll be in the kitchen. Are you sure you won't have a cup of tea?'

'Go on, so I have a half-cup!' Laughed the priest.

Maggie walked out of the room, making eye contact with Joe. He smiled weakly at her. She stood in front of Joe. 'Do you want a cup of tea as well?' she asked him in a condescending tone. He nodded. Maggie left the room.

Joe sat down on the chair, facing the priest.

'How are you doing, Joe?' the priest asked, glancing at Joe's unbandaged hand, 'How is your arm holding up?'

Joe flexed his stiff hand and remembered taking the bandage off to show the fairies. The symbol looked as if it were freshly branded.

Joe sat for a moment in silence, trying to prepare his story.

Father Waldron also sat silently watching Joe with curious eyes, waiting for an answer. The silence was continuously interrupted by the obnoxious tick-tock of an ostentatious grandfather clock in the corner of the room, dripping seconds into the deep lagoon of quietness.

Finally, Joe inhaled, and the priest sat up in his seat with eagerness.

'Do you believe in fairies, father?' Joe asked.

'Why, of course, I do,' answered the priest, anxiously awaiting the follow-up question.

Joe was silent again, rubbing his sore hand; 'The fairies have given me a task I must complete,' Joe said, not looking the priest in his eyes. 'They told me I have to stop the banshee.'

'How did they tell you?' said Father Waldron in a tone of fascination. 'Did they leave you a sign?'

Joe felt relaxed at the priest's interest, glad he didn't start laughing at him as he expected. 'I saw them; they brought me to a strange place.'

The priest leaned forward in his chair, 'Please, Joe, tell me everything.'

Joe smiled; he sat back comfortably, attempting to recall his curious story from the past hour that felt like a dream from another life long ago. He didn't overlook any details.

Maggie entered the room, holding a tray with two cups of tea and a few ham sandwiches. She placed the tray on the table between Joe and Father Waldron. Joe thanked her and reached for a sandwich. The priest looked as if he had just seen a ghost. Maggie cleared her throat.

'Here you are, father,' Maggie said, handing the priest his cup of tea.

'Oh, thank you very much,' Father Waldron said, receiving his cup of tea. 'You didn't have to make me sandwiches.'

Surely you didn't expect me to give you a dry cup of tea?' laughed Maggie, and she left the room.

'And are the fairies... okay?' asked the priest concerned.

Joe was filled with a deep sadness. 'I am not sure,' he answered, an isolated tear streamed down his cheek, 'I couldn't help them, father.'

The priest nodded in understanding. 'Of course not, so you have this tablet and dagger? Where are they?'

Joe grew suspicious at this question and became defensive. 'I would rather not say father.' Fearing Father Waldron might try to steal them.

'Joe, you know you can trust me, my boy. I want to help you; would you please let me see these instruments?' Curiosity consumed him, sweaty palms and a higher pitch in his voice made his genuine wish to help look like guilty greed.

Joe nervously ducked the question, and instead, he asked the priest a question: 'How did you come you by that book?'

Not appreciating the sudden change in topic, Father Waldron anxiously fingered his empty cup. 'I found it one day when I was a child, playing in the woods.'

'What woods? '

I grew up in Galway,' the priest answered. 'Do you have it handy? Perhaps we could read it?'

Joe shook his head. It burst into fire while I was reading it.'

Father Waldron blessed himself. 'Bless us all, were you hurt?

'No.' He stared at the ground anxiously. 'Father, did you ever read it?'

The priest finished his sandwich. 'Yeah, but there was nothing in there about a ritual.'

Joe fidgeted with his shirt sleeve, covering the mark. 'Was there anything in there about an Underworld?'

'The Underworld? In biblical terms, it's called Hell.' He shuddered.

'No, not Hell, the Underworld; it's the name of her realm.'

Father Waldron leaned in, hungry for new knowledge. 'Is that right? I'm sorry, I know nothing of it. What do you know?

'Not much more than you, I'm afraid,' he said gloomily.

Silence pressed itself against the walls and floor, filling the room.

'I have to get back; there is a mass at six,' Father Waldron declared while standing up. 'I will see you again soon, Joe.' He left the room and headed for the kitchen.

Joe retreated up to his room, and he was not seen by anyone living for the rest of that day.

<u>VII</u> THE LONG ROAD

As she poured the potatoes into a pot of boiling water, humming along to a song her mother taught her years ago, Father Waldron entered the kitchen, carrying the tray she had brought into them. Maggie noticed with a wry smile the sandwiches were eaten.

'Thank you again, Maggie, for everything,' Father Waldron said, laying down the tray on the mint-green counter next to the stove. 'It was lovely.'

'No problem, father, are you off?'

'Yes, yes, I have a mass at six. I will call again in the next few weeks.'

Maggie took some bacon from the press and started cutting it, with the knife that cut Matt... *no, stop thinking about that!* 'How is he doing?'

'H-h-he's doing great, getting better all the time.' He laughed nervously.

'Have you noticed he is in a nasty mood.' She chuckle. 'He is so angry with me, father.' Maggie quickly turned to face the priest, knife still in hand, almost plunging it deep in his guts. 'I can't talk to him.'

She was no longer smiling. She housed a dangerous glint in her eye. The priest took a step back from the sharp blade.

'He has been through a lot, poor boy. God will set him straight trust Him.' He smiled, 'give him space. I will be praying for him.'

'Thank you so much, father.' She hugged him.

Maggie showed him out. She stopped at the foot of the stairs.

'Have you heard any news of Tommy?' the priest said; his name was an unwelcomed echo around the lifeless halls.

'The last I heard about him they were taking him away to be hung for murder and the attempted murder of both our children.' Maggie sniffled. 'Where is Joe?'

'He went upstairs.'

She glanced up the sleeping stairs and nodded.

The priest turned back to Maggie, 'I will be around soon to say some more prayers' the priest smiled, 'again, thank you for everything you have done, Mrs McNeeve. Goodbye for now.' And with that, Father Waldron climbed into his wagon, equipping his black cap. He ushered his Pinto mare forwards, leaving the orchard. Whistling

When she entered the house, her eyes were pulled up to the top of the stairs, wanting to go up and check on Joe but suddenly remembering the priest's advice.

Give him space.

She returned to the kitchen to continue with dinner. She stopped at the table in the hallway and picked up the family portrait. Tears dropped from her face, drowning the tiny, smiling faces of a happy family a lifetime ago.

She patted her puffy eyes and blew her nose with her napkin, which was pretty much as much a part of her hand as her fingers. She placed the picture back on the table and felt a mournful smile in her heart, easing, for a moment, the emptiness of her life, for so is the power of memories.

Trudging to the kitchen over to the boiling pot of potatoes. She strained the water into another pot and despaired; when she realized the potatoes were burned black. Anger welled up inside her as she took the pot of potatoes in her hands and fired it across the room to a smashing crash. Tears streamed from her red eyes as she slowly sunk to the floor with her back against the wall. She was crying maniacally. She decided there would be no dinner that day.

Emotions buried her; as she thought about Tommy. She had not treated him as good as he deserved, and for that, Maggie will always bear the guilt in her heart. Replete with frustration, she began pulling wildly at her hair, wishing Tommy were there and she was gone. Her mind conflicted with the doubt that Tommy would ever harm his children, but her eyes would not have lied to her. She saw it; he held the bloody knife over Matthews's body, haunted by the image she balled. *He was dangerous*! *Ohh, Tommy, please come back*! She begged the silence. *Please.*

When her tantrum was over, she climbed back to her feet. *You are a good man Tommy*, she sobbed. Y*ou would never hurt your children. A sickness clouded your mind. I will do what I can to bring you back home, I swear it!* Fixing her hair and her and dress, standing up. 'And as for you, Matthew, I will bring you home tomorrow; the doctors will have fixed you; it will be like nothing ever happened to us, and I swear to be a better mother!'

With that personal promise, Maggie regained her composure and left the kitchen, passing through the hall.

Taking in a breath of cold wind and kissed by a gentle rain, Maggie looked around the deserted orchard and, out of habit, decided to harvest some apples. She spied some virgin apple trees in Robin Field and smiled.

Approaching the toolshed to get a pair of loopers, she gently pushed the door, and it swung open, screaming with effort; without looking around, she approached the wall with the loopers hanging on it and took them. She noticed a sack laid on the table. She thought nothing of it and left.

The sombre sky was filled with grey rain. The silence in the air pronounced a lack of cheery birds. The prosaic fragrance of apples did nothing for Maggie's sullen heart.

She retrieved an empty box at the beginning of the lane of apple trees and slowly began filling it. Not even examining the apples before collecting them, cutting down any loose apples she could see, and throwing them in the box, her mind relived the horror of the accursed night.

'I cannot perform the surgery, leave him here with me, and I will have him transferred to Castlebar hospital tomorrow morning; they can operate on him.' Maggie recalled the conversation with the doctor the night Matthew was maimed.

'Will he live, doctor?' she asked, shakily, drenched in Matthew's blood.

'The laceration is not too deep, and I have slowed the bleeding,' the doctor said encouragingly, 'but he has lost a lot of blood. It is difficult to know if he is beyond saving or not; still, we will try!'

Maggie turned to John and cried on his shoulder. She was staring through blurry eyes at the image of Matthews pale complexity against the bloodstained sheet in which he was carried in.

'We better get back to the orchard,' John said sympathetically, rubbing Maggie on the back, 'the Guardaí will be waiting.'

'I need to be here with my son!' Maggie snapped.

'You need to be at home with Joe,' retorted John.

'John is right,' said the doctor, 'there is nothing you can do for him, and tomorrow he will be brought to Castlebar. The hospital is a long drive from here, so I don't imagine you will be able to check on him regularly; call up to him mid-September, I will go with you; give them time up there to treat him, and they will inform you what will happen next,' the doctor said; gently laying his hand on Maggie's shoulder and looked in her saturated eyes. 'I am truly sorry Maggie; he is a very sweet child, he did not deserve this.'

John threw his arm around a distraught Maggie; and guided her from the doctor's office, passing through into the sullen dark void.

Maggie snapped back to reality with a jolt; realizing she had come to the end of the lane of the field, looking at her full box of apples; full of sadness and anger at what happened; she threw the full box
of apples onto the ground in a rage and stamped them one by one, screaming and crying.

Maggie no longer cared about the orchard; she did not care if it went out of business. All she cared about were her children; falling backwards onto the ground, she continued weeping. 'Matthew will be okay; tomorrow, I will bring him home. He will be fine.' She told herself as convincingly as she could but doubt ever gnawed at her hopes.

She looked up at the house, to the window of Joe's room, and thought she saw his silhouette through blurry eyes. '*I must help Joe*, she thought, climbing back to her feet. *He needs me; he needs his mother. Pull yourself together, Maggie!*

Leaving the loopers lying in the dirt, she left the field. In the distance leaning on a tree in the woods, Maggie thought she could see the shape of an old woman; a gentle weeping poisoned the silence. Maggie wiped her cloudy eyes and looked more clearly at the trees; whatever it was, was gone; the crying was replaced by the harsh whoosh of the autumn wind sundering the remaining summer's warmth. Hugging herself and rubbing her arms to repel the ever-groping fingers of the biting chill, Maggie continued to the house.

She climbed the stairs; standing now outside of Joe's room, she inhaled, wondering what to say. 'Joe, sweetie, are you okay in there?' The blatant silence reinforced the looming tension. 'Joe, are you alright?' Maggie's voice jumped with anxiety. Aggressively pounding on the door and calling Joe's name got no reply. Fearing the worst; - as was her forte recently - panic blinded any rational judgment; as Maggie repeatably screamed for Joe to respond. A muffled cry could be heard. Maggie halted her attempted breach to listen.

'I'm fine, mum, go away,' Joe's voice called out.

'I am sorry about our fight earlier on; can we please talk?'

'No,' answered Joe instantly. 'I don't want to talk. Just leave me alone, please.'

Maggie despairingly stepped back. 'Are you hungry? Do you want dinner?' Maggie said then she remembered there was no dinner.

'No!' said Joe with an irritated voice.

Defeated, Maggie retreated and made her way downstairs, distracting her gaze from the family portrait on the table. She passed through to the kitchen.

Maggie looked around the room curiously, wondering what she could make for dinner. After a brief look through the cabinets and hasty consideration, she decided it would be too much effort to start dinner again. Instead, she decided on a cheese sandwich. She took out enough ingredients to prepare two sandwiches, one for her and one for Joe when he decided to come out of his room. She poured herself a glass of water from a half-empty bucket, resting on the mahogany countertop. Maggie sat down at the table eating her sandwich, staring mournfully at the spot where Tommy slit Matthews's throat, unable to banish the memory from her mind. *How could he have just picked up a knife and slashed at our poor boy?* She thought to herself. *There is no reason Tommy would do that*; unless… *no, it's not real.*' Maggie momentarily considered the existence of the mythological being but quickly shut that idea out of her head.

She finished her meal and realized a sudden weariness had washed over her. With a yawn, she glanced out the window to see the sun was vanishing, bringing its fading light with it. It still felt early, but the long summer days were over. She felt both tired and dismal. Deciding an early night would resolve her problems. Throwing her dishes in the empty sink, placing the burden of cleaning up on her future self, she headed for bed. She passed from the kitchen and up the stairs.

She entered her bedroom—a bright room with a hopeful cream and violet floral wallpaper, a pristine, shiny boarded floor. The wavey white and red duvet clothing the king-sized bed matched the long curtains, along with the white closet and end-tables, made the room look somewhat soft and lordly, once upon a time. She flicked on the light switch, brightening up the room with a glistening glow. Maggie pulled off her dress and kicked off her shoes, and put on her nightgown.

Turning back and switching off the light, she staggered like a blind man to her cold, unmade bed and crawled in. As Maggie lay there in the silence and never-ending dark, staring with wide eyes at the nothing that surrounded her, she began to weep. She thought of Tommy; maybe because she could still smell his scent on his pillow or maybe because she could feel the empty indent on his side of the mattress.

116

The painful memories of that horrifying night came flooding back; Maggie tried her best to think of happier thoughts, rolling around to and fro restlessly in the oversized bed, which brought her no comfort. She kept imagining she could hear Matthew screaming and crying; soon she noticed, she did not imagine the screams; she held her breath to remove all sound from the room so she could listen intently. Once again, the shrill scream filled the room. Maggie tucked herself in tightly to her bedsheets and cowered. She wondered if Joe could hear the screaming; and what he thought.

Maggie did not feel the sleep creeping up on her. She laid there for hours or a lifetime. She was not sure; in the impenetrable dark void, haunted by her memories. Just before she fell asleep, she thought she could hear someone walking around the house; figuring it was Joe going down for some food, she passed into a dreamless sleep.

The next morning Maggie woke up and lay in her bed staring at the roof; slowly recollecting her thoughts, she sighed in despair, realizing the last few dreadful months were not just a nightmare.

Getting out of bed, she approached her wardrobe and took out her best dark blue dress and comfortable shoes, knowing today, she would have to go to Castlebar. Shaking with anxiety, she threw on her clothes and left the room. Stopping in the outhouse before breakfast.

Maggie walked into the kitchen, and to her delight, Joe was sitting at the table eating breakfast. She hesitated to speak with him, wondering if he would still be mad.

'Good morning, Joe,' she said while preparing breakfast.

He lifted his head, 'Good morning, mum.' He shuffled awkwardly in his seat; wanting to reconcile his marred relationship with his mother but too embarrassed to attempt it

Maggie sat down at the table with her breakfast and a glass of water. 'I have to go to the hospital today,' Maggie said, looking at Joe, 'I will be leaving soon.'

'Can I come?' Joe asked eagerly.

'No,' Maggie said sternly; I will be picking up Doctor Murphy from town; there will be no room for you. I am bringing the two-seater wagon. You will go to Cleary's farm.'

Satisfied with the news, Joe smiled, thinking about spending the day with Mary. His smile then vanished. 'Do you think Matthew will be alright?'

'Maggie finished her breakfast, 'He'll be fine. He's a McNeeve.' Maggie laughed but did not know for sure if Tommy or David was Matthew's father. She sipped guiltily at her water.

Joe swallowed his pride, 'Mum, I am very sorry about the way I acted yesterday; I'm just so scared and confused. I know I shouldn't take it out on you. Please forgive me.'

Maggie rose from her seat smiling and approached Joe, hugging him from behind. 'There is nothing to forgive, sweet boy; I am scared too. But things will get better, I promise!' she stated with as much assurance as could be mustered.

'Joe smiled, 'Okay mum.' Standing up from the table. 'Would you like a cup of tea?

'I would love a cup of tea; would you make me one while I get ready?' she said, stopping in the doorway and turning around, 'Also, there is some bacon and cabbage in the press for dinner. Would you mind having it on when we get home?'

Approaching the stove. 'Yeah, no bother.' Joe placed the kettle on the stove; he lit the hob and left the kettle on it.

Maggie passed from the kitchen, upstairs, to her room. She tied her hair up in a ponytail and retrieved a bag from her wardrobe: a faded maroon travel sack. She headed back to the kitchen.

In the kitchen, Maggie began preparing four ham sandwiches for the journey. One by one, placing them in the large pocket of the bag. She picked up an empty bottle and filled it in the pot, lowering it into the side pouch. Then the kettle began to sing in a high pitch, signalling it was boiled.

Joe made Maggie a scalding cup of tea. She sipped at it cautiously.

'Thank you, Joe, Tis' lovely. sniffing the earthly perfume of the brew, wrapping her cold hands around the hot cup. 'Would you be a dear; and get the wagon ready while I finish this?'

Joe nodded and left the kitchen.

Maggie looked out of the window; the nervous sun peaked out over the moist rolling hills. Knowing she was alone, Maggie allowed herself to cry. Tears of worry and uncertainty painted her cheeks. She took a mouthful of the boiling tea and swallowed it stoically; It burned her all the way down to her stomach. She stared out of the window, welcoming this feeling of pain like it was family, a distant cousin overstaying her welcome.

Maggie stepped outside, shouldering her travel sack containing the journey's rations. Joe had indeed prepared the wagon. He had just finished connecting it to the strongest horse the McNeeves owned: a large black workhorse, Matthew named Giant.

The fading cologne of apples was almost effaced by the cruel autumn winds carrying the fragrance of dead leaves and blatant cold.

'Thank you, Joe,' Maggie said while climbing up on the wagon and throwing her bag in the empty box behind her.

Joe stroked Giant on the forehead before climbing up on the wagon himself.

'I already told you, you could not come,' Maggie said, visibly frustrated.

Joe sat back and buttoned up the collar of his jacket against the cold. 'Can I not get a lift to the road?' He laughed.

Maggie whipped the reins, and Giant began trotting forward. She pulled on her black leather gloves, grey wool cap, and striped scarf.

The flowers dotted around the orchard seemed less bright and happy; maybe because it was the end of their ephemeral existence, and they spent what was left of their time shivering in the brutal cold and reminiscing of days when they were surrounded by friends and family.

The few birds that flew around in the dull sky did not sing anymore. They flew reticently as if they were afraid to wake some unspeakable evil. The dearth of bird song and colourful flowers dampened the hearts of all who crossed that land.

'What time will you be home?' Joe asked quietly, afraid to disturb the ominous silence.

'I do not know; I will be as quick as I can; Doctor Murphy said it was a long drive, so I don't think I will be back before seven,' Maggie replied in a low voice.

Giant whinnied and slowly pulled the cart to the end of the track, to the main road.

Maggie slowed the cart to a halt.

Joe dismounted. He turned to his mother, smiling and waving. 'Bring Matthew home.' And he began walking up the road.

Maggie steered Giant left and continued down the road. Not quite understanding the conflict in her emotions. *I will bring him home,* she thought. *I will bring him home dead or alive.*

The further Maggie drove away from the orchard, the more life seemed to pour back into the world. The refreshing breeze felt like it cleaned her dusty lungs, the colourful flowers almost blinded Maggie, and the birds sang and laughed while packing for their winter holiday. The obstinate leaves clung on with all their strength to their branches, not wanting to leave their summer vacation.

Grey clouds loomed in the distance, slowly approaching.

'An umbrella!' Maggie said loudly. *I forgot to bring an umbrella; hopefully, it won't rain. I am sure the doctor will have one.*

Maggie continued driving down the road into town, enjoying the soothing breeze and the chatty nature of the birds. The sun was standing high and proud in the sky, shining through the rude clouds trying to hide her.

When Maggie pulled up in town, she felt somewhat comforted, seeing all the people tending to their shops and walking around hither and tither. The busy life directly contrasted her present isolated, dismal existence. She looked around the town and was awestruck by the beauty it held; the damp drops of condensation being pronounced by the sunlight made the straw roofs of the buildings look like honey adorned with diamonds. The cheerful flowers dancing in boxes on the windowsills enjoyed both the warmth of the sun and the refreshing hydration of the cool silver droplets. Maggie could not help but smile at this fairytale-like atmosphere.

She stopped outside of the doctor's clinic and stepped down off the wagon, stretching her legs and arms. With three knocks on the doctor's door, she stepped back and looked around at the busy town, wondering where everybody was going and what they were doing.

(Remember when you and John dragged Matthew through here when he was dying, and he was bleeding, and he was DYING!)

STOP THINKING ABOUT IT!

Doctor Murphy smiled at Maggie. He was dressed in his usual horn-rimmed glasses, exaggerating his brown eyes; he wore a brown sweater vest over a white shirt with dark dress pants, he flashed a smile at Maggie.

'Good morning, Maggie, how are you this day? said the doctor, 'How is Joe doing?'

'Morning Doctor Murphy, I am fine, thank you for asking, Joe; he is not doing too well; his arm troubles him awfully some days, and he still has no strength in it. 'Maggie noticed Doctor Murphy nodding along to Joe's symptoms, 'and he gets so angry sometimes.'

'Perhaps you should bring him into me someday, and I will examine him.'

Maggie nodded in agreement.

'So,' said the doctor clapping his hands together, 'are we ready for this big journey we have ahead of us.'

Maggie nodded, 'Indeed I think we are. I have packed sandwiches and water for when we get hungry.'

Doctor Murphy smiled, and with a laugh, he raised a brown leather travel sack from his foot to show Maggie. 'I have also brought sandwiches and refreshments.' Looking over Maggie's shoulder, Doctor Murphy spots the small wagon she rode in on.

'You can park your cart around the back and put the horse in the stable he will be alright for a couple of hours,' said the doctor stepping out of his clinic and walking around the side of the building.

Maggie looked perplexed, 'Are we not taking my cart?'

The doctor stopped and turned to Maggie. 'One of the perquisites of being a doctor; is that you get to ride around in style.' The doctor laughed. 'Besides, the three of us will be cramped on that small wagon. I have already buckled my horses to my wagon. I will be ready to go shortly; bring your horse and cart around back. They will be okay here.'

Maggie climbed back up on her cart and steered Giant behind the clinic, where sure enough, there was a small barn.

Doctor Murphy exited the barn on his beautiful wagon: a high driver seat it had, with a roofed carriage behind it. Painted on the the carriage were detailed caduceus. The two seats in the carriage, one at the back and one at the front, so, if two people were to sit on both sides, they would be facing each other. It was beautifully padded with royal red leather. The carriage was drawn by two shining white steeds.

As Doctor Murphy passed Maggie, he smiled at the look of awe on her face. 'A wagon fit for a queen.' He laughed.

Maggie had never seen a wagon so elegant in her life; when Doctor Murphy was out of the barn in his glamorous wagon, Maggie ushered Giant and her unfashionable cart inside.

She climbed down off the cart and began detaching Giant's harness from the carriage shaft.

Like a delicate shadow, Doctor Murphy silently strolled in beside Maggie and tapped her on the shoulder. She stepped away from Giant with a sigh of frustration.

Doctor Murphy, who could see Maggie was having difficulty detaching the horse, decided he would perform the strenuous operation.

'I will take care of the horse,' the doctor said, 'you just go ahead and put all your belongings in my wagon.'

Maggie smiled and retrieved her bag from her cart; carrying it over to the doctor's wagon, she opened the carriage and placed her bag under the left bench.

Upon climbing out of the carriage, she came face to face with Doctor Murphy, who had now stored Giant away; Maggie jumped back startled.

'Sorry,' He laughed, 'do you want to ride in the back carriage or the driver's seat with me?'

Maggie hesitated, admiring the beautiful carriage; 'I will ride up top with you. Your company might make the journey shorter.'

'Or longer.' He laughed again.

Maggie laughed while the doctor helped her climb up to the passenger's seat. He then walked to the opposite side of the carriage and climbed up; holding the reins in his hands, he tenderly flicked his wrist with two encouraging clicks from his mouth; the two glistening horses drove slowly on to the main street of town; to anyone who saw them, it must have looked like a splendid boat rolling on a white sea.

Doctor Murphy and Maggie both smiled down on the fascinated townsfolk, waving, feeling like royalty on their dazzling carriage. The people watched as the carriage slowly rolled out of town, out of sight.

Remembering the purpose of the trip, Maggie sat back uncomfortably, 'Do you think there's any hope for Matthew?' she said, 'I am so afraid of losing him, doctor; I would trade my own life for his.'

Seeing the terrified look on her face, 'The boy will be fine; the hospital is known for succouring people back to health. After all, he is a strong kid, and he will be fine,' Doctor Murphy said in his most calming voice, but he hid a look of doubt from Maggie.

Trying to relax, Maggie stretched her arms and took a drink of water from her bottle. She looked out to the right where there was a small wooded area, the pine trees flailing in beat to the soft breeze, their perfume painting the air. A shape leaning against the nearest tree caught Maggie's attention; she squinted her eyes from the sun to better discern what she was looking at. And then she saw it. She screamed and jumped back, nearly knocking the doctor from the wagon: he stopped abruptly.

'What's the matter?' he shouted with a mixture of confusion and worry.

'There by the trees; don't you see it?' Maggie cried and pointed wildly, hiding her face in the doctor's shoulder.

Doctor Murphy strained his eyes, scanning the trees; 'I don't see anything. Is it still there?'

Maggie built up the courage and looked over her right shoulder to the trees. A look of perplexment twisted her face. 'It's gone; I swear to you it was there a moment ago, I saw it.'

'What was it?' asked the doctor with a twinge of terror.

Maggie slowly turned her head to face the doctor. 'An old woman; she wore a black gown with a veil covering her face. She was crying.' Her eyes opened wide, full of terror, and shot with hope; not an optimistic hope, rather a hope she was wrong.

'It was the banshee. Maggie said with assurance.

Upon saying the name, a crack of Thunder ripped apart the peaceful day; and a heavy rain drowned the world. A flash of pale lighting snapped just overhead, so close. They could smell the burning electricity.

'Good Lord!' Doctor Murphy almost fell off the wagon again. He looked up, and his eyes quickly filled with rain. He was breathing in short bursts, he reached under the seat and pulled something out, handing it to Maggie.

She looked down, and to her amusement, it was an umbrella, she opened it and held it above her and the doctor, with a quiet chuckle, she thought '*I forgot to ask him to bring an umbrella. It's a good thing he's a doctor.*'

The sweaty horses were thankful for the refreshing rain on their hot skin, they whinnied and continued to drive the carriage along the dirt road to the hospital.

<u>VIII</u> KINDLED HEARTS

Joe trotted down the road, skipping with joy, knowing he would get to hang out with Mary and later Matthew would be home, everything would be fine.

The cool breeze kissed Joe's limp arm, which he removed from its sling to allow air at it. The glorious day filled him with a desire to sing. The hot sun did its best to shine through the thick clouds to illuminate the gay flowers and to remind Joe that it would be foolish to give up hope. The birds sang to each other from different trees in different keys.

He strolled merrily along the road until he came to a gate beside a large chestnut tree. This was the field he and Matthew cut across to get home a lifetime ago. Joe had not been up this road since.

He stopped going to school after that horrible night, mainly due to his dominant arm being rendered lame. He could no longer write, so he figured he might as well give up school.

He missed his brother deeply, and the shadow of grief and doubt flooded him, but he soon banished those fears, knowing Matthew was going to be home later and he was going to be fine, then life would go back to the way it was. Even without Tommy being around, he would find a way to bring his dad home.

He continued along the road until, at last, he spotted Cleary's farm sitting just beyond the bright fields.

He slowed down to a walk as he got closer to the house when suddenly his passage was barred. Joe stood motionless, staring with unblinking eyes at the sentinel.

Joe smiled, and in one smooth motion, he cried, 'Hello Sam.' and ran over to the dog, petting him vigorously behind the ears. Sam rolled over on his back, allowing Joe to give him a belly rub, which he did.

After a few moments of monkeying around with Sam, Joe got up and made his way to the house.

He knocked on the door three times and waited a moment.

Teresa wore a smile from ear to ear.

'Hullo Joe,' she said with exuberance, 'come in, won't you? I have just boiled the kettle. Would you have a cup of tea?'

'Yes, please,' he answered.

Joe took a seat at the table while Teresa made him a cup of tea. Handing Joe his tea and keeping a cup for herself, she sat down across from him.

'I've been saying a rosary for your family every day,' Teresa said, sipping her tea, 'When your mother asked me to look out for you today, I was delighted that I could help; if there is ever anything you want me to do, just ask.' Teresa smiled.

'Thank you so much for everything,' Joe said, awkwardly sipping his tea. He had not quite got the hang of using his left hand. She had made his tea with milk; Joe only drank black tea, but it was too late now. He had to drink it. 'This is a lovely cup of tea,' he lied with a smile.

Teresa smiled gleefully, 'I would offer you a biscuit, but we don't have any left, would you like a sandwich or anything? Are you hungry?'

'No, honestly I'm fine, I'm just after eating breakfast, the tea is fine for me, thank you.'

Teresa's face twisted with disgust. 'If I make you a sandwich, will you eat it? There's nothing worse than a dry cup of tea.'

Joe laughed. 'That's what my mom says as well.'

Teresa rose from the table and began preparing a ham and cheese sandwich. 'It's awful what your father did to poor Matthew; how are you and your mother taking it?'

Joe was surprised by how candid Teresa was being and was not comfortable talking about that with her; he shifted in his seat. 'I suppose we are...' the words tangled themselves in Joe's throat, 'we are... well, things will be fine.'

Teresa realized she had crossed some sort of line. 'If you want to wait right here and I'll go get Mary; she's in her room.' Without waiting for an answer, Teresa hurried down the hall. She left Joe alone with his repulsive cup of tea.

Joe jumped up out of his chair and snuck over to the kitchen window holding his cup of tea; he opened the window and began pouring the tea out. After the cup had been emptied he shut the window, and carefully placed the cup beside the sink and finished making the sandwich that Teresa had begun.

Mary hurried into the room, followed by Teresa. She ran over to Joe and hugged him.

'I've missed you so much,' Mary said.

Joe was confused with emotions; he had never seen Mary this way before. She looked beautiful with a yellow bow in her hair. 'I am... you look, I missed you too,' Joe fumbled.

Teresa and Mary both looked at each other and giggled; Joe's face boiled red in embarrassment.

'School has been so boring without you,' Mary said, 'do you ever think you will come back?'

Joe shook his head, holding his sandwich.

'How is your hand?' Mary asked.

Joe regained his senses, 'I think they might have to chop it off.' Joe smiled, expecting his joke to rouse laughter but instead resulted in worry and pity.

'Can't they do anything to help? Surely they won't amputate your arm without trying everything else? Does it hurt you?' Teresa interjected.

Mary stood there, grief-stricken.

'I was only kidding. It doesn't hurt,' Joe awkwardly said.

Teresa did not laugh, and Mary exhaled loudly, mimicking a chuckle for Joe's sake.

Joe bit into his sandwich. Mary placed her hand on Joe's arm. 'Do you want to go for a walk?' Mary said with excitement.

Joe wanted nothing more than to leave that room after his failure of a joke, 'Yeah, I would love to,'

Joe and Mary were on their way. A cry from behind them made Mary stop and turn around.

'Don't forget you have chores to do, young lady,' Teresa said.

'Okay, mum,' Mary shouted back.

'And be careful, you two!'

'We will, mum!' she shouted back, and with that, Mary. She led Joe to a field behind her house; she stopped and turned to Joe.

'There is a lake a bit of a walk from here through these fields,' Mary said, 'are you able to walk to it?'

Joe looked down at his arm in its sling, 'The last time I checked,' he said, 'I didn't walk on my hands.'

Mary laughed and climbed over the small stone wall into the field, followed by Joe.

At the end of the field, there was a narrow dyke; there was no crossing in sight. Mary looked at Joe with eyes starved of adventure. 'We'll have to jump it,' she said, 'it's not a far jump, and the water is not too deep. But if you want to turn back, I'll understand,' she said menacingly, knowing that would egg Joe on.

Predictably Joe took the bait. 'Ladies first,' he said.

With a smile, Mary gracefully leapt over the dyke and landed perfectly on her feet. She turned back to Joe and curtseyed.

'That wasn't bad, but wait until you see this.' Joe clumsily stumbled over the gap. He landed roughly, and his feet began slipping on the wet grass. He called for help as he fell backwards into the stream.

Mary fell over laughing; when Joe picked himself up and climbed out of the dike dripping wet.

'I meant to do that,' Joe said, patting down his soaked clothes.

'Why would you purposely fall into a stream?'

'Because I wanted to make you laugh.'

'Why would you want to make me laugh?'

'Because I like your laugh,' Joe said, looking into Mary's grey eyes. He felt something deep down that he never felt before.

Mary stopped laughing and slowly approached Joe

They stood silent for a moment face to face, looking deep into one another's eyes; both filled with an unexplainable feeling, unsure what to do, but knowing they did not want to be anywhere else in the world; but right there, right then. Joe slowly leaned into Mary's lips.

Suddenly he was knocked to the ground by a powerful force. He looked up to see Mary laughing uncontrollably; it was Sam. Sam must have followed them, and being a good guard dog, prevented anyone from touching Mary. Joe picked himself up, laughing. Mary was scratching Sam behind the ears. Joe dusted his drenched pants with his hand and approached Sam, crouching down; he petted Sam.

'Sam, you have to stay here, good boy,' Mary said in a commanding voice.

Sam sat down, his tongue dangling, panting heavily.

'Good boy, Sam, we won't be too long,' Joe said.

And with that, he felt himself being pulled to his right; confused, Joe looked around to find what caused this weird sensation. He then realized it was Mary holding his lame hand, leading him on through the field.

Mary looked back to Joe and noticed the surprised look on his face.

'This is your bad hand, isn't it,' Mary said quickly, dropping his hand, 'I am so sorry.'

'It's alright,' Joe said in a dreamy state, 'I can't feel it.'

Mary looked Joe in the eyes and whispered, 'I wish I could make it all the better for you.'

'You can,' whispered Joe, and with that, he placed his good hand in Mary's hand and smiled.

Mary returned the smile, and the two of them went skipping through the fields, holding hands and dancing in the wind to the joyful songs of the birds.

They passed through a small, wooded area and emerged from a bristly thicket onto a small clearing beside the lake. Mary led Joe by the hand onto a large rock overhanging the lake; they both sat down at the precipice, and Mary removed her shoes and dipped her feet in the water. Joe mimicked this action and felt the cool, refreshing water on his tired feet. Joe continued clutching Mary's hand as he gazed out upon the still mirror-like lake, painting a beautiful upside-down picture of the landscape. The gentle wind caused soothing ripples in this otherwise unanimated body of water. The reeds and long grass touching the edges of the lake attempted to join in the water dance but could not quite get the hang of it. The sun began to cool.

Mary and Joe sat for a while, talking about school, chores, and weather. In fact, it did not matter what the topic of conversation might have been; neither of the two had ever felt such serenity and happiness.

When the clouds once again blocked out the sun, covering everything in a dim filter, Mary looked down at her hand in Joe's. She smiled and brought her gaze to meet Joe's eyes. She wanted to say a thousand things and at the same time wanted to say nothing. She had never felt such a powerful feeling in her stomach. She did not know what it was; she only knew that she never wanted that moment to end. She would happily spend the rest of her days sitting right there, hand in hand with Joe.

Joe stared back into Mary's eyes, filled with happiness. He was never much good at expressing lovey-dovey emotions, but by God, he felt it! He wanted nothing more than to kiss her soft lips, but he was afraid, afraid if he did that, she would run away and never speak to him again. He sat there feeling ecstatic yet full of sorrow, knowing this moment was only a transient reality.

The sun broke out of her clouded prison cell to illuminate the lake. A black and orange painted butterfly soared over their heads, gracefully wavering from flower to flower. It landed on the rock beside Joe, gazing out at the calming lake.

Joe watched the butterfly sitting peacefully beside his leg; his thoughts went to Matthew, and then his father, and then the Banshee. His arm burned in a pain that simply infuriated him. The burning sensation filled Joe with a fit of unquenchable anger; he wanted nothing more than to bring his hand down hard and crush the life out of that butterfly. Joe struggled for a moment with that inner-conflict, finally being consumed by the fury he prepared to strike.

Mary spoke, distracting Joe:

'How are you holding up, Joe?'

Confusion warped his face, 'If my troubles were as far apart as my grannies teeth, I would be happy out .'

Mary laughed, 'I know these last few months have been hard, and I have never really spoken to you since. I care about you, Joe.'

Joe released his grip on Mary's hand, glancing to the butterfly; it had gone. He stood up laughing; he picked up a loose stone on the rock and skimmed it on the calm lake.

'Do you know what happened?' Joe asked, not looking back at Mary.

Bemused by the question, Mary looked out at the lake for an answer. 'Someone told my dad that your dad went crazy and tried to kill you and Matthew.' Mary shot a concerned gaze at Joe; he was still not facing her.

Joe laughed. 'That's not what happened; why does everybody think my dad is crazy? He's not! I suppose they say I'm crazy too?' Joe aggressively threw a large stone as far into the lake as he could: it landed with a heavy splash, sundering the peaceful water.

Mary stood up, 'As I said; I really care about you, Joe, you can tell me anything; I will help you any way I can.'

Joe looked back and weighed Mary up, feeling vulnerable. 'You wouldn't believe me if I told you,' Joe said with a sigh of despair.

Mary approached Joe and grabbed hold of his hands; she looked deeply into his innocent sapphire eyes. 'We have been best friends since before we started school. Of course, I will believe you, Joe.'

He breathed heavily; he did not want to involve anybody else in his plan, especially not her; he knew he could not protect her. He stood in silence for a moment, then decided he would not involve Mary.

'Joe? Are you going to tell me?' Mary whispered gently.

Joe inhaled; *I can't tell you.* was cemented in his mind, but when he met her eyes; they seemed so caring and supportive; Joe lost himself in her deep grey eyes, filled with a strengthening weakness that could only be love, he ignored all his mental red flags. 'Alright then,' he said with a sigh; not knowing where to start, 'sit down,' he said, 'I will tell you everything.'

They both sat back down, dangling their feet in the water. Joe pondered on how to begin his story. After a few fleeting moments, he began his tale the day Matthew was playing by the well. Mary listened intently to every word spoken; she seemed to have been interested and did not believe Joe was lying.

Joe concluded his story with, 'That's the truth.'

Mary sat puzzled for a moment, trying to process what she had just heard. Joe stared at her, hoping she would believe him but anticipated her bursting out laughing.

'Okay… so… it's all,' Mary stammered, completely lost for words, 'the fairies are real?' she asked at last.

Joe was elated she believed him. 'Yes, the fairies and the banshee are real, and I have to stop her,' Joe said, exhaling, only now understanding how insane it sounded.

'I cannot believe there is a fairy circle behind your house; can we go and see it?' asked Mary hopefully.

'What?' Joe snapped back, full of irritation, 'Were you not listening? The fairies are gone! The banshee found them. They are either dead, or they have fled,' Joe cried, 'they can't help me,' he said, weeping.

Mary placed a comforting arm around Joe's shoulder, 'You don't need their help; I will help you,' she said, getting on her feet and pulling Joe up, 'We need to get back to the farm. I have chores to do.'

Following Mary away from the lake, his mind was deep in thought about the ritual and how he was going to do it. As they walked back to the wooded area behind the lake, the clouds obscured the sunlight, and darkness crept slowly back into the world.

Emerging into an open field, Mary slowed down to match Joe's pace.

'So how are we going to stop the banshee?' she naively asked, ignorant of the danger she could get herself into, 'I mean, do you have any plan? Do you have to like… stab her to get the blood?'

Joe slipped out of his thoughts and looked at Mary, who was smiling. 'Why are you smiling? This isn't a game, Mary; this is dangerous, really dangerous,' Joe snapped, 'if you think this is going to be fun, or that I am joking; maybe I don't need your help.' Joe continued walking.

Mary stopped walking and watched Joe with furious eyes. 'You do need my help; I am stronger than you, Joe McNeeve!' Mary yelled.

Joe allowed himself a smug smile, 'You are not stronger than me.' He laughed cockily. No sooner had he said these words before he was tackled to the ground; he struggled with all his might to push Mary off him and get up, but he could not.

Mary pinned his arms to the ground and laughed, 'Come on so, get me off you if you're so strong!' She laughed as Joe exhausted himself, squirming around, trying to push her off. At length, Joe lay still, breathing heavily, with fatigued muscles. He focused his vision on Mary, who was staring down at Joe, looking deep into his eyes. Joe looked back into Mary's eyes. And before he knew what to do next, Mary kissed him. It was not the same kind of kiss he got from his mother; this was on the lips, and it filled Joe with a feeling most unfamiliar.

Suddenly a boom of thunder ripped Joe and Mary from their ethereal paradise, and as they looked at each other, with hearts filled with fear and gladness, they laughed.

Mary stood up and pulled Joe up by the hand; she held his hand tightly, all the time smiling, and led Joe back the way they came. 'So, you stab Her with the dagger, put Her blood on the tablet, throw the tablet down the well while chanting a spell?' Mary looked perplexed, 'Do you know the spell?'

'No,' Joe said, looking now at Mary, wondering if they were going to discuss the moment they just shared. 'but the fairies said I would know it when the time comes.'

Mary did not look too convinced, 'You will know it when the time comes? Do we have a plan as to how we're going to do this?'

Joe's heart glowed with happiness when he heard Mary say, "we". 'I don't have a plan yet,' Joe vaguely answered, 'Are we boyfriend and girlfriend now?' he asked with the excitement catching in his throat.

Mary released Joe's hand and continued walking, 'I have no time for a boyfriend; I have chores to do,' she shouted back without looking.

Joe stood still bemused for a second. He jogged, catching up to Mary, 'What about that?' Joe pointed back to the spot where they kissed, 'Did you not feel the same way I did?'

She stopped and looked Joe in the eyes. 'I don't know why I did that; please don't tell mummy.' Mary's eyes filled with fear, 'I hope I don't have a baby.'

Joe laughed uncontrollably, 'That's not how babies are made.'

'Yes, it is! When two people love each other, and they kiss, they have a baby.' Mary sank to her knees, crying.

Joe continued laughing, 'No, it's not! You need to have—' Joe blushed, 'sex.'

'Sex? What's sex?' Mary asked, truly bewildered.

Joe shifted uncomfortably, 'When a man and a woman get naked—'

Suddenly! a heavy rain fell from the heavens, washing out the uncomfortable moment.

'Come on quick!' Mary shouted, running with her hands on her head. Joe followed, not in too much of a hurry because his clothes were still soggy after falling into the dike.

Wait, did she just say she loved me too? he thought giddily.

Joe and Mary returned to her farm and took shelter from the rain in the chicken coop, water dripping off both.

Mary removed the wet hair from her eyes, 'What is sex?' she persisted.

Joe awkwardly gestured with his good hand, 'It's when a man and a woman get naked and—' Joe almost felt too embarrassed to continue, 'they kiss.'

Mary sighed in relief. 'So, we had to be naked? Thank God for that, but I would never get naked with anybody!'

'Me neither!'

'Where did you learn that?'

'David told me.' Joe's heart sank in sadness, mentioning the name of his departed friend.

The heavy rain beat loudly on the galvanized roof.

Soon after, the heavy beats became a gentle trickling, the sunlight radiated, pronouncing every landed raindrop making the world look as if it was covered by a sparkling silver blanket. In the distance, Joe spotted a rainbow. He smiled, thinking back to Mary's pot of gold. Joe stepped outside into the soft drizzle. He looked back at Mary, standing in the coop looking out and smiled.

'It's OK, it's only light rain,' he said, stretching his arm out and embracing the water; his other arm was tucked neatly away in its sling.

Mary stepped out. 'Will you help me do my chores?' she asked earnestly.

Reluctantly Joe nodded his head. 'What do we have to do?'

Mary smiled. 'I have to feed the chickens, I have to clean out the barn, feed Sam, feed the sheep, and finally milk the cows.' She listed them off one by one with her fingers.

This was not the way Joe wished to spend his day; however, since he had nothing else for doing, he figured he might as well do something. 'I will feed Sam, the chickens, and the sheep; where can I find the food?' Joe asked.

Mary pointed across the yard to a small shed, 'The door is always locked; the key is in the house under the... ask mummy. Are you sure you don't mind doing all that? Would you prefer to milk the cows?' said Mary.

Joe laughed, 'I never liked milking cows.'

'No, it's fun and really easy. I'll show you,' said Mary with a twinge of excitement.

Joe hesitated. 'Yeah, sure, you can show me later. I am going to get the key. I'll speak to you later.' And with that, Joe made his way to the house.

Mary approached the barn and passed through them; the barn was a lot more spacious than it looked, housing six cows, four of which were out grazing, two were closed in their stalls waiting to be milked. She picked up the wheelbarrow beside the stall and drove it down the barn to the first empty stall; picking up the shovel that lay in the wheelbarrow, she passed into it. Ten years of working on a farm with the animals, left Mary immune to the noisome stench of cow manure.

She shovelled up the cow dung and dropped it in the wheelbarrow; all the time thinking about her kiss with Joe. *I am glad I won't have a baby… yet.* she thought, *I wonder what Joe would look like naked*, she shook her head trying to banish these blasphemous thoughts; over the cows gently groaning, she could hear Joe shouting, 'Sam… Sam here boy, dinner!' Accompanied by a whistle. She smiled and continued cleaning the stall. Unaware that Joe was feeding Sam, thinking the exact same thoughts about her.

An hour later, Mary left the barn and saw Joe approaching her from the field; he was holding a sack of sheep feed. When he came within shouting distance, Mary said, 'Put that bag back in the shed. and put the key back inside; then meet me in the barn.' Mary turned around and disappeared behind the wall.

Joe grunted. He placed the bag back in the shed on the shelf where he found it and made sure he returned the chicken feed and dog food. He stepped out and locked the door. He walked over to the house, knocked, entered the kitchen.

Teresa was cooking dinner, standing at the stove when Joe entered. With alacrity, she jumped over to Joe. 'I'll take that, don't worry about it,' she said with an opened hand.

Joe dropped the key in her palm, 'Thank you,' he said, exiting the house.

Joe made his way to the barn where he passed by a marching troop of clucking chickens, no doubt on their evening stroll after dinner. Joe laughed at how uniform they presented themselves. He looked to his left, and at the end of the long driveway, Joe saw a wagon approaching. It was Stephen, Mary's father.

Mary was leaning against one of the stalls when Joe entered; 'It's about time,' she said impatiently.

Joe did not answer but continued approaching Mary. She opened the latch and swung it open, beckoned Joe to enter before herself, he did, Mary followed.

'Take a seat on that stool there, beside Bessie,' Mary commanded.

'Bessie?' Joe marvelled as he sat down on the three-legged stool.

'Yeah, Bessie; she's mine, she has a gentle heart, and she is very calm, perfect for you to learn how to milk her,' Mary said as she stroked Bessie's back.

Joe sank onto the stool, 'I know how to milk a cow. I have done it before,' he said while placing a stainless-steel bucket under the cow and gently pulling her udders.

'Whoa, whoa,' Mary interrupted and carefully stopped Joe. 'What are you doing? First off, you didn't even clean her udders; that's what this bucket with hot water and soap is for.' Mary pointed to the foamy bucket. 'And second, that's not how you milk a cow. You use both hands to—' Mary looked at Joe's limp hand in the sling and looked back into his eyes. They were wet but determined to remain strong. Regret distorted her face. 'I am very sorry, Joe.'

Joe brushed it off with a joke, 'I guess I'll never be a handyman.' They both laughed, but deep-down, Joe felt like a waste of life.

Joe got up off the stool, 'Maybe you should do it,' he said, 'I'll watch.'

Mary took a seat on the stool and washed the udders before milking them. Joe stood over her shoulder watching her, but his mind was a million miles away thinking about Matthew.

Later, Joe's conscience returned to him, and he realized he was in a different stall with a different cow Mary was milking. He did not remember moving, but evidently, he did.

He looked out the window at the setting sun, 'I would guess about two hours of sunlight left today.'

Mary finished and wiped her sweaty brow, 'Are you staying for dinner? she said, rising from her stool and carrying the full bucket of milk with her; Joe followed. She picked up the second bucket outside of the stall and left the barn.

'No, thank you,' Joe said, 'I better get back and have dinner ready for mum and Matthew when they get home.'

'Ohh,' Mary said, with a hint of sadness; she carefully placed the bucket on the ground and walked over to Joe.

Standing face to face with him, Mary wanted nothing more than to kiss him again. Joe cleared his throat.

'Thank you for such a fun day,' he said, 'and thank your mum for me, for giving me the tea and sandwiches,' Joe said, and awkwardly turned around and started walking down the driveway.

Mary slumped in sadness at the sight of Joe leaving. 'What about our plan with the banshee?' She carelessly shouted to Joe.

Joe whipped around, flailing his arm wildly and looking around nervously, 'Don't say that name so loud! I will let you know the plan when I figure it out,' he said, turning around once again and continuing down the driveway.

The sun was sinking behind the distant mountains, taking its light with it. The silent world was disturbed by a vicious biting wind that sliced Joe's bones. He was alone but could not shake the feeling that he was being watched, hounded, and potentially hunted. He picked up his pace to a slow jog. Whenever he was with anybody, he would always act like a brave warrior of old, but when he was alone, it shocked him to learn what a coward he really was. The mundane flowers blended into the monotonous hedges, and the haggard birds fell dumb as Joe ran by them.

The shrill wind whistled in a sound Joe swore resembled his name; fear took him, and he ran as fast as he could; which was not as fast anymore, because of his arm being tied up in the sling, he found it difficult to balance himself as he ran so he had to compensate by running slower and more carefully.

The light grew ever fainter when Joe finally reached his house. He was never so happy to see the stone-arched gate in front of the orchard. He ran up to the driveway, panting, to the front house.

Quickly, Joe lifted a potted plant by the door and retrieved the house key from under it; fidgeting with the key, trying to place it in the keyhole, terror grabbed hold of him; when the wind became a resonant screech, which sounded like the wail of the banshee. He opened it, passed through. He was instantly relieved.

Joe closed the curtains; breathing slowly, he presently mastered his fears, remembering he was asked to get dinner started for Maggie and Matthew when they got home. Quietly, he crept into the kitchen, closing the curtains hoping to avoid being seen by any threatening eyes that might be watching.

Joe rummaged in a bag of potatoes under the sink, picked some out, and threw them into a pot on the stove. He collected the bacon and cabbage from the press and put them in separate pots.

The crackling from the boiling water in the pots drowned out the omnipresent silence in the house. Suddenly Joe heard the footsteps of a horse approaching, followed by the noisy rolling of a wagon. His heart skipped a beat. As quick as his feet would carry him. He jumped outside to where his mother and the wagon were. His hungry eyes briefly scanned the wagon for Matthew, but he could not see him, Joe looked at his mother, and tears welled in his eyes. He dropped to his knees.

Maggie walked over to Joe and lay a hand on his shoulder. She smiled. 'He is in the barn; getting hay for Giant,' she said, 'would you mind unhooking him and bringing him into the barn? You can catch up with Matthew.'

Joe's heart soared on a cloud. 'He's alright?'

'Yeah, although,' she said hesitantly, 'he has a grotesque scar on his neck... and...' tears flooded her cheeks. 'He will never speak again!' Maggie broke down and squeezed Joe in a remorseful grip. Her tears fell on Joe's shoulder.

Joe rubbed her back, 'It's ok, mum, as long as he's here.' He smiled and wiped the tears from his mother's face. 'I started making dinner; could you go in and finish it?' He unhooked Giant from the wagon and led him down the road to the barn. Maggie retreated into the house.

Joe entered the barn with Giant; standing with his back to Joe, laying down a bale of hay, was Matthew.

'Matt?' Joe said hesitantly.

Matthew turned around, smiling ear to ear, and ran to Joe and hugged him.

Joe could see him trying to speak, but all that left his mouth was an gurgling sound.

Joe's soul wept, but he was glad to see his brother. He untied Giant, leaving him in the barn with his hay, and threw an arm around Matthew, leading him out of the barn and back to the house.

'We have a lot of catching up to do. I missed you, Matt.'

Matthew made a sound resembling a muffled laugh.

'Don't worry; I'll do the talking; you can do the walking!' He laughed.

'The McNeeve brothers are back!' Joe shouted, bravery or forgetfulness rendered him fearless to the looming threat. Joe and Matthew passed into the house and eagerly waited for dinner.

IX BROTHERLY LOVE

His eyes shot open as he was pulled from a deep sleep by three steady knocks. His blurry, groggy eyes scanned the dark room, trying to locate the origin of the knocking when the creaking and groaning of his bedroom door alerted him. Fear consumed him. The only action he could manage was to pull his bedsheets over his head; perhaps if he could not see the threat, it would not see him. There Joe lay motionless, daring not to breathe or move. He heard footsteps approaching; he wanted desperately to be brave, to get out of bed and run, but he could not; he was supposed to be the man of the house, but deep down, he knew he was just a coward. The footsteps grew louder, finally stopping just in front of him. He felt a hand grab the bedsheets he was hiding under; his heart leapt with fear.

Suddenly the blanket was jolted down. There, standing face to face with Joe, was Matthew. He smiled enthusiastically. Joe lazily fell back onto his pillow and sighed with relief. 'What are you doing in here at this hour?' he asked.

Matthew silently went to the window and opened the curtains, filling the room with a powerful light and the cheery song of hard-working birds.

'Ohh, it's morning already?' Joe sounded surprised. The last thing he remembered: was lying in bed, quivering at the distant screams he could only imagine were the banshee. He did not remember falling asleep; he was having a nightmare, he was standing out at the well, and the banshee was slowly walking towards him with malevolent intentions. The golden dagger shattered when he plunged it into her chest. But that was only a nightmare. Joe shook his head to clear his mind.

Matthew gestured with his hand for Joe to get up.

'Alright, alright, I will get up now in a minute,' Joe said, rubbing his eyes. Matthew left the room.

Skipping to the top of the stairs and carefully making his way down, he skipped with heavy footsteps into the kitchen. Matthew was not able to speak, but he compensated for that silence with extra loud movements. It had been ten days and two since he returned home from the hospital, and despite the itchy pain in his neck and the fact that he was now a mute, it did not seem to diminish any of Matthew's cheer.

He passed into the kitchen where Maggie was standing at the stove, making scrambled eggs. She noticed Matthew entering.

'Did you wake him?' she asked, without turning her head to see Matthew's response; because she had the utmost confidence that he would succeed in his task.

Matthew nodded his head.

'Good boy,' she said, 'how many slices of toast would you like with your scrambled eggs?' This time, she turned to him.

Matthew erected two fingers. Maggie nodded and turned back to the stove, singing.

Joe entered the kitchen yawning. 'Mornin', he said.

Maggie placed Joe's breakfast on the table beside Matthews. 'Good morning, sleepyhead. It's nice to see you bothered getting out of bed today,' she said with a slightly sour tone.

147

'I didn't get much sleep,' said Joe, getting started on his eggs.

Maggie sat at the table across from Joe holding a freshly made cup of tea, 'I hardly slept myself. That wind was terrible last night.'

Joe sat back startled, 'You heard it?'

'Of course, I heard it,' said Maggie, 'the wind was screaming all night.

(That wasn't the wind.)

Joe stared at Maggie with surprise, 'that wasn't wind; was last night the first time you heard it?'

Maggie slowly sipped her tea, not understanding what Joe was implying. 'Then what was it?'

Joe looked around nervously. It was her,' he said in a hushed whisper.

Suddenly Maggie dropped her cup, and it landed with a smash on the floor, the tea pooling on the ground like blood at a crime scene. An energetic round of applause was gifted by Matthew, who seemed to be enjoying the breakfast show; Maggie got up and retrieved a towel from the cabinet and cleaned up the mess.

When she was finished, she looked at Joe with dangerous eyes; 'Don't ever mention her again, she is not real she can't hurt us.'

'She is real!' Joe argued, 'You have seen Her once; do you remember Anne Sullivan? That was her in a different form. She has many forms, dad saved me from her, and it's your fault he's gone!' Joe did not mean to shout the last part, but an unforeseen rage built up in him as his arm started burning.

Dumbstruck by the sudden change in her son's attitude and hurtful accusation, impulse drove Maggie's hand suddenly across Joe's cheek.

Regret filled her, 'I'm so sorry, Joe.' Sorrow was replaced with fear when she saw anger in Joe's eyes.

Joe saw red; he wound his fist back and retaliated, almost knocking his mother out with a punch.

She fell to the ground crying, not at the pain but the fact that it was her baby boy who hit her. She ran out of the kitchen wailing, tailed by an upset Matthew, who pressed his hands to his ears.

Joe stood still, still clenching his fist. His arm stopped burning, and the rage died down. The realisation of what he had done struck him like a knife wound in his chest. Tears streamed down his face, air came arduously to him, now gasping hard, slow breaths now breathing rapidly. He could not apologize for his behaviour his mother would not believe him; besides, he had not had the heart to look on her anytime soon. Wiping the tears from his eyes, he left the house and made his way into the woods to answer a question pounding his mind.

Through the trees, Joe prudently stepped, swimming in the fragrance of the evergreen and pine trees, listening to the few remaining birds shouting departure plans at each other. The air was close in the woods but waited outside of the trees with a vicious bite. The sun slept behind thick clouds that threatened a gloomy deluge.

Joe passed through the familiar thicket to the glade. The overwhelming silence was the first thing to greet him; followed swiftly by the vacant ambience, the place did not just feel abandoned. It felt empty, truly empty, as if there was never any life of any kind that ever dwelled there.

Joe approached the pond, already knowing the answer to his question but hoping he was wrong. He stood beside the pond hesitating, wondering what to do. He then crouched down and plunged his head into the cold water.

Joe shut his eyes tightly and listened very carefully, all he could hear was the deep rumbling of the disturbed water. He opened his eyes as much as he could, hoping against hope to see a fairy, but alas! All he could see through the water was the bottom of the pond. Desperate to take another breath, Joe pulled his head out of the water.

Coughing and choking, Joe sat back on the ground and pulled the wet hair from his eyes. A deep sadness echoed in his soul, and he wept, 'I need your help, fairies,' he shouted, 'I don't know how to stop her! Please help me.' There was no answer.

Joe did not know how long he sat there, but his hair was almost dry. He knew he had to go and try to make amends with his mother, convinced she would not believe him, but he had to try. He got back up to his feet and left for home.

The walk home seemed to be a lot quieter; the birds finally fell through on their plans and left, the wind was silent, waiting for the right moment to strike, like a disciplined beast. Joe emerged from the woods and approached the back of his house; when he saw Matthew waving him over. A smile crept across his lips. 'Hullo, Matt, what are you doing out here? Are you playing a game?' As he got closer, he realized Matthew was not smiling. Instead, he looked shocked and fearful. 'What's going on, Matthew? What's happened?'

Matthew beckoned Joe to follow; as he turned around and ran, Joe followed closely on his heels.

They ran towards the well. Joe stopped as soon as he realized where they were heading, 'Matthew,' he shouted, 'don't go that way. Come back!' Matthew kept on running.

Cautiously Joe followed him; Matthew got to the well and kept on running past it. Matthew was now approaching a waist-high stone wall that separated the McNeeve orchard from the neighbouring fields. He quickly climbed over it and continued running. *Where is he going*, he thought. *Matthew has never been this far down this field. Why was he down here? And what did he see?*

Joe stumbled over the wall and followed Matthew over the crescent of the hill. The lazy sun was sinking out of sight, filtering the fields in a crimson tint.

Matthew finally stopped running; Joe pulled up close behind him, breathing heavily and rubbing his tired legs. 'Why did you bring me out all this way, Matt?' he said, gasping for air, 'Did you just want to race me? Fine... you won.' He laughed; that's when he noticed Matthew was standing still pointing at something in front of them. Joe shielded his eyes from the setting sun and focused them on the shape down the field.

It was an old two-story house. It looked as if it had been abandoned long ago. The large house had a big hole in its weathered galvanized roof. The windows were either gone or broken, the front door was split in half, and the walls were made with dirty forgotten stone. Joe got a very uncomfortable feeling that he should not be there, and worse, somebody was watching him or something. Joe gulped in distress. 'Very nice, Matthew,' he said with a trembling voice, 'now let us away home.'

Matthew ignored Joe and darted into the house; before Joe could stop him.

Joe stopped, wondering if he should enter or not. He had to. It was his brother; Joe gritted his teeth. Just before he entered the house, he could hear feeble laughter coming from above him. He took a step back and looked up at the windows. Joe almost screamed; at one of the top windows looking down was an old woman, motioning with her finger for Joe to come in. Joe fell backwards in fear; when he climbed back to his feet and looked at the window, the woman was gone. Joe knew what it was. It was her. In the loudest shout he could muster, he called for Matthew to come back.

Silence.

Joe pushed himself into the house. There was no furniture, no way to tell which room was for what purpose, not that Joe cared; he just wanted to find Matthew and get out of that house as quick as he could. Joe entered the hallway. He knew it was a hallway because of the ruined, broken staircase connecting to the second floor. Joe glanced up; he saw the banshee standing on the second floor, peering over the cracked bannister. Her crimson hair hid most of her face, but he could see her mouth. She was smiling ear to hollows ear. She then screamed. A piercing wail echoed around the rooms of this empty house.

Joe fell to the ground blocking his ears from the deafening screech, his eyes turned bleary as he looked up to where she was, but she was gone. Joe quickly jumped to his feet fearing she was still around. That's when he noticed he was no longer in that squalid house. He was now standing in the great hall of a Victorian-style mansion.

The long clean red carpet flowed down the endless halls in every direction, covering the flawless wooden floor. The long hallways were lit by strong candles hanging on the dark wood-panelled walls. All the grand windows looked out into an infinite nothing. His wrist was burning, but he ignored it. Joe swallowed any bravery and rationality he had and looked up. A large brass chandelier dangled from the high roof like a uvula of a monstrously large angry beast.

He was terrified and confused but equally confident and sure. He admired the dark engraved columns supporting the upstairs balcony, which were carved to look like strong men struggling to hold up the roof with bulging muscles. Exquisite craftsmanship.

There were more hallways upstairs. Joe stood still on the marble tiles of the grand hall, slack-jawed and wide-eyed. He could not remember why he was in the hall. *Ohh yes,* he thought *mother asked me to acquire her pearls for the concert.* He climbed the elegant staircase and down one of the long hallways, lit by the mounted candles, creating flickering shadows to fidget on the walls. His footsteps fell silently on the expensive carpet. He glanced out the big windows traced down the hall, the darkness pressing against the glass, trying to force its way in. *Beautiful day,* he thought.

'Joe, hurry up. We're going to be late.'

'I will be down in a minute Matthew,' he shouted over his shoulder.

Suddenly three realizations hit him: 1) He had two functioning hands. 2) Matthew could speak, and he sounded uncharacteristically urbane - And 3) This was the one that freaked him out. That was not his life. He was not Joe McNeeve from the orchard.

As he entered the grand bedroom, it was half a splendid Victorian bedroom with a grand four-poster king bed and a black marble fireplace housing a roaring fire - and half an empty, run-down small room. Joe's mind could not fathom what it had to explain. The best way to describe it: it was as if Joe existed in two universes, and somehow his minds merged. He belonged neither in any of the two worlds just then, it felt like he was in both places at once, and his mind tried to rationalize both existences into one.

Crouching in the middle of the floor was a woman. She had Her back to Joe, and she was crying. The scene was unusual to both Joes because he felt nothing but confusion and slightly afraid. 'Who are you?' His voice trembled. The woman stopped crying; she unfolded herself and stood. Up she rose higher and higher. She now towered over Joe. She was ten feet tall if she was a foot. She turned slowly dressed in a tattered green gown, torn revealing decayed flesh all over. One of her eyes was missing, and half her mouth had no skin, revealing dried-out pointy teeth. Her blood-red hair flowed down to Her elbows. She screamed and advanced on Joe. She was taking very long strides. Joe turned and bolted. Turning to see if he was being followed. The banshee had to crouch low to pass through the doorway. She was laughing. Joe kept running, heart thumping in his chest. He darted down the stairs, skipping every fourth step. He turned a corner in the grand hall, and suddenly he was in a dark shabby room with a cracked and broken wardrobe. Being the only thing in the room, he darted into it and pulled it closed.

Moments later, he could hear the wheezing breath and silk shuffling that could only be her coaching through the door frame. The loud, long footfalls faded, following the banshee from the room. Joe noticed a green glow from his sling. *Sling! I'm me again*. He removed his arm and saw through the bandage that the symbol was glowing again. It was burning badly. S*he uses deception! This is not real.* He thought *it's not real!* He ran to the old shabby hallway with the broken stairs. He wondered how he got up or down.

A whispering humming coming from upstairs drew his attention; it was the same song Anne Sullivan always sang. The banshee was coming down the stairs, floating down, not walking. He watched frozen as she hovered over the gap in the stairs where it collapsed.

The fight or flight instinct half worked, Joe ran back the way he came. Bemusement captured him when he saw that's the layout of the house completely changed; the way he came was not familiar to him, he looked around confused, no longer worried about getting Matthew; this would not be the first time she used Matthew to get what she wanted *that must have been what she had done with dad*, he thought. *She made him think Matt was her! That's why he tried to kill him... my wrist was glowing the night too!* His wrist was glowing very dimly. *It glows when she is using deception.*

He passed through another open room and looked around; there was no exit to this formidable place. Every room just seemed to lead to another room. Joe impatiently ran from room to room, trying to find an escape. He stopped to catch his breath, and lo! At the edge of his peripherals, he saw a shape, sitting in the corner of the room: it was Matthew, with his head between his knees crying. Joe hesitated to approach him, but worry overwhelmed fear, 'Matthew, is that you?' he called in a whisper.

Matthew lifted his head, and terror was in his eyes. He jumped up and ran to Joe, holding Joe's hand in his, hoping his big brother could rescue them both.

Joe held on tightly to his brother's hand, his other hand in its sling, 'Come on, we're getting out of here,' he said with all the courage he could muster. He spied three empty rooms, wondering which was the best way to go.

A sound from behind made them both turn; She lowered her head a great deal to be able to pass into the room next to the boys. Joe puzzled no longer. Still holding Matthew's hand. They must have passed through eight monotonous rooms; when suddenly, Joe saw an exit. Painfully gasping for air, he pushed himself on until he and Matthew were out of the house, and he kept running.

When Joe felt he was a comfortable distance from the house, he stopped and turned around to see if they were being followed. They were not. Joe faintly saw in the top window of the distant house; an old woman watching them leave. He dragged Matthew back the way they came back to the orchard. When they were back at the stone wall leading into their property, Joe turned around to Matthew. 'What the hell was that!' Joe shouted, 'Why did you bring me out there, Matthew?'

Tears gathered in Matthew's eyes and fell while he was shaking his head in uncertainty.

Joe continued to raise his voice, 'You are not supposed to go that far. You could have got us killed, Matthew!' He could feel his anger rising, and his arm began boiling in its sling once again.

Matthew whimpered silently, shaking all over.

Joe's arm was now smouldering hot. His rage could not be subdued anymore. Seeing red, he clenched his good hand into a fist; and swung for his brother's jaw. It connected with a snapping crack. Matthew fell to the floor with fewer teeth; Joe could not stop himself. He climbed on top of his helpless brother and kept pounding. Blow after blow; he dealt until his hand was bloody and sore. His fury subsided, and he could now see what he had done. He climbed off his brother, crawling backwards, appalled at what he had just done. He stared at his brother lying unconscious on the ground, a layer of blood masking his distorted face. Joe held back a vomit. He cried loudly, now looking at his brother, now looking at his limp arm.

Joe cried slowly and attempted to lift his brother over his shoulder with one arm but could not. He ran back to the house, crying for his mother to help.

Joe barged in to find Maggie sitting in the living room weeping. She said nothing, ignoring Joe. She was obviously still distraught about Joe hitting her earlier.

'Mum, you have to come quick, please it's Matthew!'

Maggie jumped off the couch. 'What's happened to him? Where were ye until now?' she demanded.

'I…' Joe said haltingly, 'I beat…I beat him bloody, mum! I don't know why I get so angry, but I can't control it! I swear!'

Maggie stepped back from Joe in fear, not knowing her own son anymore.

'Mum, please, Matthew needs our help right now, I don't know why I get so angry, but I think I know how to stop it; we need to talk later. Follow me.' With that, Joe exited the house and ran over to where Matthew was lying followed by Maggie. They both crouched beside Matthew, and Maggie cried.

'Oh, my poor baby, what do I do?' She was afraid to touch his mushy face.

Joe tucked both Matthews legs under his good arm, 'you grab his arms, and we'll bring him inside.'

They struggled to carry Matthew back into the house and lay him on the couch. Maggie wiped the blood off his face to examine the damage. Both his eyes were puffed up and sore, his nose appeared to be broken, and his lip was busted severe swelling and open wounds on his face almost made him unrecognizable. Maggie left the room and returned momentarily with a basin of water and a towel. She cleaned his face as best she could; Joe sat on a chair with his head tucked into his knees, trembling, wondering why he could not control his anger.

The room was filled with the sound of Maggie weeping. She spoke. 'Why did you do this to him?' she asked, not looking at Joe.

'I didn't mean to mum, I swear,' he said with a strain of uncertainty gripping his voice. 'I get so angry; like I did this morning; I am so sorry for what I did to you. I didn't mean to, mum, you have to believe me. That night when dad... the banshee grabbed my arm and left some strange symbol.' He rolled up his sleeve and undid his bandage, there was no visible mark. 'It is there sometimes, I swear. Sometimes it burns, and when that happens, I get so angry I can't control myself. Please believe me, mum, I need help.' He cried like a helpless child. 'And sometimes it glows... a-a-and when that happens, I see things that aren't real! I think anyone around me does!' -pause- ' I know how to stop her.'

Maggie exhaled deeply, processing the ludicrous information rather easily. She dipped the bloodstained towel back in the water. 'How do we stop her?'

Joe was surprised and thrilled that Maggie believed him. 'You believe me? Have you seen her?'

'I'm not sure,' she said, carefully wiping Matthew's face with the towel, 'The day I brought Matthew home, I think I saw her. It was an old woman, crying by a tree, and then she was gone. I am not sure if she's real or what these noises I hear at night are, but if you are telling the truth, and Tommy knew about her, then we need to stop her.' She examined Joe's arm where the symbol was. 'How can we stop the anger?'

Joe swallowed audibly, 'It only happens when my arm starts burning, so if I cut my arm off. It can't hurt me anymore.' He winced when he thought about it, 'I have to try.'

Maggie's face twisted with terror, and she became a mother again, 'You are not cutting off your arm, are you gone stupid?' Her tone transitioned into an angry whisper. 'The doctor will have a look at your arm, and he will know what to do. I don't know if I believe in this banshee. I will not have my children kill each other or self-mutilate over it. I will go to the Gardaí on Monday. And as for Matthew, get the carriage ready; I'm bringing him to the doctor right now, and he will look at you as well.'

Joe felt his arm beginning to smoulder. He jumped to his feet and quickly ran to fulfil his mother's request.

Joe walked down the long driveway to the barn; darkness crept around, slowly consuming that remaining daylight. The air's chill cut into Joe's soul. He found Giant in his stall, eating the hay Maggie left out for him earlier that day. He set a harness on him and guided him from the barn back up to the house. Joe left Giant standing outside of the house while he hurried into the garage and dragged the small carriage out. He hooked Giant up to the carriage and made sure it was steady.

Joe looked down to his arm in its sling; and fell into deep thought. *Maybe mum is right*, he thought. M*aybe cutting my arm off wouldn't help; besides, I couldn't cut my arm off. I don't have anything sharp enough.* He thought back to the golden dagger. *No, no, I would pass out before I got through the bone; and then my mom would find the dagger and take it off me. I can't ask the doctor, he would never just cut my arm off for no reason, and he wouldn't believe me. I would have to injure it, very badly.* Joe had a lot to think about. He had to do something about his arm based on his mother's reaction to the banshee. She could not be trusted with the secrets of the ritual. He would get no help from Maggie. *Maybe Mary?*

Joe went back inside and told Maggie the carriage was ready; Maggie and Joe both carried Matthew onto the carriage and headed into town. Lanterns were lit on the carriage to guide the way through the hungry dark.

The journey was long and cold but completely necessary, knowing the doctor would be willing to do a check-up on Matthew; even though it was well after he closed, he was never one to turn away needy patients. Maggie thought hard about what she was going to say happened. She could not just say he fell, but she couldn't tell him that Joe almost killed him. That would get the Gardaí involved, and she wasn't ready for that. She pondered, and she pondered.

On the outskirts of the town, Maggie stopped the carriage; Joe looked at her, 'Why have you stopped, mum?'

She stared blankly at the argent moon, 'What will I say happened to him?'

Joe pondered momentarily, 'Tell him I beat him,' he said.

Maggie sniffed, 'And you walking in beside me with him? No. Then he will get the guards involved; I don't want that to happen, maybe I should just turn around; come in Monday and buy some medicine and look after him myself,' she said more so to herself than Joe.

Joe thought up a lie, a bit too quick. 'Tell him I beat him earlier on, and the guards are at the house right now dealing with me. I will stay out of sight, and you can pick me up on the way home.

Maggie nodded, 'What about your arm? I wanted him to have a look at it.

'We can deal with that some other time, right now all that matters is Matthew; if he asks, tell him the guards helped you get Matthew onto the carriage.' With that, Joe jumped off the carriage, making sure Matthew was steady enough sitting on his own without support. He disappeared into the dark. Maggie continued driving the carriage to the doctor's office.

Joe sat behind a dark tree, hidden in tall grass. He rubbed his arm in its sling and contemplated his quandary. He did not know how long had passed; when he heard the rolling of a carriage come up the road, he peered out through the grass and saw his mother. He leapt out to the carriage and saw Matthew was not on it; his mother said gently, 'He is going to keep Matthew in there for a few days. I told him the guards were with you. Hopefully, he doesn't go into the gardaí and ask about it. Come on, let's go home.' Joe hopped on the carriage, and on they went.

When they were almost home, Joe spotted in the distance an old woman hunched over on the side of the road muttering to herself. Maggie saw her too. When the wagon rolled closer, the feeble, haggard voice of the woman broke the silence. 'Could I have a lift?' she asked.

Maggie looked nervously to Joe and then back to the woman, 'No, I'm sorry; we don't have any room,' she said.

The old woman remained silent and watched as the wagon drove on.

Joe looked over his shoulder at the woman, and anxiety twisted his stomach when he saw the woman staring at them, just staring, not moving. Joe shook his mother's shoulder and whispered, 'She's watching us.'

Maggie turned around to look, so did Joe, surprise took them. Neither of them could see the woman; she was gone.

Maggie nervously whipped the reins, and Giant brought them home quicker.

They pulled into the driveway and parked the wagon outside of the barn. Joe unhitched Giant and led him into his stall, leaving the wagon outside of the barn; Joe and Maggie both walked back to the house quickly, fearing the impenetrable dark and what lurked inside of it. As they approached the house, Joe's eyes shot to the shed where his dagger was; he wanted nothing more than to get it and the tablet and banish the banshee, but it wasn't the night to do it, he knew this; if his mother saw the tools, she would take them off him, and he would never see them again.

'It's too late for dinner; would you like tea and a sandwich?' Maggie asked when she closed the last curtain.

'Yes, please,' Joe answered, following Maggie into the kitchen.

Maggie went to the stove and put a kettle full of water on the hob, and lit it. While the kettle was boiling, she started preparing two sandwiches.

Joe sat at the table, deep in thought. At length, he spoke, 'Do you think that old woman was the banshee?' He whispered the name.

Maggie stopped what she was doing and turned to Joe, 'No, I don't think so; it was just a woman... looking for a way home.'

'You can't be serious, mum, have you ever seen that woman before? Why would she be out here alone at night? And how did she just disappear like that?'

Maggie slammed the buttering knife on the counter loudly. She turned to Joe; anger twisted her face, 'I don't know Joe, I don't know, okay? It wasn't the banshee because the banshee doesn't exist; she is just a story that your father has poisoned you with!'

The kettle whistled, cutting the looming tension in the room. Joe got up and poured two cups of tea. Maggie left the sandwiches on the table and sat down; Joe made two cups of tea and brought them over to the table, giving one to Maggie and one for himself. He sat down, and they both ate in silence.

When they had finished with the tea and sandwiches, Joe asked, 'What is going to happen to dad?'

Maggie hesitated, 'I am not sure. His court case is coming up soon; they will figure out what they're going to do to him then.'

'Why aren't we allowed to go and see him?' Joe asked.

Maggie was silent, admiring the cup in her hands.

'Mum, do you think he went mad?' Joe persisted and saw the doubtful look in his mother's eyes. 'It was the banshee that made him do it; why won't you believe that?'

Maggie snapped and shouted, 'Your father is a sick man; if he wants to believe in fairy tales, he can, but he will not harm my children! There is no banshee, Joe. I need you to understand that. Speak to me no more of it.'

'Do you even want him home?' Joe asked.

Maggie stared at her plate, 'I don't know, I thought I did, but now I don't know; he is dangerous Joe, Look what he did to your brother, look what he did to you. You are always angry, and he poisoned your mind with this chimerical fancy.' Maggie looked into his eyes, 'We need to find a way to get this orchard back producing. Have you any ideas?'

Joe sighed in defeat. 'I'll think about something, I'm going to bed, goodnight.' And with that, Joe brought his dishes to the sink and passed from the kitchen, upstairs, then he went into bed, waiting for a dreamless sleep to take him.

When he awoke, it was still dark. The shining glow of the pale moon seeped through the curtains. Joe held his breath, fearing he was being watched. In the deafening silence, he could hear muttering coming from outside, walking around the house. Joe built up the courage to peek out through the curtains and out of the window to see who was outside. Terror froze his soul when he saw it was his mother, in her bed robe, walking around heedlessly muttering to herself. It wasn't courage but worry that drove Joe outside.

Wearing his pyjamas, his bare feet not feeling the rough stones, he walked around the house until he found his mother. She appeared to be in a trance, babbling nonsense. Joe cautiously approached her and placed his hand on her shoulder. 'Mum?' he said in a trembling voice.

Maggie stopped moving. Joe walked around in front of her to see her face. He jumped back, gasping. Her eyes were pure white as if the life was drained from them; she did not seem aware of anything, and it was only then Joe was able to discern what she was saying:

'She is real, she is real, she is real,' Maggie was chanting in a monotonous voice.

Panic gripped Joe as he vigorously shook his mother, trying to wake her. Over her shoulder, Joe saw the banshee. She was no longer very tall but was now the old lady, with her untidy crimson hair, standing still, looking at Joe. Maggie turned away from Joe and slowly walked towards the banshee; Joe grabbed his mother's arm tightly, pulling back with all his strength. She effortlessly marched onwards, dragging Joe with her. Joe released Maggie, thinking about the golden dagger and the tablet, Joe sprinted back to the shed.

He was running too fast to slow down, he shouldered the shed door with all his momentum, the hinges snapped on the impact, and it came crashing down; Joe lifted the sack from the table and retrieved his items. He ran back toward the banshee.

When he got back, he cried with anguish, Maggie lay motionless on the ground; and the banshee was nowhere to be seen. Fearing the worst, Joe approached his mother and fell to his knees at her side. 'Mum?' he said while shaking her, 'Mum, please wake up.' His tears landed on her face. Maggie's eyes shot open; this time, they were her eyes. She looked around cluelessly,

'Where am I? What am I doing outside?' Weariness took her as she began slurring her words, her questions becoming unclear. Joe helped her up to her feet and brought her upstairs back into bed, tucking her in.

Joe went back outside to where he dropped his dagger and tablet; he picked them up and surveyed the empty darkness that surrounded him. He felt eyes on him but could not see them. He pondered where to bring his ritual tools; he couldn't leave them in the open shed anymore, in case the wrong hands found them, he gripped them tightly and decided to bring them up to his room. Storing them under his bed, he collapsed back into bed and closed his eyes, and it was a long, sleepless night; Joe could not stop wondering what the banshee did to Maggie.

'I was thinking about what you said the last day; about getting the orchard back up and running,' Joe said to Maggie as she was cooking eggs for breakfast. It was now three days after that horrible night. Maggie seemed to be herself; if the banshee did anything to her, it did not appear to affect her.

'What were you thinking?' Maggie asked curiously.

'If we start advertising in the paper, we might have better luck; I mean, not everyone could have heard about what happened here, right?'

'Good thinking, but where will we get the money for an advertisement?' she said while dishing out the eggs onto Joe's plate.

Joe thought about selling the gold dagger under his bed; he quickly scrapped that idea and quietly ate his breakfast.

Maggie jumped up from the table and stood still, listening intently. Joe was about to ask her what the matter was when he was abruptly forced into silence by Maggie quickly pressing a finger to her lips. Joe listened too. The sound of a wagon pulling up outside could be heard. Maggie peered out the window; it was Doctor Murphy's carriage.

Maggie ran back into Joe, 'It's the doctor; quickly hide, you can't be seen here, he must think the guards took you with them. Away!'

Joe ran upstairs to his room. Maggie opened the front door and met the doctor.

'Good morning, doctor, how fare you this day?' She greeted him with a friendly wave.

The doctor alighted his carriage and helped Matthew down. 'I am terrific. Thank you for your concern, and Matthew here is great too, albeit a little sore.' Matthew ran over to Maggie and hugged her. She held him tight, 'Oh my poor baby,' she said, tears of joy welling up in her eyes.

The doctor cleared his throat, 'He suffered a broken nose, a fractured eye socket, and four missing teeth; nothing requiring surgery, let him rest for a few days.' He smiled at Matthew, 'and as much ice cream as he can have; that's the doctor's prescription.'

Matthew clapped his hands and ran inside the house.

Doctor Murphy stepped closer to Maggie and whispered, 'That's terrible news about what Joe did; have you heard any news on him or where they have taken him?'

Maggie nervously shook her head. 'They haven't told me where they brought him, and I am terribly worried about him, doctor.'

Doctor Murphy looked flabbergasted and outraged. 'What do you mean they haven't told you; they have to tell you where your son is. . You have the right to check on him. I will speak to them as soon as I get back to town. That is complete—'

No!' Maggie interrupted, 'No, you don't have to... I just remembered they did tell me where they brought him,' Maggie said hesitantly, 'They put him in some institution in

Galway. I am allowed to go and see him anytime I want; I will go next week.'

The doctor did not look convinced, 'Right,' he said; 'well I better get back into town, keep an eye on Matthew and bring him back into me if the pain persists; just make sure he gets plenty of rest, and give him these painkillers every six hours.' Doctor Murphy handed Maggie a small container. He tilted his grey derby hat in a gesture of farewell and climbed back onto his carriage, and left.

Maggie retreated inside, hoping the doctor would not go inquiring about Joe to the Gardaí, but knowing deep down he would. She leaned against the wall and collected her thoughts.

Joe ran downstairs, 'Where is he?' he asked Maggie.

She pointed to the kitchen. Joe ran into the kitchen to greet his brother.

'Matt!' he shouted with open arms. Matthew cowered behind the table; Joe has never experienced a more painful blow in his life, 'Matt?' Joe said in a calm voice, slowly approaching Matthew. Matthew sprinted out of the kitchen to his mom's side. Joe followed him out to the hall. Matthew was cowering behind Maggie's skirt.

'Matt, it's me,' Joe persisted, 'I didn't mean to hurt you. You must know this.' Joe's voice trembled at the sight of seeing just how terrified his brother was of him; Joe was always there to protect Matthew, he was always his armour, but now, Matthew saw him as a threat. Joe's soul felt colder than ice, fearing he would never have his brother's trust again. The bruises on Joe's hand ached.

Maggie reached a mental decision; she would go into the guards and try to explain to them the situation and maybe make them understand the morass she found herself in. She stepped away from Matthew, 'Joe, I must go back into town;

do you think you will be able to keep an eye on Matthew?' As much as she loved Joe, she did not fully trust him. Joe felt his mother's lack of trust and was pained by it. He nodded.

Maggie tried to leave, but was pulled back by Matthew, who insisted on not letting go of her, and Maggie patted his head, 'Sweet boy; I will not be gone long. You have your brother here to look after you.' She knew Joe was not very predictable recently, but he had been fine the last few days, and she didn't expect to be gone too long. This journey would be vitally important. *I could bring him.* 'Should I bring him with me?'

'No, please. I need to make up with him.'

'Okay,' she said slowly. 'I won't be long.'

Matthew sniffed back a cry as Maggie left for town. Joe slowly approached Matthew, laying his hand on his shoulder.

'I hope you're okay, Matthew; you have to believe me when I say I didn't mean it. Do you believe me, Matthew?'

Matthew nodded, remembering the reverence he had for Joe. Then he hugged him.

Joe smiled, 'I have an idea, Matt.' He lowered his voice to a menacing whisper, Matthew pulled closer to hear. 'We have some peanut butter left in the cupboard since Christmas; we are only meant to eat it at Christmas, but what do you say we get a bit now?'

Matthew jumped in excitement and danced to the kitchen, Joe followed. He climbed on the counters to reach the top shelf of the bountiful cupboard, using his hand to blindly feel around for the desired contents. A smile crept on his face as his hand gripped a jar. He retracted his arm, which was now holding a half-full jar of peanut butter; Matthew applauded as Joe jumped down. He collected two spoons from the cabinet, giving one to Matthew. He opened the jar. The McNeeve boys had the tastiest feast they have ever had, finishing the jar. Feeling an equal combination of tired and satisfaction. They relaxed on top of the table, bloated with the abundance of peanut butter they just had.

Before he got too sleepy, Joe wearily climbed to his feet and stood in front of an enervated Matthew, smiling deviously; he tapped Matthew on the shin. 'You're it!' he shouted and darted out the back trailed by Matthew.

Hours passed as the two boys played games with one another; at first: they played tag, where Joe learned that not only was Matthew quicker than he, but he seemed to have more stamina than him too. Then they played a few rounds of hide and seek, where Joe would always win. Matthew always chose to hide in generic spots, whereas Joe had a particularly creative mind when it came to hiding. As laziness grew heavier on them, Matthew and Joe resumed their favourite pastime and caught butterflies.

They lay down behind their house and watched the sun setting behind the golden mountains. Hand in hand, Matthew kissed Joe on the cheek. Joe looked at Matthew.

'Does this mean you forgive me?' he said. Matthew nodded his head enthusiastically. Joe closed his eyes, smiling, focusing on the jubilation he felt deep down.

Matthew gently shook him awake; when he finally opened his heavy eyes, he realized it was getting dark. He must have nodded off.

Joe looked at Matthew, 'Let's go back inside,' he said, throwing his arm around his brother and leading him inside. Inside they went before the insatiable darkness consumed the remaining light. Joe had just exited the outhouse after relieving himself when he heard a noise. Assuming it was Maggie back from town, he went to the greet her. It was indeed Maggie, but she was not alone. Joe's heart somersaulted as Mary emerged from behind her and approached him, hugging him,

'Hullo, Joe.'

'Hi.' Joe's voice cracked. It sounded similar to a crude stroke of a violin, making her giggle. Joe's face glowed red.

'We met your mum in town; my parents have to go to Dublin for the week on business, and your mum said I could stay here.'

Joe looked to Maggie. She smiled warmly while heading to the kitchen.

'Where is Matt?' Mary asked, 'your mom told me about him not being able to speak anymore; that is so sad. Is he okay?'

'Yeah,' Joe said, 'he's better than okay. He's happy out! Nothing can dampen that boy's mood!' he said smugly. Then there was worry in his voice, 'Did she tell you what happened to him a few days ago?'

'No,' Mary said in a concerned tone, 'what happened to him?'

Joe wanted to tell Mary the truth, but how could he. 'He fell down the stairs and messed up his face.'

Mary covered her mouth, suppressing a gasp. 'Ohh my goodness, that is awful!'

Joe nodded, 'but he's alright, I promise, come on in you can see him if you want.'

'That's fine,' Mary said.

She followed Joe; she met Matthew at the kitchen table. At first, she felt scared, not of Matthew but of his injuries. He was too pure and innocent for the horrible damage he had suffered. Matthew ran over cheerily to Mary and hugged her. She hugged him back.

Maggie announced she was going to get dinner ready. Matthew, Joe, and Mary sat at the table talking. When dinner was eaten and stories were told, it was time for bed. Mary would sleep in Joe's room, in the bed, while Joe found some extra blankets in the upstairs closet and made himself a sleeping area on his floor.

Darkness clouded the room, and Mary was still incessantly chatting to Joe about nothing in particular. Joe enjoyed Mary's company, but sleepiness felt heavy on his eyelids. Whenever he would reply, it was a short response. Mary was so thrilled about the week-long sleepover; she didn't notice Joe was asleep.

'I haven't been over here since Christmas,' she said, 'I'm so happy I don't have to go to school this week, we can spend the whole week playing and adventuring; doesn't that sound wonderful, Joe? Joe...? are you asleep?' Mary rolled over on her side and finally decided to follow Joe to sleep.

'Joe... Joe, wake up Joe,' Mary whispered.

Joe's eyes peeled open. 'What's wrong, Mary?' he asked in a groggy voice. He looked at his bed with blurry eyes and noticed the shape of Mary was no longer there; he quickly stirred, rubbing his eyes, 'Mary, where are you?' he asked, panicking, he could see her silhouette behind the curtain looking out the window. Joe wearily climbed to his feet and stood beside her. He gazed out the window and froze.

Standing outside staring up at them, with her red hair obscuring her facial features, was the banshee.

'It's her,' Joe cried.

The banshee pointed a long crooked finger at Mary. She winced as a freezing shock ran down her spine. Joe thought of the golden dagger under his bed. But before any move could be made, the banshee screamed. Such a terrible loud screech had never been heard before or indeed after; Joe and Mary fell to the ground with their hands pressed against their ears. The scream woke even Matthew and Maggie, setting fear and panic into the hearts of anyone who heard it; Maggie shook as heavy sweat cascaded down her brow when it was over. Joe quickly looked out the window again; there was no sign of the banshee. Mary looked at Joe with petrified eyes. It seemed she finally believed him and now understood the terror of what they had to do.

<u>X</u> THE FAMILY WHOM I SERVE

Joe stirred from a restless sleep. He sat up and rubbed his misty eyes as morning filled the room. He looked over to his bed and saw Mary sitting with her back against the headboard staring at the window with bloodshot, haggard eyes.

'Haven't you had any sleep, Mary?' Joe asked while yawning, ' Do you know what time it is?'

Mary did not seem to hear him; in fact, she did not even seem to be awake. She just stared, unblinking at the window. Joe rose to his feet with a jolt of panic. He went over to the bed and shook Mary. 'Mary... Mary, can you hear me? Are you okay?' Mary snapped out of whatever trance she was buried in.

'Joe? Sorry, Joe, what did you say?' she said, rubbing her eyes, 'I am so tired; what time is it?'

Joe made his way over to the window to look out, 'I'll know what time it is now, by the angle of the sun,' Joe said while smiling; he reached out his hand and grabbed the curtain but just before he pulled it back...

'Don't open that!' Mary commanded, shaking in fear; memories of the banshee standing outside the window last night flooded her. 'She is still out there. I know it. I can feel it.'

Joe ignored her and pulled back the curtain. Mary screamed, diving off the bed for cover; a radiant flash blinded

Joe momentarily while the bedroom was engulfed in a golden light. The sun retreated behind the clouds, retracting her pleasant, warm gloom, returning the world to a mundane grey.

'Them clouds are threatening thunder.' Joe sighed, 'it's in or around nine o'clock unless I have lost my wits.'

'Is she out there?' Mary asked, terror gripping her voice.

Joe looked out the window again, 'No, no, she's gone,' he said, walking back to Mary.

Mary climbed to her feet, 'That thing last night; was that the banshee?' Her voice shrunk to a whisper at the name, 'That was so scary; I thought you made all of it up.' Mary felt comforted at the dim light penetrating the window mixed with Joe's presence. 'So, were you telling the truth about everything else? The ritual.' Again Mary's voice adopted a hoarse whisper.

Joe nodded his head. 'I would never lie to you, Mary, but now you see what I must fight… we must fight, I can't do this alone. You are here for the week, right? That means this is the week we must banish her; I don't know how, but we must!'

Mary stiffened up her upper lip and grabbed Joe's hand, 'We will Joe; we will beat her, I promise; you don't have to fight her alone. You have the tools already, right? so all we need to do is fight her at the well.'

Joe smiled; remembering the tablet and the dagger hidden under his bed, he reached under and pulled them out, showcasing them to Mary. She grabbed hold of the tablet and examined it.

'What does it say?'

'I don't know what it says or what it means; all I know is that the fairies told me I would be able to cite the spell when the time comes.'

The Family Whom I Serve

Mary gave Joe the tablet back, taking the dagger; she had never seen real gold before and marvelled at the gems encrusted in it. 'This is the most beautiful thing I have ever seen.' She looked seriously at Joe, 'the fairies told you this would work? Do you really think it will?' Concern worried Mary's face.

'Yes, I really believe we can do this. It will work, I promise.'

Mary kissed Joe on the cheek. His heart danced, and an uncontrollable smile embellished his rosy cheeks. Joe opened the bedroom door and ushered Mary out before himself. She smiled, and the two of them left the bedroom to get breakfast.

Maggie reached the end of the driveway, where the mailbox was; she opened it and retrieved a letter from inside. It was sent from the high justice court in Dublin written in a high flown, jet-black text. Her fingers shook as she clumsily opened the envelope, sliding out the letter and reading it carefully. Breath struggled to come to her as she fought back the tears. When she was finished reading the letter, she crumpled it up and stuffed it into her pocket, wiping tears from her heavy, mirky eyes. She stood at the end of the driveway looking back at the house weeping, her mind replaying the loud scream she heard last night. She did not know for sure what it was, and she would not accept the possibility that there was a banshee haunting her family. *The banshee doesn't exist, Maggie,* she told herself, *it is only a silly story told to scare people.*

She had to go back to the house and get breakfast for Matthew. His throat was not yet fully healed; he could only eat soft food to avoid further damaging himself. She wanted to just lie down, curl up in a ball, and shut herself off from the world, but she couldn't. The love she bore for her children made her a mighty, fearless woman. It was not a question. She had to be there for them. With her newfound confidence, she returned to the house.

She came into the kitchen and began preparing a bowl of soft food for Matthew. In one hand, she gripped a hot cup of tea, in the other, the breakfast. She carried them up the stairs. When she reached the top of the stairs, she glanced over to Joe's room, shrugging her shoulders, *Mary and him can look after themselves,* she thought; and continued to Matthew's room, went inside to find he was still asleep.

Matthew stirred as Maggie roused him from his sleep, his eyes familiarizing themselves with his room. When they landed on his mother, he smiled, his eyes showed Maggie he did not sleep too well, she wondered if he had heard the scream as well, she glanced at the scar on his neck and was gripped by an burning pain, a combination of both fear and regret as she contemplated whether Tommy was telling the truth or if he was just trying to kill Matthew.

Maggie stroked Matthew's forehead and began feeding him, softly singing a song she did not remember hearing, but she knew it from start to finish.

> *Sing me a song*
> *a song of magic and wonder,*
> *where the stars glimmer and the oceans thunder.*
> *Far away, a distant light*
> *warm as a touch from the rising sun,*
> *as it devours night, another battle won.*
> *But in the end*
> *darkness will haunt your dreams,*
> *late at night, when you hear the banshee's screams.*

Maggie's smile disappeared when she realized what she was singing, but she could not stop herself.

> She uses your fears
> she drinks your tears, and she feels your name.
>
> McNeeve, carved in her heart like an unquenchable flame.

Maggie slowed into silence, a cold fear grasped her soul, and she placed Matthew's almost finished breakfast beside his still hot cup of tea on the bedside locker. She stood up and stepped back from the bed, even Matthew, who barely knows what is going on, seemed to understand every word as he stared unsettled at Maggie. She backed out into the hallway and bumped into Joe and Mary.

'Good morning mum, how are you today?' asked Joe in a cheery tone; he didn't wait for a reply. He made his way down the stairs to the kitchen.

'Good morning Mrs McNeeve,' Mary said sleepily, trailing after Joe down the stairs.

Maggie watched Joe go downstairs. She placed a hand in her pocket where the crumpled-up letter was. She removed her hand and descended, It was better to say nothing. She followed them downstairs into the kitchen.

Joe was frying four eggs when Maggie walked into the room; Mary sat at the table politely. Joe noticed instantly; his mother looked sallow, like she would be sick. She was very cold to the touch; the way she wavered around the kitchen, swaying as she stood grabbed his immediate attention.

'Are you okay, mum?' said Joe, 'Have you eaten this morning? Would you like an egg and toast?'

Maggie stirred as if from a long deep dream, 'Hmm? No, I am fine, Joe, thanks for asking.' She stared out the window while talking.

'Are you sure, Mrs McNeeve?' said Mary, 'You don't look too good; you can have one of my eggs if you like.' Mary stood up and pulled a chair out for Maggie. 'Would you like to sit down for a moment?'

Maggie stood there smiling, wobbling back and over. With a crash, she collapsed onto the floor. Joe abandoned his cooking to pick his mother up. Mary came to help Joe.

'Mum, mum? Are you alright?' said Joe, laying his hand on his mother's freezing forehead. 'What do I do, Mary? What do we do? What's wrong with her?' he said, panic plucking his voice.

Mary looked bewildered, 'I don't know! Help me get her on the chair,' she said, grabbing Maggie's left arm; Joe helped pick up his mother, and they set her on the chair. Without support, she just slumped over and threatened to fall on the floor, so Joe agreed to hold her while Mary ran upstairs and got blankets and a pillow.

Moments later, Mary returned to the kitchen with blankets and a pillow and set them on the floor, making a soft spot to lie on. Mary and Joe set Maggie down carefully on the floor; resting her head on the pillow, Joe looked down at his mother and wept; Mary wanted to comfort him, but her attention was shifted abruptly to the sizzling eggs in the pan. She ran over to the stove to try and salvage breakfast. The eggs were burnt but not inedible. Mary continued making breakfast and tea while Joe knelt beside Maggie dabbing her sweating forehead with a towel muttering to himself.

'How can this be?' said Joe. 'She is freezing to the touch, and yet she is sweating.' Joe took a moment to process his unspoken fear. *Witchcraft*.

178

'She did this to her; a few nights ago. She did something, and I don't know what she did!' Terror strangled Joe's words, 'I have to stop her! we have to stop her to save my mum.'

Mary stood bemused for a moment before she plated up breakfast, 'I don't understand. Should we not bring the doctor out to examine her?' said Mary optimistically.

'No, absolutely not,' spat Joe viciously, 'the doctor won't know what to do, and she might be dead before he even gets here.' Joe eschewed the real reason he did not want the doctor at the house, because as far as the doctor was concerned he thought Joe was locked in a mental asylum; Joe would not get help from anyone outside the house.

Matthew walked into the kitchen fully dressed, though his shirt was on backways; his smile faded when he espied his mother on the ground. He went over and knelt beside her; he cupped her freezing hand in his.

Joe placed his hand on his brother's trembling shoulder, 'She is fine, Matthew, don't worry; she just went to sleep for a while. She was very sleepy,' said Joe as calmly and assuredly as he could manage.

Mary handed Joe his plate with eggs and two slices of toast. 'Your tea is on the counter,' she said. Matthew got up from the floor, looking hungrily at the toast.

'No, Matthew, you are not allowed to eat hard food,' said Joe, filled with remorse, 'you can have a cup of tea if you would like but no toast.'

Joe swallowed his breakfast and tea, thanking Mary. He left the kitchen and went up to his bedroom. He retrieved the dagger and the tablet from under his bed and decided to bring them downstairs and leave them on the table in the hall. He knew he would have to access them easily in the next few hours. He set them on the table and covered them with a white sheet, and returned to the kitchen.

'Matthew, I left a white sheet on the table in the hall', he said, looking at Matthew and glancing at Mary, 'don't go near it, do you understand?' Matthew and Mary, both in sync, nodded their heads.

'Matthew,' said Joe. 'Help Mary clean up the dishes; I am going to go outside for a while… alone,' he said, looking at Mary.

Matthew nodded his head and got to his feet, picking up the dishes on the table and carrying them over to the sink.

'Joe,' said Mary grabbing his arm as he left the room, 'do you think it's a good idea to go out on your own?'

'I don't know,' answered Joe honestly, 'what I do know is waiting here for something to happen is a bad idea; I won't be gone long or far, don't worry, I will be back soon.'

And with that, Joe smiled and passed from the kitchen to the hallway; he stopped at the table and decided to bring the golden dagger with him.

A chilling autumnal breeze penetrated Joe's bones, and he shivered; the distant chirping of birds and a fragrant of dead apples clouded the air. Joe took a deep breath and looked around; he could not help but feel he was being watched. Although he could not see by whom, he scanned all the landscape within eyesight but could see no one. Joe took a few steps forward, down off the porch, groping the dagger firmly in his good hand, physically but not mentally prepared for a confrontation with the banshee.

Joe continued walking to the woods behind the house, which was once home to the fairies. Joe had recently been there, hoping the fairies survived the onslaught, but when he checked last, there was no sign of any survivors; still, he decided to check again, hoping against hope, something could aid him.

The wind felt heavy, but the air felt light, and the clouds darkened; Joe knew this was the sign of an oncoming storm. He picked up his pace and trudged carelessly through the naked trees, all the while feeling a growing intensity of eyes staring at him.

Presently Joe emerged through a thicket into the fairy circle; fear stupefied him as he saw, sitting on the rock dipping her beautiful feet in the clear pond, Anne Sullivan. She looked at Joe and smiled warmly.

'Sing me a song, a song of magic and wonder,' she sang softly as Joe approached.

'What have you done to my mother?' Joe shouted, raising the dagger.

Anne admired the golden dagger with the shiny gem-encrusted hilt, 'That's a beautiful knife; wherever did you get it?' she wondered aloud, 'And you had better watch your manners, young boy, or poor mummy might get a lot sicker.' She laughed.

Rage, this time a natural rage, blinded Joe's fears as he took three hasty steps forward and aimed the dagger at Anne. 'What do you want from me?' Joe said angrily, 'Why are you haunting us?'

Anne Sullivan laughed vehemently, 'Silly boy; I have been with your family for decades, centuries even, since the start; I am the McNeeve banshee!' She jumped down off the rock and landed gracefully, a few feet in front of Joe and curtseyed low, 'When the fairies first made me; I was forced to obey your family and to warn you of uncertain tragedies and possibly even preclude your untimely death. Needless to say, I grew tired of this, and you want to know what I realized? It is a lot more fun to take life rather than protect it.

'Once I exterminate you and your brother, there will be no pure McNeeves left, no family to bind me, don't you understand, Joe? I will be free!'

Joe was perplexed; a hundred questions swam around his tormented mind, 'Then why don't you just kill us?' he asked unwillingly. Afraid of the response, he gripped the dagger so hard his knuckles turned white.

She laughed again, 'You are either very stupid or deaf to the words I am speaking; I will, fret not, I am growing more powerful by the day.' She opened and closed her hand as if displaying an unseen power, 'after I consumed those fairies that you so kindly gifted to me; I grew more powerful than I anticipated; why do you keep coming back here, Joe. They are gone, they are a part of me now.' She laughed maniacally, 'I never asked you by the way; how is your arm doing?' She smiled.

Joe looked at his lame arm sitting in his sling. He was aware of Anne creeping slowly towards him; 'Don't come any closer, do you understand?' said Joe, trying to sound as threatening as his terrified heart would allow, brandishing the dagger again, trying to appear dangerous.

Anne laughed. 'You cannot harm me; I cannot be harmed by anything you have.' She smiled confidently. 'Now, let me see your arm.'

She outstretched her hand and reached for Joe. Instinctive fear drove him as he thrust the dagger forward at her arm, grazing the flesh. A thin, wet black line appeared on her arm where the blade cut her. Oily black blood dripped on the grass, singeing the soil. Anne stared at the laceration on her arm with surprise and disbelief; she stumbled backwards and screamed, not her usual ear-shattering scream. This was a scream of fear, a cry of terror; Anne slowly morphed from the beautiful Anne Sullivan to the old woman with long unkept crimson hair. A grotesque creature, wearing a horrifying facial expression. Joe wanted to run away, but an unexplainable strength burned in his veins, he had wounded her; he could kill her.

The banshee continued stepping backwards, cradling her injured arm, weeping and cursing in a forgotten tongue, as if the cut on her arm was burning into her soul. – or lack thereof - Joe lunged forward with haste and stabbed wildly at the banshee. She screamed and cried, trying to fight off the attack. Blinded by rage, he stabbed and stabbed, connecting multiple times with the banshee, until exhaustion slowed his arm; he stumbled back and gasped for air.

The banshee fell to her knees. Joe looked at the dagger, which was now coated in the banshee's black blood. Joe smiled. He wanted to run back to the house, get the tablet, rub the blood on the stone and throw it down the well and be rid of the banshee once and for all. But the urge to kill her right there and then swiftly overcame him. He took one last deep breath and charged towards the banshee. To his shock, the banshee swiftly rose from her knees and stood straight. She seemed to have doubled in height, inky black blood streamed down her body from multiple lacerations and stab wounds; the blood pooled on the ground, it vanished into smoke, killing the grass it saturated.

The banshee no longer looked frightened. She looked dangerous and very angry. She rushed at Joe with speed unimaginable, Joe closed his eyes and stabbed blindly in front of him. He felt the knife shooting out of his hand when the banshee disarmed him, before he could open his eyes, he was forced to the ground, crushed under an unyielding weight. Joe tried to call for help, but he couldn't even breathe, he could feel his insides slowly being crunched together

(like that dream when I was a giant)

183

The pain was unbearable. Suddenly! He felt a very sharp pain in his left ear, followed by a warm liquid flowing down his face, despite not being able to breathe, he screamed. The banshee had taken Joe's ear in her mouth and ripped it off; he felt the sharp pinch on his head a second time, now a third; she was eating him alive! All Joe could do was cry.

As his eyes darkened and the pain became numb, he thought of the fairies; how much he wished the Guardian was there to save him now. Then he felt the weight being lifted off him. He inhaled deeply, catching his breath. He could not hear anything because the only ear he had left was clogged with blood. He rolled over on his back, staring up at the sky; from the corner of his eye, he saw something that resurrected his hopes.

It was the Guardian, in its big beastly form fighting with the banshee. It called to him in many voices. Joe wiped the blood out of his ear to hear the message.

Joe! Retrieve the dagger and run! It commended with all its voices. *We cannot stop her! Go now!*

Joe jumped to his feet and frantically looked around for the dagger, all the while ducking and dodging the stray swings of the fight of the fairies. At last, he found the dagger at the bottom of the pond, holding his breath, he plunged his head and arm into the clear water. It quickly clouded in a red mist. His fingers tightened around the hilt, and he resurfaced. He got up and ran as fast as he could, looking back only when he passed through the thicket. The sight of the banshee fighting with the beast was enough to frighten even the bravest man. Joe once again turned his back and walked away from the fairies in their moment of need. He wept uncontrollably, fearing that was indeed the end of the Guardian. It could not defeat the banshee. The howls and cries of battle soon faded as he left the woods and stumbled back to the house.

Joe leaned on the back door with all his weight, and it swung open; Joe fell to the floor. Mary and Matthew, who were sitting watching Maggie, who was still unconscious on the floor, jumped to their feet in horror.

'Oh my God, Joe!' said Mary stooping down to pick him up. 'What happened to you?' She picked up the towel they used on Maggie from the floor and gently rubbed Joe's bloody face with it; she carefully dabbed the blood away and found the hole in Joe's head where his ear used to be. She covered her mouth with her hand and cried.

Matthew was horrified at the sight of the bloody mess that was his brother. He blocked his ears and ran out of the room, upstairs, presumably to his room. Joe used whatever strength was left in his body to rise to his feet, he was very dizzy and stumbled over to the counter where he held on for stability, he could see Mary's lips moving, but he could not hear her speak. All he could hear was an incessant ringing sound. Joe dipped his head in the sink and prudently washed away the blood from his face and ear, doing his best to avoid the excruciating injury; he washed out enough blood from his ear to be able to hear. He turned to Mary.

'Joe, what happened to you?' said Mary. 'Was it the banshee?'

Joe nodded and smiled; adrenaline pumped through his veins. 'There was a fight, Mary. The other fairies weren't gone. They helped me.' A tear fell from Joe's cheek. 'I was stabbing her, Mary! I got some of her blood!' Joe smiled from cheek to cheek and examined the dagger he cupped intensely in his hand. The golden blade sparkled. There was no blood on it; Joe fell to his knees and cried. 'It must have been washed off in the pond. That was all for nothing! Why didn't

I just come back when I had the blood? Why did I feel I had to kill her?' Joe bawled.

Mary knelt beside him, hugging him; she felt grateful Joe was still alive. 'Don't worry, Joe, you made it back; that's all that matters,' she said reassuringly. 'We will get another chance, and we will succeed; we must.'

Joe cried on Mary's shoulder; then wiping his eyes with his sleeve, he looked at his unconscious mother lying on the ground, and he noticed something in her pocket. It looked to be a note or a slip of paper. On his knees, Joe waddled over to Maggie; he lay his bloody hand on her still cold forehead and sighed, carefully removing the paper from her pocket. First noticing it was balled up; as if it were rubbish, Joe straightened the paper out and read it.

Mary watched his face as it twisted with curiosity, then into worry, now perplexity and now shock; his eyes darted back and over the last line as if he was trying to read a different language. Tears welled in his eyes as he dropped the note.

Mary swiftly made her way over to him and put her hands on his shoulders. 'What is it, Joe?' she said, her heart breaking as she looked into Joe's tormented eyes.

'It's… they…' Joe stammered through his tears. 'My father is dead.' Saying the words aloud seemed to smash his heart like a glass bell being struck by a sledgehammer.

Mary read the letter; confirming what Joe had said, she hugged him. 'I am so sorry, Joe.'

Joe broke out crying once again. 'They killed him for a crime he didn't even commit He didn't kill David; and he didn't mean to hurt Matthew, and now he's dead,' he said sobbing. 'The death penalty, justice they called it!'

Mary sat beside him on the floor, feeling his sobbing convulsions.

At length, Joe stood up and again stumbled backwards; falling onto the table. He rubbed the left side of his face with his hand and realized his head was still bleeding heavily: dripping onto the floor; he fell back into a chair trying to stop the bleeding with the towel.

Mary ran over to his side. 'Where do you keep the first aid kit, Joe?' she urgently said. Joe pointed to the back hall connected to the kitchen; Mary ran out and returned momentarily. She set the kit down on the table beside Joe and opened it. She soaked a rag with Dettol and dabbed the left side of Joe's head, disinfecting the wound. Joe screamed in agony but did not try and fight Mary while she succoured him. Joe struggled not to pass out from the pain. Mary continued dabbing Joe's head until the bleeding slowed. She removed a large bandage from the kit and wrapped it around Joe's head multiple times, tucking it into itself when there was no more to wrap. Joe looked rather comical with a lame arm and a white bandage wrapped around his head, like a turban covering a bloody hole where his ear once was. Mary's dexterous hands did a great job on the bandage, making sure Joe's vision was not affected.

Mary brought two cups of tea over to the table and sat down across from Joe. She looked him in the terrified eyes and said: 'That should stop the bleeding for today, but you need to see the doctor as soon as possible.'

Joe was staring out the window, silently debating with himself about all the things he could have done better. Finally, he met Mary's eyes. 'I spoke to her out in the woods.'

'You did?' said Mary, genuinely surprised. 'What did you say? And what did she say?'

Joe winced in pain from his head and sipped his tea. 'I asked her why she doesn't just kill us. And she said: "I will. I am getting more powerful every day." Do you understand,

187

Mary? We have to banish her today.' Joe tried to smile gallantly. 'She will be much too powerful soon. She was very surprised that the dagger had injured her. Maybe she doesn't know about the tablet or the ritual. We have to go out to the well tonight and challenge her. Hopefully, she will take the bait.'

Joe stared at the gem-encrusted hilt of the dagger, carefully rubbing the broad side of the blade with his thumb. Mary noticed he was deep in thought.

'What else is bothering you?' she asked in a concerned tone.

'It's just…' Joe stared out the window, trying to catch a memory. 'She said: "when she exterminates Matthew and me, there will be no more pure McNeeves left." how did she know my dad was dead… unless—'

Joe turned around quickly in his chair to look at Maggie. She was sitting upright staring at Joe, listening intently with poignant green eyes where her brown eyes once were; she cackled maniacally.

'Do you miss your father, Joseph?' she said in a voice that was not hers.

Joe and Mary jumped to their feet. Maggie cackled again.

'I have already won; I have killed your father, your mother is mine, your brother is pretty much dead already, and you Joe? I can make you do whatever I want. I can even make you kill your mother.'

Suddenly, a burning rage flowed through Joe; coming from the radiant green symbol on his lame arm, he rushed for the golden dagger he left on the table and picked it up approaching his mother, she sat there laughing. Mary dove in the way and tried to wrestle the dagger out of Joe's hand. He shouldered Mary hard. She flew back into the counter and crashed to the floor with a cry.

'How dare you try to stop me!' said Maggie, not laughing anymore. 'How about I kill you first?'

Joe turned his attention to Mary, who was lying on the floor. He approached her and climbed on top of her very swiftly, pressing the tip of the blade against her throat, and he pushed as hard as he could; Mary was pushing against his arm with both hands with all the strength she had, but it was not enough. The dagger slowly penetrated her neck, digging deeper and deeper. Mary cried helplessly.

Suddenly, Joe was knocked off to the ground.

Matthew stood over Mary heroically, watching Joe, ready to fight him again if he tried to hurt his best friend. With a sigh, Maggie slipped back into an unconscious dream. Joe sat up and gasped.

'Thank you so much, Matthew.' He climbed to his knees and swiftly approached Mary, who was lying down crying. 'Mary, I am so sorry—'

Before he could finish his sentence, Matthew pushed him to the ground again as he got too close to Mary.

'Matthew, stop. It's me!' he said, holding his hand up. 'It's me, I swear; let me help her.'

Matthew nodded and stood down.

Joe cradled Mary in his arm and wept, 'What have I done? Mary, please forgive me; I had no control.' He carefully wiped the blood off her neck with his sleeve. It was a small cut and by no means fatal. Still, Joe felt sick.

Mary wearily got to her feet and approached the first aid kit once again. She opened it and disinfected her wound, then covered it with a small band-aid. 'If we don't end this soon, we are going to run out of bandages.'

Joe laughed and said: 'I couldn't agree with you more. We are going to end this tonight, but first I must get some rest.'

With that, Joe passed from the kitchen into the hall, returning the dagger beside the tablet on the table and covered them with the sheet, and then went into the living room. He crashed down on one of the couches and swiftly fell into a doolores sleep.

XI A LIGHT IN THE DARK

Hope remained distant as she removed her hand from Maggie's forehead; it was still gravely cold to the touch. She remained still on the floor, apart from that episode she had a few hours ago, there had been no life from Maggie if that even was Maggie. Mary shivered to think about it.

She got back to her feet and sat down at the kitchen table beside Matthew he stared out the window, she briefly wondered how much of everything he understood, did he understand his mother was gravely ill, did he understand his father was dead, a pitiful chill ran down her spine.

She lay her hand on Matthews and said: 'Are you alright, Matthew? Are you hungry? Would you like a sandwich?' She then remembered Matthew could not eat solid food. 'Do ye have any soup in this house?'

Matthew looked Mary in the eyes and wore a smile.

She rubbed him on the back. 'I will go and wake, Joe. He will know what to do.' Mary got up and walked to the kitchen, looking down at Maggie, hoping she would get up, but there she lay, dead or asleep she did not know; she knew only, she could not help them.

Mary passed into the darkening hallway, the sun was setting through frosted glass, merging tall shadows into the night. She passed by the table covered in a white sheet and sighed.

She stepped into the living room and noticed that the curtains were not even pulled closed; the room invited the sun in to say her goodnights. The noisy silence was interrupted by the deep tick and tock of the hurrying arm of the ancient grandfather clock, a family heirloom Maggie would not part with. Its clean, maintained glass face shielded an immaculate snowy clock face, with ebony limbs pointing at *7:23*.

Mary looked upon Joe, sprawled out on the couch, a large bandage wrapped around his head and his arm tucked away in its sling. She quietly crept towards him and gently roused him from his sleep: 'Joe, wake up. It's getting late,' she whispered.

Joe stirred, opening his eyes, 'Mary?' Bemusement stupefied him as realization slowly caught up. 'What time is it?' he said groggily, yawning and stretching.

Mary stepped back from him. 'It's about twenty past seven. Do you know if there's any soup in the house for Matthew? I will make sandwiches for you and me.'

Joe swiftly got up off the chair. 'Don't be ridiculous; I'll get sandwiches for us and look after Matthew.' Before Joe left the room, he turned around to Mary. 'Has there been any movement from mum?'

Mary looked him in the eye and shook her head. Joe nodded in disappointed understanding.

He passed through the hall trailed by Mary, pausing at the table and looking down at it, 'After we put Matthew to bed, we have to go looking for her, and end this.'

Mary could almost feel the fear in his words. She tacitly agreed.

Joe came into the kitchen and twitched nervously when he looked down at Maggie on the floor. He espied Matthew sitting at the table and smiled. 'Are you hungry, buddy?'

Matthew nodded vigorously.

Opening one of the top cabinets, Joe pulled out one of many tins of soup; he held it up to his face. 'Looks like you're having vegetable today.' He smiled.

Joe opened the soup and poured it into an empty cup; he placed the cup on the stove and turned on the hob. He then proceeded to make ham and cheese sandwiches for him and Mary.

'Are you sure you don't want me to make them?' Mary asked awkwardly.

'What kind of a man would I be if I made the guest make food?' Joe laughed. 'Besides, you're not my wife; you don't have to make my food.'

Mary blushed at the thought of marrying Joe.

After a few moments of pointless chitchat and fumbling around trying to make food for everybody with one hand, Joe cleared his throat and said: 'Dinner is ready, Mary could you give me a hand bringing it over?'

Mary quickly jumped to her feet and joined Joe in bringing over the sandwiches and soup, and cups of tea. She placed the bowl of soup on the table in front of Matthew and left her sandwich on the opposite end of the table, going back for the three cups of tea. Joe carried over his place with the sandwich, unfortunately, he did not get the hang of carrying multiple things in one hand.

The group of three sat down to a wonderful dinner, if that is indeed what you want to call it, and Maggie was still unconscious on the floor beside them. For the moment, the children acted like children, laughing, joking, and messing around. For the first time in a long time, the house hosted booming laughs as the inseparable youths engaged in banter. When they had cleaned their plates and bowls and drained the last mouthful of tea, they all sat back in their chairs, feeling satisfied, still hungry but satisfied.

Joe briskly got to his feet when Maggie sat up, before he touched her, he checked her eyes, they were Maggie's beautiful brown eyes once again, but they were haggard. He helped her up to her feet and sat her down at the table. 'Mary,' said Joe, 'would you mind making a sandwich and a cup of tea for mum?'

Mary went to the cupboard again, pulled out the last bit of ham and cheese and began making the sandwich, laughing to herself. *Maybe I am his wife*. Her cheeks glowed red.

Joe quickly fetched a cup of water for Maggie, she drank the whole cup full in one breath and gasped.

'What happened to me?' said Maggie, her voice little more than a whisper. 'Oh my God, Joe! What happened to your head?' She slowly reached out a fragile arm.

Joe held her hand. 'Don't worry about me, mum. I'm fine. You need to rest. After you eat, I'm putting you straight to bed.'

And so it was; after Maggie had slowly nibbled on her lunch, Joe threw one of her arms around him and carried her upstairs to bed.

When he returned to the kitchen, he stood behind Matthew and lay his hand on his shoulder. 'It's time for bed, Matt. Go upstairs and put on your pyjamas. I will be up in a few minutes to read a story,' said Joe.

Matthew made a dissatisfied gurgle in his throat and pointed at Mary. Joe looked bemused at Mary and guessed the possible reasons for the dissatisfaction.

'What's wrong?' he said, 'You don't want Mary to see you in your pyjamas?' Matthew did not reply. 'You want me to sleep in your room tonight?' Again, Matthew was unresponsive. 'You want Mary to help you to bed?'

Mary lost her cool. 'Joe,' she interrupted. 'I think Matthew wants me to read him a story tonight.'

Matthew nodded his head excitedly and ran upstairs to the to bed.

Joe smiled. 'That was my next guess.'

'I'm sure it was.' Mary laughed.

'In his room, just across from his bed, there is a cabinet.' Joe gestured with his hand. 'There are about six short fairy tale books that he loves; just pick any of them and read until he falls asleep, then meet me down here and we will go outside to the well and finish this.'

Mary nodded and passed from the kitchen.

Joe gathered up the remaining dishes from the table that Maggie used and carried them over to the sink; watching the water slowly fill up the sink, he added some washing up liquid and smiled at the bubbling surface. Bubbles always calmed him. There was just something about a little bubble careless floating through the world with no cares or worries that just warmed his heart. Joe allowed himself to feel the last possible fraction of happiness he could, after tonight, he might never feel it again.

Presently he cleaned the dishes, one plate at a time; perhaps spending longer than needed scrubbing, he was not focused on the dishes, his mind was playing out all possible outcomes of the fight to come, prudently considering all strategies that could be used to give he and Mary the upper hand. Joe disappeared into a deep fog of hopes and dreams.

Matthew briskly climbed into bed and vibrated with uneasy anticipation, eagerly waiting for his story.

Mary walked across the room to the cabinet Joe spoke of and opened it, it was full of clothes and old toys Matthew no longer played with. There was a shelf on the top of the cabinet holding six short children's books. Mary took them out one by one, reading the titles:

195

The Dwarf and the shooting star
Nippy Nip's secret
The Bear, the King, and the magic wand
Babba Doo's adventure
Upside down land

And lastly:

Ghost the dog.

Mary chuckled at the funny names and the accompanying cover art with the title. She carried all the books over to Matthew's bed and sat on the end of it, smiling at Matthew, who was now tucked away snugly in bed, fidgeting excitedly for the story.

'Which story would you like to hear?' Mary said cheerily, displaying the books for Matthew to point to whichever one he wanted.

Matthew sat there smiling ear to ear shrugging his shoulders in excitement; Mary took this gesture to mean it was the dealer's choice. She glanced down at the books, deciding which one to read. They all looked very entertaining, but Mary loved the cover art of *Babba Doo's adventure*, so that was the one she chose.

'Right, we'll read this one,' she said, opening the book. 'Lie back and close your eyes, Matthew; it will help to imagine the story.' She smiled.

'Once Upon a time, there was a little green elf with a wild mane of silver hair and a matching great big bushy beard. This elf was named Babba Doo. He lived in a magical village named Obanab. One day Babba Doo got tired of making magic potions, which he did, so he left his village and went on a quest to find the amulet of flowers...'

Mary was a great storyteller; she rose her voice to indicate to Matthew when he should anticipate something.

She lowered her voice and changed her tone for every character she portrayed.

Matthew proved to be a very enthusiastic audience. His jaw dropped in disbelief at parts, he gasped, he smiled, and sometimes he would make this low gargle sound in his throat, which Mary soon took for laughter. Even though he did not understand the story, his reactions were mainly to Mary's social ques.

Half an hour later, Mary was coming to the end of the book. Matthew had nodded off to a gentle sleep some time ago, but Mary continued reading, more so for herself. She had got very interested in the story and had to find out how it ended.

'Babba Doo held the amulet high above his head, and it glowed magnificently bright. Suddenly, the great spikey tree turned into a giant sunflower. All the elves came out of their houses and cheered, "Babba Doo, you saved us." but it was not over yet; Babba Doo again wore the amulet around his neck, feeling all the power from the flowers, he looked dangerously at the warlock Grubble and said: "You evil orc, I will turn you into a beautiful rose bush!" he held out his hand...'

Mary eagerly turned to the next page.

'I will make you regret getting involved with the McNeeves, Mary Cleary.'

Mary stopped reading with a jolt of shock; she almost dropped the book in disbelief. After a moment of recovering her composure, she opened the book again and quietly continued reading: 'I am the daughter of the devil; I will blind you, Mary.'

She stared down at the book with incredulity as the page was slowly being filled by a crude sketch of the exact sight

Mary was looking at last night, the banshee standing outside pointing at Mary through the window.

She dropped the book in horror and jumped to her feet. Matthew twitched in his sleep and rolled over. Mary felt gravely threatened, she did not feel comfortable leaving Matthew on his own, but she needed to tell Joe. Finally, she assumed Matthew would be okay on his own, She shot out of the room, not tidying up any of the books she left on the floor or even finishing the tale of Babba Doo's adventure.

She ran downstairs as fast as she could into the kitchen, there, she found Joe sitting at the table staring at the golden dagger and tablet, a look of concern painting his face. Mary was gasping for breath.

'I'm not sure if we can do this, Mary,' said Joe, slowly with a broken tone.

'What made you change your mind?' said Mary, presently forgetting the horrifying experience she just had, trying to understand Joe's sudden change of heart.

He sighed and brushed the engraving on the tablet with his finger. 'What if I won't be able to say the spell? I don't know what any of these words mean or how to say them. What if when the time comes, I can't say it?'

Mary sat down beside Joe, taking the tablet from him and looking at it: 'I don't know what these words are either, but I do know one thing for sure...' Mary waited to continue until Joe met her eyes. 'If there is anyone who can do it, it's you; you are the bravest, strongest person I know, Joe, we will be able to beat her.'

Hope returned to his heart, and a smile decorated his face. 'You're right... you are right, Mary. I don't know what came over me. Of course, we can beat her; we must. Are you ready to go over the plan?'

Mary nodded enthusiastically and placed the tablet back on the table.

'Right, this is what we have to do.' Joe used an old cup stain on the table-top to represent the well. 'Once we get her blood, we wipe it onto the tablet and throw it down the well, saying the spell, that is our mission, so the closer we are to the well, the easier this will be, so I think we should wait right here for her.' Joe tapped his finger beside the stain. 'The only way we can get her blood is with this dagger.' Joe held up the dagger. 'All I have to do is stab her with this and smear it on the tablet, but here is when things get really difficult… I am not sure how to call her, or if she knows to stay away, or anything. I am just hoping if she sees us out there, she will take the bait and come to kill us.' Joe exhaled with frustration.

Mary reached out and cupped Joe's trembling hand, looking him in the eye and flashing a reassuring smile. 'It will all go according to plan; I am here with you every step of the way.' Mary looked down at the tablet. 'Would you like me to carry the tablet? You can bring the knife; I would more than likely kill myself with it anyway.' She laughed.

Joe smiled in response. Then his thoughts sank into a deep pool of questions. 'I think…' Joe wondered aloud. 'I think it needs to be me who cast the spell.'

Mary nodded. 'Did the fairies tell you that? If you want, I can hold onto it and stay close beside you?

Joe pondered for a moment, then nodded. 'Yeah, maybe you should hold onto it; but stay as close to me as you can; when I stab her and get her blood, the rest will have to be done very quickly before she has time to react.' Joe tried to master his fears. 'I wish we didn't have to do this; I wish the fairies could help us. It was me who led the banshee there and got them killed.' Joe wept.

Mary tried to comfort him. 'Why do you say that?'

199

'Because she told me herself,' he cried. 'She possesses me through my arm.' Joe tried to lift his flaccid arm but couldn't. 'Even if we banish her, will she still live through me? What is going to happen to mum?' Joe cried uncontrollably. 'Maybe she has already won? Should we even bother trying?'

Mary turned Joe's jaw with a slap; it was the only way she could think of to snap Joe out of his pessimistic state. Joe slowly peeled his eyes towards Mary. She sat dangerously still, nursing a threatening expression. He swallowed loudly and nodded. No words needed to be spoken, a silent understanding had been reached with a single look.

Outside, the wind howled aggressively like a hungry, treacherous beast. The cold rain beat against the window like drums of war. Joe and Mary sat quietly at the kitchen table, both knowing it was almost time to go, but neither of them wanted to make the first move. Joe hoped that maybe if he sat quietly for long enough, there would be some sort of divine intervention that would preclude his inevitable fate, but deep down in the dark, dreadful pit at the bottom of his heart, he knew he had to do it.

A deafening silence pounded in his ear as he sat there trying to mentally prepare himself for the fight. Instead of growing braver, he shrank more and more into cowardice, his vision seemed to become cloudy he felt as though he had lost control over his body, he could just about see the world around him, but he was no longer a part of it; he could feel his heartbeat knocking against his ribs. His phantom ear burned profusely, and his lame arm felt abnormally cold. Saliva caught in his throat when he tried to swallow. He was not able to guess how Mary was feeling, mainly because he could not even understand how he was feeling.

Mary sliced through the silence when she cleared her throat: 'When I was reading Matthew a story—' she stammered. 'The banshee... she... threatened me.'

Joe's fearful face twisted into an angry, sullen look. 'She threatened you?' Joe's newfound rage gave volume to his voice. 'What happened? How did she threaten you?'

Mary cast her mind back to what felt like an eternity ago. 'I was reading the book, and just before I finished, the last pages were empty, but writing appeared on them, her writing, saying my name, and that she will blind me.' Mary burst out crying, finally feeling the fear in these words.

The sight of Mary crying and shaking in fear was enough to infuriate Joe.

'She killed my dad, she killed David, I don't know what she has done to my mum, Matthew will never speak again. She has tried to kill me, and she has threatened to kill you... no more!' Joe stood up and brought his fist down hard on the table, almost splitting it in two. 'She will not bother us anymore after tonight; I promise you that Mary, we will stop her once and for all.'

Mary sat up straight and proud. 'I am with you, Joe, together we can beat her.'

Joe looked at Mary with bewilderment. 'Mary...' he said gently. 'Why do you want to be a part of this fight? You know what she's capable of doing. Why don't you just run and save yourself?'

Mary was flabbergasted by that question. 'What and leave you here on your own to fight her, you need me, and I would never leave you,' she stated.

'But why?'

'Because I—' Her face became a rosy shade of embarrassment. 'I... I love you.'

A heavy silence filled the room. Mary turned so pale she looked like a ghost, and Joe sat in bemusement; he had said those exact words to her once, but it wasn't real then, now—it felt real.

Mary buried her embarrassed face into her hands, 'I should not have said that. God, I'm so stupid. I am sorry, Joe.'

Why did Mary feel bad when he was the one too afraid to speak his mind? *Love,* he thought, *is that what I feel for her? Is that why I feel so happy and safe around her? Love?* Joe stared at the tablet.

After a few moments of composing herself, Mary said: 'Maybe we should go up and check on Matthew before we go outside?'

Joe nodded. 'I'll go,' he said, 'you stay here until I come back; try to find a way to conceal the tablet, we don't want her to see it cause she might know our plan if she does, but make sure you can access it quickly when the time comes.' Joe picked up the dagger from the table and tucked it inside his pants, and covered the hilt with his shirt. He nodded once again to Mary and left the kitchen, climbing the stairs.

Joe returned nervously into the kitchen where Mary was standing at the table, a bulge protruding from her pants, where she has stuffed the tablet, getting her inspiration from Joe. She figured the banshee would not know what it was.

'Are you alright?' said Mary, only now realizing Joe had turned pale. 'Is Matthew okay?' Worry hit her like a lightning strike.

'Yes, Matthew is okay, flat out asleep,' Joe said, then his voice trembled with concern. 'It's mum; her bedroom is open, and she's not in bed. I checked all around the house for her.' He wiped his sweaty brow with his hand. 'Have you seen or heard anything down here?'

Mary shook her head. Joe now paced back and over the kitchen, muttering to himself. A terrible dread penetrated Mary's mind. She paid close attention to Joe's face, who looked like he had the same thought: Maggie was under the banshee's control again. They both feared it to be true, but they did not know for sure.

'We will search this floor very quickly,' Joe said, finally voicing a plan. 'Then we have to go outside and end this.'

Mary nodded, and seconds later, they split up, searching the bottom floor of the house.

A few short moments later, they regrouped back in the kitchen, Joe with the dagger tucked into his pants and Mary with the tablet. A fearful look was shared between them, confirming neither of them had any luck finding Maggie. Joe looked Mary in the eyes.

'Are you sure you want to do this?' he said. 'I don't know what we are in for, and I can't promise we will survive, I will do whatever I can to make sure you do, but I can't be sure.'

Mary blushed warmly. 'I am with you, Joe; whatever happens, I will not leave you alone.'

Joe was once again filled with... well, love; a powerful instinct drove him to wrap Mary in his arms and kiss her lips. She kissed him back, and at that moment, with everything that was going on for those six seconds or less, nothing mattered.

Moments later, Joe and Mary stopped kissing and took a step back, giggling. One was as red as the other, but it was not embarrassment. It was happiness, deep happiness.

Playtime was over. Joe knew it and regained his composure, adopting a stern face. 'It's time to go outside and end this; then we will look for my mum.'

Joe went outside, nonchalantly fingering the hilt of the dagger with anticipation. A biting chill was the first thing to meet them, followed swiftly by darkness. They could not see two inches beyond their noses. It was unusually dark; there did not seem to be any stars or moon in the sky. There didn't even seem to be a sky; it was as if a pitch-black blanket lay over the orchard, smothering any type of light, any type of hope that dared to shine through.

Joe removed his hand from where the dagger hid and grabbed Mary by the hand, which she gripped tightly. Joe made a left turn as soon as he left the house. Mary's teeth were chattering, and Joe was breathing heavily. He tried to remember a warm fire in the hearth of his house, being wrapped up in warm sheets in bed, but he could not remember anything. The wind screamed and cursed all around them.

Joe bumped into something solid, he used his hand to feel what it was, the cold stone told him it was the well. He turned to Mary and nodded, she could just about see his head moving, but then she knew they were at the well. Her eager hands gripped the tablet under her shirt, and she waited. Joe stood still for a minute, wondering what to do next. At last, he cleared his throat and bellowed:

'Here we are! Come get us!' Joe pulled out the dagger and held it fast.

Mary stood stiffly behind him, ready to rip out the tablet at a words notice.

They stood quietly amid the whistling cold, too afraid to feel the gnawing wind. Joe strained his eyes to try and penetrate the ever-growing darkness, feeling the omnipresent gaze of an unseen threat. Suddenly! A thin beam of light emerged a short distance away; it was difficult to make out the figure cloaked in the dim light, but the more Joe squinted, the more discernible it became. It was Maggie, walking away, towards the woods.

A Light In The Dark

Without hesitation, Joe bolted after her. Mary remained at the well screaming for Joe to get back. Either he could not hear her, or he ignored her. Either way, he did not return. Mary was alone at the well, no weapon to protect herself, Joe was gone, and she could not see anything through the omnipotent dark. She wept at how vulnerable she was, panic smothered her, and every breath felt like lifting a boulder off her chest. A high cackle surrounded the air around her; she dropped to her knees in fear as her anxious eyes scanned left and right for the source of her doom. A long flash of lightning illuminated the world. Then she saw her, the banshee, an old crone with long dark, blood-coloured hair wearing a long tattered green dress; she could not see her face. But she felt the insatiable stare and a formidable smile. Mary shut her eyes and screamed for help.

Joe gasped for air, the sharp wind like cold knives stabbing him in his exhausted legs; he did not understand how his mother was moving so quickly or where she was going, he persistently followed the dimming light.

The light came to a stop in the distance. Joe ran quicker towards it. Maggie seemed to be levitating ten feet off the ground. Joe called for his mother while slowly approaching her, worrying about this new devilry.

The world lit up as a lengthy flash of lightning sundered the darkness. Joe screamed in horror, and his eyes filled with freezing tears. It was his mother levitating, well, not so much levitating.

Her lifeless eyes stared out into nothing as she hung from a high branch on a tall tree by the neck. Joe stared in disbelief at his mother's pale dead body. His mother was hanged in the back garden. Joe roared and cried in agony, but nothing could change what happened. The world returned to darkness, and Joe fell on the floor, ready to die; suddenly, a scream for help echoed in the thick air, 'Mary!' He remembered how he had just abandoned Mary; he could not let anything happen to her. Joe jumped back up to his feet and sprinted back to the well, clutching the dagger.

<u>XII</u> DEEP IN THE WELL

Joe ran as fast as he could, the razor-sharp wind slicing his face with its freezing claws, tears streamed from his eyes and turned to ice on his cheeks; Joe could not see what was directly in front of him, but he did not slow down, Mary needed his help; he had just lost his mother. He was not going to allow Mary to join his parents. The dark clouds parted just enough to harbour a faint glow of pale moonlight that did little more than pronounce the silhouettes of looming shapes, but it was enough for Joe to make out what he was running towards. The dagger glinted gold in the silver light.

He was now close enough to the well to discern the scene; he could see two shapes at the well, one on its knees, the other seemed to have a grip around the first one's throat; fearing the worst, Joe readied the dagger in his hand, he was approaching the banshee at too quick of a speed to plan an attack, so he charged her, screaming.

The knife was now inches from the banshee's face and closing. Time itself felt as if it had slowed down; Joe was watching as the knife slowly made its way to the banshee's temple. It seemed to take a long time. The banshee did not seem to be affected by the slow motion of time. She turned her head to Joe and looked him in the eye, Joe could see through the thin veil of her crimson hair, her bloodshot eyes staring at him; she was smiling. Just as the knife was about to penetrate her head, she vanished in a cloud of black smoke. Joe was so committed to the swing when it did not connect, all his momentum swung him around and made him fall onto the ground. He caught his breath and looked over to Mary, who was kneeling beside him, crying, with a raw handprint on her throat.

Joe quickly stammered to his feet, pulling Mary up by her arm; he quickly bent down and recovered the dagger that he had just dropped.

'Are you all right, Mary?' he said, not looking at her. Instead, he was franticly surveying the area for the banshee. 'Do you still have the tablet?'

Mary regained her composure, she brushed her hand along her waistline and felt the bulge. 'Yeah, I still have it,' she said, standing now back-to-back with Joe to cover all angles.

The wind rose again, resembling a harsh whisper. The weak glow from the moon was sheathed behind heavy clouds.

Suddenly, the world was filled with the most horrific blood-curdling scream. Mary fell to her knees, blocking her ears with her hands, followed by Joe, who dropped the dagger so he could block his only ear with his hand. Joe clenched his eyes shut, trying to cushion the intensity of the head-splitting scream. When the screech died down, Joe opened his eyes and realized Mary was gone.

Panic enslaved Joe as he stumbled around the well screaming Mary's name, not wanting to divert all of his attention away from the ever-present threat. Fearing she was gone forever, and he would be next, he gripped the dagger as tightly as he could to his chest, waiting. He figured if he was going to go, he was going to take the banshee with him.

A cloud of wind and smoke swirled around in front of him and cleared, leaving the hunched figure of the banshee smiling at him. Joe had an outburst of anger, no longer feeling any fear; *this is the end* he thought, *I may as well go out as a fighter.*

Squeezing the dagger and pointing it at the banshee while running at her, he roared like a warrior of old. The banshee remained still, smiling at him. He plunged the dagger with great force where her heart should be, but again, the dagger did not connect. In fact, when he blinked, he was no longer at the orchard. He did not know where he was. It was as if he went blind; Joe could not even see his hand. He could still feel the dagger clutched tightly in his grip. He called out for Mary feeling hopeless. But it was not Mary's voice that answered him.

'I told you I would consume your soul Joe,' it said in a cruel whisper, 'and now here you are.

All Joe could do was listen; then, he recognized the voice.

'Come out and fight me, Anne,' Joe said, trying to sound braver than he was feeling.

A menacing laugh rumbled like Thunder. 'So, you can cut me more with that cursed dagger? I think not,' she said, with a flicker of fear in her voice. 'Here you will dwell, alone, for the rest of time, remembering everybody you failed.' She laughed again.

The never-ending curtain of black was torn by a powerful green beam. The light became more and more bright. Joe truly was in a realm of emptiness. As the world became brighter, Joe realized there was nothing as far as the eye could see. He then realized the light was being emitted from the symbol on his limp wrist. He stared at it in wonder for a moment before removing the bandage; the mark glowed a blinding green. *I'm not really here!* He thought *it's another trick, an illusion I'm not here.* He looked around the empty oblivion again and then at the golden dagger, shinning a sludgy green, gold in the light. He did not know why, but he aimed the pointy end of the dagger at the symbol and swallowed the oncoming pain. He pressured the dagger through the green lines, and with a snap and a flash of green, he was back at the orchard, where he last stood at the well. He heard the shrill, surprised cry of the banshee.

Joe caught a glimpse of her, lunging at him with long claw-like fingers. He dodged backwards, almost losing his footing, reading the dagger for the next surprise attack. The banshee seemed to notice Joe was ready to strike because she did not swoop in again; she seemed to be gravely fearful of the dagger.

In a flash of green light, Mary appeared on her knees in front of the banshee. She held a long claw to her throat and smiled at Joe.

Joe tried to hold a straight face, but the banshee noticed his mouth quivering.

He stared at her noticing the grotesque cuts and scars on her body from their last conflict. His mind raced. *I should just run at her and stab her get her blood, and banish her,* he thought. *No, I don't have the tablet; Mary does.* Joe was silent for a few moments until: 'Let her go!'

A high-pitched cackle like metal rubbing off metal punctured the scene. Then the banshee was clouded in smoke, emerging as Anne.

Joe held his stern face.

'Where are my manners? Come to my Underworld, and we will settle things.'

'Let her go!' Joe bellowed. 'And I will go to your Underworld.'

No, Joe don't!' Mary cried

She pulled Mary's head back by the hair. She squealed, then was silent.

'Deal.' She morphed back into a very tall decaying crone. She raised her decrepit arm and pointed a long-crooked finger at the well. She grinned, showing horrible, jagged teeth. Joe took a step back and peered down the deep abyss in the well, refusing to take both eyes off this deceptive crone.

She could sense that doubt in his heart. Her eyes grew wide. Large yellow lamp-like eyes shot with lines of blood.

She poked Mary's neck carefully, drawing a fresh blob of blood. Mary screamed when the freezing point broke her skin.

Joe screamed and ran at her, brandishing the dagger. The knife grazed her cheek as she swooped aside swiftly. She turned around to Joe and screamed. He fell on his back, clutching his ear, feeling like his head was about to implode. The banshee quickly leapt over to Joe, gripping his throat and grabbing his empty hand. Joe could not retrieve the dagger an inch from his fingertips. She held him up high with a strength she did not look to have; and turned around, carrying him to the well. Joe's vision was fading to black as he struggled for breath. Joe could see a figure swiftly approaching him. He did not know what it was.

He was dropped to the ground and jolted back to consciousness by a piercing wail; Matthew took a step back from the banshee, holding a blood-soaked golden dagger; with a dark flash of green light. The banshee once again disappeared, bringing Mary with her. However, the threat of her still lingered, and although she suffered a pernicious wound, thanks to Matthew, she still felt dangerous, if not more dangerous now.

Joe was surprised to the point of tears when he saw that Matthew was not alone, Matthew was accompanied by Maggie, who looked very exhausted, and she swayed on the spot where Matthew left her. Feeling foolish for falling for yet another deceitful vision and overjoyed that his mother was still alive, Joe ran over and hugged her. She could hardly believe her eyes at what was happening, and the words caught in her throat.

'It's okay, mum,' said Joe. 'you're okay.' Joe wheeled around to face Matthew, still supporting Maggie. 'Thank you, Matt, you saved my life.' Joe noticed the blood on the dagger, and his heart nearly leapt out of his chest. 'Matthew, give me that dagger.

A resounding panic drummed Joe's animated heart as he eyeballed the well. Wondering if, indeed, Mary was down there, he had to try. Joe wheeled around to his mother and Matthew and said: 'I have to go down the well to get Mary, both of you must get back inside and don't come out. No matter what!' Joe considered leaving Matthew the dagger but decided against it, as it was the only way he had of harming her.

Joe reached the rim of the well and looked down; he could not see the bottom. In fact, he could not see anything. It was as if he was looking up at the starless night sky full of nothing but darkness. He swallowed his fears and tucked the dagger into his pants to free up his hand, throwing one leg over the ledge, then the other, he sat on the edge breathing heavily before looking over his shoulder at Matthew and Maggie standing there staring at him; begging him, with their eyes not to go. Joe gave them a final smile and carefully climbed down the well.

After a long, arduous, and treacherous descent, Joe could no longer feel a wall continuing underneath him. He awkwardly shifted his feet around, trying to locate the next footfall. Suddenly his hand slipped off the wet stones, and he lost his grip, plummeting into darkness. A strange force engulfed him. For a moment he felt icy cold, and his fall felt, slowed. Just slow enough to make sure the fall wouldn't kill him. So it was that Joe passed the portal to the Underworld.

He landed awkwardly on his back and lay there quietly for a moment squirming in pain. A few moments later, he sat up, opening and closing his eyes, wondering if he had gone blind; he could see nothing in front of him or in the distance. He got to his feet slowly, wondering if or not he should call out. He called for help. Piercing the eerie void with a resonant yell that seemed to shake the very foundations of the world, that's when Joe realized why the air felt so enclosed, and the darkness was impregnable, he was still in the well, or some dark hole, he could not tell, but he knew it was a confined space by the vibrations of his yell.

Joe began shifting around and waving his arm up above him, trying to feel for something significant to pull himself up on; his hand finally reached what felt like a ledge of some kind. He pulled on it hard to make sure it was sturdy. It was. Joe slowly began pulling himself up out of the hole. It wasn't a particularly long climb. Finally, Joe threw himself onto solid ground, panting heavily. When he regained his breath, he opened his eyes again.

The world that met Joe's eyes was completely peculiar, he would not be able to describe it because he did not understand it. It was dark but in a bright kind of way. The sun in the sky, if you could call it a sun, was a deep black hole engulfed in a radiant white flaming ring. This dark orb in the sky seemed to be sucking in the light rather than emitting it. Joe felt no wind on his face, but he could hear the low whispering of a distant breeze, or perhaps it was a low moaning of some unseen ethereal residents. He shivered to think about it. Joe did not care to find out. He had to find Mary and get out of there. He looked around carefully, only now noticing there was some life in this sinister place. He could see he was surrounded by trees and flowers stretching out to the distance. It was a queer sight to behold. Much like the sun, they too were a solid black interior that could only be distinguished by the flaming white outline surrounding them. Joe found this forest to be oddly beautiful. He decided to look down at his own hand; he jumped with surprise realizing his hand too was pitch black with a burning white outline. He cautiously moved his hand to his face and realized the white fire was, in fact, cold. The world was not completely dark, it was touched by a dim glow, painting the sky with a monotonous grey. Joe was still transfixed by the objects in this world; the shape outlined by a thin, radiant white flame, and inside the fire was the pitch-black shape of whatever it was. Joe wondered if they were solid shapes. Finding a stone at his feet, he picked it up, feeling it and throwing it, still amazed at its appearance. The well was indeed a portal that teleported him into some sort of inverted universe—the Underworld.

Joe looked around this alien realm and noticed monstrously large dark trees, swallowed by pale fire, filled the world. Like some kind of colour abandoned forest. He looked directly up and was amazed to see the well floating above the ground; about twenty feet up, floating beside it, was the massive oak tree. He could vaguely see a starry sky in the well. *That must be the way back,* he thought. He was stepping prudently to avoid falling back into the hole. At length, he decided to look around for Mary.

Joe carefully strolled through the inverted dimension, followed by a creepy, incessant susurrus. He quickly picked up the pace when a terrifying feeling of being followed overwhelmed him. He now began to panic. Where would he even start looking? How would he hope to find Mary here? These questions began to smother him. The fear of being followed abruptly became too much for Joe to handle. He remembered he had the dagger tucked away in his pants; wheeling around while unsheathing the dagger, he stood stoically, waiting for the danger to reveal itself. Nothing was there. He noticed the dagger grew in size at the touch of his hand to a long golden sword. It was not the mysterious inverted colour of everything thing else around; it was still a shiny golden colour; maybe even shinier now, it seemed to radiate a rich yellow tint. It filled him with a warm feeling of power. A cold, terrible cackle filled the air, followed by a very frightened scream for help. It was Mary. The screams were very frequent, as if Mary were in immediate danger. Joe wasted no time and sprinted off towards the screams.

He ran over the precipice of a hill, and his heart almost stopped at what he saw. A dark silhouette of a person engulfed in a radiant white flame which Joe easily recognized to be Mary, was being held and suspended off the ground by a giant spider-like creature covered in red hairs. Joe knew this entity to be the banshee. The nightmarish monster had a big body about fifteen feet tall with a large bag-like growth protruding behind it, six hairy legs sprouted out from the body like a spider. At the end of these six legs were razor-sharp claws, like it was walking on knives; but most abominable: a large horned head with two very large, pointed yellow eyes, fixed unblinkingly on its prey.

Joe gave a horrified swallow looking at that thing, but once again, Mary screamed for help, animating Joe's bravery; he charged the nightmarish fiend with a bellicose roar, plunging the sword deep in its back. The creature dropped Mary instantly, spinning around in shock and fear and centring its stare on Joe. He could not tell if Mary was alright because he could not see her. She was just a dark silhouette engulfed in a white flame. Joe fixed his eyes on the large monster who was now charging at him. An unknown instinct kicked in as he dodged the creature's leg, slashing at another. It collapsed to the floor with a scream but shortly got back up, leaning primarily on one side. It jumped at Joe, mashing with large, jagged teeth at his face; Joe stepped to the side, tracing with the sword a long horrendous laceration down the creature's face. He smiled, feeling a power he never imagined possessing. The creature cowed away from the golden blade in Joe's hand with a venomous hiss. Joe could hear a muffled voice shouting: 'Joe? Joe, is that you?' It was Mary.

Joe looked around the dark plain for a sight of Mary. Before he could call out, the creature was on him again. This time it used her claw-like legs to slash at Joe.

He elegantly danced between all the slicing legs, without feeling tired or challenged. He laughed at how easy it was; Joe was figuring out where to land his next precise incision when he felt a burning agony in his right arm, the creature stepped back, holding its scarified face while making a terrible gurgling sound resembling laughter.

His arm burned hotter than he had ever felt, and quickly he looked down, thankfully his arm was in its sling covering his chest. If not, the claw would have pierced his heart. A glittering silver-like liquid cascaded out of the wound Joe had just sustained; a searing pain progressively flooded Joe's body. He collapsed to the floor, breathing heavily, unable to cope with the pain; his eyes darkened.

'Were you truly naive enough to think you could slay me! Here!' a cruel voice resonated from the darkness. 'The venom is not fatal...' she said, 'but I am.'

When the voice died down, the creature lunged on Joe, pinning him to the ground. Joe struggled, looking for the sword he dropped, his eyes dimming. The noisome odour of rotting corpses choked Joe as the creature prepared to bite his head off. Joe closed his eyes.

Suddenly, a screech pierced the gloom, followed by a loud crash. Joe felt a tremendous weight crush his chest as if a wagon had been dropped on him. He moaned in discomfort and opened his eyes. He saw up close a reflection of himself, a dark figure engulfed in white flame; his reflection was cast by looking in the large evil eye of the creature, it got up and spun around shrieking, Joe spied a deep painful gash in its side. Mary was standing there looking heroic in a bright white fire. She was amazed she dared to approach the hideous demon.

The cold voice screeched with astonishment. 'You will rot here forever!' it cried while it thundered away through the trees.

Joe ran over and hugged Mary tight.

'Joe, you're bleeding,' she said.

Joe looked down at his arm, observing the silver liquid flowing heavily down his body, 'You have got to get out of here,' Joe said, stumbling to the ground. 'It is too late for me; please, Mary, go, take the dagger with you. Do you still have the tablet?'

Mary lifted her shirt, revealing the tablet, then she removed it from her pants and inspected it. It, too, did not lose its colour, but it glowed a faint purple. Her eyes thoroughly checked every engraving on the stone until her finger landed on a specific one. '*Abhaile*,' she spoke in a clear, sonorous voice.

A tear in the world opened up before her: a thin oval window surrounded in purple water-like goo, with a lucid view of the orchard. Her heart soared with relief; she didn't know for sure where it would take them, but anywhere was better than there.

She wrapped Joe's arm around her, dragging him slowly to the portal. She held her breath and was about to jump through when behind her, a scream echoed in the gloom.

'No! You will not escape!' the cruel voice once again screeched.

Mary stepped through the portal dragging Joe with her and the sword and the tablet.

As simple as stepping into a house, they were back at the orchard.

Mary cheered with relief. 'We did it, Joe!' she exclaimed. 'We're back!'

Joe was struggling on his feet. The coursing pain flowing through his veins had stopped, now only his arm hurt, where he was still bleeding from, a healthy dark red liquid. Mary helped him.

'Mary, give me the dagger; I'm going to end this.'

In her relief of returning, she almost forgot about the mission. She handed Joe the pristine knife, holding the tablet out to Joe so he could finish the ritual; he dragged the dagger across the tablet, hoping to smear some unseen blood on it, but nothing happened. Anxiously he tried again and again to no avail. He looked at Mary with a sea of panic in his eyes.

'The banshee's blood must have vanished when we went through the portal,' he said, his voice reflecting the panic in his face.

'What do we do now?' Mary said, equally anxious.

Joe slowly glided the dagger across the stone with no result. He sighed in desperation. 'Maybe we need to stand by the well?' His voice dabbled on a hopeful tone. He limped over to the well with Mary at his side supporting him. Once again, Joe slid the blade across the tablet, nothing. Joe dropped the dagger and snatched the tablet out of Mary's hands. He examined it closely, turning it over and back again, leaning on the rim of the well.

He handed the tablet back to Mary and sliced the silence with a terrified whisper: 'There is nothing for it. We need to get her blood again.'

Mary tried to look brave, but Joe could feel the terror screaming in her eyes. 'How do we get it? I don't want to go back into that well, Joe.'

Just then, their attention was drawn down the well, where they could hear a coarse whispering coming from the bottom and slowly rising. Joe stooped down and picked up the dagger, then he and Mary stepped back, adrenaline pumping.

They watched as two pale, harsh hands emerged from the well, followed by a head hidden by crimson hair. The banshee collapsed onto the ground in a disfigured heap and remained still for a moment. Joe was telling himself right then to quickly close the distance and start stabbing her, but he was frozen in fear. Then a cracking snapped through the air like gunshots as the decrepit figure twisted itself back into shape. It rose ten feet tall. Joe and Mary stood petrified on the spot. The banshee screamed, knocking them on their backs. Mary instantly climbed back to her feet and was swiftly assailed by the towering banshee. Mary felt a burning grip around her throat as she was lifted high off the ground. Unable to draw breath, she opened her eyes wide and looked ahead; she was face to face with the banshee, two large, horrendous yellow eyes shot with blood looking back at her. Mary was not able to scream.

The banshee plunged a long, sharp finger through Mary's right eye, laughing cruelly as she did it.

The lack of oxygen and the excruciating pain was enough to set Mary's body in a limp state. She felt ice-cold liquid running down her cheek. Then she could just make out a finger nearing her other eye; then she saw nothing.

The banshee screamed in anguish, dropping Mary; Joe had picked up the knife and buried it deep into her leg. She dropped to her knees, and Joe removed the knife, plunging it in her lower back. The banshee could no longer scream, as the dagger seemed to be dealing more damage, the angrier Joe got. He rose to his feet, twisting the dagger as he stood; the banshee appeared to be shrinking in front of Joe as he stood taller and angrier. Joe again pulled the dagger from her back, hobbling around to look her in the eyes, to watch the realization of being beat contort her face as he killed her; he was about to bury the dagger in her face when She surprised him with one final strike; the banshee, as quick as lightning shot a hand towards Joe's throat, but instead, it caught his lame arm in its sling. She squeezed as hard as she could, imbedding her long claws into Joe's wrist. He screamed loudly, feeling his arm being torn off from the elbow. Suddenly, she disappeared into a cloud of green smoke with a pain-induced cry, bringing with her Joe's lower arm.

Joe quickly looked around, feeling he was soon going to perish; he could see Mary's body lying on the ground. He wanted nothing more than to make sure she wasn't dead, but it was not over yet, the banshee was not yet banished; Joe found the tablet on the ground in proximity to Mary's body, he kneeled on the ground and smeared blood from the blade onto the tablet. To his delight, the inky black blood painted the stone, and the dull engravings now radiated a neon green. Holding the tablet tightly, Joe's jolted to his feet and ran to the well.

Holding the glowing tablet over the abyss in the dark well, he felt a powerful, warm shock surging through his bones; he closed his eyes and heard a deep voice voicing the incantation:

'Bí spiorad beidh tú i do chónaí anseo go deo níos mó. Cuirim cosc ort'

Joe opened his eyes and dropped the tablet down the well. He heard a distant, shrill cry.

After he had dropped the tablet down the well, he stumbled back to the ground, only now feeling the intense pain of his phantom limb. He looked back to Mary with eyes flooded with tears. She was lying on the ground as still as a corpse, blood jetting from dark eye sockets down her pale, peaceful face. Joe painfully crawled over beside her and lay his hand in hers; he closed his eyes lying on the cold ground, smiling.

'She may have got us, but we got her.' Joe choked on a celebratory chuckle. 'We got her,' he repeated until a long undisturbed sleep took him.

The banshee had been banished, breaking all spells and ties she had to that world. Maggie shot up off the kitchen chair, feeling renewed. Matthew jumped to his feet to his mother's side; she pushed him off.

'Thank you, Matthew, but I am fine, come with me outside quickly. Joe needs our help.'

Matthew nodded, and they both headed outside. Maggie broke into a run at the sight of her son's body lying on the ground beside Mary. She kneeled hugging him and crying, staring at his injuries; then she noticed Mary's eyes or lack thereof. How she didn't faint is beyond her; she kept her head and turned to Matthew. Time was against her. Joe and Mary needed immediate medical treatment; Maggie could not lift them onto the wagon and haul them in to the doctor on her own or even with Matthew's help. She grabbed Matthew by the shoulders and looked him dead in the eye.

'Matthew listen to mommy very carefully,' she said sternly. 'I need you to run down the road to Luke and Geraldine Quinn. Do you understand me so far?'

Matthew nodded along with Maggie, anxious to remember his orders, a look of pure steel determination glinting in his eyes.

'Get them to follow you. Don't come back here without them, do you understand? You will do this for me,' she said reassuringly. 'Mommy has to stay here with Joe and Mary, but you can do this on your own, can't you?'

Matthew nodded frantically, drool falling off his chin.

'Okay, my love, go!' she said, pushing Matthew towards the road. 'Remember to bring Luke and Geraldine and Dick if he's home. Don't come back without them!' she shouted as Matthew disappeared down the dark road. It was a very dangerous gamble: sending Matthew on his own, but she had no choice; Maggie ran back inside to retrieve any medical supplies she had left in the house. Grabbing all the towels and blankets she could find, she had to slow the bleeding; she kneeled by her son and dressed the wounds as best she could, waiting for Matthew to return with help, every second as long as the life span of an oak tree. Crickets sang a eulogy in the feeble moonlight; the harsh wind held its breath.

<u>XII</u> I   PHANTOMS

The distant sound of low voices and people shuffling back and forth grew ever more clearly to his ear, he tried to open his eyes, but a sudden beam of blinding light forced them to close again. He felt a painful itch on the palm of his right hand. Instinctively, his other hand shot over to scratch it; it was then when his left hand landed on his right hand but felt nothing did Joe open his eyes, ignoring the brightness in the room. Joe surveyed the scene with his lethargic, blurry eyes. There was a bandage wrapped around his left elbow, and beneath that that there was nothing. Joe jolted up, heart racing, a million questions buzzing around in his head like an agitated beehive. His gaze was drawn to his bedside, where his mother tried to comfort him.

'Joe, Joe, be still,' Maggie said, propping herself on the bed beside him and wiping his forehead. 'I thought I lost you, my sweet boy.' Tears pooled in her eyes, dripping down her pale face.

'Everything hurts, mum,' said Joe.

'I know, I know. I am so sorry this happened to you, and I am so sorry I didn't believe you.' Maggie almost suffocated Joe in a tight hug. 'I now know how you felt. Nobody will believe me. They…' Maggie got up off the bed, covering her mouth and walking to the window. Her mind replaying Tommy's last words:

Please believe me.

'Mum, what's wrong? Mum?' Joe slowly and painfully propped himself up to a sitting position.

'They are going to take me away.' She crept across the room and pressed her ear to the door. 'Ohh no! They are coming.' She stepped back.

Joe's heart was now thumping against his ribs almost as intensely as the headache he now realized he had. 'Who is coming, mum? Where am I?' Joe screamed at his mother.

'Ssshhh Joe, it's okay, be still.' Maggie sat beside Joe again, rubbing his arm, trying to pacify him.

Two men in lab coats came flooding in the room, followed by three women in surgical masks. Joe squirmed restlessly in his bed. The three women held him down, speaking some jargon as one of the men uncapped a large needle. He flicked the top and approached Joe. The other guy had a hold of Maggie; the women grabbed Joe's arm and held it very still. Joe let out a blood-curdling scream as the long needle penetrated his skin, poking his bone pouring magma into his veins. The hot serum immediately took effect, Joe's vision instantly became blurrier, all the chatter in the room became muffled and started echoing like Joe was slipping into an alternate reality, he could no longer hear the sounds, but he could feel him. Just before he lost consciousness, he slurred out the words: 'Isz Maarrii alllllliiii—'

He blacked out.

The next time Joe opened his eyes, it was dark in the room, the insipid white walls kindled by the feeble light of a gas lamp. Joe lay there quietly, fearing the banshee was going to appear at any moment and finish him. *No, no, I've banished her. She is gone forever,* he thought, but the feeling of safety eluded him.

He called for Maggie to answer the question that bothered him and soon realized he was on his own. Panicking, he called out for help. There was no reply. He needed to know if Mary was alive; there was nothing else for it. He had to find her.

Joe prudently peeled the blankets off himself and sat on the edge of the bed, his bare feet touching the cold floor. When he stood up, he instantly stammered and caught the side of the bed to steady himself. He was not sure if it was the burning venom that made him dizzy, or the feeling of losing an arm and an ear that affected his balance. He found a pair of crutches standing at the end of the bed; not being bothered figuring out how to use them, he decided to take one of them and use it as a walking stick, leaning heavily against it to compensate for his maimed balance.

He hobbled unsteadily across the room to the table with the gas lamp; he wanted to pick it up, but he could not hold the lamp and the crutch in one hand. He put the crutch on his other arm, strapping it just above his elbow, but he was not able to use it properly. It felt incredibly erroneous not having a hand to hold the crutch. He swallowed a painful gulp of sadness, knowing he would bear that phantom limb for the rest of his days. He abandoned his desire for bringing the light with him, hobbling towards the door, breathing in the empty dark corridor.

Leaving the light inside of room 26. The corridor was very poorly illuminated by the recycled reflection of a cold, tired moon, poorly painted silhouettes of the chairs and desks. Joe took a deep breath and shivered in his surgical nightgown. Looking up and down the interminable gloomy corridor, he decided he would start down the left side and work his way up, the crutch hammered on the ground in inconsistent rhythm like a deaf percussionist in an orchestra. His bare feet slapped on the sheet vinyl flooring, followed by the peeling sound of tearing the skin away, followed by the booming thud

225

of the crutch; thankfully, being quiet was not a priority because the echoes of his movement thundered around the walls in the vacant corridor.

Joe reached the first room down the hall, *22*. It was dark and empty. A gust of wind slithered its way out of the room through Joe's legs. He felt lonelier and more scared than before, imagining he could hear the incessant whispering of a demon in the dark.

He continued hobbling up the corridor. *23* was locked, as was *24*. Feeling very lonely and somewhat petrified, Joe hurried his pace, pretty much running to room *25,* which swung open, but Joe wished it wasn't. Inside was a very dimly lit room. The embers in the gaslight were haggard remnants of a bright flame that had finished its work.

Four monotonous white walls enclosed the room, with only a boring small window to accentuate the end of the room. There was a dark bed in the room. Joe had to strain his eyes to confirm what he was seeing. The sheets on the bed were saturated with blood; the blood dripped off the side of the bed onto the floor, where it trailed towards the furthest, darkest corner in the room.

Joe very slowly approached the corner. No matter how hard he squinted his eyes, he could not see anything beyond the impregnable dark. Aside from the sound of the crutch on the ground, Joe could hear very faint wheezing coming from the corner. It grew louder the closer he got; something was squatting in the corner, but he could not tell what it was. Joe tried to call out to whatever was in front of him, but the words 'caught in his dry, terrified throat.

The thick silence was shattered by a low ghastly rumbling, like an old smoker, chuckling at his own bad joke. Joe saw the darkness slowly moving; he turned around as quickly as he could and hobbled down the corridor. *26* was locked, *27, 28*. The faster Joe moved, the louder the whispering became.

There could be no mistaking it; a sound like a heavy chain being dragged up the corridor pierced the darkness. Joe spun around so fast he almost fell over. The screeching of the chain on the ground got louder, accompanied by resentful wheezing. Joe strained his eyes again thanks to the weak glow of the moon could just about make out the scene. A very tall, cloaked figure shuffled towards him. It was bound in heavy chains. It stopped; the musical jingle of its chains faded. It just stared in silence. Joe could feel his chest lifting and falling in fearful anticipation.

The tall figure sprinted directly at Joe, its chains once again sang, his heart froze, but thankfully his muscles reacted; he quickly shouldered the crutch like a baseball bat, waiting for the right time to swing; the cloaked figure was right on top of him, Joe closed his eyes and swung hard. He wheeled around and fell painfully to the floor. Joe opened his eyes, panicking. He knew he missed the swing, so he darted his eyes around the dark corridor, looking for the threat. Nothing was there. Looking down the endless, dark hallway, he saw no other shadows and heard no chain scraping the ground. Feeling a bit more confident, Joe climbed to his feet, forgetting the crutch or no longer feeling he needed it. Joe continued down the faintly lit corridor; he entered an opening. Dark silhouettes of desks and chairs reminded him of an office or a lobby.

Joe searched the desks and the cabinets for a light or even something to tell him where he was. The cabinets were just full of apples and bottles of fresh well water. Irritation slowly grew in him as he frantically searched through the desks throwing away all the negligible components he found, pens, paper clips, balled up paper, and for some reason, a compass that only pointed west. Joe just finished searching the bottom drawer finding nothing but cobwebs, when a voice rang out:

'Joe, please help me.'

Joe jolted in shock and quickly looked around. There was nobody there. Again, the distressed voice called out for help. Joe searched around the room sporadically, looking for the person needing help.

'Where are you?' he called out. 'Is that you, Mary?' A tone of hope twinkled in his voice.

Joe rushed around the room with peeled eyes looking for Mary. Finally, he found her, at least he thought it was her, what he saw was a dark silhouette wearing Mary's shape; she was standing in the dark corridor facing the wall, she was making a very consistent clicking sound, like a leaky, rusty tap slowly dripping into a dirty sink. Joe slowly and prudently approached her, feeling somewhat fearful and even threatened. The moonlit up the corridor enough for Joe to see she was not making a clicking sound with her mouth. There was blood dripping onto the floor. Joe slowly raised his hand to lay it on Mary's shoulder and gently spoke to her.

Quicker than Joe could blink, her head snapped around, the bones in her neck cracking and popping. Joe screamed when he saw Mary, two gaping black holes dripping blood where her eyes should be.

'Look what she did to me, Joe,' Mary said with a demonic echo. 'You promised you would protect me! You lied!' Mary wept, blood cascaded from her eye sockets to the floor, pooling on the ground: the pool became a shallow river and quickly began rising. Joe was now knee-deep in blood. He stepped back from Mary, turned around, and ran away, trudging through the stream of blood.

As Joe was hobbling away, the corridor was ignited by a radiant blaze of fire. Joe was no longer in the corridor. He was now in a room; in the centre of the room was a large chair with a man sitting in it. The chair was surrounded by people watching as the man in this chair was being shocked to death. He was smouldering. After the man went flaccid in the chair, he lifted his head to look Joe in the eye.

'Watt's up, Joe?' said Tommy, laughing uncontrollably. 'What's the matter, boy? You look a bit shocked!' He continued laughing.

Another voice chimed in belonging to a half-eaten corpse. 'at least you're cooked. I was eaten raw.' David laughed.

The room exploded into cheering and applause.

Joe turned around and ran away, leaving the dying echoes of the laughter ringing in the distance. The faster he tried to hobble out of this burning cave he found himself in, the sooner he realized he was being pulled back by something he could not see. Gasping for breath, he stopped running. He felt an unrelenting force push against him, knocking him to the ground. A large, decayed hand pinned Joe to the floor; he looked behind him in time to see he was being dragged into a deep dark abyss housing a whirling firestorm. Unable to move, Joe screamed as the edge got closer... closer, Joe slipped off the edge, falling an endless fall.

Joe was screaming as a man in a lab coat was kneeling on the floor beside him, patting him on the back. Joe opened his eyes and saw he was sitting on the floor in the corridor while a whole audience watched him with concerned eyes, some in uniform, others in casual attire.

'Where am I?' Joe lethargically asked the man.

'You are on the second floor at Castlebar Medical House,' he said with a deep calming voice. 'Let's get you back into bed, young man.'

Joe grabbed onto the doctor's extended hand, and he pulled him up, gently holding him as he went back to bed.

'Do you know if my friend is alive?' Joe weakly asked, getting back into bed. 'Her name is Mary Cleary. I think she was with me when I came here.'

His bright blue eyes cowed behind his thin brown framed glasses. 'She was in a very critical state when she came in. I have not seen her since. I'm unsure of her present condition.' Seeing the broken look on Joe's face; he added: 'I can find out for you if you wish?'

Joe gave the doctor a morose smile and nodded his head.

'Do you need help with anything for now?'

'I'm fine,' Joe said in a hoarse whisper.

The doctor nodded and left Joe to his spiralling thoughts.

Hours later, the room door opened again, and Maggie hurried in, followed by a sleazy man wearing a burgundy suit. Joe sat up in the bed.

'Joe sweetheart,' said Maggie rushing over to hold Joe's hand, 'how are you feeling, gentle boy?'

'I'm as solid as water.' Trying to get loose from the bear hug his mom was suffocating him in. 'You haven't seen a doctor with glasses anywhere, have you?'

'No,' she replied. 'Why, what's wrong? Do you need help?

'No, nothing like that. I'm fine, but he told me he would let me know how Mary is; nobody will give me a straight answer! Is she alive?' Joe felt his temper rising when he noticed his mother eschewing eye contact and staring quietly at the floor. 'Please just tell me, is Mary alive?'

Maggie wiped the moisture from her cheek. 'I don't know sweet-pea, I hope she is, but I honestly don't know; they won't let me see her because I am not her family.'

Joe sunk into his pillows with a sigh of frustration; a small cough came from the opposite side of the room where the man in the suit cleared his throat. Maggie and Joe lent him their attention,

'I'm sorry to interrupt you, Mr McNeeve,' he said in a nasal voice. 'my name is Emmett Hopkins; I am a lawyer representing the criminally insane in Mayo.'

Joe was equally bemused and uninterested as he looked at his mother.

'I will keep this candid for you,' he said, flashing a smug smile. 'Your mother has attempted to kill you, your younger brother, that girl Mary Cleary and she probably pinned the story on your father Tommy, getting him killed.'

Joe attempted to lunge at Emmett but was to exhausted to commit. 'That's a lie!' he lazily snapped. 'It was the banshee who did all of this. My mom was trying to help us.'

Mr Hopkins gave a bored shrug, lifting a crumpled pack of cigarettes to his mouth, putting one in his mouth and then stuffing the pack back in his trousers pocket; he glanced at Maggie and then to Joe looking for some sort of tacit disapproval; no reaction was all the confirmation he needed, he raised a cheap red lighter to his mouth, four clicks and a deep inhalation expelled the on-coming jitters in his hands. He pulled a chair from the corner of the room in front of Joe's bed and sat on it, crossing his legs, his shallow brown eyes smiling.

'Look, Mr McNeeve.' He paused to fill the room with secondhand smoke. 'can I call you Joe?'

Joe gave a nod that Emmett did not see.

'Your mother, Joe,' he continued, 'is in a lot of trouble, yeah? Now you might not believe this, but I am here to make sure she doesn't meet the same sticky fate as your father.' Another deep drag, blowing out the smoke. 'When her court case comes up in a few months, she can plead insanity.' Shooting a sideways nod at Maggie. 'She will probably live out her days in an asylum… Hopefully. But you can visit her whenever you would like, but because you are not quite eighteen, Matthew being younger still means neither of you can claim the orchard until you come of age, you follow me?'

Joe grunted in confusion as Mr Hopkins took another drag.

'This is where things get really complicated,' he said, running a hand through his long brown hair. 'after your mother's court case, you and your brother will be living alone in the house; that's not a problem with me, but because none of you are adults, and there will be no adults living with you, that puts us all in a delicate position.' Another long drag. 'We would need to send agents to you regularly to make sure you were doing okay. Got it?' One final long drag and a sigh of relief that told Joe and Maggie he was craving that cigarette all day. Mr Hopkins stood up from the chair, flicking the cigarette butt into an open bin in the corner of the room. It bounced off the rim and landed on the floor. Emmett did not even glance to where it landed. He bowed low to Joe. 'Mr. McNeeve, it has been a privilege.' Facing Maggie. 'Mrs. McNeeve, I will speak to you later to finalize some things.'

Mr Hopkins took his leave.

Joe lay there speechless. Maggie finally worked up the nerve to speak:

'He said he will make sure I will be safe.' Maggie tried to smile.

232

'Mum, I am not going to let them take you.' Joe's eyes filled with tears. 'the way they took dad.'

Maggie sat down beside Joe, hugging him. 'I wish I believed your father I had been so stupid and selfish; I thought he had lost his mind; I thought he was going to kill Matthew because of David...' she paused.

'Why would dad kill Matthew because of David?' Joe's face boiled with wonder.

Maggie looked into Joe's radiant blue, judgmental eyes; she could not bring herself to admit how monstrous she had been to Tommy. 'I am not s-sure... but wherever I do end up, I probably belong there. I am sorry for being so pathetic. Please look after Matthew, please.' She broke into tears.

Joe tightened his arm around her. 'I will, mum, you know I will.' Joe knew it would be a waste of time to persist in questioning his mother. 'We will come to visit you as often as we can, I promise.'

A promise he kept for little over a year.

Maggie unscrewed herself from Joe and blew her nose on her sleeve. 'Get some more rest, Joe. I better go with Mr Hopkins and finalize my defence.' She took a long sorrowful look at her son before she left the room.

Joe was once again left alone with his boggled mind. He quickly got used to having one ear; his hearing was good enough to be sufficient even at half capacity, but only one arm, the phantom limb he could never get used to. It really felt like it was still there, burning with pain, but when he would try to scratch his nose with his hand. Nothing. Even though it had been disabled for the last few months of its existence, it was a horrible feeling losing it all the same. Joe dozed into another restless slumber.

This time Joe did not hear the door open. He was roused by a gentle, concerned voice.

233

'Joe, how are you feeling?'

Joe jolted, and his eyes flashed open; sitting on the chair beside his bed was Teresa Cleary, Mary's mother. She was shocked to tears to see Joe in this bloody state.

'Hullo Teresa, I'm holding myself together as good as a fat man's belt.'

Teresa snuffled.

'How is Mary?' Joe asked recklessly. 'I have not seen her since I got in here.' Joe was afraid to hear the answer, but he needed to know.

Teresa held onto Joe's hand and looked at him with her wet, grey eyes, which made Joe think of dreary mountains in the rain. A feeble smile wrinkled her face.

'She will live.'

These words fell into Joe's ear and filled his heart with happiness. He momentarily ignored the intense pain he was in to truly appreciate this angelic news. He contorted a wide smile.

'Can I see her?'

'I will see if I can bring her to you. You better stay in bed.' Teresa stood up, but before she turned, she burst out crying.

'Teresa, what's wrong?' Joe's voice was twisted with worry.

Teresa moaned through her wails, finally catching her breath. 'Mary... s-she is blind Joe.'

Joe's heart felt as if I had just been trampled by one hundred angry horses. He promised her he would keep her safe, and he didn't. Does she hate him now? Does she blame him; maybe it was better if he never spoke to Mary again. Teresa left the room before Joe could say anything. There he waited, not knowing if Mary would be delighted to speak with him or would she detest him and not show up. Joe anxiously lay back, staring at the door, snakes twisting in his stomach, waiting, waiting.

Joe must again have dozed off, or else he was so deep in thought he must have zoned out of existence momentarily; there was a gentle knock and Teresa Cleary entered the room, followed by her husband, Stephen Cleary. Stephen was pushing a wheelchair, sitting in the wheelchair, with a fresh, slightly bloodied bandage around her head covering her eyes was Mary. Joe's heart turned to steel and dropped into his stomach at the sight of his best friend. Stephen and Teresa forced her smiles. Mary was wheeled upside Joe's bed, Joe wanted to speak to her, to hold her as tight as he could and cry, but he was filled with aloofness and blame. It was Mary who sliced open the uncomfortable tension in the room:

'Are we there yet?' Mary said, turning her head side to side, waiting politely for a reply.

'I'm so sorry, Mary, yes we are here,' said Stephen, who could not get used to the fact his daughter could not see anymore. 'I am so sorry, sweetheart. I keep forgetting that you can't—'

Mary cut him off with a nonchalant wave of her hand. 'Are you here, Joe?' She extended her hand near to Joe.

This was it. The person he cared for most in this world besides Matthew was about to rip out his soul with the blame he knew he deserved. Why did he ask Mary to help him? He knew what he was getting into. She was about to declare how she hated him and never wanted to speak to him again; Joe had lost his arm and ear, now he was about to lose his heart, and that was going to hurt more than both of them combined.

Joe extended his left hand, meeting Mary's and held it tightly. 'I am here, Mary,' he said, fighting back the tears.

She sighed and relaxed. 'Thank goodness you're alright, Joe. I was so worried.'

Mary's reaction caught Joe completely off-guard. Judging by the look on Stephen's face, he, too, expected a furious outburst from his daughter. Joe's brain still hadn't caught up to the surprising denouement; Joe felt his tense muscles which were bracing for an emotional disaster, slowly relax.

'I was very worried about you too,' Joe said. 'I am so sorry about your eyes, Mary.'

'Don't worry. It's not your fault.' As if she could read Joe's mind. 'at least I don't have to see your ugly face anymore.'

Everybody laughed at this, even Joe, who couldn't even feel offended with how happy he was.

'Is it true your mother has to go on trial?' said Mary.

Joe nodded grimly, instantly remembering Mary would need audible confirmation from now on. 'Yeah, it is true. I have no idea what to do.'

'I don't know why nobody will believe us when we say it was the banshee,' said Mary.

Hearing the name still sent shivers down Joe's spine.

'Luckily, my mom and dad, believe me, so they will help us convince everybody it was not your mum.'

Joe glanced quickly at Stephen and then to Teresa, noticing how they stared at the floor and shifted uncomfortably.

'What's going to happen to you and Matthew if things go bad?' Obvious concern decorated Mary's tone.

'We will be fine. We can still live in the house, although we can't work the orchard until I'm eighteen. I think they said they will send people now and again to check up on us.'

'Me, mum, and dad would always be checking on you.' She smiled. 'What about your mum?'

'Your man reckons she will be put in some sort of insane asylum, said me and Matt can see her whenever we want. So, I guess it could be worse.'

Mary heard the sadness in his tone and repeated. 'It could be worse.'

Matthew pulled off his bedclothes, stretched, and got out of bed. he slipped on the same clothes he wore yesterday, visiting the outhouse before breakfast.

'Good mornin Matt!' said Joe, pouring out two cups of tea.

Matthew smiled and hugged his brother, Joe, who stood in anticipation wrapped his arm around him. Matthew sat at the table, waiting patiently for breakfast. Joe adeptly carried over a plate of eggs, resting on his left wrist below his elbow and a hot cup of tea which he gripped with his hand, over to the table setting them before Matthew, he smiled and patted him on the back.

'Do you know where we are going today?' Trying to encourage excitement, bringing his own eggs and tea to the table.

Matthew stared at the roof, deep in thought.

'We are going to see mum.'

Matthew raised his arms and bounced up and down in a hyperbolic reaction.

It had been seven months this day since Maggie's court case landed her in the insane asylum, as planned. Joe and Matthew have been living in the family home in the orchard where Joe had assumed the role of taking care of him and Matthew. He swiftly became very dexterous with his left hand but still felt the chill of his phantom limb, his hearing was still going strong, and Matthew, while unable to speak, had conjured a sort of jargon sign language understood only by him and Joe. This would be the third visit Joe and Matthew had had to Maggie, who now resided in the *twisted nut park asylum for mentally unstable cases.* - Joe never realized how degrading that name was - Only three visits in seven months, not even a quarter of how many times Joe wanted to see her, but the asylum was in County Cork; the journey took the best part of two days to make, meaning even if Giant were able to haul the wagon carrying Joe and Matthew without getting jaded, Joe would have to stay awake for two consecutive days, in a bumpy wagon; it was illogical to think of.

So instead, Joe carefully mapped out a track they could follow, passing by two inns along the way. It was a very strenuous journey, but the refreshing sleep and hot dinner made the trip a little easier for them and Giant. Not only was the journey onerous, but it was also very toilsome on the money.

Every week after Tommy had brought the apples to sell into town and shopped for the weekly groceries, he came home and stored whatever money he had left in his upstairs safe inside his bedroom closet; he did not trust banks. Some weeks he would sell many apples, it always depended on the time of year, but little by little, his little stash became a small fortune. The day he died, there was £415.74c. Joe had felt like a millionaire when he saw his family legacy.

The password, Joe, is the year you were born.

He could remember the day as if it was yesterday, still feel his father's hand on his shoulder, hear the birds singing jovial jingles through the meadow. If he closed his eyes and imagined it, he could feel the wagon rolling over the ignorant rocks.

I won't be around forever, Joe; when that time comes, you will be the man of the house. You will keep the orchard thriving. You will look after the family. I have some money saved. On the second shelf in the closet in my bedroom, there is a safe. The password to the safe is one-nine-zero-eight, the year you were born.

That was the day they had tracked Giant to a meadow and brought him home, a splendid thirteenth birthday. Tommy was great with horses, so Giant did not cause any trouble as he was lassoed, brought home, and trained to be a hard worker.

Not being allowed to get the orchard operational until he was 18 meant there was no income for Joe and Matthew for two years, they had to live on what their father had saved, which seemed at the time like a lot of money, but it quickly dwindled. The first time Joe went grocery shopping, he was surprised and appalled at the cost of food and milk, but it was the price of tea that made his jaw drop. £2.24! An ounce would satisfy him and Matthew for maybe three days if they were a bit more strict. All-in-all it cost roughly £12 a week for groceries alone. Even with Mr Burke's pity discount, it was too much to spend. Then it cost money for clothes, upkeeping the horses, the dreadful bills but worst of all were the trips to visit Maggie. 4 nights bed and breakfast for two lads plus Giant, food for the journey: these visits cost £40 give or take a tenner, after the fifth visit, Joe calculated how long the savings would last at this rate. Not long enough.

That was going to be the last time Joe and Matthew visited their mother; Joe did not dare to tell her they would not be coming again until he got money. Anytime Matthew would point to a picture of Maggie, Joe would always say, 'We will visit her soon.' But they never did, Maggie rotted away in her cushioned cell, alone, forgotten; always hoping today would be the day her children would remember to visit, every day she was disappointed.

As the months dragged along, Joe quickly realized being an adult was not as fun as he had imagined. He had to cook dinner for him and Matthew every day; bacon and cabbage, for the most part, Teresa had also taught Joe how to cook chicken and even roast beef, it took a bit of training with the one hand, but he slowly got the hang of it. Cooking was oddly relaxing, but the washing up, not so much, then once a week there was washing the clothes, feeding the horses daily, making sure they were okay, making sure Matthew was okay, and lastly, remembering to take his tablets to sooth the pain in his phantom arm and ear. I am sure there was a bunch of other miscellaneous tasks that you don't want to hear about.

Every night at 10:00, Joe would collapse into his bed despite his pain would fall briskly into a deep sleep for 9 hours, where he would awake the next morning into a new day with the same jobs.

Every Saturday, like clockwork, Teresa and Mary visited; Mary was always equipped with a Mahogany walking stick to navigate through the endless dark world she now existed in. She always wore a smile under the bandage wrapped around her eyes, even though deep down Joe could sense her frustration and anger, and Joe always wept, feeling a burden of guilt. Teresa would make dinner and keep an eye on Matthew while Joe and Mary stole away to take a walk in the woods. No matter how tight Joe held onto Mary, she would still trip over some roots and brambles. She always laughed it off and made a joke about it, saying: her walking stick shrunk, or she was testing Joe's reactions, but Joe only heard one thing: *I will never be able to see because you didn't protect me.*

They always found themselves in the fairy glade where they would sit on a log for hours and talk and kiss, but don't tell Teresa! Subconsciously Joe always brought them to this spot, hoping against hope the fairies would come back and maybe they could help Mary see again. He did not care about his arm or ear. He only cared about Mary.

Life continued in that fashion until Joe's 18th birthday when the bank finally gave him back the contract to his orchard. He began selling apples again and tending to the still extant apple trees. It was very difficult to employ people to help out. Stories about the orchard were bruited far and wide across Ireland; nobody in their right mind would come in proximity to that haunted land. Joe once again disappointed his father because the orchard never thrived again, he never spoke of his mother to anybody, but he did not forget her, and often he dreamed about visiting her again. But he never had the time or the money, and now it was so long since he last visited it would be very awkward to attempt to fix the broken relationship.

X IV THE BROKEN MAN (1962)

Down a quiet street on the outskirts of Dublin city, a pale moon emitted a ghostly light between egotistical clouds. A gentle rain surfed on the controlled breath of a sleepy night. Down the squalid, seemingly abandoned alleyway, there was light in the front window of a storefront, being hammered softly by a polite but intrusive rain. The faded midnight purple lettering standing above the door read:

BUCKS BOOKS AND MORE BOOKS – If your desired novel is not here, then book a book from Buck.

What an idiot name for a bookstore. Buck was an idiot, he thought, but he was the only idiot who would sell his idiot book so he wouldn't have to work for his God damned idiot father anymore. He closed his lips on his last Benson and Hedges fag. He threw the empty box aggressively across the alleyway. He struggled to light the cigarette in the rain, but thankfully he found refuge under a protruding lip that I guess you could call a roof, maybe.

His hands were shaking because of the cold wind brushing his face, the stressful scenario he just took a recess from, or maybe it was knowing if he could not grit his teeth and deal with these book signings, he would be back working for his "magnificent" Father *Jack O'Brien,* manufacturing "life-changing" gas heaters. "*If it ain't O'Brien heat, it ain't heat!"* Mark shuddered; he could still visualize the smile on his father's face when he invented that motto. Suppressed memories started emerging in Mark's head.

If it ain't O'Brien heat...

...it ain't heat! Jack had said while holding his hands above his head with his palms facing outwards and a complacent grin, looking like he had just ended world hunger. Calvin and Nicolas or just Nick - as everybody called him - clapped and cheered to their father's brilliancy, then they all clinked glasses and drained their champagne. Calvin and Nick were Mark's older brothers; Calvin was 27, Nick was 25, and Mark was 22 that Christmas Eve night in 1959. His father, Jack, had that classic O'Brien appearance he passed down to all three of his sons; shiny black hair, hazel eyes, a long nose with a toned body; unfortunately, they all had his hairpin temperament when things didn't go right. The chair beside Jack was empty, empty as it had ever been for the last twelve years. Mark always felt so alone at these family get-togethers. It was only his mother, Penelope, who seemed to like him at all. Maybe it was because he was the youngest, maybe it was because he was always tired and falling over because he was born with *neuromuscular disorder* that had deteriorated his body, forcing him into a wheelchair at the age of 16; the weakest link, a stigma on the O'Brien name, an easy target; and a target he was for as long as he could remember.

Calvin and Nick always bullied him in school and at home; his mother always tried to protect him and make the boys stop picking on him, but his father Jack tacitly encouraged it.

The O'Brien's were a very rich family. They owned four mansions around Dublin city, one for each of the lads and one for Jack and Penelope; naturally, Mark got the smallest and most run-down house of the bunch, but he didn't mind, he lived there with three servants: one maid, a gardener and a full-time live-in butler, Dominique, because no matter how independent Mark felt, he still needed help.

Mark started working with his father's company when he was 16. Back then, they were making gas lights, the pay was very good, but is your pride and dignity worth a payday. If anything ever went wrong, it was never Calvin's or Nick's fault. It was always Mark's, always. When Mark turned 24, he decided: *damn the family company, damn Calvin and Nick, and damn my father.* He would pursue his wild dream of becoming an author.

Penelope had always forced Jack to guarantee Mark a job at the company, even if it was just cleaning toilets, which it usually was. So, you can only imagine how patiently and eagerly Jack waited for Mark to come crawling back and say, *my dream is a bust. Can I please come back and work for you, dad? You were right this whole time; I am just a mess up.* Little did Jack know Mark would sooner drink himself into an early grave than give his father the satisfaction.

'Mark.' Mark shook the terrible memories from his head, then he realized he had let his cigarette burn out. Annoyed that his father could still ruin the night while not even being there, he flicked the charred remnants of his cigarette at a nearby bin.

'Mark are yez coming back in tonight, or wha'?' The voice held a potent Dublin accent, an angry little man appeared, his thick black glasses exaggerated his greasy, balding hair, which he tried to hide by combing over four long dark strands. It didn't work.

'Yeah, sorry Buck oi was just avin a fag,' Mark said as he zoomed around the alleyway back into the book shop on his motorized wheelchair. A gift from his father - the only gift he had ever given Mark - but boy was it a lifesaver; they were very recently invented, but Jack being Jack, managed to get his hands on one.

Buck briskly stepped aside in his second-hand maroon two-piece suit. 'Yez shouldn't smoke. It will kill ye someday.'

'Don't worry, Buck. Oi would neva get tha' lucky.' Mark drove inside from the cold, windy night through the back of the store. Open boxes of poorly organized books and unused posters were laid peacefully on the dark table and the floor in the backroom.

Mark inhaled deeply for three seconds and exhaled for three, opening the door. There was a large group of fans of his book hanging around, smiling, chatting incoherently amongst themselves. The book signing was for the book Mark had just published: *The Ghost of Hell Hollow.*

It was a factual story; well, Mark said it was factual, although he might have twisted the truth a little bit, or a lot a bit. It was a Ghost story; much like the Bible when nobody can positively state something as spurious, it sells for a lot more; writing 101. The story follows Mark and his partner *Daniel Bloom;* not his romantic partner Mark did not swing that way, neither did Daniel, who was married and had a little boy and another child on the way.

Three years ago, Mark had been at a pub drinking his sorrow's away one night when he overheard a conversation between two men behind him. They were talking about a haunted Manor in Laois called *Mt. Hollow. T*he men were saying how the family is haunted by a ghost. Then they started arguing about the existence of ghosts. Long story short, this inspired Mark to write his first story. He spent weeks on the phone, calling in favours – until finally, he got into contact with Mt. Hollow. He explained how he was from the papers, writing a story covering the paranormal events - not completely false, only he didn't work for the paper - and how he would need accommodation for two people for two weeks. They agreed. Within three days, Daniel and Mark were travelling to Mt. Hollow.

Mark had met Daniel ten years ago at a book convention in the heart of Dublin, where they instantly clicked and became best friends; they both had a dream to become famous authors, and here was their chance at last.

Mark realized soon that most of the people at the book signing were women. Most of them cared nothing for the book and only bothered coming to admire the handsome author. Mark was a well-dressed, well-groomed man. His burgundy 3-piece suit exaggerated his bright hazel eyes. He had a midnight black pompadour and a thin moustache. While signing an autograph on a newspaper from the trash for a middle-aged, bald man - who looked as though he accidentally stumbled into the bookshop - he declared loudly and slowly how Mark was the best writer the country had had in a long time, told him how he was very impressed by the book and then; mentioned a story he had heard a long time ago, about a family in the mid-west who were terrorized by a banshee. His breath was fetid with weekend whisky, and his eyes, though haggard and distant, looked honest.

Mark, who had heard of the banshee but had never encountered one, was intrigued. He desperately needed to get this story and write about it, got as much information as he could from this drunken man. Mark made a note in his trusty notepad of the 'McNeeve orchard' and about its location, "somewhere in Mayo". The man was finally pushed aside and lost in a sea of impatient women, staggering into a bookshelf knocking over Buck's precious books. The rest of the humorous show was blocked off by the storm of lovestruck women.

Mark answered the same questions over and over again. *Did you really see the ghost? How did you survive?* And *Where is Daniel tonight?* And of course, the most common question of all *would you like to go steady with me?*

Daniel much preferred being at home with his pregnant wife Sarah and his four-year-old son, Luke. That indeed was where Daniel was. *I don' fancy spending my night in some rundown shop shaking hands with old biddies* had been his exact words, but Mark figured he would be better off not telling them that.

He felt Dan's intentional absence would upset some people, so he came up with an excuse.

'Daniel is quite sick tonight. He sends 'is regards and gratitude to everybody.'

As for the questions of authenticity about his book, Mark obstinately claimed it was true, and since technically, nobody could prove it was fictional, he got away with it. It wasn't the money Mark was after; it was the success, the fame, the ability to attend the next Christmas Eve dinner with his family and look at the surprised faces of his father and brothers when they realize he was not just a liability. It was very petty, Mark knew it, but it is often the tree that is starved of sunlight that wants to grow the tallest. And Mark was a tiny tree, a tiny tree hidden in the shadows of his brothers.

Mark flipped out his golden pocket-watch from his jacket and checked it: *11:25 pm*. He announced to a shrinking crowd of women that he would be leaving in five minutes. A choir of disappointed moans filled the shop. The last five minutes were spent hugging and kissing a crowd of middle-aged women who thought he was just the cutest thing alive. Nobody even seemed to care about the book anymore. *You are the best-looking man I have ever seen. You are so cute.*

I'm not cute! He thought *I am the best-selling author you'll ever know you, peasant.*

Moments later – he wished the remaining fans goodnight and made his way out. He was then struck with questions about his motorized wheelchair. Amidst all excitement, everybody must have forgotten about the alien machinery Mark was operating. As the last few women stared at the chair with dumbfounded expressions, somebody finally asked the question: 'What is that chair?'

Mark stopped and turned around to face the crowd. 'It's a wheelchair, of course.' Mark opened the door and headed out. *They are far too stupid to understand the ingenuity of this machine.*

'How did you get one?' a voice bellowed out,

Once again, he stopped but did not turn around this time. A wry smile crept across his face. 'Oi am Mark O'Brien.' He left the store towards a long black car parked on the road just outside.

His live-in-butler Dominique - also his driver, opened the back of the car, waiting under an umbrella.

'How was your night, Mista Mark?'

'Ohh, it was absolutely fantastic' Mark headed to the car waiting for him, hands shaking anxiously for a calming cigarette, but he remembered he smoked his last one. Dominique helped Mark into the car. He closed Mark in and folded up the chair, placing it in the boot of the car. He then sat in the car and drove home.

It was a thirteen-minute drive from Mark's house to the bookstore, but the time seemed to drag on and on as if every second were a month of Sundays. Mark groped around the back of the car restlessly, searching for a bottle of Jack Daniels or some other potent sedative to mollify his frustrated nerves. After a few minutes of a frivolous search, Mark began frantically clawing at seat cushions and pockets in the back of the car for a stashed drink. He found nothing.

When Mark's teeth were sore from grinding them together, he finally accepted he could not find anything. He cleared his throat: 'Eh Dom, oi don't suppose we 'av any whiskey left in the car?'

'Ah ha-ha, no, no Mista Mark, no whisky, not here.' Dominique retorted in his exotic accent.

Mark had ordered his servants to call him Mr Mark, never Mr O'Brien, that was his father's name, and he was not his father.

'D'ya 'av any fags left?' Optimism saturated his tone.

'Sorry, Mr Mark, I do not smoke anymore.'

Mark sat back in the seat and sighed a long exhalation. His head lulled lazily to his shoulder as he watched the window, faintly lit shapes of trees and buildings and streetlights went zipping by, reminding him of an old black and white film. Imagining he was at home, in the bathtub, washing away all the filth of those commoners touching him all night: *why did they have to touch me?* He wondered, *couldn't they just enjoy my book and ask me a few questions instead of touching me and kissing me all night? They didn't even care about the book. Nobody cares about my book. I mean, really, why did they all feel a need to touch me? One or two of them were gorgeous, but most of them...* he shuddered; *sweet Jaysus, I need to wash their disgusting presence off.*

Mark enjoyed the company of tall women, but desperation often blunted his libido, and he would end up bringing home any woman who wasn't afraid to get real nasty behind closed doors (*and I don't mean girls who pointed out that without money, I wouldn't stand a chance with them – get it Mark? Stand, cause you're crippled*) when nobody could see them, or laugh at Mark if he wasn't able to please her; which was never the case, but the fear was always there, looming over him like a shadow of terror; if he ever failed to satisfy a woman and his brothers found out, he may as well find out how to tie a noose.

The car pulled up to a large stone archway. The large black-iron gate was closed. It had a stainless-steel M connecting the gate in the middle; it reminded Mark of a villain's lair, and he laughed. Dominique stepped out of the car, opened the gate, and returned. At this time, Mark's mind was fixed on the liquor cabinet in his study. The soothing sound of a car slowly rolling over loose stones accompanied Mark up the long driveway to a large two-story mansion.

When the car stopped and the engine was turned off, it clicked and purred into silence. Dominique stepped out of the car and walked around to the trunk, Mark who had his eyes closed, followed his footsteps with his ears. He heard the trunk being opened, his wheelchair been removed and unfolded. Dominique stretched out a hand, and Mark gratefully accepted it. Prudently helping him onto his chair, Dominique asked:

'Did you have a good night tonight, Mr Mark?'

Mark smiled when he was sitting in his wheelchair. 'It was particularly jejune Dom if I must be honest, not to mention blatantly intrusive on my being, not many people cared about me bleedin' book and the few who did had this vexatious crochet of lecturing me in the most supercilious manner about how they would write my book using a more grandiloquent font.'

Dominique smiled. 'Yes, yes, Sir, very good.' He laughed.

Mark knew Dominique did not understand anything he just said. He rarely did; truth be told. Dominique knew very little English. Just his smile and his "yes yes, Mr Mark" was enough to gladden Mark's heart. He loved Dominique. Even if there was a language barrier, he understood Mark, maybe not linguistically, but he was very dependable and kind. For that, Mark greatly appreciated him.

Dominique pushed open the two massive doors. Mark thanked him for everything and entered the house, trailed by Dom. He looked around the familiar commodious hallway. At the ambiguous paintings hanging on the wall, hoping someday he would be able to look upon the art and make sense of it. He then gawked up at the large chandelier hanging from the ceiling. Its intricate designs and the warm glow it emitted always made Mark feel safe and curious. Mark looked up the grand oak staircase, wondering if he would ever someday get to see what was upstairs. A woman silently emerged on the top of the staircase, dressed in a tidy black skirt and shirt and a frilly white apron. She looked down at Mark.

'Greetings, Mr Mark,' she spoke proudly and properly with a London accent. 'it is great to see you again. I have finished cleaning the kitchen, the bathroom, and the hallway. I steered clear of your study just as you asked, will there be anything else, or am I free to go home tonight?

Mark smiled as he always did when in the presence of Elizabeth. 'Actually yeh, oi hate to be a pain, but could ye'ever run a bath for me, oi really wish to bathe as soon as possible.'

'Of course, Mr Mark,' she said in her smooth tone as she walked downstairs.

Mark watched her fondly as she walked down the stairs, her curly brown hair bouncing with every step, her beautiful green eyes watching Dominique going back outside to lock up the car, her pretty hand gently brushing the bannister as she descended. She smiled at Mark, showing her pearly whites as she walked beside him, going to the bathroom. Mark stared at her desirable figure as she walked away. Those long, glabrous legs in that skirt and heels drove him crazy, her tall, slender figure. She looked no older than 24… Mark knew he was not the first man to fancy his maid, and he would not be the last. He also knew she was way out of his league. This thought depressed him, making him crave a large glass of anti-sad juice.

Mark entered a dimly-lit room with wavey crimson wallpaper and a polished dark-wood floor. The tall bookcases had been recently ransacked, judging by the blatant gaps in the uniform layout and the many books scattered listlessly on the tables and desks around the room. He approached the empty fireplace, unburdening the mantelpiece of the nearly empty bottle of Jack Daniels sitting idly on it. He uncapped the whiskey, picked up a glass on the table beside him, and then returned the glass. *I will just drink from the bottle,* he thought and took a deep swig.

The hot liquid coursed through his veins, giving voice to his concerns and strength to overcome them.

'Maybe oi should just tell her how oi feel about her,' he said quietly, 'maybe she feels the same way.' He shook his head. 'No, of course, she doesn't, look at her! And look at me,' he said with a defeated sigh. 'She could never love me, nobody could; she is the most beautiful woman on the planet, and oi am just a crippled son of a successful man.' He wiped a tear from his eye, feeling he was not good enough for Elizabeth, which was almost as painful as the worst experience of his life, which was not the day he went into the wheelchair, but the day he realized he would never leave it. He numbed this painful actualization with another mouthful of his comforting sedative.

Moments later, the tall, slender figure of Elizabeth appeared.

'Your bath is ready, Sir; would you like my assistance, or would you rather be alone?'

Mark placed the empty bottle on the table. Elizabeth would usually help Mark take a bath by helping him in, washing his arms and legs and back, and helping him out and get dressed. The thought of being naked in front of Elizabeth surprisingly never discomforted him until recently, until he started to have… stirrings for her. Since then, his face would always glow a magnificent red. He always wondered, did Elizabeth feel turned on or did the sight of him naked repulse her.

'Could ya help me please, if ya don' mind?'

Elizabeth nodded and left the room. Mark pulled off his suit jacket, emptied the pockets, leaving his notepad on the table, and followed Elizabeth.

He entered his bathroom behind Elizabeth, a very large room it was bigger than his study, brighter too. A simple purple seashell pattern infused with wooden panelled wall and white marble tiles lit by four candles: one in the centre of each wall and a gaslight on a small Ebony table beside the bathtub, in the centre of the room. Yes, Mark's bathtub was in the centre of the room. It was a bit larger than a bathtub, big enough for three people to bathe, big enough for him to drown comfortably in, not that he ever thought about doing it… anymore. After he found out it was a lot harder to drown yourself than to drink too much or "accidentally" shoot yourself in the face with the .32 you kept on the top shelf of your desk in your study. Mark was embarrassingly familiar with the taste of that steel barrel, but his thumb would never tighten harder on the trigger.

He stopped behind Elizabeth beside the bathtub. Without any reluctance, she began undressing him, helping him take off his shirt, slowly peeling off his pants. Mark watched her face carefully as she did this, hoping to see any kind of expression, fearing to see her shudder. Nothing, he had to hand it to her. She was a hard worker. This drove him even crazier. He needed to know how she felt about him. She needed to know how he felt about her. The whiskey was giving Mark a burning strength. He was going to do it. He was finally going to come clean with Elizabeth, lovely Lizzy. Lizzie O'Brien did have a ring to it.

What will you do when she says no? A cruel voice echoed in the back of his mind. *You will make her feel awkward and laugh at you and quit, leaving you alone in this bathtub. Maybe you can try to drown yourself again.*

Shut up. Why do you always shatter my confidence?

I am here to protect you from making stupid decisions. You know she would never fall in love with you. You are nothing, just a cripple wearing a fancy suit complete with a fake smile… you are nothing, Mark. Nothing.

I will treat her right. I will make her laugh. I will make her smile. I can be the man she needs.

Don't make me laugh, are you hearing me? You are in a wheelchair. You are a broken man. No matter what you do for her, it will never be enough. You can never be the man she needs. You need her, don't ever forget that, Mark. You are the one who needs help with everything… until you finally grow the balls to rid the world of your useless presence.

Elizabeth must have noticed the cold sweat dripping down Mark's sullen face. 'Is everything alright?'

'Yeah, yeh course it is.' Mark had strength in his legs, and with the help of Elizabeth, he lowered himself safely into the warm bubbly water. She got a sponge from the table, dipped it in the water, and began gently scrubbing his chest.

Usually, by now, Mark would have slurred some licentious joke about this situation. Elizabeth was very uncomfortable in the awkward silence, so she decided to cut the tension herself by making a joke: 'So when are you going to bathe me for once?' She laughed.

Mark's mouth twisted into an awkward smile, and he held his arms stiffly out in front of him to be washed.

Knowing Mark would never eschew a good flirt session, she knew something was bothering him.

'What happened tonight?' All the playfulness drained out of her tone.

'Nothing, oi'm just very tired after the book signing,' he muttered; *I'm depressed that I will never be good enough for you* played around in his subconsciousness.

'Were there many people there tonight?' she asked politely, scrubbing his calves washing up to his thighs.

Mark was busy deeply scrubbing his face with a warm cloth to wipe away the dirty scummy saliva of the Commonwealth. When she reached his thighs, he stopped what he was doing and lay back, closing his eyes. *Elizabeth, I need to tell you how I truly feel about you: I love you; do you think you could ever love me?* 'There were a few people there, isn't there always? Oi doubt half of them even read me book; nobody seems to care about me hard work.'

'I care, Mr Mark.' Quickly switching from his thighs to his back with the sponge. She poured a jug of water on his head, washing his hair. Mark could tell from the expression Elizabeth was hiding behind that she had something she needed to say. He craved desperately to open his heart.

What's the worst that could happen, he asked, *losing her forever,* he answered.

Elizabeth helped Mark out of the bathtub and back onto his chair, drying his legs and making sure he got his dressing gown on before leaving the room.

'Would you like me to help you get into bed, Mr Mark?' she asked.

Mark had buried his head under the towel and was frantically drying his hair with it. 'Yeh, wait no; oi'm going to go into me study awhile, oi have some work to do.' His mind torn between absolute honesty to Elizabeth and researching the banshee at the McNeeve orchard he had heard about.

'Alright, I guess if that's everything, I might as well go home.'

'Perfect, thank you for yer help, and oi'll see you tomorrow.'

She took note of how Mark didn't go in for a hug, which she didn't care about. She only worked for him. *What would a man like that see in a girl like me anyway?* She often asked herself.

'Goodnight, Mr Mark, I will see you tomorrow.' And with that, she left the bathroom, got her jacket and hat from the rack in the hall, and disappeared from the house, until tomorrow that was.

Mark bit down on his tongue, feeling disappointed in himself for once again being a coward while also feeling relieved he did not push Elizabeth away. He made his way with haggard eyes to his study, closing the door behind him to retain what little heat was in the room. Slowly driving to the table, he picked up his notepad: The McNeeve orchard. Somewhere in Mayo, he smiled. 'Better start somewhere, oi guess.'

The Broken Man

He sat down at the table with both of his hands busy: one holding the notepad, the other groping for a full bottle of Scotch. he brought the bottle up to his face smiling a sad smile, he was sad because he felt like he always needed to be drunk to feel even a tiny shred of happiness, and every time he took a drink it saddened him to know today wasn't that spiritual day he was constantly promised where *things would get better.* Uncapping the Scotch, he filled the glass halfway and left the bottle down, picking up the glass and sipping at it. 'Alrigh' so... How do oi start 'ere?'

If your man wasn't just talking pure muck, it would probably be in the news, so check the newspaper. 'Grand, one problem we're in Dublin, The News up here doesn't cover Mayo; oi would have to pull some strings to get a newspaper from the west, and another problem... Oi forgot to ask him for a date; when did this even happen?'

Mark slammed his fist hard on the table, causing the bottle of Scotch and the glass to sing in harmonious twinkles. He caught the neck of the bottle before it tumbled to the ground and placed it firmly on the table, cupping his face in both hands. He then began aggressively thrusting the palm of his hand into his forehead. 'You stupid idiot Mark! Why didn't you get the date? You really are just a terrible excuse of a human.' He sat back, stretching out one hand to the heavens and the other lifting his glass of Scotch to his lips and swallowing an impressive gulp.

He pulled a pearly black telephone from the opposite side of the table, fingering the rotatory dial in the middle, which was adorned by a cast gold M, Just like the one on the front gate, the one on the front door, the decorated stone M in the flower patch in the front lawn, and on every other significant item in the house, Mark loved seeing his initial around his house, it made him feel important.

He collected a thick copy of the Yellow Pages from the top shelf in the desk and opened it to D. Dancing through the names with a giddy finger. He stopped on *Darren Durkin,* editor of The Dublin Stories; Darren was a friend of Mark, and if anyone knew where to start digging through old news stories, it was him. Mark cited the accompanying number and spun his finger on the dial accordingly. The call rang out. Mark tried again, the same outcome. Finally, he looked up at the birchwood grandfather clock in the corner of the room: 1:32 am. He swallowed the last gulp of Scotch in his glass, feeling like a fool, promising to pick up the work first thing in the morning. He headed for bed.

Mark's bedroom was a small, cosy room. A large painting of a lion standing proudly on a rock adorned the wall, a comfortable chocolate carpet hugged the floor. A large four-poster-bed sat against the wall facing the picture of the lion. Beside it, a large black-stone fireplace devoid of fire since Mark moved in. *The O'Brien gas heater warms the room. What would I need a fire for?* Mark stripped off his nightgown, peeled back the mint green silk sheets on the bed, and planted himself in bed using the helping rail he had installed. He switched off the large, brass intricately carved lamp resting on the oak tree table stand married to his bed. He shut his eyes and faded from reality for a few hours.

<u>X V</u> PREPARATIONS

The loud, obnoxious ringing of an enthusiastic alarm clock on the opposite oak tree table stand pulled Mark out of the lewd fantasy he was having of Elizabeth. Mark crunched his face up trying to fight off real life and continue existing in the reality where Elizabeth loved him… it was too late it was gone, she… her love vanished, leaving Mark alone in bed, in a world where he was just a cripple, 9:02 AM he slapped the alarm clock silencing the incessant screaming, he gently massaged both sides of his head, trying to mollify the percussionist orchestra warming up for a grand extravaganza.

Right on cue, same as every day, Dominique knocked and entered, smiling his jovial smile, almost skipping around the room, opening the curtains, painting the dark room with optimistic sunlight. He always waited a few minutes after nine until entering. After all the abusive tirades he got for not letting Mark "wake up properly" or waiting too long and making Mark "waste the day," he soon discovered 5 minutes after nine is neither too late nor too early to go in.

'Good morning, Mr Mark. How are you today?'

Mark grunted while sitting on the edge of the bed pulling on his underwear. 'Ahh, y'know yourself.'

'Yes, yes, Mr Mark.' He laughed, 'I think you no should drink anymore.'

Mark's blood bubbled. *Go away, dad. I will do what I want!*

Dominique helped Mark get his silver suit pants on, button up his black shirt, and put on his silky green waistcoat. After he got his shoes and socks on, he lifted Mark onto his chair.

'You want the same breakfast as always?'

Mark nodded. His breakfast nowadays consisted of a hot cup of coffee and three aspirin tablets, "a cure for yesterday's shenanigans," he often called it.

'Could you bring it to my study? Oi have a lot of work to do,' he said, leaving his room.

'Yes, Sir, very good Sir,' Dominique said as he left.

Later that morning, after Mark had finished drinking his hot coffee and swallowed his three pills, he hung up the phone after talking to his friend Darren Durkin at the Dublin Stories, requesting Darren to ask every contact he had belonging to the Irish news to pinpoint The exact time, location and story behind the McNeeve orchard. He said he would do it - for a hefty chunk of change - which Mark agreed to, no problem. A small investment of £50 for a multi-million-pound story like a banshee. *Let's hope people like banshees.* He drew out some imagined storyboards for how he thought the book would go.

Five days later, mid-autumn, as the world was losing its tenuous grip of the suns warmth, it was still early in the morning, but the fluffy blanket of the grey sky made it look late in the afternoon. The flowers and trees in the garden were at the end of their short lifespan. Whenever Mark would look out the window at the dying landscape, he wondered if Mother Nature enjoyed killing the flora; was it a mercy killing or was it her way of dealing with the anger of coexisting with a species slowly succeeding in destroying her home.

Preparations

Mark was sitting at his desk in his study, his hair was messy and unkempt, his shirt was half opened and painted haphazardly with unknown stains, and he was clouded in a fetid order, The smell of a man who has been drinking whiskey for the last five days - 6 empty bottles sat on his desk - and somebody who has been too busy to bathe this week. One hand pressed the phone to his ear while the other held a lit cigarette, tracing the air with the translucent silver line.

Please, please, please, he muttered under his breath.

'Hello, yes, this is he. Am oi coming through clearly?'

A muffled, husky voice escaped from the telephone: 'Yeh, how can I help ya?'

'Oi'm writing a book and oi have been desperately desiring a tranquil holiday in a bucolic setting and oi was wondering nay hoping you could accommodate say one or two people to stay for say three weeks? Oi have been informed you still have residencies; would this be acceptable for Monday next? And how much would the admission be?'

-silence-

'What exactly are ya asking me?'

Mark bit down on his lip. 'A friend and me want to book three weeks at your resort next Monday, to write a book on the banshee, oi was hoping to get the story from you. Can we do this?' Mark spoke slowly like a child reading a passage from them Dr Zues books, or whatever they were called. It only then clocked him that he would have to abandon the sophisticated speech of the city and adopt the crude country mumbling for the duration of his stay.

-Another brief silence- 'Next Monday, for three weeks? Can do. It will cost £200. You will have a bed, running water and a cooked dinner every day.'

Mark took a celebratory drag of his cigarette. His excitement quickly died. 'I forgot to ask, is it wheelchair accessible?'

'Wheelchair? No, no, I'm sorry it's not. I can make it so it can have a wheelchair, but I would need a week to install some things. Is there anything, in particular, you would need?'

'Not really, my friend will be staying with me as oi have already said, just a couple of handrails by the toilet, the bed.

'Alright,' the phone continued, 'if you and your friend can come down on the seventeenth of September, that's Friday week, everything should be sorted.'

'Al-ry, splendid cheers.'

'Make sure to have the money. What's your name again?'

Again? I never gave it to in the first place you country bumpkin 'Mark O'Brien is moi name, and me friend is called Daniel Bloom. Don't worry; oi will have the money.'

'Okay, see ya then, Mark, goodbye.'

'Bye, Joe.' But the call was already disconnected before he got to finish. *Business mustn't be going well if he needs the money so bad, never mind. Okay, I've booked our vacation, now comes the hard part.*

Later that evening, there was a knock for the third time. Elizabeth answered it to a man in a stylish grey suit standing under a black and white striped umbrella, shielding him from the violent downpour that seemed to recur during this cold, misty September day. His combed-over hair and well-groomed beard complimented his deep blue eyes. Elizabeth welcomed him and beckoned him inside. Once in the hall, she gestured to the end of the hall. 'Mr. Mark is in his study.' The man thanked her and made his way to the down. He knocked twice and entered.

Preparations

When the man entered the room, the first thing he noticed was the mess—piles of newspapers stacked like a small paper town scattered around the floor. The man shuffled carefully through the paper labyrinth to a desk with precisely placed newspapers with names, and important facts circled in red pen. On the table also are several mugs, some with coffee offal at the bottom, and some were full of coffee embellished with a layer of days-old neglect on the surface. Empty bottles of whiskey littered the floor like a pebble dash of drunken dilapidation.

The man looked on top of the desk. Leaning against the wall was a chart-board with pictures and cut-out headlines from newspapers all connected by strings. Like an intricate spider web, written across the top of the board was *The Banshee*. The man stared at the board, trying to understand it, then there was a resonant shout behind him: *Daniel!* Daniel turned around to see Mark among the mess of papers. He was sporting an unkempt stubble and seemed to be staring through Daniel with enervated eyes.

'Where have you been? Oi called yez days ago,' said Mark picking up a mug off the table, finishing the cup of... something, maybe coffee.

'You called me not three hours ago,' retorted Daniel, staring concernedly at Mark.

Mark gagged and regurgitated the drink back into the mug. A look of disgust twisted his face.

'Mark, wa'z going on here?'

Mark made his way to the desk. He pointed to the board. 'That Daniel is our next book.' His fervent excitement mixed with his squalid appearance made him look truly insane.

'The banshee?'

'Correct, it wasn't easy getting all the information, but oi did it.' His excited chuckles sounded to Daniel like a chicken. 'Oi even called Joe McNeeve, seeing if we can stay there for three weeks and write the book. He said we could, it will cost two hundred pound, but we can go half each. He needs a few days to caterer the place for a wheelchair.' Mark slapped the arm of his wheelchair. 'He said to come on the seventeenth.'

Daniel stares at Mark with dumbfounded disbelief. 'Wait, wait, wait… what did you just say? The seventeenth? That's in like two weeks, isn't it?

'Friday week' Mark interjected coolly.

'Did you say two h-hundred pound?' Daniel continued stuttering over his shock. 'You already b-booked it? Why didn't you ask me before doing something stupid? I leave you for two weeks and—' Daniel caught his breath and calmed down. 'Yer gonna have to explain the whole thing to me.' Mark was swiftly growing tired of repeating himself. 'Look, oi'm going writing a new book about a banshee, there was a case of a banshee haunting an orchard in Mayo thirty-eight years ago, we are going down there to find out what happened and to write about it, it will cost two hundred pound so a hundred each. We are going Friday week for three weeks.' He paused, watching Daniels's bemused expression. 'Did that penetrate your mind, or do you need it in writing?' A drop of venom seeped into his tone.

Daniel fidgeted uncomfortably with cold hands for a while. 'I mean, if it's already decided there isn't much I can do about it, is there?'

'No, not really.'

'Righ' so I better get off home and tell the missus. Friday week? I'm assuming yiz expect me to drive?' He shot Mark a cheeky smile.

'Unless yeh want to sit on me knees for two weeks.' He laughed.

Preparations

Al-ry, I suppose I'll pick you up next Friday at ten o'clock in the morning, yiz better be ready on the button!'

'Oi will oi will.'

'Okay, I'll see yiz then, be safe.' Daniel left the house.

Mark knew Daniel had a family now. His place was at home; that was not, however, where his heart truly was. The adventure was what he yearned for. Many times he had had to fight to suppress the voice that called, begged for excitement. *He wouldn't miss it for the world. Something tells me this story will be the best thing we have ever heard.*

For the first time all week, Mark allowed himself to relax. He sat back in his chair, closed his eyes, and breathed steadily. Suddenly the poisonous perfume of dried whiskey, cigarettes, and hygiene neglect lacerated Marks's senses.

'Oh my God,' he complained quietly, cringing up his nose. 'Elizabeth, I need a bath now!' he shouted and left the room.

Later that night, Dominique called Mark and Elizabeth to dinner; he had prepared a dish his mother taught him to make, indigenous to his country. Mark was no gastronome, and he wouldn't be able to pronounce whatever it was, but boy did it taste good. It tasted like duck, smothered in an orangey, creamy gravy... I'm not doing it justice but believe me, it was spectacular. Quite frequently, Elizabeth would audibly moan in satisfaction while eating to stroke the ego of an already bombastic butler. It was constantly met with a 'Are you enjoying this?'

'Oh my God, Dominique, it's simply ammmmaaaaaazing.'

'Yes, yes, thank you, my mother teach me to make it.'

Every forty seconds!

Mark was enjoying it too, but he wouldn't dare say anything. *Okay, okay, we get it. Your mother taught you to*

265

make it; it's very tasty. Now let's enjoy it and stop talking, please.

'Dominique, I might just marry you and get you to cook for me every day.' Elizabeth laughed, Dominic did too, but Mark did not. The thought of Elizabeth marrying somebody who wasn't him made a black hole open in his chest and swallow his heart.

'Oi will be going to Mayo Friday week for three weeks.' It came out in a squeaky mess. He wanted to change the subject before Elizabeth got any permanent ideas, but he had no idea the stress of this potential ceremony would spill into his emotions.

'What did you just say, Mark?'

'Friday week oi'm going to Mayo with Daniel for three weeks.' He watched Elizabeth's sombre face. 'Will yeh miss me?'

'Yeah, right, three weeks off! Why don't you stay longer?' She and Dominique laughed.

'What will yez get at for three weeks without me!' He joined in on the joke.

'We might start new lives.' She laughed, 'we might have to get new jobs, working for someone else. Hopefully, he treats us better.' Dominique roared with laughter at the banter Elizabeth was suppling. Mark's merry mood sunk into annoyance at that disgusting comment. She was only joking, of course, but Mark always prized himself in the generosity he gave to his employees, unlike his father, who cared for nobody but himself; Mark was different, altruistic even. He wanted (needed) people to know that. In his mind, Elizabeth inadvertently accused Mark of being his father.

'Oi don't think you would ever find anybody who treats you as good as oi do,' he said in an agitated tone.

Preparations

Dominique and Elizabeth stopped laughing. 'We were only having a laugh, Mark. We meant nothing by it.'

His anger was uncontrolable 'Oi'd like to see anybody else give you a week off because your sister broke her arm!'

'Mark, please…'

'No if oi'm not good enough for you, go find this better man!' he bellowed, and brought his fist down on the table with such force he spilt his glass of milk and shook everybody's plates; the calming jingle sang up to try to sooth his anger. Mark left the room, not finishing his dinner, and he got no dessert.

Mark retreated to his study as he often did, either to work or to shield himself away from the big bad world for a few hours. Unfortunately, he was getting more and more comfortable with the latter. At least twice a week, his father would come by and tell him to stop lying around, doing nothing all day and get back to work for him. *I am not doing nothing; I am writing a book. -you? Writing a book? I'm surprised you can even write your name.* he then sneered in his condescending way. He never even asked what the book was about. He never cared. Never. His brothers didn't care much either, Elizabeth on the other hand, seemed to nurse an interest. As small and fake as it was, it was better than nothing.

Mark picked up a copy of his published book and read the title page:

> *The Ghost of Hell Hollow*
> *A true story experienced and written by*
> *Mark O'Brien*

The longer Mark stared at it, the more lucid his father's ghostly laugh became. He could imagine his father buying the book just to leave it on a shelf collecting dust. *Excuse me, Mr O'Brien… is it your son who wrote the book? -no, he's not my son, a distant relative or something;* he would probably tell the press that ask him at his next press conference for whatever garbage he was about to sell. Mark groped for the bottles of whiskey scattered around the room; they were all empty, he even searched his emergency cabinet, but that too was empty. His hands began shaking, and deep in his skull, fury began vibrating. No smokes and no booze. He wouldn't dare ask Elizabeth to get him some right now or Dominique. Remembering the interaction from 5 minutes ago pushed him over the edge of sanity. 'Well, if oi can't drown the pain, oi will fight it.' Blow after blow hit him on the top of the head, the side of his face, his nose, and his temple, every time he landed another painful hit, it made him madder, which in turn made him hit harder; It looked like a comical pantomime of self-loathing. 'Why did you make me like this?' he screamed at the roof at a God he did not believe in. 'Why can't you just kill me?' The slapping died down as the aggression left his body morphing into depression. He could taste blood with every hard swallow, but he did not care. Tears mixed with blood running down his face. He roared in agony, not at the self-inflicted wounds that would heal next week. He cried because he was a pitiable man born to a family who was disgusted by him and the knowledge that he would never amount to anything was ringing in his hot, sore ear.

He folded his arms on the desk and tucked his painful head smugly between his biceps. The heaving dampened down until it was little more than distorted breathing. His nose stopped bleeding, and his eyes stopped watering. Pretty soon, he sat there, curled up in himself like a hibernating bear, in silence. He stared through slobbery eyes at the chart-board: *The Banshee* he raised his head, used his sleeve to clean the remnants of blood, snot, and tears that lingered on his face, and took a deep breath. *You don't get to choose the boat you are stuck with. All you can do is keep sailing and hope it can bring you to where you need to be.* That had been a quote from Mark's father, Jack, the year of the great O'Brien fishing trip in 1952.

The sun cracked the sapphire sky, and all the fallen fragments dazzled in the gentle, precious waves of the quiescent blue-eyed Sea Serpent. This had been a day Mark was longing for the past three months. Jack had planned a fishing trip for him and his three sons: Calvin, Nick, and Mark. It was gonna be a twelve-hour fishing trip in the sun-kissed trawler Jack had rented for the day. Mark needed some time away from life right now. He had just been diagnosed with neuromuscular disorder earlier that week, finally understanding why his body was betraying him; he got tired quickly from walking, running even standing, he fell over a lot. He just felt like he was fading more and more out of existence. School had become almost unbearable for him. His school bag seemed to get heavier as the days dragged by, although realistically, it was getting lighter because Mark had started removing the heavier books. He slowly fell from the top of the class to the bottom - still higher than his brothers - because he always "forgot" his homework and schoolbooks. Little did the teachers know; he never forgot them. It just became too great of a weight to haul. Becoming enervated from the simplest things came with a high risk of being susceptible to bullying for a small boy. Between classes, the other boys always had a great laugh in slightly shoving Mark and watching him fall to the ground. Calling him names like "wibbly-wobbly-wonder", "jelly legs" and their all-time favourite: "Matt", they called him "floormat", but that was soon shortened to

Matt. Mark was very indignant over the way he was treated, but what could he do; especially with his brothers Calvin and Nick being the ones enforcing the name-calling and bullying, Mark often wondered why they hated him. Maybe it was because he was smarter or had a better personality. Either way, his brothers detested him, and his father acted like Mark was a stigma on the O'Brien name. '*Come on, Mark, just lift it onto the table!' 'For goodness' sake, Mark, get up. Why are you sitting on the floor like a dog?' 'How are you tired already? Look at your brothers. They are strong lads. That's what you need to be… stop being weak and get UP!'*

Jack had always assumed his son was just being lazy and difficult, so he encouraged Calvin and Nick to bully him into his senses. Penelope, on the other hand, always treated him with patience and kindness. She always knew there was something wrong with Mark, but she died before anyone could confirm it. He would often stare up to the heavens with pain-splashed eyes: 'She was the only person who loved me, and you took her away! I hate you, God! WHY DID YOU DO THIS TO ME?'

It was the day of the fishing trip when Mark truly understood the life that was forced upon him. He had been looking forward to this day all week, not only because he was diagnosed with a terrible, life-altering condition a few days prior and he needed an escape, but because he was spending the whole day on a boat in the middle of the ocean with his two brothers and his father; he expected a formal apology from all three of them, how bad they felt now that they realized it was never his fault, none of it. And maybe he would now be treated with reverence and finally be accepted into the O'Brien family. No, no, he was not. If anything, being diagnosed with a disease made everything worse, he was used to verbal and physical beatings, and at that time, nothing seemed worse until now. He was being ignored by the crew of the *Nibbler-nabber* trawler. His father had shown Nick and Calvin the proper way to use a fishing rod: 'Use your index finger to gently hold the wire, then release it to cast the line. swing with your wrist, not your arm.'

Mark tried to learn from looking under Brains outstretched arm, leaning on the rail for support, but he couldn't see where to put his finger and when he asked Jack if he could show him, his father continued fishing, pretending the wind picked up and that had drowned out Mark's voice. He asked Calvin and Nick to show him how to do it, but they continued chatting and laughing amongst themselves, ignoring Mark.

Ten hours of sitting on the starboard side of the boat, his father and two brothers on the port, laughing and bragging about who caught the biggest bass. Mark caught nothing. He didn't even understand how to cast the line; it kept getting tangled in itself or on his jacket. One particularly temerarious swing nested the hook behind his ear, and when he flicked his wrist, the hook caught his ear, almost ripping it off. He had to bandage himself because his cries fell on deaf ears. He could still remember his father driving the boat back to the dock when the day was done, and most of the fish were kidnapped. The trawler, good ol' reliable Nibbler-Napper; kept cutting out, the coughing engine was as dependable as Mark was; but for some reason, his family was overly supportive of the sick boat. 'Come on, old girl, you can do it, just a bit further.'

When Jack had got the boat safely tucked into its dock, he turned around to his boys. 'You don't get to choose the boat you are stuck with. All you can do is keep sailing and hope it can bring you to where you need to be.' Calvin and Nick got off the boat with their coolers full of fish and hearts full of joy, laughing away to themselves. Jack hauled his heavy cooler, packed with smallmouth bass, off the boat, returning for his 5lbs brown trout trophy fish. He pulled Mark to the side, eyeing his empty cooler. 'You didn't catch anything?' Disappointment hushed the applauding sea.

'You wouldn't teach me how to cast the line,' Mark retorted gloomily.

'They say a picture paints a thousand words.' He sighed, 'sometimes a few words can paint a thousand pictures.' Jack had made a very audible tut-tut in his throat. 'Just because you are sick does not mean you will get special treatment or a pardon for being a waste.' He carried his brown trout off the boat, beckoning Mark to follow to the car. The whole car ride home, he sat undisturbed, staring out the window of the car at the starless sky, like a deep black ocean. His heart sank deep in it. *You are a waste,* the voice of his father echoed in his mind. *You are a waste.*

He no longer got pushed around at school or knocked to the ground. Now it was much worse. Calvin and Nick had convinced everybody at school that their brother Mark had a very contagious disease, people treated him like a leper, nobody talked to him, nobody looked at him only behind his back when he would hear them sniggering, "There he is, that's Mark O'Brien! Don't let him touch you."

Mark forced the memories out of his head; he was back in his study staring at the chart-board *The Banshee. I am not a waste, dad. I will show you.* Mark clenched his fist as tight as he could, leaving nail marks in the palm of his hand. He felt tired and cold and desperately desired to be snuggled up in bed. *Yesterday was yesterday,* he thought, remembering the fishing trip. *Tomorrow is tomorrow,* he thought ahead to his journey to Mayo. A twinge of excitement for his new book comforting his aching head.

Preparations

However, before going to bed, Mark knew he had to reconcile the relationships he had marred with Elizabeth and Dominique. He found Dominique in the kitchen washing up after an abrupt ending to a glorious dinner.

Mark cleared his throat: 'Dominique, oi need to apologize for the way oi acted at dinner.' Mark stared at the floor, trying to remember the speech he had fabricated on the way to apologize. 'Oi know you are always doing your best, and oi really appreciate it—'

'It's okay, Mr Mark. I love working for you, and I'm sorry if I made you angry.'

'You have nothing to apologize for, Dominique.' Deciding his apologetic speech would be a waste of time. 'You meant nothing by it. Oi was just in a bad mood. Why don't we just forget about it? Dinner was lovely, by the way.'

Dominic smiled. 'Yes, yes, okay, Mr Mark.'

Mark turned around and left the kitchen, wondering where Elizabeth was. Probably the sitting room. He found her in the hallway.

'Elizabeth, oi'm very sorry for the way oi acted earlier.'

Elizabeth approached Mark, her beautiful tall, slender figure towering over him, her long curly brown hair bouncing with her steps and her deep green eyes shining with the despair of wounding one whom she cared about. 'I was just looking for you to apologize.'

'You apologize? Oi need to apologize to you... oi shouldn't have got so angry, you were only joking, and oi lost me temper. Oi'm sorry.'

Elizabeth hugged Mark; it wasn't a hug your sister would give you after seeing you for the first time in three years. It was a hug that said I was so afraid I lost you. I never want to lose you. She stepped back, and for a moment, their eyes locked. Time itself felt like it had frozen solid. Mark felt a hot sensation of joy originating from his heart and coursing through his body right up to his head; however, when it reached his brain, that terrible part of your body that remembers, the terrible organ that makes you understand a situation, it felt as if though an icy river of grief flooded the hot, happy juice. He was just a cripple, *a waste.* The fleeting hope of both of them living happily together forever was swept away like the dead leaves of a cherry blossom tree in a hurricane.

'Well, oi better get to bed, oi'm very tired.'

Elizabeth awkwardly rubbed her hands on her skirt. 'Ohh, right, yes. D-do you need any help?'

Mark was sore and a bit dizzy from the whooping he punished himself with earlier. So, he accepted.

When Mark was in bed, he was just about to turn off his bedside light when Elizabeth stopped and turned back to him.

'Mr Mark, are you sure you're not angry with me?' He watched her shoes fidget uneasily. 'It's just… I li… you mean a lot to me, and I would never forgive myself if I hurt you.

Mark watched her curling her hair around her finger. *She doesn't want to lose you as a friend… a friend, nothing more, I promise you.*

His lips tightened into a weak smile. 'Don't worry, Elizabeth, it was me own fault. We're grand oi promise.'

Elizabeth left the room. Mark switched off the light and lay back in his bed. Darkness and regret filled the room. *If you were waiting for a time to tell her how you feel, that was it.* He soon slipped into a dream where he was a respected author, respected by his father.

X VI THE JOURNEY TO MAYO

Tuesday morning, Mark had been eating scrambled eggs and rashers that Dominique had made him for breakfast. *Three days until we go!* A bright ball of excitement radiated deep in his soul. He would soon be writing a new book about a banshee! That was an exhilarating topic. Mark had always been fond of ghosts and urban legends. Although he did not believe such things existed - except the night when his mother died, that bright woman came to him - *no, she isn't real)!* they were still very fun to write about, and with all the credulous people around, it had seemed like a lucrative concept to tackle. He was enjoying his slightly burnt, greasy rashers - the way he liked them - remembering all the stories about the McNeeve orchard he read in archaic newspapers his friend Darren had got for him.

Tommy McNeeve Had been arrested and sentenced to death for the murder of an employee David Henry and the attempted murder of his mentally disabled son Matthew McNeeve. A cold chill crept up Mark's crooked spine as he imagined his father trying to kill him because of his physical disability. Then a few months later, Maggie McNeeve, their mother, was sentenced to life in an insane asylum for the attempted murder of her sons Joe and Matthew and their friend Mary Ward.

The Banshee

Tommy and Maggie both pleaded not guilty for their actions, both claiming it was the work of the banshee, a specious theory advocated by both Joe and Mary, which was overruled due to both of them sustaining head injuries and the fact the three children were almost killed by folklore was nonsensical.

Mark had finished his breakfast and was sipping happily at his tea, rembering all the stories he had heard of the banshee. He had always found Irish mythology to be interesting: leprechauns, fairies, dullahan, the púca, even the banshee, but they were only stories for children at Halloween. They were not real. The banshee certainly was not dangerous as far as he could remember, an old red-haired crone she was described, she would wail through stormy nights, and if you could hear her, somebody in your family or even you were going to die. Mark stretched his memory as far back as it would go to when he heard about the banshee in school when he was five. *How did legend say you died? Was it her that killed you?* Mark shook the childish fears out of his head and convinced himself it was not real. It was just a story, but he would be sure to make her the most dangerous thing in the world, in his book, believe that.

Mark had just finished drinking his cup of tea when Dominique appeared in the kitchen.

'Excuse me, Mr Mark, your father is here.'

Mark hung his head. Of course, it was Tuesday! Jack's weekly visit to relay Penelope's wish to get Mark back in the O'Brien factory with his family, Penelope's wish not Jacks', he could not care less in fact, he was probably happier not having to work with Mark.

'Show him into the sitting room. Oi will be right out.'

'He has already shown himself into your study, Mr Mark.'

Mark bit down on his gum hard tasting blood. Any hope of a secret escape to Mayo to write his book was now gone. *I should really lock that door or clean up after myself.* There was no point worrying it was done now. He may as well see his father. So, he left the kitchen, making his way to his study. Cold sweat streamed from his brow.

He entered his cold study. Jack O'Brien was standing in there, with his back against the O'Brien heater. In his hands was the chart-board with "*The Banshee*" written across it. He wore a £100 black suit, his salt and pepper hair neatly gelled to one side and on his face, bemusement, as he studied Mark with curious hazel eyes.

'Do I even want to know what this is about Mark?' he said, flaunting the chart-board.

'Hullo dad, great to see you as always,' he replied in his customary, dull greeting.

'You know why I'm here.'

'Yeah, and the answer is still no, oi don't want to work with you.'

Jack began pacing the room approaching the table to leave the chart-board back where he found it, staring bewildered at all the connected charts and newspapers. 'Mark... what in God's name are you doing here? Have you finally lost your mind? When do you plan on growing up and coming back to work at the factory?' He sat on the edge of the table with his hands on his hips. 'Did you know Calvin and Nick were invited to Paris to negotiate selling heaters in France?'

There it is. 'Good for Calvin and Nick. Hopefully, they remember not to open the window on the plane for some fresh air. Well, hopefully, they do open it,' he spat with venom. 'As for the factory, oi am never coming back. Oi've discovered my calling, writing books is me life.'

His father towered over him, looking dangerous. 'Ever you insist on being a stain on the O'Brien name. Why couldn't you be a hard-working man like your brothers? Just because you have an illness doesn't excuse you for being a waste, put aside all this hippy-dippy rubbish behaviour and come back to work, wear the family name with dignity.' Jack could see the amount of emotional stress Mark was now carrying. 'I will send a car to pick you up at seven o'clock tomorrow morning, and you will come back to work—no more of this foolish book-writing nonsense. You are an O'Brien; you are not some child of doctor Sues. You are my son.'

Mark suppressed a terrible rage.

Jack made his way to the door. 'I will see you tomorrow morning. Nick's wedding is Monday the twenty-seventh. You will be there, so get yourself a haircut and a new suit and a shave, and make sure you bathe, for goodness' sake.'

'Oi won't be here.' Mark spoke in a weak whisper.

'Excuse me?' Jack turned around, shocked and awed that his son had the audacity to speak to him after that. 'What did you just say?'

'Oi won't be here, oi'm going to Mayo on Friday for three weeks.' His voice grew more powerful with the adrenaline surging through his rebellious veins. This was the first time he had ever disobeyed his father face-to-face, and it felt great. 'Oi'm writing a new book; Oi need to go to Mayo to study every detail of my story.' His eyes were glued to his father, his mouth hung open, inhaling deep breaths of cold oxygen in case he needed to fight to the death.

Jack stood as still as stone as if the very idea of someone defying him petrified him to the core. His face was stupefied, and his voice was commanding yet broken: 'If… if you g-go to Mayo f-fr-Friday. Consider yourself expelled from this family.' He pointed a very minatory finger at Mark. 'I am not joking, Mark. I will cut you off from my funding, you will be evicted from this house, and I will cut all ties with you. Do you understand me.' It wasn't a question; he spoke very slowly and sternly to make sure his point hit home.

Mark chose his next words rather honestly but carelessly: 'I was never a part of this family anyway.' He sat there watching his father intently with anticipation.

Jack audibly swallowed and locked eyes with his son. 'I mean it, Mark, sort your life out, or you're gone.' And with that, he swirled around and left the study and the house.

Later that day, at dinner with Dominique and Elizabeth, silence echoed in the room, broken only by the clinking and clanking of knives and forks abetting each other, slicing the roast chicken into pieces and the uncontrollable masticating of a soggy mouthful of potatoes saturated with gravy.

'So, oi was speaking with me father earlier on.'

Both Dominique and Elizabeth lifted their heads eagerly to listen to the announcement.

'Or, what oi guess oi should call him from now on, Jack O'Brien. He said if oi go to Mayo Friday, oi won't be allowed to come back to this house, or have any of his money, or talk to any of my family anymore.'

Elizabeth clapped her hands to her mouth. 'He can't do that, can he?'

'Are you kidding me? He's Jack O'Brien. He can do anything.'

'What uhh mean this for us? Dominique's finger was alternating between him and Elizabeth rapidly.

'It means.' Mark looked at Elizabeth and blinked away a tear. 'You won't be able to work for me anymore, as oi won't have a home.'

Elizabeth's mouth quivered. 'He can't do this. It's against the law.' She tried to rationalize the situation. 'You can bring it to court. He is bullying you.'

Mark guffawed. 'Elizabeth, he is the law... he's got the court in his back pocket. Any fight would be pointless, oi could tell from the look in his eyes he wants me to go, so he has a reason to ostracize me, just like he always wanted. You two are just going to have to find other jobs. This is the end of us. Oi hope you enjoyed our friendship as much as oi have.' Mark left the dinner table and went to his bedroom sobbing.

Mark didn't want any help getting into bed that night. After a long and arduous struggle to get undressed and transfer safely into bed, the way Mark was feeling that night, he didn't care if he fell and split his head. Mark lay in bed staring at the emerald canopy roof of his four-poster-bed and wept. All through his life, his father had been bullying him and saying horrible things to him, which had cut him deep, but he always bounced back. He was going to be somebody. He would show Jack... but this was a whole new level of malevolence.

His eyes were growing heavier and heavier as the reflection of the tenebrous moonlight dancing across the canopy roof shrunk until it felt awkward being there, then it faded into black. Time itself fell away as Mark was dragged into another exhausting dream where his family were standing on high pedestals circling him, laughing, throwing rocks, and disgusted looks. Mark, whose legs were clamped to the floor, could only attempt to shield himself from the projectiles with his arms while crying, p*lease, I'm sorry, I never wanted to be born*.

The next few days were very hard. Dominique and Elizabeth looked around, hoping to find other employment. Mark avoided them as best as he could, keeping to his study, not out of spite but because he was so scared and anxious about what was going to happen to him. Every time he saw them, he was reminded of the upcoming doom. So, he did what any coward would do; he stayed in his private area, drinking his worries away with the finest wine he could buy. He may as well have spent the last bit of money he had.

'Surely your grandmother would not let this happen to you. She would find a place for you to stay, right?' Elizabeth had inquired out of concern yesterday.

'Oi really don't know Elizabeth, sure me gran likes me, or maybe she just hates me less than the others. She always listens to my dad, and he wants me gone. Oi can't imagine her defying his order for me.'

'Well, can you say with your brothers? Surely they won't leave you homeless.'

Mark burst out laughing in a sort of sad way like a crazy person being asked his name. That was enough to answer Elizabeth's inquiries.

Thursday night. The last night in the house, Elizabeth was bathing Mark. He stared at her through the blurry eyes of an inebriated conscious. *Seeing as tonight is our last night together, why don't you get in the tub with me?*

'W-why, whi dun yu j-joyn me, Lizzzybisssh?'

Elizabeth had to keep pushing his head back to stop him lolling over and drowning in the bath. An aura of strawberries or cherry mixed with an array of toxins and ingredients Elizabeth could not discern or afford emitted from his mouth.

'How much did you drink, Mark?' she asked in a like a mother chewing out her rambunctious teenager for drinking instead of being at school.

The Banshee

'All of iiisshhh!' He laughed to himself, 'No waish theresh one bockle lefth, a gifth fur Jo an hisshh family.'

'That was very thoughtful of you.' She scrubbed his back with the sponge.

His mood turned gloomy. 'Oi am shuch an idiot, Lillabish.'

'Why is that Mark?' Pouring water down his head and hair.

'Becuz oi never toul ya how oi really feel.'

Elizabeth stopped what she was doing and looked Mark in the eyes. 'How do you really feel?'

He leaned forward splashing her with water. 'Oi tink yur te phrisiesht prishist… beautifulish woman in te world. Oi jush wanted you to love me back.' He sat back weeping.

'Why didn't you ever tell me?' Elizabeth asked, full of longing and happiness.

'Becuz you would jush laugh at me. You are gorjush, and oi'm jush a cripple, a whaste.'

Elizabeth's heart sank to the bottom of the tub she was washing Mark in. *How could somebody that perfect think of themselves as a waste?* Tears sprinkled her cheeks just thinking about what Mark had said. She wiped her eyes on her sleeve. 'You are not a waste. So don't you ever think that. The truth is, I have had strong feelings for you since I started working here.' She looked up at Mark, wearing a nervous smile. Only to find that Mark had passed out. He was snoring lightly with his head drooped back on the lip of the tub, mouth hanging open. Elizabeth sighed. *I thought we were getting somewhere. Maybe he might remember in the morning. Most likely not.* She sighed in frustration again and let the water out of the tub. She left the bathroom to find Dominique to help her get Mark into bed

Mark fingered his pocket-watch impatiently. He grunted and impetuously ran a hand through his freshly styled pompadour. A cool breeze forced the nearby trees to shake with discomfort, and the fragile light of the sun tried its best to penetrate the inviolable heavy clouds. Birds could be heard but not seen in the distance, probably complaining loudly about the weather.

He had already said goodbye to Dominique and Elizabeth for the last time. A terrible mix of grief and the hangover hung over him. He had lost the two people in his life that mattered most to him and, on top of that, his head! *Oh my God, my head, Jesus Christ, that wine could split a stone wall.*

A big black car appeared into view from the gateway up the curvy driveway. The car pulled up beside Mark. The door swung open, and Daniel stepped out, shivering in the cold. 'Sorry I'm a bit late. Sarah and me we're having a bit of a fight; she doesn't want me going all the way to Mayo for three weeks. She can be terribly intractable sometimes. "You are just going to leave your pregnant wife? What about your son!"' Daniel Tutted

Mark chuckled guiltily while putting his suitcase in the back seat of the car.

Daniel takes note of how Mark is dressed. 'What's with the fancy attire? I thought we're going to an orchard?'

'Ohh, we are, but oi believe presentation is half the introduction. And this may well be the most important man we will ever meet.'

Daniel looked confused but helped Mark into the passenger seat. When Mark was in the car, Daniel examined the wheelchair with his eyes. He then looked at the boot of the car, puzzled. Mark could see Daniel struggling, so he extended an olive branch: 'It will fit in the boot. Just pull it up in the middle, and it will fold up.' Daniel did so and was surprised by how easily it folded.

'That is incredible.' When the car was packed, Daniel enters the driver's seat and drives off—leaving Mark's mansion as a shrinking image in the rear-view mirror.

Mark opened his jacket and retrieved a brown envelope, holding £100 in big bills. He turned to Daniel: 'Do you have your hunnit?'

Daniel pulled the car over and reluctantly counted £85 in clumsy bills. 'I'm a bit, short pal.'

Mark sighed and added £15 from his satchel to the envelope. He sealed it and returned it to his pocket, silently.

Daniel drove on.

Mark was curiously looking out the window, watching the passing landscape and architecture feeling a distant sadness. He started rooting around in his satchel until his curious fingers gripped their target. He pulled a bottle of wine out of the bag. He twisted the cap and lifted it off, taking a few large gulps.

'Steady on,' said Daniel 'it's a four-hour drive, and we are not taking any breaks.'

Mark recapped the bottle and dropped it back in his satchel.

'You seem to be in a bit for queer humour, and when did you start daytime drinking? Is everything okay?'

Mark carefully contemplated whether he should tell Daniel the situation with his father or not. He stared dumbly at the passing trees hoping for an answer to be carved in the trunks. He figured he might as well tell him, so he began with the visit from his father two days ago. Not shying away from any childhood stories, the more wine he drank, the more he was willing to say. The wine was like a key to a door Mark had kept closed, never daring to open it, afraid of what he would find: a mirror to his soul.

The sun had begun setting. The tress and fields of the bucolic setting got ready to turn into shadows. As the sun abandoned them, silence buzzed in the car. Daniel looked at Mark with concern. 'So, what are you going to do when we get back?'

Mark stared with vacant eyes out the dark window. 'Oi'm going to write this book, and it's going to be the best book that was ever written. That's why oi want to impress Joe. Oi need him to tell me everything that happened, or at least what he thinks happened.'

'You really think a suit and a suave diction is going to impress a countryman?' Daniel laughed. Mark shrugged his shoulders. 'You never did tell me what happened on this orchard.' said Daniel.

'You never asked.'

'I'm asking now.'

'Fair enough,' Mark sighed, 'the family at this orchard has... a tragic past.'

'What sort of tragedy?' Daniel chimed in.

Mark began citing everything he had learned about the orchard's history in the newspapers he read over the last week.

When Mark had finished speaking, Daniel exhaled loudly in shock. 'What the Hell are we doing, Mark?' Daniel stopped the car.

'What are you doing?' said Mark.

'We're going home. You have lost your bleedin' mind, Mark!'

'No, no wait, oi didn't tell yeh the best part.'

Daniel stared at Mark with disgust. 'The best part? This is not one of your made-up stories. This actually happened.

Do yeh hear me? How can you embarrass and vilify this poor family?'

Mark rooted around in his satchel. He pulls out a tattered, cut-out headline of an old newspaper. The headline reads: *The Banshee Strikes Again.* Mark handed it to Daniel, looking complacent.

Daniel read the headline and turned the piece of paper in his hands, looking bemused. 'What am I supposed to be looking at here?'

'Joe swears there was a banshee terrorizing his family, but everybody laughs at him and thinks he's mad. So, if oi write this story, we prove his sanity while making a name for me.'

Daniel laughed. 'There he is, mercenary Mark. You don't care about this family; you just want to write a good book.'

Mark shrugged contently.

'Are banshees dangerous?' Daniel said.

Mark looked at Daniel with disbelief. 'There is no such thing as a banshee.'

Daniel turned off the car, the engine droned and spluttered. 'Then what in God's name are we doing?'

'Writing a story Daniel… a story.'

'Why can you not write it from home?'

Mark sat back. 'Oi won't have a home to go back to, besides stories sell better if people believe they are real. Look at The Ghost of Hell Hollow.' Mark pulled out a copy of his book from his satchel. 'This book wouldn't have sold half as much if people didn't think it was real, Daniel.'

Daniel looked perplexed. 'But that story was real. I was there!'

Mark returned the book to his satchel. 'Real, was it? Tell me, did you see a ghost?'

Daniel was taken aback. 'Well, no. But you did. Didn't you?'

Mark shot Daniel a doubtful look. Daniel sighs. 'You wrote it! You said it's a true story.'

Mark rubs his haggard eyes and yawns. 'Exactly, oi wrote it! Nobody can prove it's apocryphal.'

Daniel puffed heavily in disbelief. 'I cannot believe this. All this time, you have been a charlatan, writing phoney stories.'

Mark looked emotionally distraught. 'Not phoney, exaggerated. Why does it bother you so? I'm not hurting anyone, and people believe we're ghost hunters.'

'We are nothing more than liars.'

Mark got comfortable in his seat and closed his eyes. 'Whatever you say, Daniel. Just please drive on. I need to get some sleep.' Just like that, Mark's exhaustion caught up to him and carried him to sleep. Daniel stared out the window, watching the sinking sun pull the light from the world. He sat quietly, contemplating the news he had just received. As he weighed up his choices, Daniel slid Marks's book from his satchel. *The Ghost of Hell Hollow, a true story experienced by Mark O'Brien* Daniel, returned the book. He ruffled his hair with his hands and took a few heavy breaths. In a swift motion, he turned the keys in the ignition and started the car. Listening to the engine click and hum itself awake. He looked both ways on the barren road he stopped on, then tore off, leaving the unsettled dust dancing in the sunset.

XVII BREWING STORMS

The sun had all but abandoned the world as they finally arrived at the orchard. As Daniel slowly drove the car under the great arched gateway, he nudged a snoring Mark on the arm to rouse him from his slumber. Mark woke with a grunt, looking around, trying to shake off the state of sleep. Mark had now mentally caught up on the journey, rubbed his heavy eyes, and yawned. He gazed up in time to observe the arched stone gateway

McNeeve Orchard est. 1892

In its prime, the McNeeve orchard was a booming farmland, with many employees that produced the best apples in Ireland, but after many years of neglect and fear, it had fallen into ruin. The once bountiful fields of apple trees were now defunct. Dead saplings now littered the once fertile grounds. It looked to be isolation that created the stillness at the orchard - but to Mark, who felt an unknown dread while looking out at the dark fields, swimming in a late fog. He felt, for the first time a shiver, crawl up his spine.

Everybody except the McNeeve family and a few very desperate workers had left the orchard, and fewer ever even came to visit out of fear. And so, it was without much help available the orchard could not tend to or produce many apples and was now teetering on the edge of closing.

This almost abandoned land was still inhabited by the McNeeve family. Joe was very adamant about staying in his family home, hoping to someday revive the family business.

The car slowly rolled up the beaten track, which was once a well-traversed road in and out of the orchard as they approached a dark silhouette taking the shape of a house. Daniel and Mark noticed the house was almost in complete darkness, save for one or two dimly lit torches on the porch and in the bottom window. Mark peered out the car window to see the abandoned, squalid bunkhouses. All but two of them seemed unliveable and ruined, with boarded-up windows and chocking in unkempt grass and weeds.

One of the houses had what looked to be a crudely made wheelchair ramp aligned to the front door. Mark smiled with comfort, knowing his needs were taken care of. His gaze was then drawn to one of the windows. He thought he could see the outline of a person in the dark window. He squinted to improve his vision, confirming his superstition. Mark could see the shape of a woman, standing at the window, staring out at him. Not thinking too much of it, Mark continued silently gawking. Thinking maybe it could just be somebody finishing up arranging the cabin, but as the figure still stared, motionless. Mark started feeling uncomfortable. He strained his eyes to attempt to discern more of the figure. As Mark watched, unblinking at the shape. It looked to start lighting up slowly as if glowing ever so dimly. The shape became slightly more discernible, enough for Mark to see it was a woman with straight silver hair. As her face slowly came into the cold light, Mark realized whatever was staring at him was not human, well it could have been human, but she was

289

beautiful, like an angel. Her radiant blue eyes shined brighter than her glowing white body.

She's not real. She's not real!

As Mark watched the glow diminish out of reality, again, there was a dark flash, like reverse lighting, followed by a high-pitched scream. Terrified, Mark shielded his face in his hands and screamed. Daniel swerved the car but quickly stopped it sideways on the road before he could crash. Breathing heavily, he looked over to Mark: 'What happened? Why did you scream?'

Mark unveiled his eyes and looked up to the window again. He wasn't surprised to see nothing was there. It was not the first time that ghost-thing appeared to him.

She's NOT real!

He sat back, frightened at what just transpired. Mark finally controlled his breathing. 'Sorry Daniel, oi had a bad dream.' Breathing now slower,

Daniel clutched the car wheel and continued driving to the house.

The car came to a stand-still outside the two-story house in the centre of the land. Daniel turned the key, and the car went to sleep, shutting off its lights, humming, and clicking as all exhausted cars do.

Daniel climbed out of the car with a grunt stretching his back as he slowly made his way to the trunk of the car to retrieve Mark's wheelchair. Mark opened the door to the car and let the icy cold country air wash over his face and cleanse him from the drowsy journey. A cry from behind him made him open his eyes: 'Uhh, Mark, who was meant to pack your wheelchair?'

Mark's eyes bulged in both anger and fear; the same feeling you would get if you left the oven on before you went on holiday, only it wasn't an oven left on; Mark left his legs behind. Panic began suffocating him. *Oh my God, what do I do? We have to go all the way back up; I need my wheelchair. How could I have left without it? Why did Daniel not listen to me?*

'Daniel, we have to turn back. Oi need that wheelchair. How could you have left without packing it?' Mark's voice began to break as tears considered jumping out of his eyes. 'Why didn't you listen to me?'

Daniel emerged beside Mark unfolding the wheelchair. 'I was only winding yez up.' He laughed cruelly.

Mark laughed with tremendous relief. 'That was not funny oi damn near had a heart attack.'

'If it's not funny, why are you laughing?'

'Oi'm not.' Daniel helped Mark sit in his wheelchair. Mark surveyed the landscape and nodded to himself. 'The terrain seems to be acceptable.'

'Fine time, I'm thinking of it, but did you bring the battery to charge it?'

Mark nodded, and, at that moment, the front door of the house opened, and a tall, hefty man with a greying-black beard and tangled hair ambled down from the porch to Mark. He extended his hand; his left hand, the sleeve of his green plaid shirt, was rolled up to the elbow on his right arm. Mark saw there was no hand there and wondered to himself if anything had happened or was he born like that. Then Mark spied under his messy hair, scars around where his left ear should have been; then decided something had happened to him.

'How aya now?' said Joe shaking Mark's hand. 'I'm Joe McNeeve. Welcome to my orchard.'

Mark beamed happily at him. 'Oi'm Mark O'Brien, and this is...' Mark's hand wavered around trying to find Daniel, who popped his head up around the back of the car and smiled at Joe. 'There he is, this is my friend Daniel Bloom. Thank you for letting us stay here and write about your perspective on the banshee attacks.'

Joe shuddered to the core, hearing the name. 'Before we do anything, can we handle the…' Joe grunted and rubbed the tip of his primary fingers with his thumb.

Mark stared at this ambiguous gesture. *Money!* 'Oh yes, yes, right of course, oi have it here somewhere.' Mark fumbled in his coat pockets, finally extracting a brown envelope and handing it to Joe.

Daniel rolled his eyes at the transaction and continued unpacking the car.

Joe counted the money. At least Mark thought he was counting. He was running his thumb through the notes while muttering.

At last, he lifted his radiant blue-eyed gaze to Mark, and his face split into a wholesome smile. 'I hope you enjoy your stay, my wife Mary an' me will give you a full account from our perspective.' He lowered his voice and looked at the windows of the house. 'Mary still struggles to try to talk about it, but we will do our best. Hopefully, people will believe us at last and stop avoiding us like we're daft in the head.'

Mark smiled, unsure how to react.

'Come on in, meet the family; the kittle jus' boiled, d'ye drink tay?'

I'm sorry?' said Daniel.

'Sorry tea, T-E-A; we call it tay.'

Mark chuckled. 'Of course, sorry about our ignorance. We're city boys.'

'Shur nobody's perfect.' Joe wheezed with laughter. 'Come in, come in. See if you can get that wheelchair up this ramp I built. I copied the sthyle off the one at the doctor's clinic downtown. The same kind I used for yur bunkhouse

292

there.' Joe pointed to the cabins. 'We'll check it out after a drop a tay, see if it's good enough for ya. Come on.' Joe shot up the stairs, watching Mark ascend the ramp unabated. 'Jaysus, that's a fine wagon you got there, hah?' He marvelled at the chair.

'It gets me where oi want to go.'

'I'd say so.' Joe disappeared into the house, followed by Mark and Daniel.

They followed Joe into the hallway. Joe stopped at the foot of the stairs and shouted up for whoever was up there to come down and meet the new guests. Mark's attention was pulled to the portrait sitting on the table in the hall, he recognized Joe in it, but he looked young, much younger than the man standing in front of him.

'Is this your family?' said Mark.

Joe glanced over and picked up the portrait, staring at it with glassy eyes for a moment. 'It is yeh; that's me fadder Tommy, me mudder Maggie, my brother Matthew and me.' He pointed to each one. 'This picture was taken two years before me fadder died.' Joe blinked away a tear.

Daniel, who hated awkward pauses, chimed in: 'You look just like him.'

Joe smiled weakly. 'Yeh think so? I would be happy if I were half the man he was.'

The creaking stairs amplified two sets of footsteps descending. All three of them turned around to the source of the sound.

Joe boomed out merrily: 'Here they are now. This is my daughter Caoimhe,' he said, pointing to a teenage girl; she had curly shoulder-length brown hair, it looked ginger in some lights. She had her mother's grey eyes and freckled nose. 'and this is my son Mark.' A young boy with short black hair and grey eyes followed his sister down the stairs. 'Jaysus, yer name is Mark too.' He laughed, slapping Mark's arm. 'Kids, this is Mark O'Brien and his friend Daniel Bloom. These are the lads I was talking about that will be staying with us for a while; say hello.'

'Hello,' they chorused awkwardly. Caoimhe waved with a bandaged hand.

'Honey, what happened to your little paw?' Joe said while examining Caoimhe's hand.

'Nothing, dad. I just scratched it playing outside.' She pulled her hand away abruptly and continued to the kitchen, followed by Joe, who couldn't help being inquisitive about his daughter's injury.

Mark followed but couldn't help himself goggling at Mark's wheelchair. He had never seen anything so alien in his life and was fascinatedly fixated on this phenomenon.

'Hello, Mark.'

'Hello Mark.' They both laughed.

'Have you ever seen a motorized wheelchair before?'

Mark shook his head.

'It is a pretty cool machine. How old are you, boy?'

Mark stuck up all his fingers.

'Ten? That's a great age. Come on. We'll go into the kitchen for that cup of tea.'

They passed through to the kitchen. Mark ran by Mark to sit in his seat at the table. Caoimhe was already sitting at the table beside another man. The man got up silently and approached Mark and Daniel. He shook both their hands vigorously, studying them with his careful green eyes.

'Hello there,' Mark said.

-silence-

Mark looked over to Joe, who was pouring tea and buttering some sandwiches.

'Oh, sorry.' He dropped the buttering knife to join Mark. 'This is me, brother Matthew. He's not able to speak.'

Mark smiled warmly at Matthew. It was then he realized Matthew had a very crude-looking scar across his neck. A very realistic fear grew in Mark's heart. *That was where his father cut his throat when he tried to kill him.* It was no longer a story he read in the paper. Now it became real. Daniel must have felt it, too; he shivered.

'Please help yourself to sit wherever you can fit.' Joe laughed and turned to his sandwiches.

Mark and Daniel took their places at the edge of the table. Mark was not able to tuck the wheelchair comfortably into the table, so he sat at an angle.

'Mary tea is ready. Come on in.' Joe shouted, moments later, there was a thumping sound coming from the hall. A controlled banging, like an adroit carpenter driving a nail. - boom... two beats of silence, boom... two beats of silence.

Mark and Daniel stared into the hall in breathless anticipation, waiting to see what kind of monstrosity would emerge.

It was a woman, a rather personable woman with flowy brown hair and a nose embellished with freckles. She looked like her daughter.

Joe gently held Mary's hand (not the one clutching the walking cane scouting for any displaced objects) and guided her to her seat. Mary wore a black bandana around her eyes. *I am sure I don't want to see what's under there.* Mark thought, knowing it would send a jolt of unexplainable fear through his body.

'Hello Mary, moi name is Mark O'Brien, and this is me friend Daniel Bloom. Thank you again for letting us stay at your home.

Mary's head rotated very accurately to Mark. 'My boy's name is Mark too, isn't it?' she laughed and turned her head to her son's seat, and young Mark made some kind of agreeable chuckle. 'It's always exciting to have visitors here, and you're from the city, I heard? You will have to tell me all about city life; is it as loud as the wireless makes it out to be?'

'Louder Ma'am,' said Daniel.

'Fascinating,' she whispered under her breath.

Joe approached the table, wheeling a breakfast cart that held plates of sandwiches and seven cups of tea. He began distributing cups of tea to everybody at the table with practised hands. Mary, he noticed, was impeccably drinking her tea and eating her sandwich with better coordination than he had. *She has adapted well to her missing sense.* Surely, she wasn't born like that. *No.* Something must have happened to her, like Joe and Matthew. Mark was both excited and fearful to learn the story.

The room was clouded in a thick quiet. The flame of the candle in the middle of the table wavered to and fro as if bending to the force of some unseen formidable power. Mark could almost feel Daniel's discomfort at the brooding silence through his staggering breath. Who was going to tear apart the peace? Mark thought. *Who is going to forfeit the quiet game?*

'So, how was the drive up here?' Joe said between bites.

'It was—'

'It was grand,' Daniel interrupted Mark. The awkward pause made him long for conversation. 'we were lucky enough, there was no traffic, and surprisingly the weather held together.'

'The weather held? Now that's a miracle for Ireland!' Joe roared out laughing, joined by his son.

'Definitely an anomaly,' said Mark.

'A-wha'? said Joe.

'Anomaly, it means something unexpected. Peculiar.'

Joe smiled warmly, and another silence breezed through the room.

About half an hour later, when the sandwiches were eaten, the tay was drunk, and the small talk was had. Mary sent Mark, Caoimhe, and Mathew up to bed. She stayed in the kitchen with Joe, Mark, and Daniel for a little while longer.

The candlelight began to diminish as silhouettes of monsters and formidable things smothered the light in the room. Joe went to the kitchen press and returned with a new candle, which he lit. It emitted a more powerful glow, filling the room with a particularly appropriate ambience for sinister conversation.

'I suppose yeh want the complete account from start to finish of our experience with the ba... the woman in the well,' Joe said, studying Mark.

Mark began flustering in his pockets. 'Oh, oi was expecting to start tomorrow, but no matter. Oi have it here somewhere. A-ha.' He produced a small book from his jacket pocket and a pen. glancing at the surprised look on Daniel's face, he smiled. 'All good writers always carry a diary with them, just in case.' The first thing he jotted in the diary was: *He won't refer to it as the banshee, rather the woman in the well. – Why? Fear?*

'I am not entirely sure how to do this.' Joe laughed awkwardly.

Mary squeezed his hand in hers reassuringly. 'Maybe if you start from the start?'

Joe smiled and looked to Mark for confirmation. He nodded. Joe began spinning his recollection of his traumatic history. Mark recorded interesting points in his diary while gasping and showing questionably spurious empathy. Daniel listened intently while watching the fear grow and waver in Joe's eyes as he reexperienced memories he had until then, blocked out. Mary also gasped at parts of the story she never heard and subconsciously rubbed Joe's arm to comfort him and begged him to say no more than he was comfortable with when his voice faltered. The candle had to be replaced two more times in the telling of the story. The moon was falling from the sky, about to be given leave for the night from the sun.

The smoke of the candle buried the kitchen in a light cloud of and a perfume of burned-out conversation. Daniel struggled to keep his eyes open, and his head was uncontrollably lulling to his chest, making him jump in alert. It was difficult to tell if Mary was awake or asleep. She was sitting perfectly still. Her eyes were wrapped up. Mark was fighting off exhaustion, trying to hold his incredibly heavy eyelids open by rolling his eyes with every yawn. Joe looked like the only one who wasn't tired. In fact, Joe looked like he was not going to sleep for the next week. His eyes were wide and bloodshot, his body was asleep, but his mind and his fear were not.

'It's very late. I think we should go to bed,' Daniel moaned through a yawn.

'Excellent idea,' Mark agreed, his haggard face seeping with gratitude that Daniel was here to suggest a recess. 'we will pick this up tomorrow, or whenever you're feeling up to it.' Stuffing his diary back in his pocket along with his pen and stretching his cramped hand.

'O-rhi', but wait here a minute, I have to get Mary into bed. I will show ye to yer cabin.' Joe gently roused Mary and told her he was taking her to bed. With no reluctance, she swung her arm around Joe's neck, and he led her up to bed.

'It's no problem, sir. We will find it ourselves,' said Daniel.

'No, I insist,' Joe said, momentarily pausing.

Mark and Daniel exchanged a tired, bemused look and waited quietly for Joe to return.

In what seemed like an eternity later, Joe returned downstairs and met Mark and Daniel in the hallway.

'Sorry for keeping you up,' Joe said. The sound of heavy rain hammered the windows. They stepped outside onto the porch.

The orchard was slowly being lit by the waking sun. Darkness still crept in the open fields. A heavy layer of fog swam along the ground as the rain continued to deluge, intensifying the mist. No birds sang, no critters complained about the rain. There was a very unsettling silence crushing the orchard. A silence Mark could somehow feel.

'Right,' said Joe, 'see the closest cabin there? That's where we're going. Should we just run?' He caught a glimpse of Mark in the wheelchair. 'Just go as quick as we can, I mean.'

Mark was too tired to tell Joe he didn't mind the "run" comment. He had heard worse. 'D'ya have a towel or something?' he said. 'Anything oi can cover the panel with, so the rain doesn't get to it.' He pointed to the control panel of his wheelchair.

Joe retreated inside and returned moments later with a small rag and handed it to Mark.

'Ya ready, lads?' said Joe hiding a smirk.

Daniel and Mark nodded. they lined up, side by side on the porch, ready to make this 200-meter dash through the ice-cold rain to their cabin. 'GO!' Joe boomed. All three of them took off, tearing through the wall of water. In the middle of their run, a flash of lightning lit up the sky, a terrifying pale white, illuminating all the dark shapes lurking in the darkness, followed swiftly by a ground-shaking rumble of thunder, which hastened their journey.

Joe reached the door first and pushed it open, followed by Daniel and then Mark, who confirmed that Joe's DIY wheelchair ramp worked. Once they were all standing in the relatively small living room, Joe decided to show them around.

'This is the living room. You've got a small kitchen over there in the corner; the cupboards are empty. There's a shop downtown a few miles away that way. You have a kettle and running water. The bedroom is that way. There are two single beds.' Joe turned to Mark. 'You can push them together if you would like.' He winked.

Mark was much too tired to explain his and Daniel's relationship. He just shook his head.

'The outhouse is out behind the cabin., I have put a rail at the toilet. Yeh can let me know tomorrow if it needs adjusting for you.' He ended with a sigh.

'Well, thank you so much, Joe, for everything. We will see you tomorrow and hopefully learn a bit more.'

Another crack of thunder shook the windows, making them all stir uneasily.

Daniel helped Mark to bed.

'Goodnight, Dan.'

'Noite,' Daniel responded through a yawn.

Seconds later, they were in a dream they would unfortunately remember tomorrow. A few hours later, a blood-freezing scream echoed around the quiet orchard; waking everybody up with a jolt, they all felt terribly afraid, not understanding why. There was only one man who knew why they should all be afraid. A man who lay in bed haunted by memories of a malignant being. He was not surprised to hear the scream. He did not forget what it was. He never wanted to admit it, but deep down, he knew sooner or later he would come face to face with her again. He clutched his scared wife in his arm and comforted her. She wept softly between sleepiness and a half-forgotten fear. It then occurred to Joe; Mary also remembered what it was.

X VIII BLOOD AND SILVER

The next time he opened his eyes, the room was significantly brighter; a few hours had passed, but it was still very early in the morning. Figuring there was not much point lying in bed, turning and twisting and sweating any longer, he decided to get up and maybe take a walk to relax his nerves.

Joe carefully climbed out of bed, cautious not to wake Mary,
he slipped on his faded blue jeans and his green plaid shirt. He threw on his brown wellingtons and tiptoed down the stairs, prudently dispensing his weight on the stairs as not to pressure the creaky steps. When he reached the bottom of the stairs, he made his way to the kitchen. He thought about making himself breakfast and a cup of tea. *No, I'm not hungry. H*e sat down at the table where his father once sat and gazed out the window. Watching the early sunlight creeping along the fields shining on the water droplets in the grass, remnants of the cold night's condensation, making the green fields look like they were littered with sparkling glass.

A strange whim came over Joe, more like a powerful urge, a desire he had not felt for many a year; he wanted to go to the glade in the woods and see if the Fairies ever came back. It was not that he missed them per se, but the scream of the banshee had awoken his most unrelenting fear: *she is back, and there is no way for me to stop her this time.* Not even with the golden dagger, which he had kept in a safe in his closet, feeling he would need it someday but hoping he wouldn't. Temptation hounded him some nights when he thought about how much money he could get for that dagger to the right hands and how far that money would go toward the orchard, but no, what if he needed it someday, what if she came back. But he could not perform the ritual to banish her again. The tablet was sent down the well with her. *Maybe it's at the bottom of the well. Maybe I just have to climb down and get it and banish her all over again.*

His back ached just climbing the stairs, and his legs were not as pliant as they once were, plus the mere memory of the Underworld in the well terrified Joe. He felt if he ever had to go there again, he would not come back. How did she get out, he wondered? He tried his best to remember what the fairies had told him.

(only the blood of a McNeeve could break the spell)

I haven't been near the well for years –' then, like a hot knife through the brain, a horrendous thought festered. *'Caoimhe!'* She had cut her hand playing outside yesterday. Surely, she wasn't playing by the well. After all the warnings he gave his children about never going near it, surely his daughter didn't cut her hand on the boards covering up the well, surely a few drops of her blood didn't seep through the cracks: unleashing a most terrible curse.

He laughed. *Of course, she didn't. I'm just imagining it again,* but there was only one way to be sure. He had to check it out for himself. Joe stood up, trembling a bit. This wasn't the first time he had thought he heard the scream or imagined seeing the banshee. But like every other time before that, he had to make one hundred per cent sure it was not just his post-traumatic stress disorder.

He stepped out onto the porch. The first thing to hit him was the unforgivable cold air that blew aggressively, cutting through everything in its path. The early morning clouds did their best to hide the sun as she got ready to warm up the world. Joe folded his arms and tucked them into his armpits shielding his chest from the cold wind. He shivered and made his way to the well. On his way there, he glanced over to the cabin where Mark and Daniel were staying and wondered if they had anything to do with— *no, no,* he thought *it is all in my head. She is not back; she can never come back. She is gone. Pull yourself together, Joe.*

Joe pressed on to the top of the hill until he was standing under the ancient oak tree; he stared up at it and was flooded by uncomfortable memories of Matthew playing on the tree after their father specifically told them never to go near the well. Then a thought hit him: *why did dad always forbid us to go near the well? Did he know about the banshee? No, he couldn't. Maybe he just thought it was dangerous? Yeah, that was it, right?* Doubts continued to enslave his mind until he trusted nothing.

He stood beside the well and peered down the hole, and to his shock, the wooden boards sealing off the well were shattered. The remaining bits and fragments of boards were slightly bent towards the top, meaning something was pulling at the boards trying to get into the well, or more unsettling, something in the well was pushing to get out. Joe continued to examine the scene with trembling hands and horror in his heart. On the rim of the well, on a jagged stone, there was a small bloodstain, dried blood, but it looked fresh enough, maybe a day old, maybe three days; there was no way of telling. But the dried blood trailed down into the deep dark of the well. Caoimhe was his first thought. She would never understand the gravity of what she had done. Joe could feel his heart beating like a war drum. He collapsed onto his knees and wept. *This can't be happening. It can't be. What am I going to do? We just about got rid of her the first time. She will kill us all.* Then he thought about his family with a sober mind. *No, she won't. If she threatens my family, I will kill her with my bare hands.* Adrenaline now pumped through Joe's veins. He thought about the fairies again and hoped maybe if the banshee was back, maybe they would be back too, but he doubted it. Still, it was worth a try.

Joe rose from his knees, made a fist out of his one hand. Courage burned through his body. She would not touch his family. He would not allow it. He could not feel the cold breeze anymore as he stormed into the woods behind his house to the fairy glade.

Joe felt as though he had not been through the woods in a lifetime. The skeletal shapes of naked trees filled him with dread. Just like the trees died this time of year, he too was very likely to die this autumn. He quickly shook that ostensible fear from his mind. The beaten track he had made in his youth was gone, it was grown over with weeds, and wild grass, The wet, dead leaves buried on the forest floor made the going slippery and crunchy. It was like walking on brown and orange ice. The path which was unfamiliar to Joe seemed a lot more strenuous to traverse under all of his awoken stress and fear. He did not even realize the deafening silence in the trees, how every step he made echoed through the woods like gunshots. He was oblivious, locked in a cell of this own imagination, hoping against hope that the fairies were there and they could help again.

Joe scrambled through the brambles and the defoliated shrubs of the circular thicket surrounding the glade. The once poignant scene of colourful flowers was barren. The crystal-clear blue pond where so many flowers and colours once bathed was poisoned with scum and dirt. Joe felt his heart drop into the pit of his stomach when he realized: he was alone. He thought this every time he came up here since he first dealt with the banshee, and still, every time, he convinced himself *maybe they were back now*. Joe walked over to the pond noticing the lack of the magical buzzing sound he·had been accustomed to hearing a long time ago. He was going to dip his head in the water as he had done before to transport himself to the fairy realm, but he stopped himself when he stared down at the fuliginous pond. It looked diseased. It looked like if Joe stuck his head in that water, he would be cursed, and he would be sick for the rest of his life.

Tears started in his eyes. He fell onto the squishy floor in the fetal position and wept. 'Please, please, somebody has to help me. I can't fight her again, please I'm begging you, anybody.'

Mark opened his eyes with great difficulty. That was not the most comfortable night sleep he had ever had. Every time he opened his eyes, the room seemed to be a tiny bit brighter, as if he was viewing a slideshow on the evolution of the sunrise on an old timber wall. He rubbed his sticky eyes and checked the time on his trusty pocket watch: 8:37. He rolled over on his opposite side with a grunt to face Daniel. Dan was either in a very deep sleep or perhaps dead, the former being more likely. Mark lay on his back and stared at the roof, trying to recall what had made him so afraid last night. Why had he woken up sweating and shaking? It was very uncharacteristic. The growing urge to go to the toilet quickly overwhelmed his comfort. He peeled off the bedsheets, slipped on his suit pants and shirt and his shoes. - he always slept with his socks on - And pulled himself onto his wheelchair, quietly leaving the room. While in the outhouse, he tested the rail Joe had installed at the toilet for Mark. It worked impeccably. He wondered if he had to install rails in the outhouse for his wife, Mary.

The hunger soon became unbearable, so he went to the press to fix himself up a nice country breakfast. When he opened it, he was met with a nettling reality; It was empty, completely empty, not even a crumb of bread. Mark felt slighted. He had paid an exorbitant fee for accommodation, and Joe wouldn't even supply a loaf of bread. He swiftly banished any odious thoughts of spite and checked his own suitcase, hoping he packed something he could eat. If not, he would have to starve until Daniel woke up and drove them into town, where they could buy some groceries. *Will the shop be open on a Saturday?* He was sure it would. Fumbling through his suitcase, he found his last bottle of wine, which was meant to be a gift to the McNeeve family, but since Joe didn't even have the decency to gift his visitors even an apple... on an orchard! Mark decided he would keep the wine. In case that was all he had for breakfast, there was no point in being frugal with the portion he would allow himself. This had not been the first time Mark had had alcohol for breakfast; like he always says: "'This will be the last time."'

The more wine he drank, the more discernible his nightmare the night prior had become:

he was running through a dark field towards a small stone wall. Rain beating down on his head, filling his eyes with water and blood, he was being chased by some... thing. He could feel its ice-cold breath spitting on the back of his neck. It was about to kill him, he just had to make it up the hill to the wall, but the closer he got, the more he realized it wasn't a wall; it was a well. Then whatever was behind him screamed. Not an ordinary high-pitched scream. This was a ear puncturing screech, not something you could just hear but something you could feel.

Now Mark remembered; the scream had woken him up, but the weird thing was even when he was awake, he could still hear it, and he could still feel it, he put it down to some sort of sleep paralysis; maybe some kind of homesickness. Slightly drunk from the wine and still shaking from his horrifying experience, Mark decided it was unjustifiably necessary to go check out the well he saw yesterday going into Joe's house, the one beside the big tree. He thought about writing a note for Daniel explaining where he was gone, but then he decided not to. He would only be outside.

Mark opened the door and rolled outside; he inhaled a deep breath of cold fresh air; it smelled like dying leaves with just a suggestion of apple. The chilling breeze gently murmured along with the distant squawking of crows. He surveyed the silent orchard. In the distance at the barn, a man with grey hair and a matching beard was pushing a wheelbarrow towards the field. Mark assumed that was Mr Conroy, the only farm hand who dared to work at the orchard. Mark read that Mr Conway was a convicted petty criminal who chose to work here instead of doing time in jail, but he didn't believe it. Still, he was happy keeping his distance.

On top of a hill, in a field beside the McNeeve mansion, was a thick, pale oak tree. It stood almost naked in the morning sun but still looked proud and strong. Beside the tree was an old abandoned well. Carefully placed moss-covered rocks were stacked on top of each other in a circle around this well. There didn't seem to be any sort of pulley system built onto the well with a bucket for the water, and if there was, it had been removed long ago. Mark wondered if there was any water at the bottom of the well. Maybe that was where the tree got all the water from to make itself huge and powerful.

The well gave off a sinister, almost evil aroma that Mark did not want to come into proximity with. The curiosity and the desperate desire for adventure carried him against his better judgment. He studied the terrain of the field for a moment, pondering if the wheelchair would get stuck in the wet grass. He figured it was quite possible, but it wasn't like he was exploring the hidden caves of The Grand Canyon. Somebody would see him. It was worth the risk.

The wheels on the chair slipped and struggled up the silver-coated hill. Once or twice Mark thought he got stuck, but the chair had some power behind it and refused to stop. Finally, he reached the well. He could hear a murmur. It sounded like whispers, but Mark being rational, swiftly decided it was just wind blowing in the well. An unprecedented shiver shot through his body when he looked down the well. Broken boards lay across it bent upwards, potentially meaning something very powerful was held against its will in the interminable darkness and had gotten out. Mark's pragmatic mind worked overtime to try to come up with a reason for this oddity. Maybe the strong wind forcing itself against the wood for years had finally won the fight and escaped. He nodded to himself. Looking down the seemingly bottomless pit of black, Mark wondered on how deep it was. *Is there anything down there?*

A strong feeling of being watched made his eyes shoot upwards. Staring at him from a nearby tree line was a shadowy figure. Mark waved at it and got no reply. A cry from the well sounding like a distressed plea for help, snatched his attention. He shouted down the well and was wrapped in silence. He then looked back up to the figure, but there was nobody there. Cautiously Mark approached where the figure was standing. His wheelchair skidded and tore at the wet soil as he went. He searched around aimlessly to find any trace of whatever he had just seen but found nothing unusual. After taking a note in his pad: *am I going crazy, or was there somebody here?* He slipped his notepad back in his jacket pocket with bemusement and looked back at the well. A cold sweat painted his forehead and made his body jolt with fright when his eyes detected what appeared to be a red-haired woman sitting on the well rim humming a song; it sounded more melancholy than eerie.

Mark floated back to the well, towards the song, like one who has been enchanted, oblivious to the wet soil trying to hold the wheelchair in place. When he was within talking distance of the woman, she stopped singing. Suddenly, she fell backwards into the well. Mark cried out in alarm. He hurried to the well, looking down, calling for the woman. While he stared down the well, the whispering started again, growing louder. He could make out the shape of a woman climbing slowly up the well. As she got closer to Mark, he realized her skin was decayed and rotten. She could not be human. She aimed a malicious stare at him, exposing a truly horrifying face behind the veil of streaming blood that was her hair; Mark could see terrible yellow eyes shot with red streaks. Her mouth opened abnormally wide, and she let out a spine-shivering, almost metallic scream. Mark, who was petrified, quickly plunged himself out of the shock instinct and tried to get away as quickly as possible. He tried to reverse from the well, but his wheelchair got stuck in the mud, forcing him to sit and watch this horrific act unravel. Mark tried everything to get his wheelchair mobile to no avail. A growling sound from the well made him freeze in terror as two hands emerged from the pit. Slowly, red hair came into view. The woman spilt out onto the ground in a heap. She was wearing a tattered green dress. She maintained unwavering eye contact. Her disgusting posture paralyzed Mark. Her head was locked in place staring at him, and her long limbs dislocated and relocated over and over again to propel her forward in a strange crawling motion. The sound of crepitating joints was mingled with wheezing as she approached Mark.

After what felt like a lifetime, she reached Mark; placing both her hands on each of his knees, she pulled herself up, so she was face-to-face with Mark. The banshee once again dropped her jaw and pierced Mark's skull with a scream. His eyes, a once bright curious hazel, were pale as if the scream had drained the colour from his eyes. When he opened his eyes, she was gone. The wheelchair escaped the clutching ground. Mark raced back to the cabin shouting for Daniel.

He was about to rush into Daniel and wake him and tell him what just happened to him, then he hesitated. *He's not going to believe me; I don't even believe me. Did that really happen?* Mark looked over to the table and saw his half-empty bottle of wine. He slapped himself in the forehead. *That didn't really happen*; he thought *it must have been the wine. That's the only reasonable possibility*. He vowed right there to never take another drink and decided not to wake Daniel or act like anything strange had happened to him. He pulled out the notepad from his pocket and began scribbling in it, thinking about the encounter he had just had. He assured himself it was just his drunken mind replaying the nightmare. He was imagining things. Things that didn't really happen. He needed to get a grip of himself and write down key points for his book; the book that would make him a famous author, the book that would finally earn him the much sought-after reverence from his father. There was no excuse. He had to write this story.

Daniel stepped out of the bedroom and spotted Mark sitting at the table. 'How long have you been up?' he said, stretching.

Mark shrugged his shoulders and continued to stare ahead, dreamily.

Daniel sat beside him and watched him quietly with concern. 'Are yiz alright? You haven't even been here a day, and the country life has got you bored to the point where you're staring at the wall.' He laughed.

'Yeah, oi'm fine,' he said at last, 'Oi'm just really hungry; there's no food here.'

'Ahh, stop! Nothing in there whatsoever?'

'Nope'

Daniel opened the cupboards and closed them with a slam. 'What does he expect us to eat?'

'Each other.' He laughed. 'He said there's a town a few miles away. Would you mind driving down to the grocery store and getting us some food we can live off?'

'Yeah, sure, I guess I'll have to,' he said reluctantly. 'Do you not want to come?'

'No, oi'm gonna stay here awhile see if oi can get started on me book.'

'Okay-dokey, I'll see you soon' Daniel headed off.

'You didn't hear a noise last night? Sort of like a scream?'

Daniel turned around; a bead of cold sweat stood on his brow. 'Now that you mention it. I do remember hearing something last night, like when you rub metal on metal. I thought somebody was in the room with us. Scared the holy hell out of me!' He laughed awkwardly. 'Wait, do you mean to say you heard it too? I thought it was just a dream, what do you think it was? A fox or something?'

'Oi don't even know what sound a fox makes.'

312

'Me neither. Anyway, my stomach is rumbling, boy. I better get these groceries. Is there anything yiz would like me to buy?'

Mark instantly thought of more alcohol but shortly expelled the notion. 'Nah, oi'm alri' cheers, just make sure you get bread and milk.'

Daniel saluted and left the cabin.

Mark continued to replay the encounter with the banshee over in his mind. *If it was just a nightmare, how did Daniel hear the scream too?* Thoughts became doubts, and doubts became fears. Mark brooded in silence for a while, listening to the engine of Daniel's car become quieter and quieter until it finally faded into nothing.

The sound of the petrol engine leaving her yard woke her up. She opened her eyes, but the world stayed black and dark. She gently let a hand fall on the vacant spot where her husband slept. Sitting up in bed for a moment, she began rubbing her throbbing head, shaking slightly and trying to remember what happened to her last night. She had been woken with her heart beating against her chest like a hammer on an anvil. Suddenly it came back to her. It was... *her.* No, it couldn't be. She just imagined it again; it would not be the first time. The last thing Mary ever saw on this earth was the yellow, bloodshot eyes of the horrific demon before it stabbed her eyes out. The image of the banshee smiling at her, holding her with long, sharp dagger-like fingers was the last thing she saw so. Naturally, she remembered the image every day, and every time she heard tyres screeching on the road or Joe whistling for the horses or any high-pitched screeching sound, she immediately remembered the malignance of the banshee.

The Banshee

She sat on the side of the bed and pulled on her brown polka dot dress. She could not tell if it was backwards or not, and she cared nothing of it. She slipped on her shoes and tied her black bandana around her eyes. She groped for her walking stick, getting up from the bed and she stepped out into the hall, barely using the stick. She knew the layout of her house so well she didn't need her eyes to navigate it. She stopped outside of Mark's bedroom and knocked lightly, no response. He must still be asleep. She continued down the hall a bit to Caoimhe's bedroom and again knocked gently. 'Morning, mum, I am awake. I'll be down in a minute.'

Mary continued her journey to the top of the stairs; she inhaled deeply before descending.

Christmas day 1953, Mary was making her way downstairs that morning to join her children and her husband in the sitting room under the Christmas tree opening the presents Santa gifted them. When her mind was momentarily distracted, she misplaced her foot. Falling painfully down the stairs, thankfully, she did not break any bones or succumb to any serious injuries, but it nested a fear, a fear that would serve as a precaution when she thought about using the stairs anymore.

Using her walking stick to precisely measure the drop in each step, she carefully planted one foot before the other in a slow, methodical way, before finally reaching the bottom. She continued to the kitchen.

She carefully waved her arms around the countertop until they found the kettle. It felt a bit light, so she filled it with water from the tap before placing it on the stove. It didn't take long to figure out how to use the stove blind; experience is the best teacher, after all. While the kettle was boiling, she moved over to the press and opened it. Feeling inside for a bottle of milk, she found it and took it out. Next, she opened the breakfast cabinet and pulled out a box of cereal she assumed was Bran Flakes. She had learned to always taste test if she was not sure, after one horrible morning when she poured orange juice into her Weetabix instead of milk. She sniffed the tea bags to confirm it was tea she was holding and dropped them into cups. Two cups because Caoimhe was on her way down. When everything was ready, she carried them over to the kitchen table and broke her night-long fast.

Caoimhe ambled into the kitchen and kissed her mother on the cheek. 'Morning, mammy.'

'Good morning, sweetie; I have made you a cup of tea; it's over there.' She pointed to the stove. 'How did you sleep?'

Mary could not see it, but Caoimhe's eyes widened at this question as if she recalled a horrifying memory. She stumbled silently over to the stove, got her tea, poured herself a bowl of Bran Flakes, and joined Mary at the table.

'I had a really scary dream last night,' she said at last, 'But I can't remember it now. I just remember waking up in the middle of the night, sweating. I dreamt I could hear a loud scream.'

Mary was silent.

'It was just a scary dream, but it felt so real at the time. Do you ever get dreams like that, mom?'

Mary sat quietly, deep in remuneration, frowning under her bandana. She wanted to speak honestly with her daughter, but she wouldn't dare frighten her child with the traumas of her past.

'Yes, I get them too sometimes. They are only dreams, sweetheart. Dreams can't hurt you.' She delivered the last

315

line with whatever confidence she could muster, which wasn't a lot.

'Mark is still asleep, is he?'

'I guess he is. I knocked on the door, and he never answered.'

'He is so lazy.' She laughed. 'What about dad? Is he still asleep?'

'No, your father was not in bed. I don't know where he's gone. He probably went out to check on the horses again. It wouldn't be the first time Joe snuck out of bed early to start some jobs around the orchard.

'Have you and Mark finished your homework for Monday?

'Not yet. I will do it later after my chores,' she answered between bites.

'Good girl.' Mary smiled. 'Them lads woke me up this morning driving away in that loud car of theirs.'

'What do you make of them, Mama?'

Mary honestly answered: 'I don't know what to make of them, city boys. They are quite handsome, though.' She laughed and smiled at Caoimhe, who returned a guilty giggle. 'Please tell me they're handsome at least?'

'I suppose they're cute enough.' Caoimhe laughed like a little girl. 'But I wouldn't know I'm only sixteen.'

'That's my girl. There will come a time when boys will be breaking your heart every day.' She smiled weakly. 'Like me now, your father and your brother have my heart broken. Where is Mark? He should be up by now.'

'He is probably still very tired after all that walking around he did last night.'

'Walking around?'

'Yeah, I could hear him walking around the house after my scary dream woke me up. I thought somebody broke into our house, but then I heard him mumbling to himself, so I figured he was just getting up for a cup of water or something.

Mary hoped her true feeling of panic and concern didn't show on her face. There was no way *she* could be connected to these happenings in any way. She was gone, banished by her and Joe. Still, superstition gnawed at her heart. 'Caoimhe dear, would you ever check on Mark for me, see if he's still in bed?'

Caoimhe got up and went upstairs, Mary following her every footstep in her mental map. Shortly after, she came downstairs and stood in the kitchen.

'He's not up there.' Her voice was as calm as if she was reporting on a misplaced can of beans. 'Matthew hasn't seen him either. Maybe he went out with dad?'

Mary's soul turned to ice. 'Yeah, maybe he did.' *But maybe that wasn't just a dream we had last night. Maybe we are all in grave danger.* 'Come with me outside. We will go looking for them.' A terrifying fear pooled in Mary's stomach: *I hope Mark is not in danger. I hope she didn't get him.*

When he had just exited the tree line behind the house, he heard his name being called. Wiping his moist eyes, he looked up to see his daughter Caoimhe waving at him, linking his wife in her arm. He made his way over to them.

'What brings you out here today?' he said, trying to sound cheerful.

'Is Mark with him?' said Mary.

'No.'

'Mark?' Confusion mixed with worry as Joe read the mood of the group. 'Mark was never with me. Is he not in the house?'

317

'No, he's not. Caoimhe said she heard him last night walking around the house, and now he is not there.'

Joe's eyes widened. He managed a hunch at what might have happened to his son, but he prayed he was wrong. He didn't want to say anything to his wife to worry her, but judging by the tone of her voice, she had the same thought as he did. *She is back, and she has taken my son.* 'Okay, we won't get anywhere by panicking. Caoimhe, you said you heard him in the house last night. What time roughly can you remember?'

I heard him mumbling to himself and walking around the house after I had that scary dream. I would say it was six-ish o'clock.' Her voice was damaged and shaking from stressed nerves.

'What scary dream?'

'There was a woman.' Caoimhe choked back tears, 'a woman with red hair. She was chasing me—' Her voice was broken apart with sobs. 'She chased me up to the well, and then she screamed at me, a really loud scream. I could still hear her when I woke up.' She fell into her father's arms, crying.

Joe comforted his daughter in a warm hug. 'You heard a scream last night?' Caoimhe's crying told Joe everything he needed to know, he had heard the scream too, and Mary had heard it, judging by her sullen facial expression. The banshee was back, and she had taken his son. Joe did not know for sure, but he had an idea where his son might be. Just to hammer the last nail into the coffin, he had to make sure. 'Were you playing by the well yesterday, and did you cut your hand messing with the boards?'

Caoimhe was frantically crying, but through her sobs, Joe could feel her head nodding.

'Sweetheart, I thought I told you to never go near that well?'

'I didn't mean to—' The sobbing died down enough for Joe to understand what she was saying. 'A woman was sitting there yesterday. She called me over to her, then she disappeared. I was trying to move some boards to find her, but I cut my hand. I am so sorry, Papa.'

'Joe hugged her even tighter. *Wait, how could she have been out of the well before the blood set her free?* 'Can you remember what this woman looked like?'

-sob- 'She was beautiful daddy, like a princess. Her hair was almost touching the floor, and it was shiny silver.'

'Silver?' Joe asked, taken aback. 'Are you sure it wasn't red?'

'No, it was definitely silver. She was singing a kind of sad song; I couldn't hear the words, but it made me want to cry.'

Mary fumbled her way over to them and reached out her hand to comfort her daughter.

'We had better look for Mark immediately. Maybe he's just hiding somewhere playing a trick on us.' A tenuous smile wrinkled her face, hoping that would be enough to calm her daughter down. 'Caoimhe dear, why don't you look for him inside again? I must speak with your father, privately.' She heard the footsteps of Caoimhe hurry away, growing quietly into silence. 'Is she gone?' Mary whispered to Joe. Yup, he muttered. 'What do we do, Joe? We don't have the strength to fight her again.'

'I know. I can't believe this has happened.'

'Why didn't you listen to me when I told you to destroy the well!'

'I tried!' He lowered his voice from a scream, 'there's some kind of dark magic that lies in that well, no matter what

I tried, I couldn't move any of the stones, anything I built on top of it, even if I tried to cover it with stones, they just rolled off; it wasn't natural. All I could do was board up the hole.' He took a deep breath. 'There is no point in standing here arguing. Our son is missing; he could be in great danger. What are we going to do? There's no point calling the police. They will never help us; they think we're cracked.'

'Joe, don't say that.'

'But they do. They won't help us. I'm telling you nobody around here will.' He stood up as straight as he could. 'I need to go down the well.'

'No, absolutely not!'

'It's the only way, Mary, unless you have any better ideas?'

Mary pondered in silence for a moment. 'Them lads what came yesterday.' Mary lowered her voice. 'Don't you find it strange this all happened the day they arrived?'

Joe's face twisted into disbelief. 'Mary, for goodness' sake, you can't believe they have anything to do with this?'

Mary shrugged her shoulders. 'I'm just saying it's strange.'

The more he thought about it, the more it seemed logical. *Maybe they do know something about it.* 'Alright, I will talk to them and see what I can find out. We need to find our boy as soon as we can. Caoimhe is checking the house. After I finish speaking with Mark, I will search the whole grounds. He will be alright; do you hear me?' Joe squeezed his wife in his arms. 'I won't let anything happen to our boy.'

Mary began sobbing. 'I can't do anything to help.' Her bandana was slowly saturated with blood and tears. 'Why couldn't I be deaf rather than blind? I have never even seen my children.' She wailed uncontrollably. 'Can you believe that, Joe? I have never seen my children, and I never will!'

Joe patted her heaving back and adopted a sombre voice. 'Listen to me, sweetheart, you are the bravest and strongest woman in the world. I wish—' Joe's swallowed a painful truth that tore all the way down his throat. 'I wish it was me that the banshee blinded. But it wasn't. If it were me, I would not have survived, but you did, and you went on to raise a family, a family that loves you and think you to be some sort of superhero. You don't need to see your children to be a great mother. You always feel how they're feeling. You are always there for them. And we will continue to be there for them and keep them safe. You and me together, we are an unstoppable team. Please, honey, never think of yourself as a liability. Without you, I would crumble. Without you, we would all crumble.' He gently traced away the tear line on her face with his thumb. 'You are my strength, honey. Please, please don't give in on me now. I need you to be strong, so we can keep our family safe.

She swallowed her sadness and nodded her head with a dawning smile.

'I will bring you inside, keep Caoimhe and Matthew calm. We will speak again when I look around the orchard.'

I will get myself back, don't worry. She brandished her stick.

Just then, the humming muffle of Danial's car came into earshot. Joe looked towards it.

'That's them now,' said Mary. 'Speak with them. Hopefully, they will know where Mark is.' Joe planted a dry kiss on her cheek and left her, jogging heavily towards the cabins.

Daniel stepped out of the car and dragged a basket replete with groceries by his side. He caught sight of Joe trudging towards him against the wind. He stuck his arm up in the air and waved his hand at Joe. 'Hello there, Joe, how are ye this morning?'

Joe didn't answer until he was two feet away. Puffing and panting harshly, he managed to speak between gasps. 'You haven't seen Mark, have you?'

'Yeah.' Daniel was bemused by Joe's concern. 'He asked me to go downtown and get some groceries for breakfast because there was absolutely nothing in the cabinets.' Daniel's comment had taken a bitter tone against his intentions.

'What?' Joe crinkled his eyes against the beaming sunlight. 'No, not your Mark, my boy Mark. He has been missing since this morning. Is there any chance Mark would have seen him?'

'I'm not sure. We could ask him. Would you like me to go into town and get the Gardaí?'

By this time, Joe was already halfway into the cabin and did not hear Daniel or chose not to.

When Joe entered the musty room, he saw Mark sitting at the table. The sunshine glaring through the window exaggerated the millions of dust particles floating around the air like bubbles in dirty water. Mark did not seem to notice Joe and Daniel enter the cabin. His stare was fixated on some unseen world where people spoke in colours and bled in words. Daniel approached the press and began storing some groceries in it while preparing scrambled eggs for breakfast for himself and Mark.

Joe stood behind him and cleared his throat to get Mark's attention; he didn't budge. Joe decided to sit down next to him and lightly tap him on the shoulder. Mark ever so slowly rotated his head to Joe but kept his eyes locked on the wall where they were.

'I'm sorry to bother you before breakfast, but have you by any chance seen my son this morning?'

Mark continued staring at the wall in an enchanted kind of way. He slowly murmured: 'How did you lose your arm?'

'Mark!' Daniel turned around from the counter, disgusted by his friend's candour.

Joe turned a surprised white then morphed back into his exhausted verging on angry, red. 'Have you seen my son this morning or not?' Joe's rage tightened his pitch into a manly falsetto.

'Oi haven't seen him... but oi know where he is.'

'Where?' Joe was rapidly getting vexed by whatever game Mark was playing. 'Damn it, man, you tell me where my boy is, or I'm gonna make you wish you were never born!'

Mark brandished an evil, smug smile. 'You must understand your son is dead. Your daughter is dead, your wife and you and me and Daniel. You have killed us all.'

Joe's jaw was almost scratching the table surface in disbelief of the attitude his guest was showing him. He pretended he had no idea what Mark was talking about, but deep down, he knew what he meant, and he didn't want to admit it, but deep down, he knew he was right.

'Speak plainly, or I'm going to lose me temper!'

Daniel ignored the scrambling eggs and paid his undivided attention to the conversation.

'Oi saw her today. She showed me things, things she has done and things she is going to do, because of you.'

'What did I do?' he asked, already knowing the answer.

'You didn't kill her. Now she has come back to finish what she has started.'

'Kill me,' Joe answered in a whisper.

'No, not just kill you. She wants you to suffer for the rest of time for stopping her from becoming more powerful than any other fairy.'

Joe gulped a mouthful of stress. 'Where. Is. My. Son?'

Marks' cold eyes shot to Joe's. 'He is with her, of course, waiting, waiting for you to show up and save him.'

Joe got to his feet and stormed out of the cabin.

When the thundering footsteps faded into the whistling wind, Daniel sat down across from Mark.

'What the bloody hell was all that about?' he asked with the little patience he had left. 'Speaking pure and utter garbage and threatening our host? What are you doing, Mark?' a squeaky rage strangled his voice.

'Daniel, we should never have come here. We have been dragged into something, something we can't escape from.' Mark slowly slipped out of his enchanted state.

'What can't we escape from? Why can't we just get in the car and go?'

'One often meets their destiny on the road to avoid it.'

'What are you talking about? You're starting to scare me. Are you saying the story was true this whole time? About the banshee. You told me it wasn't real, and it wasn't dangerous.'

'Well, oi didn't think it was, but now oi know it is real. And it is dangerous.'

'So, what are we going to do? I have a family, Mark!'

'We have to find a way to help Joe get rid of her once and for all.'

Daniel stared at Mark, who stared out the window with his chest puffed out.

X IX GUARDIAN ANGEL

The whistling wind swept thick raindrops against the dusty window. The setting sun shrouded the naked trees in a golden cloak. Joe stared through the window, watching the fragile water droplets shatter on the soil, hydrating the earth. It's been five days since his son Mark had disappeared, five days of relentless searching around the orchard, chasing a ghost it felt like. The sharp clicks of Mark snapping his fingers to regain Joe's attention broke the heavy silence. Mark had a pen and a notepad in his hands, and he was watching Joe intently while Daniel had his nose stuck in a book about the fairies, which Mark had packed to brush up on his folklore.

'So, what exactly did they say to you, Joe, can you remember?'

'I told you ten times already everything I remember!' he replied briskly and venomously, wiping his exhausted eyes. Understandably Joe hadn't slept properly since his son disappeared. He was completely enervated, like batteries that had been worn out and recharged over and over again, only Joe never got a chance to recharge. He was so tired and worried. The nightmares wouldn't him to sleep; it seemed like only adrenaline fueled his body at this point. He existed in a state between consciousness and sleep. The world felt like it was zooming in high acceleration past his eyes, yet he himself could not keep up with it. His mind seemed to lag behind. Every sound felt like an echo from a large empty room in a different world.

The Banshee

'It says here,' Daniel read from the book, 'when the Milesians first settled in Ireland, they contended with the Tuatha Dé Danann until they decided to divide Ireland into two halves: the top half, taken by the Milesians and the bottom half or the other world taken by the Tuatha Dé Danann, or the fairies.

'It is said that any Irish family who can trace its roots back to the Milesians was gifted a banshee (fairy woman) as a sign of respect and peace from the fairies. These banshees were not harbingers of death, as some stories claim. Instead, she is meant to be a gentle spirit whose sole purpose is to notify the family they were assigned to of death of somebody close.' Daniel paused to flip the page and take a drink of water. 'Although many people claim to have heard or seen the banshee, she is not a very common spirit to behold, mostly because the amount of true Irish families are dwindling.

'Nobody knows for sure what a banshee looks like. They adopt many different forms depending on the news they bear. If a young girl dies in a family, she takes on the form of a beautiful young woman. If an old woman dies, she takes on the form of an old crone clad in black. If she is bringing news of somebody who will die, she—'

'Alri' Dan, we get it. Does it say anything about a well? Or where is she might dwell?'

Daniel paged through the book, scanning every word on the page with his restless eyes. 'I'm not seeing anything.'

'You won't,' Joe interjected at last. 'This is not an ordinary banshee. When I was speaking with the fairies, they told me that she was a malevolent spirit who only wanted power to destroy the fairies and my family, probably all Irish families, now that I think about it.'

'So, you must be a descendent of the Milesians?' Daniel broke in with amazement and reverence.

326

'Yeah. I remember reading that in a book once.' Suddenly, Joe's haggard mind stretched back to the day he sat on his bed reading the book about the banshee before it combusted in black flame. He shuddered. 'Any Irish family with a surname beginning with O', Mc, or Mac is a true Irish family, and more than likely have a banshee.' His lethargic eyes rose to meet Mark's. 'You are O'Brien, right? Your family should have a banshee.

Daniel's jaw dropped as he slowly pivoted his head to Mark. Mark sat there silently, pale as an empty cloud, his mind racing through his past to find some memory to corroborate Joe's theory. His eyes widened, confirming his mind had fixated on a memory of the O'Brien banshee. The night his mother died.

'You have a banshee too, don't you?' Joe was now leaning towards Mark with a bright glitter of hope burning in his eyes.

Mark nodded his head in disbelief. How could he have had a banshee all his life and not have realized it? He supposed his rational mind always debunked any sightings of her to realistic thoughts.

'Have you ever spoken with her?'

'No, at least not that oi know of.'

Joe grunted as he turned this new information over in his mind. 'Maybe she can help us. But how do we communicate with her.' Joe rubbed his chin as he recalled all encounters with his banshee and the fairies, trying to determine a parallel factor in all such cases.

'Have you got anything that is somehow connected with the fairy world?' Daniel asked.

'Not that I know of, as far as I can remember I didn't...' Joe's face split in half with a wide smile. 'The dagger! They give me a golden dagger! When I used it, I was able to wound the banshee. Maybe if you touch it, Mark, they will come to you.' It was a foolish hope, and Joe didn't believe it would work, but they had to try something before he could even process any linear train of thought. He was already halfway up the stairs to his room to get the dagger from his safe.

'Are you alri' Mark?'

Mark's complexion was almost transparent, His eyes were almost sinking into the back of his head, and his hands were trembling. 'Oi... oi can't believe oi...'

Daniel gently squeezed his shoulder.

'How could oi be so ignorant? Oi have been seeing her and hearing her all me bleedin' life. Oi always assumed it was something rational, like sleep deprivation or the drink messin' with me head. All this time... she came to me the night my mother died, Dan.'

Daniel could see the mere memory of Mark's mother machete its way through his heart. He was choking on the pain.

'Oi Always thought it was a dream oi had, oi can still remember it so vividly. Mam went out to her friends' birthday party fifteen years ago; it must've happened around eleven or twelve o'clock that night. Oi could hear this... crying, a sort of keening wail coming from outside. It was dark, and oi was scared, but oi looked anyway; oi peeled back the curtain and looked outside into the pitch-black night. It was so dark the yard was barely lit up by a lazy moon, but there was just enough light to see into the immediate yard, and if oi squinted, oi could see the tree line in the woods just beyond the gate.

'There was a very gentle pitter-patter of rain against the windowpane; oi remember looking at my reflection in the glass, the water droplets all around my silhouette, it looked like oi was some kind of giant, in space with loads of stars around my body.' He smiled like a child. 'But the sound of a woman screaming in pain and sadness soon roused me from that childish fantasy.

'At first, oi thought it was me mother, maybe she was locked outside, and she was crying because she was wet and cold, but no matter how hard oi searched oi could not find her. Oi could not pinpoint where the sound was coming from. It was very strange, Dan, it sounded like it was coming from outside, but there was nothing there, nobody was crying. The more oi looked around. The more oi presumed it was just in me head, and maybe oi was the one crying because oi was tired. Oi know it made no sense, Dan, but I was only ten. Then oi remember seeing something: a woman, a white woman. Oi'm not just referring to the colour of her skin. She was all white, glowing even. Oi thought it was an Angel. Her long, streaming silver hair seemed to float behind her as she glided from tree to tree. Oi, remember she stopped crying and shot a glance at me through the window. Oi couldn't make out her face, but oi knew she was looking at me, into me very soul it felt like. Then there was a flash of lightning, and she was gone.

'Oi ran back to bed, shaking with terror, oi was shook like a hand at mass Dan, and that's when—' Mark broke off, he was not speaking anymore, but Daniel could see the story unravel in his eyes, revisiting a long-forgotten denouement. He stared at the table as if the words to express his memory were carved into it, but only he could see them. 'Oi was lying in bed, and that's when oi could hear footsteps slapping down the hall, growing louder as they stopped outside my room. Me mind was telling me it was Nick or Calvin playing a prank on me, trying to scare me again, so oi tried to shout out and tell em to go away, but the words got caught in a ball in me throat. Oi was so afraid. The handle ever so gently got pushed down.

329

The Banshee

The door carefully squealed open. The room began to fill, with a bright ghost light coming from the hall., lighting up the corners even the sun couldn't reach. When the light touched me, oi wasn't afraid anymore. In fact, oi felt comforted. Then, shrouded in the bright light, a figure hovered into my room towards me. It was a woman. A woman oi had never saw but it felt like oi known her all me life. It was the same woman oi seen in the cabin when we first arrived. The same woman oi have been seeing all me life, her long silvery hair cascading down her beautiful figure, her bright blue angel eyes, her mellifluous voice. Oi can't believe oi ever forgot about her, Dan.

'Well, oi mean oi didn't forget about her, oi just thought it was a dream. All this time oi convinced meself it was a dream when in reality she has always been me guardian angel.' Mark smiled in a way Daniel had never seen before. He didn't just look happy he looked as content as anybody could ever be, like he finally answered a riddle he had got years ago. His face was not wide enough to fabricate a smile to mirror his satisfaction. 'She sat down beside me in bed and cradled me while singing in me ear; it was a soft, beautiful hymn, oi couldn't understand the words, but oi knew it was a sorrowful lament, only when she sang it oi wasn't able to feel sad. The warmness of her touch told me she would look after me for the rest of me life. Tears were trickling down her perfect cheeks, between that and the song she was singing, oi couldn't understand it, Daniel, but oi felt her purpose. She was telling me my mother had passed and that she would always protect me. I felt a deep struggle of happiness and sadness.

'Then she disappeared into a puff of smoke, it sounded like the flapping of dove's wings, and she was gone. Oi was alone. The next morning my dad was crying in the kitchen with Calvin and Nick, oi found out my mother had been killed in an attempted robbery at the party. She was stabbed to death for not going with a gang of strangers. Oi, guess they figured she was the key to our family's wealth. She wasn't.' Mark's smile vanished into the grave memory of his mother's funeral. 'Oi never saw her again, the Angel. At least oi didn't think so, but really oi did, but oi never believed it was her. She wasn't real she was only a dream, a magnificent dream I had when my mother died.

'But now it all makes sense. She is not my guardian angel. She is a banshee, the O'Brien banshee. And she will keep me safe; oi just have to trust her. She can help us, Daniel.'

Daniel closed the book looking at a familiar face, but on a man he had never met. A queer sensation saturated him. He had never known that about his best friend. It felt like Mark was a completely different person, a stranger. A lot of different emotions fought their way through Daniel and got all mixed up on the way out. his reply was simply: 'Ugh, I am so sorry, Mark; I had no idea.'

Mark was very sullen, but a glint of happiness or hope sparkled in his eye. He was about to say something when they could hear thundering footsteps rushing downstairs.

'They gave me this to fight her.' Joe displayed the golden dagger, wheezing heavily after his excessive stair dash.

Mark held out his hand and was given the knife. Joe took a step back, watching intently. Mark turned it over in his hands, inspecting closely the engravings that he could not make out and the gemstones which looked genuine; Mark had a fair idea what real jewels looked like. His mother used to wear them all the time. Joe studied the scene with a subdued smile. He hoped when Mark had touched the dagger, the fairies would somehow reappear and advise him how to defeat the banshee and save his son, but desperation often twists reasoning. Daniel was transfixed by the glittering gold shining in his eyes. He had never seen real gold (besides Mark's pocket watch, and of course, his own wedding ring). For a moment, his heart was trying to convince him to take the knife and sell it.

Mark met Joe's defeated gaze: 'Oi don't think that worked. What should we do now?'

Joe sat down and took the knife from Mark. 'I thought that would do it.' He studied the blade himself. 'I don't know what to do now. We can't fight her alone. She was almost too strong back then and now. I don't even want to imagine what witchcraft she has learned.'

'Maybe… maybe we don't have to do this alone.'

Joe lifted his heavy head from the pillow he had made with his arms. 'What do you mean?' He forbade hope to sink into his voice.

'When you said my family should have a banshee. We do. Oi remember seeing her now; she told me she would always protect me. Oi can remember her so vividly whereas before oi thought she was only a dream.'

Joe jumped up onto his feet: 'This is perfect, this is such great news. Can you ask her to help us find Mark? She might just be what we need.'

'I am not sure how to contact her,' Mark said. He switched glances between Daniel's and Joe's bemused faces, hoping one of them had some idea. They remained reticent. 'But she is here, in the orchard. Oi saw her.'

Joe smiled with a hope he needed to express.

Daniel returned the fairy encyclopedia back into his satchel. 'I reckon we've done enough for one day. If I have to read one more word or hear fairy one more time, I will scream louder than the banshee herself.' He accompanied that with a nervous laugh. He was not sure how long they had been sitting at the table planning things: hours, days, weeks, years. It felt like all of them put together. He was so dizzy from reading both his eyes met at the top of this nose. His head swam and crashed like a maelstrom smashing rocks together in its whirlpool. He needed to go to bed and revive his boggled mind. *Surely both of them have terrible headaches too. Of course, they weren't reading all day like me, so they're probably fine.*

Mark hid behind silence, staring at the floor so intently as if it would make him invisible. He did not want to suggest calling it a day lest he insulted Joe. That was a confrontation he would be satisfied to eschew. To both of their surprise, Joe agreed. he pinched the top of his nose between his finger and his thumb and scrunched up his face. 'Daniel is right. We are too exhausted to come up with something sensible. A night's sleep is undoubtedly what we all need right now. But listen to me.' The flame in the gaslight flickered, making Joe look very menacing. 'At seven o'clock tomorrow morning, we are getting up, and we're gonna figure something out, and we will get my boy back. Am I making myself clear.' There was no question in Joe's eyes. In that small pack, he was the alpha. Not even a fool would dare question his authority at that moment. Daniel and Mark nodded.

'Alright, get to bed.' He dismissed them with a head nudge. 'Sleep well, lads, for tomorrow, tomorrow we're gonna destroy that cursed banshee and get my son back,' he spat with pure poison. They passed from the kitchen, heading for their cabin.

'Do you really think Mark is in danger?'

She readjusted the bandage over her eyes. 'We're doing everything we can to save your brother, but yes, sweetie, I do think Mark is in danger, but I won't let anything happen to my children, do you understand?'

'Yes, mummy.' She snuggled even tighter into bed, making sure not to pull the blanket from under where Mary was sitting. 'Is this the same thing that took your eyes, mummy?'

Mary shuddered. She was silent for such a long time Caoimhe felt she might have stirred up some long-drowned memories that were better left sinking in the forgotten pools of tragedy.

At last, she spoke, slowly and thoughtfully, as if she were reliving her memories and narrating them. 'When we were younger, your father and me about your age. We were attacked by a… spirit who is connected to your father's family, she—'

'Mum, I know about the banshee, dad told me.'

'Ohh, we agreed we would never tell you or Mark about her.'

'It was my fault, mum, he didn't want to tell me, but I kept asking.' She jumped to her father's defence rather quickly. Mary thought it was a bit too quick to pass as the truth, but it made describing the current events easier, so she didn't press the matter anymore.

'To make a long story short, she, the banshee, is back and has taken your brother. I don't know

(*yellow bloodshot eyes*)

'where she has taken him or why, but your father is spending every minute of the day trying to find him and how we can defeat the banshee once and for all.'

'What if she hurts him like she hurt you and dad?' Tears began in her eyes.

'I have already told you, sweetheart. I won't let anything happen to any of you. If me and your father bested her once

(*decayed face*)

'we can do it again. We just need to figure some…

(*harsh cackle*)

'…thing out that…

(*smell of death*)

'…can…'

(STABBING MY EYES WITH COLD, SHARP FINGER)

'Mummy, what's happening?' Caoimhe screamed.

Mary squeezed her thumping head. Her ears buzzed in a monotonous drilling sound, and she felt a cold sensation pouring down from the sides of her nose from her eye holes.

'M-m-m-mum?' Her terror escaped through her voice.

Mary could feel the sharp fingers puncturing her eyes again, she cried out in pain, then the cold sensation reached her lip, and she could smell it, and taste that dreaded melted iron; it was blood, her own blood. The buzzing faded away, and her head no longer felt as if it were being cracked in half. She touched her hand to the blood-soaked rag tied around her eyes and jumped to her feet. She raced to the door, stumbling into the wardrobe, knocking over Caoimhe's favourite doll sitting on the shelf.

'Mum? Matt! Matthew help!' Caoimhe shot up out of bed and hurried to her mother's side. Mary pushed her away.

'I'm fine. It's nothing. I just need to lie down for a while.'

Matthew appeared from his bedroom wearing his light blue bear patterned pyjamas. He quickly glanced at Mary with blood streaming from her eyes and jumped in horror. Even though he was very accustomed to seeing blood and horror, it still unnerved him, made him uncomfortably frightened. He rushed over to Caoimhe, alternating between looking curiously at Mary's bloodied face and a dirty knot in the wooden floorboards.

'Help me get her into bed.' Caoimhe spoke in a clement tone. She had learned that Matthew only panics based on people's reactions, not so much the event itself, no matter how bad an incident that might have occurred, as long as you speak calmly, Matthew will believe the situation to be normal. It wasn't his fault she knew this, but she needed his help, and there was no need to panic him... that would happen soon enough, she thought. *I wonder if Matthew remembers the banshee as mom and dad do.* Now was not the time for silly questions. She had to get her mother to bed, which is what they did.

'Mum, will you be alright for a minute? I'll get dad.'

'Sweety, there is no need. I'll be fine.'

'Matt, will you stay here with mom until I get dad?'

He nodded. Caoimhe left the room and ran downstairs.

'What was all that screaming? Is everything alright up there?' Daniel asked.

'Yeah, everything is fine. Have you seen my dad?'

'He's in there.' Mark pointed to the kitchen. Caoimhe turned and darted down the hall.

Daniel and Mark exchanged eye contact and shrugged, leaving the house.

The moonlight shining on the rain made it look like somebody broke the glass sky, and all the glittering shards were falling onto the cold world. Daniel led the way and opened the cabin; Mark entered and shook the rain from his crumbling pompadour staring into the dark room. Daniel flicked the switch, and the ancient bulb flickered on and off while trying to muster enough power to hold the light like it once did.

Daniel opened and closed his mouth. He had a million questions to ask, but he was reticent. He waited patiently for Mark to speak first.

'What are we going to do, Dan? Oi have no idea how to summon me banshee, and even if I could, would she help us? Could she help us?'

'So, it's true? You really have a ... a banshee?'

Mark looked at Daniel like he had two heads. 'Of course, it's true. What, yeh think oi'm lying?'

Daniel surrendered his hands and collapsed onto a chair. 'It wouldn't be the first time you lied for a story, would it?'

He felt rage powering through his enervated veins. 'This is unbelievable. Oi, swear on me bleedin' life oi'm not playing a little prank on yiz, Dan.'

Daniel climbed to his feet as quick as a flash of lightning. 'It wasn't a little prank, Mark. Yiz had me believing there was a ghost at hell hollow! Yeh had me worrying day and night instead of just telling me yiz were making it all up. I thought our bloody lives were in jeopardy!' Daniel roared like thunder, causing Mark to flinch.

'Alri' oi'm sorry… is that what yeh want to hear? Oi'm sorry Dan, oi should have told yiz, but you made it more convincing, made it more real.' There was contrition in his heart, 'Oi swear to ye now Daniel I am not lying this is all for real and oi feel Joe is counting on me to seek aid from a spirit oi have no idea how to contact.'

Daniels's mind could not even begin to think about figuring out such an enigmatic task. He simply grunted and said: 'I think we need to get some sleep. We can worry about tomorrow's problems tomorrow.'

Mark lethargically nodded his head in tacit agreement. They were both too tired for supper and decided to just call it a night instead. Retreating into the bedroom they got ready for a good night's sleep. Their heads had barely hit the pillows, and they slipped into a dreamless coma-like sleep.

He gently pressed a towel against her face while she wept tears of blood.

'Joe, where is our baby?'

He rubbed her shoulder and squeezed her tightly in his arm, attempting to calm her unrelenting sobs. The ghostly white light of the moon veiled in early clouds forced its way in through a small tear in the curtain, illuminating a large white screen on the adjacent wall, like them drive-in movie screens. Only this was not a motion picture. There was nothing on this screen except the bottom half of a picture that hung on the wall and a creepy silhouette of a shaking tree just outside the window; It looked like a disfigured claw waving at him. Joe wiped away a cold sweat and adopted a stern, hard posture for his wife to cuddle up to. He had to appear strong for his distraught wife lying beside him, unable to sleep.

'I will find him tomorrow; we will find him, and he will be just fine.' His wavering tone did not even convince himself. 'I will take care of the banshee honey, ' he kissed her forehead, 'don't worry about it. I will get rid of her for good, and then our family will have the fearless life we deserve. Believe in me.'

Mary allowed herself a little chuckle between sobs. 'I know you will. You have always kept us safe.' She fell silent. 'Do you have any idea where she has taken our son?'

Joe stared at the dancing claw on the wall. *I would bet my life he is in the well, in her Underworld and I literally mean bet my life on it because tomorrow I am going down there. I hope he isn't there, but if he is, I hope I can get both of us out safely. But I won't get that lucky again.* 'Not just yet, honey, but I am working on it with them Dublin lads, together we will sort something out. Everything will be okay, I promise, just try to get some sleep.'

She quietly moaned and got comfortable lying beside Joe. His arm fell asleep cradling her head, and once again, he found himself wishing he still had his other hand to scratch his nose.

Suddenly, before Joe's eyes had sealed themselves shut for the night, there crossed a shadow on the screen of a very thin human-like figure hobbling from left to right. He jolted with a fright. *Wait.... we are on the second floor, and there is no roof to stand on. How could something pass by the window unless it was ten feet tall.* His mind trailed back to when he and Matthew were in that ruined house, and the banshee towered over them. Mary also hopped in shock. 'What is it, Joe?' she asked, tilting her head trying to hear any sort of movement.

He pondered his next words carefully. 'Nothing, sweetheart, I just got a cramp in my leg.'

She lay back down, but he could feel a restless tension in her. The figure was gone from the screen. Once again, Joe attempted to close his eyes. That's when they heard a scream, not the banshee's horrific, deafening scream. It sounded more... human. Without hesitation, both Joe and Mary jumped up out of bed and hurried to their daughter. Joe's mind was still in that Victorian mansion being chased by the banshee. *Why is it that you can always remember your worst experiences, no matter how hard you try to forget them he thought.*

In the hallway, he saw Matthew standing petrified outside of his bedroom, scanning the hall curiously.

The Banshee

'Matt, what is going on?' his voice was trembling as much as his hand. Matthew stared into Joe's eyes, unsure of anything.

'Joe, the door is locked.' Mary cried, fondling the handle. Joe gently moved her aside and tried the handle himself. It would not budge.

'Caoimhe, honey, are you in there?' (knock... knock... knock) 'Caoimhe, are you okay?'

Another scream and cry for help answered him. He took two large steps back, with his back against the opposite wall. 'Stand back, honey. I'm breaking down the door.'

He took two large steps forward and kicked at it with the sole of this foot as hard as he could. It remained shut, and the sheer vibration of the impact almost knocked Joe off his feet. Again, he took two steps back, then forward and kicked—the same outcome. The archaic chandelier, which seemed to emit more darkness than light, flickered, and for a moment, the world felt like it was in darkness. Caoimhe screamed again. Violent desperation took control of Joe's body, and instead of trying to kick the it down, he ran into it shoulder first with such force that could only be channelled by a desperate need, the door split in two, half of it hanging askew on its struggling hinges. The other half, under Joe on the floor.

Joe let out a roar when he saw his daughter lying lifeless on the floor. He pushed himself up like a starving beast on a fresh carcass. He lunged to his girl, with his ear on her chest, listening for a heartbeat.

Mary cautiously entered the room, groping around the interminable black searching for her daughter. 'Caoimhe? Caoimhe, where are you? Joe, where is she?' Her screams sounded almost identical to the banshees.

Matthew turned and raced away frantically, not quite understanding why he felt the need to flee. His heavy footsteps pounded down the stairs.

Joe caught his elusive breath and almost choked on relief. 'She is still breathing.' He erected his hand. 'Come to my voice Mary.' she did, and he carefully took her hand and gently pulled her to where he was sitting on the floor.

Mary rested her palm on Caoimhe's forehead. 'Is she wounded?' Mary espoused a commanding mannerism, no longer acting like the helpless blind liability she saw herself as. She was now a mother. And being a mother meant there was no room for self-pity or worry when your child needed to be succoured. It was impossible to be bothered about personal issues when your child needed you.

'Not that I can see.' He examined her inanimate body. 'Is she going to be alright?'

Mary did not answer. 'She has a temperature. Run downstairs and get me a basin of cold water.'

Joe bounced to his feet. He looked back and gasped.

Caoimhe's eyes were open; they were a cloudy white. She sat up, staring at Joe. Mary jolted in surprise. 'Caoimhe?'

A complacent grin twisted the edge of her mouth. A malign whisper echoed from her mouth: '*His flesh was sweet; his blood was warm. I hope you taste like your son.*'

The whispering came from Caoimhe's possessed body, but it felt like it came from his own head. Slowly the deep grey of her iris returned, and she had a coughing fit.

A tremendous scream came from outside. Joe stepped past Mary, who was comforting Caoimhe to look out the window, where a shrill light from the lad's cabin disturbed the dormant, moist air. The cabin stood like a lighthouse in a sea of silence, inviting all evil spirits to it. Joe's gaze was pulled to the windowsill, and his stomach filled with restless snakes. He opened the window and picked up the thing on the damp sill with a trembling hand. He turned it over, feeling a terrible threat. It was a hair comb. *It's on Caoimhe's window. She will not get my daughter. Just like she got my son. No… no, Mark is alive. She is trying to scare me. I must save Mark!*

Time was up. Joe turned and ran out of the room and downstairs, ignoring Mary's questions. When he reached the front door, he turned and saw Matthew gawking at the old family portrait on the table. His smile vanished when he locked eyes with Joe.

'Matt, go upstairs and help Mary.'

He went out and disappeared into the hungry dark.

Mark woke with a jolt feeling like he was being watched. He blinked away the groggy sleep blur and looked at the window. He froze solid at the sight that met him. It was the banshee, but not the beautiful woman, that comforted him that night many years ago. This one looked… older, angrier, and dangerous with her sharp yellow eyes and her morbid blood hair. She was watching him, smiling. Mark wanted desperately to call for help to Daniel, who was asleep on a bed just to his right, but he could not. He could not move his body. It felt as though two cold hands were holding his head still but sternly, so all he could do was stare out the window. She placed a cruel hand on the glass, and it began freezing, morphing into a clear picture of ice. Mark remained frozen in fear. Painful fright like ice picks to the heart engulfed him. *I am going to die tonight, right now! Just wake Dan up. Why can't I move? I don't want to die. I don't want to die, Elizabeth.*

The ice shattered off the glass, and she vanished as the window became clear again, but there was still a cold, eerie atmosphere lingering in the cabin. A loud thump in the main room snapped him out of his enchanted fright. He was about to call for Daniel when he heard another thump. Almost deaf from the silent suspension, the adrenaline kicked in, and he now called out to Daniel in a trembling whisper. He got no reply. He was sitting still in bed, listening intently.

A third thump was enough to shake him back into his senses. He screamed for Daniel to wake up and looked over to his bed, only to realize Daniel was not in bed. A feeling of isolation smothered him. Mark felt completely alone and defenceless, like an abandoned king waiting to get checkmated.

'Da...Da...Daniel?' he heard himself say in a voice that sounded too small to belong to a human. He quickly looked around the small bedroom for some sign of help, and that's when he found Daniel, sitting on the floor in a corner facing the wall, crying and murmuring to himself. A new feeling of terror gripped him.

'Daniel? are you al-alright?'

He continued crying and muttering something.

'What did you just say?' Trying not to sound as scared as he felt.

-silence-

The room felt somehow bigger and darker. The quiet strained the air as if the world was inhaling deeply, holding its breath in anticipation.

'She is here.'

Mark turned to see the banshee towering in the door frame. She was hunched over so that she could get her red veiled head in the room. Mark once again froze, shocked by his own cowardice in the face of a threat; he always thought he could handle stressful situations better, but obviously not.

The banshee dropped her jaw abnormally low and screamed. The scream was so loud it roused Daniel from his fit. The two men clutched their ears and tightly shut their eyes. The scream was hitting such a high pitch, it felt to the men as if their skulls were imploding, and the discharged fragments of bone were slicing their brains like a hot knife through ice cream. When the scream ended and Mark peeled open his dizzy eyes, the banshee was no longer there. However, they could hear her laughing, and with a shared glance of concern, they decided to get away from there. Daniel flicked on the cold light and helped Mark onto his chair, and ran ahead, The two men left the cabin and made it halfway to the mansion before turning around to see if they were being chased.

The night was brutally cold. The moon was not powerful enough to pierce the mist that had just spawned, strangling the minatory night. Mark and Daniel stopped abruptly, not sure which way they were facing. A distant scream originating from every direction closed in on them. They stood side-by-side, looking around frantically, trying to penetrate the wall of fog with their eyes, hoping to see some familiar landmark that would show them how to get to safety.

'What do we do, Dan? Oi can't see anything.' Shaking with fear and the cold.

Daniel did not seem to have heard him; he continued peering around. The dark fog made everything look like the silhouette of an unknown danger watching them, waiting to strike.

The claustrophobic silence was broken by an gentle whispering rising and falling on the air.

The blinding dark was sundered by a light bobbing in the void. It grew nearer and nearer. *Why did I never ask you out Elizabeth, at least I wouldn't spend the rest of time in the ground, thinking about whether we could have been happy together*.

344

The light was now bouncing in front of Mark, but he could still not discern what was casting it.

'Quick, follow me,' a voice yelled at him, but it sounded little more than a whisper against the screaming wind.

With one hand, Mark clutched Daniels's unaware hand, and with the other, he drove the wheelchair after the light. The light slowly became a silhouette of a man, then the silhouette transformed into Joe, holding a lantern. They were almost back at the house when the mist lightened, and an odious screech made them all turn around.

In an instant, the banshee fell upon them. She glided through the mist with a horrifying scream and glowing yellow eyes that trailed behind her in streaks of gold. Before Mark could process what was happening, he felt something trace across his face, something cold and wet, like when he was younger, and his brothers drew on his face with a marker pen. Only it never flowed down his face like it was now, and thinking back, it never hurt as it did now. When his senses returned to him, he realized he was staring into the evil, hideous eyes of the banshee. He was no longer in his wheelchair either. He was being suspended in the air. He realized at that moment what was suspending him and why his face felt wet and sore. The banshee had dug her claws into his cheeks and held him up. He wanted to scream and cry for help, but even a tiny movement of his mouth caused grievous pain. He could hear Daniel screaming: 'Put him down.' It sounded very muffled and far away. Like when his parents would argue in the kitchen, and he would hide under the stairs—blocking his ears.

His vision was fading into black, and the last thing he saw before passing out was a radiant white light that pushed the banshee hard enough to cause her to drop Mark and force her a few steps back. He heard another scream with ears that were about to shut down, but that scream wasn't malevolent. It almost sounded happy. It sounded like his mother. *I'm coming, mom.* His conscience left him.

<u>X X</u> THE BELLS

Joe and Daniel stood still as statues frozen in place while Mark lay on the ground in a bloody mess, unconscious. However, their attention was not on their injured friend but rather on the banshee... both of them. The banshee Joe was accustomed to seeing; the McNeeve banshee towered about 10 feet tall. She wore a tattered green dress with long red hair and glowing yellow bloodshot eyes. Her skin was all decayed and torn. Scars from the knife wounds she suffered at the hand of Joe embellished her body. Yet she seemed angrier and more vicious than ever. As if she was not idle during her banishment, rather growing in some secret power, eager for the day she got free to release her revenge on Joe, to make him rue the day he contested her.

The other banshee, however, the O'Brien banshee, was much smaller in presence. She wore a glistening white dress, which looked like freshly fallen snow kissed by bright sunlight, sparkling in a cold field of diamonds. She had long, wavey silver hair, which seemed to soak up the moonlight and shine even brighter. She was beautiful, the face of a young woman who had known nothing but sadness. Her enchanting blue eyes mixed with the heavy red of constant crying. Fresh tears trailed down a familiar line on her face and broke on the ground. Compared to the embodiment of evil which looked down at her, she didn't look like she stood a chance. It looked like she was just some angel who accidentally stumbled upon the Devil himself. But she had power, a power even she herself did not understand—a power *she* undoubtedly overlooked. The crimson banshee screamed loudly and cruelly, almost knocking Joe and Daniel off their feet, but the silver banshee did not waiver. She took two steps forward. Her naked pale feet gently dabbled the soil wet with her tears. She extended her arm and sang some beautiful spell in a forgotten tongue. Another refulgent bolt of white light radiated from her hand, pushing the McNeeve banshee further away. Daniel and Joe had to shield their eyes.

A terrible sound echoed in the darkness, like two ancient cogs of an evil machine devoured by rust were grinding against each other. The sound came from her. She was laughing, not laughing in a way that said, *this fight is going to be difficult* but instead said, *I'm going to consume you and then everybody else.*

Suddenly, malign clouds swirled in a sinister ring above the orchard, flashes of lightning painted the sky, and the snap of the electric band filled the air, not disturbing either banshee from their death stare. An enthusiastic rumble of thunder signalled the rain to start falling, and it did.

The banshee croaked out some foul-sounding words, and out from the tip of her fingers came a dark beam coated in black smoke.

She was quick to block the curse, gracefully spreading out both of her hands like the Christ the Redeemer statue. The pose activated a bright impenetrable bubble. Inviolable sure, but it was getting smaller by the second under the force of the shadow. It would soon constrict her, and she knew it. In a strenuous motion, she threw the bubble at her enemy, almost cloaking her in light.

Her reactions were laudable. She tucked her elbows into her hips and screamed. Darkness engulfed her, and the louder she screamed, the darker she became.

The Bells

What followed was a battle of lights and screams. When the banshee finally lunged at an unconscious Mark, trying to finish what she had started, and she was forced away by the silver banshee. That's when the fight became more physical. The two banshees were clawing at each other and screaming wails of pain and anger. Then she spoke in a strained but soft tone. *Get Mark inside*, she had said. The soothing voice was enough to wake Daniel up from his stupor, and he ran over to Mark, throwing him over his shoulder and running into the house behind Joe. Leaving the wheelchair overturned in the storm. The two banshees disappeared in a scream and a flash of light, the fight still going ahead. Further and further, the flashes of light appeared over the dark hills until nothing could be seen or heard.

Joe quickly led Daniel into the sitting room, throwing the extinguished lantern across the room, and gestured to Daniel to lay Mark on the couch.

Matthew emerged, followed by Caoimhe, who was guiding Mary. All of them hosted a look of terror and confusion.

'Joe, what's going on?' Mary croaked in a voice riddled with concern.

Caoimhe glanced down at the bloody couch and saw Mark lying there with half of his face hanging off. She screamed, and the sound reverberated off the walls amplifying the fear within.

Everybody jumped. 'what's the matter, sweety?' Mary asked.

'It's Mark. He's dead.'

A brief silence breezed through the room. Then Mary would have collapsed if Caoimhe wasn't holding her. 'He can't be... Joe... Joe promised he wouldn't...' her feelings mixed with what she wanted to say had scrambled into a fat frog in her throat. 'Bring me over to him.' It must have been the shock that held her calmness intact.

'It's not our son Mary. It's the other Mark, and he's not dead, but he does need serious medical attention right now. So, if you would please help him.'

Caoimhe prudently guided Mary to Mark, feeling sick, looking at his wounds.

A crash of lightning flashed into the window. Joe quickly shut the curtains, feeling it was the banshee returning after her inevitable victory.

'What's wrong with him?' Mary asked.

Caoimhe swallowed. 'His face.' She fought back the tears. 'His face is ripped in half.'

Mary quietly pondered this image for a moment. Then she guided her hand gently onto his wet face. 'Get me the basin of water, and a few towels and bandages and all the disinfectant you can find. Do it now!' she screamed at her daughter.

Caoimhe stood up and shot out of the room.

Joe placed a strong hand on Daniel's shoulder: 'I need your help, Daniel.'

'Yeah, sure, what can I do?' Sounding less enthusiastic than he tried to be. Truth be told, he was scared, very scared.

Joe hesitated for a moment and swallowed his fear. 'I need your help to get down the well. My son is down there.'

Mary looked up, and although she could not see, she looked directly through Joe. 'No. Absolutely not. You are not going down there, do you hear me?'

Daniel looked bemused, switching his gaze between both of them.

'Honey, I have to save our son. I know he's down there. I know it. I'm going to save him. I'm not asking you. Come on, Daniel.' Joe grabbed Daniel by the arm and was leading him out the door.

Mary stood and cut Joe off before he left the room. 'Joe, you know what it's like down there.' Memories of the Underworld came flooding back to her.

'Of course, I do! That's why I have to get our son out, Mary. He is down there alone and terrified. My boy Mary.' He broke out into tears. 'I need to be there to save him. I'm his father.'

Mary reluctantly nodded. 'But Joe... what if he's not down there? What if he's already de—' she choked on the thought. Loathing herself for even thinking such a terrible thing.

Joe held her tight. 'You can't think like that, Mary, don't think like that.' He kissed his wife on the forehead. 'I have to try. I have to.'

Mary sobbed, but deep down, she knew he had to. So, she threw her shoulders back and raised her chin, adopted a martinet manner: 'Alright, but you come back here with our boy Joe McNeeve.'

He released a slightly audible chuckle. *She hasn't used my full name since we were children and only when she was annoyed with me.* 'I wouldn't dare disobey you, Mrs McNeeve. I will bring him home no matter what it takes.' Joe walked around Mary, pulling Daniel by the arm.

'I'm not going anywhere without Mark. He needs to be brought to a hospital right now.'

'Daniel, you saw that thing out there. It's going to kill us all unless we destroy it first, now is the best time while she's distracted. Mary and Caoimhe will look after Mark, don't worry, he won't die... will he?' He turned back to Mary, who was once again kneeling beside Mark, trying to get a feel for his injury by gently dabbing his face.

'He is losing a lot of blood. The quicker we can get him to the hospital, the better.'

'I need your help, Daniel, please.' His supplicating eyes fixated on Daniels's tenuous gaze.

Daniel nodded reluctantly. 'I'm coming back in ten minutes and driving Mark to a hospital.' He was not asking for permission.

Joe smiled grimly and looked over to Matthew, who was standing quietly by the couch staring at the wall replaying old memories like a movie through his brain.

'Matt, you must go to and look out for your brother,' Mary commanded.

Joe looked at Mary with regretful eyes. *No, I can't risk his life too! Why did you do that, Mary?*

Without hesitation, Matthew jumped to his brother's side and followed him. Joe made a quick digression into the kitchen to collect the golden dagger, stowing it down the side of his pants before leaving.

The night still clutched desperately to the fading storm; a tired breeze flicked the light remnants off a downpour onto their faces like an awakening kiss from a cold sea spray on a tedious voyage. The transient thunder retreated into silence, bringing the lightning with it. However, the thick black sky was lit up every now and again by distant flashes over the hill. Joe swallowed nervously. He seemed to be the only one who knew what was going on. Daniel's mind was with Mark, worried about his best friend. And Matthew's mind was focused on keeping Joe safe, just like Mary had ordered him to do many years ago.

The lads stood beside the well in the shadow of the great oak tree.

'What's the plan, Joe?'

Joe looked from Matthew to Daniel, trying to buy enough time to prudently explain his intentions. Subtly was never Joe's forte. 'We need to go down the well.'

Daniel laughed aloud, mostly in disbelief.

Matthew didn't even grin. He almost always knew when his brother was joking. He was not. This was evident by his stern, slightly frightened eyes.

'Down the well? What do you mean we have to go down the well? I don't think we will all fit. How deep is it anyway?'

Joe looked bemused at Daniel. 'No, you see, the well is a sort of passage to the Underworld, to the banshee's world.' Joe watched as doubt twisted Daniel's sullen face. 'I was there many years ago, and Mary. That is where we fought her.' Joe looked at Matthew. 'The first time I was down there, I went down this well to save Mary, who had been dragged down there by her. I strongly reckon she has done the same with my Mark.' He looked up to the starless sky. The orchard seemed as if somebody wrapped it in a black sheet. Almost like there was nothing else in existence, just the orchard. No sun, no moon, no stars, no space, no time. Nothing. Joe tried and tried, but he could not conjure an elegant sentence in his mind to secure Daniel's help. 'Last time I was down there, I got very lucky in getting out., an outcome I fear I will not be able to duplicate. If you decide to come down with me, just know I can't guarantee we will leave.' Watching the doubt slip into distraught in Daniel's eyes, the fear that he might be going alone shook his commanding voice. - he refused to bring Matthew down there out of fear that he would not be able to save his brother, breaking the promise he made to his mother - 'This is the only way we can stop her; we have to destroy her in her own world. Otherwise, she will keep coming back.'

Daniel met Joe's concerned gaze with contrition. 'This is all way too much to take in. I'm sorry about your boy Joe, but if what you're saying is true, I really don't want to risk my life. I have a family at home, surely you must understand.

'Mark needs to be brought to the hospital.' Regret opened an insatiable void of guilt in his stomach. 'I'm really sorry, Joe, but I can't do this. I have a family at home, yeh? And Mark needs to get to the hospital. I'm sorry, but I can't.' Daniel turned and started walking back towards the house.

'You won't be able to leave.' The lie sprung out of Joe's mouth before he could think about what he was about to say. A lie that felt less like a lie the more he thought about it.

Daniel turned to face him. 'What?'

'You think she is going to let any of us leave? No, no, we're all in this together now. If we don't destroy her now, she will kill every last one of us.' Matthew seemed to have understood this because his eyes stirred a concoction of fresh tears and terror.

Daniel trampled back to Joe, animosity in his walk and in his heart. He moved quickly. When he was close enough to Joe, he balled up his fist and cracked Joe just under the eye, knocking him to the ground. 'You planned this! You monster, you needed us to solve your problem. You sacrificed me and my friend for your own selfish gain.' He stood over Joe with a fist throbbing with warm blood.

A sudden thump made his eye flicker open and close in discomfort. He stumbled back a step, and then before he could process what had hit him, he was struck again, in the same exact spot. He was forced to shut the restless and painful eye. Using his arms to shield his face like a boxer, he saw what was hitting him. It was Matthew. Daniel did not feel right fighting back, so instead, he pacified him. Grabbing his arm the next time, Matthew swung and pinning it behind his back, tripping him to the ground. 'Enough, Matthew! Stop it now!' he shouted while pushing Matthew's head into the dirt.

Matthew had stopped, and Joe begged Daniel to let him up.

Daniel stepped back from the two incapacitated brothers, breathing heavily, alert, and ready for a potential second round.

Joe got to his feet and helped his brother up, showing his hand to Daniel as a gesture of submission.

'There is no sense in us fighting each other. We would just be helping her.' Joe looked uneasily at Matthew, who was still vibrating with rage. 'Listen to me, both of you. We have to work together to do this. It's our only chance, do you understand?' He watched both of them, holding their aggressive body stances until eventually they calmed down enough and nodded.

'Alright then, Daniel, you will come with me down the well. We will find Mark and get out of there before she comes back.

'Matthew, you must stay right here, and if you see her coming back, let us know.' Joe began to turn around and walk towards the well.

'How the hell is he gonna let us know anything? He can't speak. Besides, three of us stand more of a chance than two, so why doesn't he come with us?'

Joe quickly tried to think of a reason to avoid risking his brother's life. He hoped Daniel would not be too inquisitive of the plan. Joe did not think it through too far, he was never the cleverest man at planning things, and that had not changed now.

'The last time we fought her, she used Matthew against us... I think there's some connection between them. It would be easier to fight her alone than fight the two of them.' A quick lie.

'Wait, couldn't he just climb down the well and attack us if she wanted to use him? Joe, this plan isn't making any sense. Why don't I stay up here and stay on guard? I will shout down if I see her coming.'

'No!' Joe shouted, frustrated that he could not outwit Daniel. 'You're right. It's better if the three of us go.' He looked at his brother, his heart as heavy as the suffocating darkness, and gently squeezed his shoulder. 'Now, come on, please, we're running out of time. follow my lead.'

Joe swung a leg over the rim of the well and began a slow, arduous descent, followed by Matthew, then followed reluctantly by Daniel, who was nursing a copious amount of dissatisfaction.

A humorously cruel thought perched itself on Joe's mind: the last time he climbed down this well, his arm was hanging lamely in a sling. Now it is gone. If he manages to escape again, he might have no arms. That would make the climb very difficult, he thought and sniggered manically under his breath, momentarily veiling the worry he bore for his son and brother getting hurt.

Joe slipped his feet into the difficult located holes and protruding rocks in the stone wall, every inch he squirmed down, it became darker - he didn't think it could get any darker than it already was, but it did - and it got colder and colder; it almost felt as though he was standing blindly in a tundra. Whispering winds slicing through him with icy blades. He could hear grunting and the occasional sound of a tenuous grip being lost on the slippery stones. Without looking up, he knew he was being followed by his brother and Daniel.

356

The climb once again felt like forever, and once again, Joe reached a point where there didn't seem to be any more well underneath him, A freezing gust overwhelmed him and he slipped, falling slowly onto the same unseen solid ground. Looking up hazily, he could see Matthew was about to drop down, followed by Daniel. The fall had winded him, and in that brief recovery time, he managed to catch enough breath to either evacuate the landing zone or shout up and warn the others; the fall was inevitable, no amount of warning could preclude destiny, so he decided to roll out the way.

Plop. Followed by an epicene scream climaxed by a thud. Joe got warily to his feet. Looking around the familiar hell, he had wandered around in so many nightmares. The last time he fell into a hole, he remembered. *It must have been filled in.* Joe looked around the distantly familiar pitch-black forest, strangled by large trees engulfed in white flames, outlining every shape and blade of grass in that world. The sun, the ebony sphere encircled in white fire, loomed above the realm. Joe wondered if the "sun" had got bigger than it was the last time he was here, but there was no way of knowing. He tried his best not to remember this place but failed miserably. It haunted his dreams. There was no sound of wind rustling through the trees, no birds singing in jovial celebrations. There was only a rising and falling murmur. Daniel did not know for sure what it was, and he did not want to know, but it sounded like the wails and cries of all the unfortunate damned souls she managed to drag there.

Daniel stood up and gawked around with equal bemusement and fright. The words were caught in his throat, but Joe knew the very questions on his mind, for they were also on his mind the first time. Matthew, who was involuntarily taciturn, was looking around in amazement. When Daniel turned his head to Joe, he screamed. Seeing Joe as nothing but a dark shape exaggerated only by a pale flicker. It was difficult to make out facial features, but Daniel must have recognized him from his missing arm.

'Joe, Wha... what in the name of all that is holy is this place?'

Joe extended his arm in welcome. 'Where are my manners? Welcome to the Underworld, lads.' The words reverberated around the void.

Welcome to the Underworld, lads, welcome to the Underworld, lads

They continued looking around in bewilderment and amazement. Briefly forgetting the horror that compelled them to go down there in the first place.

'Nobody is gonna believe me about this,' Daniel said with wonder.

'Join the club.' Joe laughed. 'people will say you're crazy if you try explaining this.'

'This place is incredible; how do we get out?' Daniel asked, fear starting to settle in his heart.

Joe pointed up. Matthew and Daniel looked up in synchronisation at the well, floating in the air. Before he could ask:

'No, I don't know how to get up,' Joe said. 'The last time I was here, the fairies got Mary and me out through a portal.'

The silence was enough to inform Joe that Daniel was completely aghast at that absurd statement that sounded entirely plausible to him at that moment. A story he was most excited to hear sometime.

'So, how do we find your son?'

'I'm not really sure. It's damn near impossible to navigate this place. Maybe our best bet is to head over towards the hill? Get a better view, see what we can't see.'

Joe pointed in front of him. 'This way and stick together. There are more dangerous things down here than the whispering voices.' Joe's memory reeled back to when he and Mary fought the monstrous demon thing. He hoped he would never see it again, but right now, it also felt inevitable. They had to find his son. He could feel Matthew's trembling hand clasping his own. He took a deep breath and led the party forward.

Caoimhe handed Mary another towel. That was the third towel in ten minutes that quickly became drenched in blood, even with Mary rinsing off the once white, now crimson towels in the basin which was once full of clear water but now transmuted into a dirty red liquid; it looked like a love potion out of a witch's cauldron Caoimhe thought. The sight of blood and gore surprisingly didn't sicken her.

'We have to stop the bleeding.' Caoimhe was full of calmness. 'How do we stop the bleeding?'

Mary was not quite as calm. Her prudent hands were shaking at the scene; she was glad she could not see. *He is going to bleed out,* she thought. *He is going to die right here on the couch, and Joe is going to die down there in the well, along with our son.*

'Hand me another towel.'

There was only one towel left, bright mango. Caoimhe hesitated in handing it over. She wasn't being niggardly with the towels. She was just concerned. That was the last towel, and Mark was still bleeding profusely. They needed to stop the bleeding.

'Mom, we need to stop the bleeding, or he is going to die.' Caoimhe handed over the final towel, taking a step backwards and looking at Mark, sallow as a corpse and saturated with wet blood, staining the couch and floor; No matter how long they spent scrubbing the sitting room, it would never again be clean, they would never remove that amount of blood from the carpet.

'Caoimhe honey, there is a sewing kit in the cabinet beside the stove unless somebody moved it. Would you look for it and bring it back to me. I will try to stitch the wounds. It will buy him a bit of time.'

Caoimhe pictured Mark sitting upright with his face stitched together from the tip of his left ear all the way around to the bottom of his right. She shivered and left the room.

She returned moments later to an unchanged scene. If there was more blood, it was unnoticeable, like rain on the ocean.

'It was still there, buried underneath a pile of yarn.' Caoimhe handed the sewing kit to her mother.

Mary fumbled with the box, trying to open it with her slippery, bloodied fingers. She clasped her hand around the two needles and asked Caoimhe if there was any thread in the box. There was not. It was in the same drawer. It had to be!

'Caoimhe, there should be a spool with thin, silver thread in the same drawer. Go!'

Caoimhe got to her feet again, and she was just about to leave the room when the lights went out. Mary didn't notice, but Caoimhe stood motionless and held her breath, fearing the worst.

'Mum?' Caoimhe whispered.

'Sssshhhh. I think I can hear something in the kitchen.'

She was right. Though it was no longer in the kitchen, and now Caoimhe could hear it too. Clumsily trudging down the hall with uneven steps, pain-induced wheezing grew louder and louder until it was just outside the door. The blacked-out house retained no light, and if Caoimhe were not already facing it, she would not know which way she was looking. Through the deep dark, the wheezing stopped. Slowly a terrible yellow light appeared in the shadows, followed by another. The lights rose to an abnormal height, almost touching the ceiling, which could not be seen.

Suddenly it screamed, so cruel was the scream it summoned an evil shine, a glow that momentarily illuminated the banshee enough for Caoimhe to notice the battle wounds she had suffered from her fight. Oily blood gushed down her weathered green dress from painful lacerations all over her body. The scream had knocked Caoimhe to the floor, holding her ears, and at that moment, the banshee swooped forward and grabbed Mary by the throat, raising her up so she could stare into the petrified eyes (or lack thereof) of her old friend.

Mary could feel the hot stench of death on her face. The last image she saw in this world was the banshee's hideous face smiling at her, an image that never left her mind; though she could not see it, that was the exact image facing her again, and she knew it. Her cold fingers were clutching tighter, Mary's body began convulsing desperately trying to spread oxygen that was not there, her hearing became muffled. She could hear Caoimhe screaming from a different plane of reality. Then she felt herself falling and landing hard on the ground. Her consciousness still swam ambiguously around her head.

Caoimhe opened her eyes just in time to see the banshee get pushed out of the house by a bright white blast. She faded through the wall. The silver banshee hurried to Mark's side; shiny chrome-like blood smeared her white dress originating from gashes all over her. She cupped Mark's head in her arms spoke a soft spell while gently tracing the cut on his face. The laceration began healing right in front of Caoimhe's eyes. His face stopped bleeding, and the open wound now sealed itself, leaving a tidy scar reconnecting his face, like a thin white bridge splitting a sea of drying blood in half.

Mark inhaled deeply like a drowning man sucking in newfound oxygen. He locked eyes with his banshee.

'You saved me,' he choked out. Then his eyes widened as he remembered what almost killed him in the first place. 'What about the other one? Is she gone?'

She stared at Mark with remorseful sapphire eyes.

You need to get down the well. Her lips didn't move, and Mark got a feeling that nobody else in the room could hear it, the soft, velvety voice of his banshee.

He nodded, then suddenly, a sound like the crack of a whip echoed in the room along with a continuous chain of dark yellow electricity. - at least that is what it looked like to Mark - It was coming from the other banshee's fingers who had just reappeared from the wall she disappeared through. The spell had caught the silver banshee, and she was shaking violently like one being shocked.

Caoimhe had tackled Mary to the ground behind the couch out of the firing line. Mark rolled off the couch and was lying still between both banshees, terrified of being hit by the yellow lightning just above him. Caoimhe held tightly onto her mother's hand and made a run for it, but the dark banshee had noticed. As soon as she had a clear shot, she took it. A dark blast, like a shadow javelin, shot out of her palm and went through Caoimhe and Mary like a bullet. They both fell to the ground motionless. A white light radiated around the room along with an intense snap, and the two banshees were gone.

Mark crawled frantically over to Caoimhe's and Mary's bodies, and no matter how much he shook them or screamed their names, he would get no response, not even a twitch of the eyes. There was no blood or wounds from the spell, but to Mark, it seemed they were dead or worse. *I need to go down the well,* he thought.

Leaving the bodies lying on the ground, he crawled to the front door, which was hanging open and saw his wheelchair turned over in the pouring rain. *How will I get down the well,* he thought, but first, he needed to get back in his wheelchair, one problem at a time. He crawled and crawled further out into the night, with no stars and no wind. It felt as though some evil was suffocating the world with its malevolent will. Cold rain trickled down on top of Mark's lethargic arms. Grabbing fistfuls of blood-stained soil, pulling himself ever nearer to his wheelchair. He was a few meters away now. He could see the blipping red light indicating the wheelchair was not in its correct position. The light flickered a sinister red glow in the wet soil. His nose, drowning in the smell of blood and putrid meat,

look

eyes screaming to close and sleep but forced open by adrenaline

look

and ears surveying intently for any sound that wasn't the gentle drib drab of rain on the slated roof or the arduous dragging sound of his body pulling itself across the ground. His arms were ready to break off with exhaustion. He had never had to crawl this far before.

look...

... at him crawling like a baby, look Nick look! Wittle baby Marky wants his chair, look he's crying! Go on, Mark, you're almost there.

The memory had flooded back into his strained mind without permission - Nick's 21st birthday. I guess he didn't forget it, not from lack of trying anyway. More like couldn't forget it.

Calvin and Nick had taken Mark's wheelchair while he was sitting on a kitchen chair at the table, eating chips and sausages. Being the good brothers, they were told Mark where his wheelchair was. Outside on top of the slide on the jungle gym. They would not help him get it, but they insisted on trailing behind him as he crawled outside to the jungle gym, mocking and laughing the whole time (or being supportive, as they called it). Mark did not know if it was indignancy that fueled him to keep going through the well-kept back garden of the O'Brien mansion. Crawling past the old swing set and tattered footballs, whatever the reason, it was a powerful drive. He could not ignore the laughs from his brothers, and the tears flowing from his eyes made it very difficult to see, but he had kept crawling. He kept crawling until he got to the jungle gym; he climbed up and up as high as he could on the blue steel ladder, not fully thinking ahead to how he would get the wheelchair down. One problem at a time. It didn't matter. He had almost reached the acme of the jungle gym, but his arms gave in, and he fell. Fell for what seemed like a week. The last thing he remembered before waking up in a hospital bed was a sharp pain in his head and a resounding *dong* from where his head had smashed off one of the metal bars. It rang out, loud and mournful like the church bells at his mother's funeral.

A very pungent pain shot through his lower left leg. He screamed in pain and turned around to see if he snagged his leg on broken glass or maybe a knife he didn't see. The long, jagged claws of the banshee gripped into his leg. *She has killed my banshee,* he thought, *nobody can save me now, she's going to kill me.* Mark had accepted death with a heavy heart knowing his banshee, his angel was destroyed because of him. He was so consumed with sadness he did not even notice the pain growing more extreme as the banshee dragged him towards the well. She picked him up by the throat. Mark stared in her yellow eyes shot with thin-blooded lines. She smiled and dropped him into the deep darkness of the well.

Joe and his party had trudged deeper into the Underworld. Every step further was more exhausting. It felt like trying to walk through some thick, viscous sludge. Joe didn't know how much further he could go. He gazed around the black world, frustration in his heart, and although the world was coated in dancing white flames, there was no heat, no wind, no time. Just lugubrious moans all around them. They were originating from some unseen sources as terrible as could be imagined.

'Joe, can we stop for a minute? My legs feel like rubber. I need a break.' Daniel gasped and sat on the ground.

Matthew must have been feeling it, too, because he also collapsed onto the ground rubbing his legs.

'No, come on, get up both of you. We can't stay here, not even for a moment. We must find my son and get out of here.

-Panting- 'Joe, I'll be with you in two minutes. I just need to catch my breath.'

'Fine,' Joe said reluctantly. 'Two minutes, then we have to keep moving. I will scout ahead.'

Daniel lay flat on his back, staring up at the big black sun adorned with a dancing white ring curiously. *If that is the sun,* he thought, *why is it not giving off warmth or light? Is it radiating life or draining it?*

'Matthew was also lying on his back with his eyes closed, breathing unsteadily.

Joe stumbled on, up to the summit of the shadowy hill. It was not by any means a mountain they were climbing, just a large hill, but it had felt like he had just scaled the tallest mountain in the world. He bent over, resting his hand on his knee, trying to suck in all the oxygen he could. He looked around from that vantage point, and his heart dropped into the pit of his stomach like a cannonball. There was nothing, absolutely nothing. The familiar sinister forest came to an abrupt end in every direction, but the darkness swept through the land as far as the eye could or could not see, but the white flame outlining and giving shape to every object in existence died out along the way. There was no way to know if there was anything beyond the final tree outlined by white fire. Joe dropped to his knees, collecting all the breath he could in his chest. He shouted Mark's name as loud as he could, expecting it to echo around the empty void but instead, the shout did not carry. There was nothing to reverberate the soundwaves, so it failed shortly after leaving his mouth. *My son is not down here.* he thought. H*e is not down here; he cannot be down here! Where is he?* Joe's heart began to beat hard against his ribs as he frantically tried to figure out where his son could be. How could he go back to Mary without his son? How could he get back to his own world? These questions tugged on his already enervated mind. He pressed the palm of his hand against his forehead and tried desperately to calm himself down.

A short time passed. Joe stood up and began to walk down the hill to Daniel and Matthew. He strutted as one unaffected by the exhausting atmosphere, by the terrifying fear that his son would spend the rest of time dead in some forgotten plane of existence.

He would find a way to climb out of the well, get back to Mary and from there decide how to find and save their son. He just had to save his son.

Daddy, do you promise you will always keep me safe? The ghostly voice of Mark chimed in his head.

He had looked him in the eye that day they went fishing after Mark had fallen overboard on the dingy paddle boat trying to reel in an aggressive pike. Joe had caught him by the ankle before he could be dragged down into the crushing depths of the lake. When he felt Mark grab hold of his arm, he pulled him up into the boat and hugged his drenched son. Between Mark's rattling teeth and shivers from fright and the cold, he began laughing. An innocent childish laugh like one that could not comprehend how close he just came to death. Joe could not help but laugh along with his son. He had promised that day to always be there for his son. *Yes, I promise to keep you safe, Mark. Only if you promise me not to be an idiot and let go of the line if you know you can't reel it in!* They both laughed again. That had been quite a productive day. They had fish for dinner that whole week.

Joe walked past where Daniel and Matthew were resting.

'Joe? Woah, woah, Joe, where are you going? Slow down.'

Daniel and Matthew climbed awkwardly to their feet and began following Joe, who did not stop walking.

'We need to go back up the well.'

'Wait up! What about your son?'

Joe walked on silently for a moment. 'He isn't here.'

Daniel and Matthew continued the strenuous trek trying to keep up with Joe.

Mark felt a cold rush through his body, then crashed hard on his already crippled legs. The snaps sounded like gunshots in a large, empty cave. The pain flooded back into his head, and a taste of hot copper made him gag. He pulled himself wearily along the dark to find something to sit up against. He found an uncomfortable rock.

He stared up at the floating well, and a terrifying thought hit him: *I'm dead, the banshee killed me, and now I'm trapped in this… whatever the hell this place is.* He looked around at the dark forest and the omnipresent white flames dancing around everywhere. His dazed head could not make any sense of it. He was slipping in and out of conscience. He looked at his legs; pitch-black hugged in a cold, pale fire, and he could tell from the wonky outline that his legs were not in a good state. Well, they never were, but now he felt they were beyond the point of no return. He sat there scared, sore, and cold. His senses were all discombobulated, but the longer he sat there in silence, the more he realized things were not making any sense. *If I am dead, how can I still feel? How can I think? I can't be dead. The banshee must have brought me to her world.* He looked up at the big black sun, embellished with a white flame. It all started to make sense. He was not dead; he was in the well and he needed to get out. He needed to see *Elizabeth*. His eyes began leaking. *Please let me see her one last time.* He begged a God he felt had abandoned him.

His weeping was interrupted by a sound inconsistent with the atmospheric moaning his ears had quickly become accustomed to. It sounded like something trying to chuckle, but it was choking. The croaking was accompanied by the sound of something heavy being dragged along the ground. The noises grew louder, indicating whatever it was approaching rapidly. To his horror, he could faintly see with the little light present in the Underworld, a long pale hand emerged from the darkness. In the shadows, two odious yellow eyes glared from the darkness. She was breathing hard and laughing. Mark jerked awake from another unconscious slip, shaking violently.

He looked up through the well and felt a crushing sense of isolation. He needed to get out of there, so he shouted up: 'Can anybody hear me? Oi'm stuck down the well. Oi need help.'

-no response-

He did not expect anything, but he hoped maybe his banshee was still alive and she could save him yet again.

Then a realization smothered him with hope. Daniel, Joe, and Matthew were down here. The well looked like the only way out. They would find him. *They will. I will be okay.*

Mark had lost track of how long he had been down there. Minutes, days, years? He did not know. A niggling awareness gnawed at his brain: *I need to get out of here, or I will die from blood loss.* He imagined himself attempting to climb the well. Realizing he could not even move, never mind jumping 10 feet to climb the slippery stones of the well. He could spend the rest of his breath screaming for help, but he felt that would be counterproductive. He needed all the oxygen his body could retain. He needed to think of a realistic escape instead of these foolish chimaeras.

Mark sat there, eyes closed, head thumping. Nothing for doing but pondering possible ways out. A biting chill crept up his legs.

Mark once again was roused from unconsciousness as the cold was now cutting bone-deep, making rest an impossible fancy.

Mark's concentration was snapped to the deep dark, where he could hear a strained breathing, like a young forest exhaling winters chill. As Mark listened intently, he wondered just how deep the forest continued. He decided to try his luck in the dark, figuring it could be no worse, mustering all the strength he could into his broken body. He dragged himself through the colourless trees. A few moments later, he was deep in the unknown of the ongoing black, drenched in a tenebrous white fire.

Mark again cried uncontrollably as he was now more afraid than ever. He called for Daniel. Among his pitiful weeping, he noticed his heaving was being harmonized by a wheezing breath, but not his. Mark held his breath and listened carefully. The wheezy breathing transmuted into a monotonous bass-like laugh. The laughing then ceased and turned into a sharp scream. Anxiety now chocked Mark's heart as he quickly tried to crawl away, frantically throwing one arm out in front of the other, feeling like he was being dragged through broken glass. His arm gave in, and he could no longer move. He lay there, neither extant nor extinct. There was tapping and shuffling behind him. It grew louder and louder still. Mark did not have the energy to glance over his shoulder, so he lay there, embracing death. His last thought was of Elizabeth's laugh.

A gentle hand on his back and a warm breath on his neck alerted him enough to hear his name being called in a frightened childlike voice. He rolled over in disbelief.

'Mark?'

'Mark, is that you? I'm scared. Where is my dad?'

Mark breathed in a sigh of relief. 'They all came down here looking for you, have you not seen them?' his voice faded into the despair he was feeling.

'No, how do we get out of here?' he asked with his worried childish innocence.

Mark hesitated and then arrived on premeditated speculation. 'We should wait here for your dad; he might know what to do.'

'But I didn't even see him down here. Should we go looking for him?'

'No!' Mark did his best to sit up straight. 'No, oi can't walk, and oi'm not letting you go alone.'

'Then what should we d... AHHHH!'

Before Mark had finished his blink, young Mark had been aggressively pulled up in the air and was being carried off into the gloom. He stared in shock as the thing that had ahold of the boy was a large black spider-like demon with red hairs coating its abominable body. It had multiple large, hateful yellow eyes. There was no mistaking it. It was her. *I had no chance of fighting her in our world when she was almost human. What chance do I have now? She must have a secret power down here.* He thought *I have to save the boy.* He rummaged desperately along the ground for something. His hand met a stone, a small black stone surrounded in cold white fire. Without hesitation, he called out for her attention then he threw it with all the strength he could gather.

The stone flew through the air and bounced off one of the huge yellow eyes of the demon, with a solid tttfffttt sound. It dropped Mark, and he landed awkwardly on his backside. The demon shielded its eyes with his four front legs. When it sensed it was no longer in danger, it roared a horrible scream and darted for Mark, who was sitting defenceless.

Before he could react, the thing was upon him. He felt a jagged claw tighten around his waist, lifting him, almost slicing him in two. He was suspended in front of the demon, eye to eyes. It mashed its long knife-like fangs. He saw in its yellow eyes a reflection of himself, but he did not feel frightened. He felt angry. He knew he was going to die, but he felt angry because he was the reason his banshee died, that demon was going to stop him from seeing Elizabeth again, and that infuriated him. He did not scream; he did not beg. He would not give her that pleasure. The demon lowered Mark towards her mouth just before he felt the long spikes tearing his flesh apart.

'Put him down!' a booming voice bellowed, momentarily startling the demon herself.

'Dad!' Mark ran over to the three shapes. Joe swiftly ran over to hug his son and secure him safely behind him with Matthew.

The demon dropped Mark and focused intently on Joe, whose silhouette appeared to be twice as large as any of the other men just then. He slipped a hand behind his back and brandished a long golden blade at her. If that was the same golden dagger, it definitely grew in size. Joe charged for her.

His movements were fastidious and precise, ducking and dodging her legs and claws, making elegant incisions around the demon's body, cutting off two of her legs and stabbing out three eyes. The others wanted to help, but there would be no point. None of them could move like Joe, who looked as though he was enchanted by some magic they could never understand. Then the demon screamed, knocking everyone to the ground. The demon transformed back into the ten-foot woman she had been before. Her sallow complexity looked alien in the shadow realm. One of her eyes was missing, and black blood flowed down her face. Her right hand was missing, and Joe smiled. *Now it will be a fair fight.*

The banshee outstretched her hand, and a thick smoke-shadow shot from her hand towards Joe, who swerved between trees dodging, slashing, dodging. It looked like a rehearsed dance to the useless onlookers.

Finally, the banshee shot a dark beam too quick to dodge. Joe caught the spell with the sword. The pressure from blocking the spell seemed to be crushing him, he yelled in agony, and eventually the sword snapped, and Joe fell to the ground consumed by smoke.

The banshee laughed a horrible triumphant cackle while looking at all the bewildered, petrified shapes of everyone reluctant to move.

Mark shouted for his father and charged the banshee. She clutched his throat and lifted him, squeezing so tight her long fingers broke his skin. He screamed.

Suddenly a bright light emerged from the well and smashed into the banshee, forcing her to her knees, dropping Mark. She screamed and wiggled but could not break the bonds binding her to the ground.

Quick, destroy her now! a voice choked from the white light forcing her to her knees.

Joe climbed unsteadily to his feet, couching and limping. He found a fragment of the shattered golden blade and stumbled to the banshee.

Tears glazed his sight of his son's lifeless body. He stood as tall as he could in front of her. 'THIS IS FOR MY FAMILY!' he screamed in a heroic, war-like cry, then he plunged the shard through the banshee's heart.

She inhaled a sharp terrified breath. Joe watched her remaining yellow eye grow dimmer. In her last burst of energy, she plunged her hand through Joe's chest. He felt his ribs being pushed out the gaping hole in his back, falling to his knees, still clutching the shard and twisting it deeper into her chest. They locked eye contact, and Joe smiled.

'I got you.' He laughed; blood streamed from his mouth. 'You might have got me, but I got you.'

He shoved the shard as deep as he could then she exploded in a refreshing wind. Everybody once again fell to the ground—the wind swept all across the land, restoring colour to the Underworld. Trees began to blossom, and flowers began to bloom out of the once dark ground. The sun turned a magnificent gold that filled the world with light, warmth, and happiness. The trees grew very tall indeed, and to everybody's surprise, all the fairies lived in small holes in the trees. Tiny, winged creatures danced in glee from the houses. They flew around, laughing and singing, and for a moment, everybody forgot the terror that ruled the world a moment ago. Water flowed through the land, a crystal-clear pool of innocence.

The light that bounded the banshee to her knees took the form of the silver banshee, mighty to look upon. Her watery sapphire eyes smiled. Although she was cut to pieces and could barely stand, she looked omnipotent. *We have done it; we have vanquished her evil heart. It is time for you to return to your world.* A portal opened beside her, the McNeeve mansion swimming in the middle of the image.

You have saved the fairies from a treacherous fate. There is no greater gift we can give than the serenity of remembering this world. If you ever find yourself anxious or worried, think of this place, and you will be troubled no more.

Mark looked remorsefully at his banshee. 'You are hurt.'

She crouched down beside him and kissed his forehead. *There was nothing you could do; she was very powerful*

'Won't you come back with us, with me?'

She laughed a gentle laugh. It reminded him of his mother. *I will always be with you in here, Mark;* she placed a hand on his chest.

374

The Bells

She turned to Daniel, who instinctively picked up Mark and carried him to the portal—looking around, for the first time in his life lost for words.

Young Mark ran over to his father and held him tight. Matthew followed and hugged Joe's body.

'Dad!' He shook Joe carefully. His blood turned to cool water and continued flowing from his chest.

Matthew cried and began to ample around in circle.

-weeping- 'Come on, mom will be so happy to see us

Mark tried to pull Joe's corpse to the portal, then he caught the banshee's eye, and she stared pitiably. Sorrow cascaded down his cheeks.

'No, please. Help him, save him.'

Everyone stared at him with sullen expressions. Everyone except Matthew, who could not accept his brother, was gone forever.

'No, dad, please.' He did his best to screech through the tears. 'Please, come back.'

Joe's cold, pale face didn't even twitch when his son's tears landed on it.

Your father's name will never be forgotten by the fairies. I am sorry, but the dead cannot be woken. Now please go.

Mark was carried by Daniel through the portal. The fairies flew around gleefully, chanting:

Joe saved us, Joe McNeeve! Joe McNeeve.

Young Mark was pulled by Matthew. Neither of them wanted to leave Joe behind. Quicker than the blink of an eye, they were back in their world. The portal had vanished, and with it, Joe.

Daniel sat Mark in his car, put the wheelchair in the boot, and went into the cabin to pack up all their luggage. Mark rolled down the window of the car and could hear

Caoimhe and Mary screaming in sadness at Joe's end. The loss of a man he barely knew also tugged at his heartstrings, but he did not belong with the McNeeve family. He would not be welcomed to mourn among them. Daniel returned to the car with three suitcases, stowed them in the back seat, and they began driving away into the sunrise under the stone archway.

Mary stood in the sitting room, tucked away in a large hug with Caoimhe Mark and Matthew. All of them full of grief. But deep down, they all knew his sacrifice was not in vain. Whatever curse dwelled on the land was now gone. The orchard seemed happier. And it would blossom like it once did, producing the best apples in Ireland. For now, she would weep, remembering that day at the lake, the day when she and Joe first kissed. How handsome he was and how bright the world was with him in it.

Mark woke up in a hospital room. His father and two brothers were sitting around the bed.

'Ello then!' he said in a cheery renewed way, convinced he was imagining them.

'Jesus Mark, you're alrigh!' Jack rushed to his son's side and held his hand.

'Dad? Calvin, Nick?' Disbelief danced in his voice. 'Oi'll be honest, yiz are the last people I expected to be here.'

'You are our family, Mark.' Calvin popped up off his chair. 'I know we give you a hard time and all, but we will never let anything happen to you. You know that, Mark.'

'Yeh,' Nick introjected. 'Besides, if anything happened to you, who will be the flower girl at my wedding?' They all laughed.

'So, oi didn't miss the wedding?'

'No,' said Jack. 'It's tomorrow, I bought you a dapper grey suit, but it might be a bit difficult to get you into it now.' He tapped the enormous cast covering Mark's lower body. 'You really messed yourself up, son. I told you not to go to Mayo.'

Mark smiled. he didn't know if it was the morphine or the fact that he was finally in his family circle. 'Will oi be able to attend the wedding?'

'I will carry you on my back if I have to,' said Calvin.

Mark looked at his father. 'Since technically oi'm not going to miss the wedding, can oi still live in me house?'

'Yiz didn't think I would kick yeh out, did ya?' He looked at Mark with an unreadable face.

Mark swallowed, He didn't know the answer, and he didn't want to know. 'Does anybody know how Daniel is?'

'Yeah, he's just outside. He's fine. We wanted to speak with you first,' Jack said, standing up and picking up his cup of coffee. 'Here I'm off now I've got things for doing.' He shot a hazel-eyed glance at his son again. 'I'll be expecting you back at work in two weeks Mark, I might even let you manage one of my smaller shops if you want.' And he left.

Classic nepotism Mark thought.

Calvin and Nick stood up.

'Hang on, lads,' Mark said, 'dad said he wants me to be back at work in two weeks? How the hell am oi supposed to work in two weeks?

'Well... you were never much good at walking anyway.' Calvin laughed.

'I guess you'll be paid for sitting around.' Nick laughed.

'Go on. We shall see you tomorrow, bro. Get well soon.' And they left the room as well, bumping into Daniel, who was coming in.

Mark looked at him with bemusement. 'Dan, oi have no idea what just happened but, my family oi think they like me now.'

'It's weird, isn't it? When I got home to my wife, she wasn't angry at me anymore. She was really glad to see me.' He sat down and fingered his empty paper cup of water. 'Do you think the fairies have something to do with it?'

'Oi don't know, maybe, hopefully. I'm sorry for dragging you through that Daniel oi had no idea.'

'Don't worry about it, man. We got through it with our lives. We should be thankful.'

'Oi am because now oi have been given a chance to be with…' *Elizabeth* 'do you have a phone Daniel oi need to call somebody!'

Daniel gave him a sly wink. 'Have you finally come to your senses and realized your maid is in love with you?'

'Be quiet and just give me your phone.'

Daniel gave Mark the phone. 'Do you need me to get her number in the phone book?'

Mark was already dialling her number.

'I guess not.' He laughed.

'Would ye mind giving me a bit of privacy?' Mark smiled at Daniel with the phone up to his ear.

'All right, Romeo, calm down. I'll be outside. Are you going to ask her to the wedding tomorrow? I know she would get on with Sarah, and we have some stories for them.'

'Hello Elizabeth,' Mark spoke to the phone, 'it's Mark. Oi'm back in town, and I was just wondering if you would like to come with me tomorrow to my brother's wedding?'

Daniel smiled and left the room.

The next day the wedding bells rang out, proud and resounding. Daniel stood beside his wife Sarah, smiling up at the altar where Jack, Calvin, and Mark were beside Nick and his newly wedded wife, Charlotte. On the way out of the church, flower petals and fake snow rained down the aisle.

Mark had never felt happier in his life, his best friend Daniel and his family around him and his new girlfriend Elizabeth holding his hand. Elizabeth moved in with him the following month, where together they lived in his big house with their recently reemployed friend Dominique who was almost too happy for words to be back working for Mr Mark.

Mark always had a fresh crate of McNeeve apples in the kitchen and would often call and speak with Mary and Mark and make sure they were doing alright. They were the first to receive a copy of his latest bestseller, The Banshee.

Mark continued writing in his free time when he was not managing his small O'Brien's heat store.

In 1965 he married Elizabeth; it was a spectacular Christmas wedding. Jack, Calvin, and Nick stood as his best men – proud of their brother, and Jack hugged him. Mark tried to fight off the tears. He finally felt like he was an O'Brien.

Whenever life became too troubling or worrying, Mark would simply sit back, close his eyes and visit the fairyland in the Underworld.

Acknowledgements

Thank you to my brother Conor for designing the book cover. It came out fantastic, and thanks for sticking to it despite my fussy demands.

Thank you to my mum and Dr Monaghan for incessantly telling me I should write a book. Here it is.

Thank you to my dog Ghost for staying with me through the writing process. I would have cracked up alone during the lockdown. Also, when I read him what I was writing, his feedback was both sagacious and honest.

Thank you to Andy Hannon for your tips.

Thank you very much to Jackie Kelly for teaching me how to properly layout a book, a lesson I will hopefully never forget. Not only did you provide unparalleled help, but you managed to put up with me.

A big thank you to Moira and Caroline Noone for your above and beyond help.

Thank you, to Lee Williamson, for taking a great picture of me, that's no easy job, you're the best.

Thank you to Mr. Thomas F Moran M.Ed, H.Dip Ed BA, NT, A.T.G. for your insight and feedback.

And lastly, thank you! You took the time to read the book, or maybe you skipped to the end. Maybe you're not even reading this. Either way, I hope you know I appreciate you, and I really hope my book entertained you.

How do I end this? Do I just say goodbye?

About the Author

Born in New York in 1996 and moved to Ireland in 1998. I've always had an interest in writing, and movie making. Tolkien and Stephen King Inspired my writing. This is my first book and I thoroughly enjoyed writing it. I hope to write more in the future.

In 2019, I wrote a short film called "Medical Aid" it's a comedy, but I have recently branched into horror.

I have always enjoyed writing and acting and reading, so I figured I would give writing a book a go.

I have never been good at talking about myself; I let my work speak for me.

Printed in Great Britain
by Amazon